MAXINE

FIRE AND ICE

SCARLET

Enquiries to:
Robinson Publishing Ltd
7 Kensington Church Court
London W8 4SP

First published in the UK by Scarlet, 1996

A copy of the British Library Cataloguing in
Publication data is available from the British Library

ISBN 1-85487-472-1

Printed and bound in the EC

10 9 8 7 6 5 4 3 2 1

PROLOGUE

New York: Eighteen Years Ago

The fourteen-year-old boy shivered in the cold November air. Alone in the passenger seat of his father's broken-down old car, he stared blankly out of the side window, watching the occasional passer-by with icy blue eyes. One old lady, pushing a pram that contained a loaf of bread, a cheap bottle of gin and a beloved marmalade cat, paused to stare back at the boy, her mind momentarily diverted from the drudgery of her life. It was not surprising. The boy was startlingly handsome, even at so young an age. Hair that couldn't make up its mind whether it was silver or gold framed a face that was appealingly strong. The old woman smiled as she took in the challenging thrust of his jaw, the high, proud cheekbones and chiselled mouth. 'Heartbreaker,' the old woman murmured knowingly to her cat, and moved on.

The boy didn't notice her arrival or departure. His eyes were fixed on the building. Red brick and eight storeys high, it looked like a run-down factory. But it wasn't a sweat-shop, as the chipped white sign fixed to the wall clearly showed. How many times had he looked at the sign now – thirty? Forty? He'd been waiting for his father for only ten minutes, but it felt like ten years. He squirmed in the hard, cracked seat, recognizing the familiar doubt that

1

began to nibble at his insides, and almost moaned aloud. Why now? Why did he doubt *now*, when it was all too late?

Again his eyes slewed to the white sign. It fascinated him, that sign, and hurt him too. 'NEW YORK STATE-SIDE', the first line read, in big black letters. Underneath, as if ashamed of themselves, smaller lower-case letters spelled out the words 'Mental Correctional Facility'.

The boy looked away, a deep sigh ricocheting through his narrow chest. Looking back, he could have done things differently, couldn't he? Oh, sure. His mouth curved into a smile so shockingly cynical that it would have made anyone watching stop and stare in amazement. It was such an old smile for so young a face, but the boy already knew more about life than a child ever should. He knew all about despair and desperation. He *could* have done things differently. He could have told his dad what was going on, and then stood back and watched him do nothing about it. He *could* have kept his mouth shut, as he'd done so often in the past. He could have run away from home, away from the slums, away from the cold.

The slums. A shudder ran through him as he recalled days spent dodging recruiting drugs gangs always on the lookout for children to make addicts of and turn into runners and dealers. He thought of days spent at his overcrowded, crumbling school where he struggled to learn, aware that education was his only hope. Oh, yes, he could have run away, but he couldn't have abandoned Vanessa. Not after his mother, on her deathbed, had made him promise to look after her.

The building door opened and the boy tensed, the cold forgotten as he watched his father walk down the steps. He was only forty, though he looked as if he had the weight of the whole building on his shoulders. But he didn't look

2

back as he walked to the car, and for that the boy was grateful. The gust of wind that blew into the already arctic interior when the door opened turned the boy's hands blue, and he quickly stuffed them into his too-small blazer. Would his father take him on to school, or would they both go home?

The car started with a dry, rattling cough, and he blinked back rapidly gathering tears. The tears surprised the boy. He hadn't cried since his mother had died, and nothing had made him cry since – not the sly beatings, nor the lies spread about him, nor Vanessa's tearful questions that always started the same way . . . 'Why?' Why? How could the boy answer his baby sister when he didn't even know the answers to his own whys?

Why had he done it? Why had he run with Vanessa in his arms all the way to the police station, knowing that he would never be able to undo it, once it became official? Had it really been fear for Vanessa's safety, as he'd first thought? Or was it his own fear that had propelled him? Had he simply grown so tired of being afraid that he'd betrayed one of his own?

The car kangarooed away from the kerb, and the boy cast a quick glance at his father's face. It was grim, and grey, and old. 'Dad . . .' he said, but stopped as his father raised a huge, gnarled hand. The gesture was at once angry and hopeless. The boy knew how he felt.

'Don't talk unless you can improve the silence,' his father advised grimly. His son recognized the old Vermont proverb immediately and swallowed back an almost unbearable sob of grief. Vermont. Oh, God, what he wouldn't give to be back in Vermont, where the view was green, and the air was pure, and he still knew what hope meant.

3

The boy might not trust his instincts any more, but he trusted his brain, which had always been bright and true. He had done the right thing for both Vanessa and himself. But, as the car pulled out into the traffic and belched its way into the grey November day, the boy's intellect told him one other thing – that he would never forget this day, or the lessons he had learned. Do what you must, and pay the price. It was a simple philosophy, but it was a truth that had been hard-earned. Oh, yes. *Very* hard-earned . . .

And inside the red-brick building, from behind a barred window, two dark eyes watched the car until it was out of sight, and the owner of those eyes knew something too. He would never let the boy forget. Somewhere, way back in the bowels of the building, someone was screaming, but it was in perfect silence that the vow was made. Never forget. Never forgive. Never let the one who had put him here live in peace . . .

CHAPTER 1

Yorkshire, England: Present Day

'Cuuuppp ... cup ... cup ... cup ... come onnnnnnn.' Her voice battled bravely against the raw March wind blowing strongly across the dale, a thin, defiant sound in the bleak landscape. Bryn Whittaker winced as a rain droplet hit her smack in the eye, then curled her hands around her mouth once more and took a deep breath. 'Cuuuuppp ... cup ... cup ... come onnnnnn.'

She had been six when she'd first asked her father why he used the word 'cup' instead of 'come', and he'd explained with his usual good-humoured patience that the harder-sounding 'p' carried farther and better than did the softer 'hum'. Now, proving as always that he was right, out of the misty blanket smothering the dale the first shapes began to emerge, and Bryn grinned happily. It never ceased to give her a thrill, no matter how many times she did this most routine of tasks. Trotting and bleating, the sheep came, tails swishing, their fat bellies, swollen with lambs, doing little to slow them down.

Walking around to the back of the trailer, Bryn lowered the rear tailboard and grabbed the first bale of hay. The red string cut deep into her fingers, but they were protected by the dirty but sturdy canvas gloves she

5

habitually wore, and she barely noticed. With a small grunt she hoisted the bale out and on to the ground, swivelling to grab the next one. She was sweating by the time she'd finished unloading all nine, but she barely paused for breath. Taking the first one to the nearest rack, she gently but firmly nudged the gathering ewes to one side and reached deep into her anorak pocket for her penknife, careful to cut the string at the knot, roll it up and put it back into her pocket so that no sheep could become entangled and choke. Then she scattered the hay along the metal containers and moved back for the next bale.

She worked methodically and with a grace that belied her considerable size. Only when she'd finished with the hay did she take a break, and leisurely cleaned her wellingtons on the side of the tractor-wheel rim before hoisting herself aboard. Pushing her glasses back up to the bridge of her nose, she started the noisy engine and pulled away, wrestling with the steering wheel on the old and cumbersome machine.

Once on the open road, she glanced at her watch. Good, she was making fair time. She waved cheerfully to old Mr Gornwell and his six Yorkies as she went past, grinning at the way the little dogs yapped excitedly.

Glancing at the sky, she estimated the chances of the weather clearing. They didn't look good, which was a shame. Bryn, with a pride that was as strong as any, knew she lived in the most beautiful of Yorkshire's six dales. Across to her east was the River Wharfe, which gave the dale its name. Over forty miles long, Wharfedale rose and undulated in valleys that gradually petered out in fertile farmland just beyond Otley. Not that she envied the lowlanders their more fertile acres. She was more than happy with the farm they had. So long as they could just hang on to it . . .

Suddenly a stab of apprehension shivered up her spine, making her bite her lip, an old habit she reverted to whenever she was upset. The post still hadn't arrived when she'd left just after breakfast, and she hated waiting, not knowing . . . She sighed deeply as she turned off the tarmac road on to the packed-rubble and dirt track that led to Ravenheights, the only home she'd ever known. Once she'd looked forward to receiving the mail – living on a lonely farm miles from anywhere, it had once been the highlight of her day, especially on her birthdays and at Christmas. Now she dreaded the mail. Just in case there was something from *him*, Kynaston M. Germaine. How she hated that name!

Nestling against the side of the hill, Ravenheights suddenly loomed into view, a low grey-stone building that squatted with a stolid defiance that never failed to raise her spirits. From the thick chimney, smoke wafted into the cold, drenched air, and, as she rattled her noisy way into the yard, Violet, their retired old sheepdog, rose from her favourite spot in the barn and shuffled over to greet Bryn as she climbed down.

'Hello, old gal. Want to come inside, hmm?' She ruffled the dog's silky ears affectionately, and moved off towards the kitchen, ignoring the chickens that pecked for stray grains of corn in the courtyard mud. In the linoleum-covered kitchen alcove she hoisted off her muddy wellingtons and hung up her coat, ignoring her reflection in the mirror on the opposite wall. She knew only too well what she'd see, so why depress herself even further?

Violet shuffled in with her and headed straight for the huge Aga, where she curled up with a heartfelt canine sigh.

Her offspring were busy working the fields for miles around, and Bryn grinned at the grey-muzzled retired collie and tossed her one of her favourite biscuits.

The kitchen was warm and welcoming, as always. The walls were a daffodil yellow that her mother had picked out over twenty years ago, and that Bryn had only re-touched a year or so ago. The floor was a checked lime-green and yellow, covered with a fleecy rug that warmed her bare toes. The table in the centre was a solid piece of centuries-old home-made oak furniture. On it rested a small bowl of the early narcissus that Fred Jacombe always grew in his greenhouse and swapped at this time of year for some of Bryn's home-baked bread. At the windows, the curtains were white with bright splashy poppies, and the same patterned material covered the table in the form of a linen tablecloth. The smell of warmth and cooking filled the air, reminding Bryn of when her mother had still been alive and she used to run home from the school bus and burst into the kitchen, so glad to be home, she could sing.

Bryn shook her head now and pulled off the green knitted bobble hat she wore. Cascades of hair the rich colour of conkers fell around her wide shoulders, but she ignored its breathtaking beauty and simply pushed it out of her eyes. She should go into the hall and check the mail, but she didn't have the heart. Instead she grabbed a bowl and went to the cupboard under the stairs, filling it with enough potatoes for six. Taking them back to the sink, she ran the water and began peeling, wincing at the sharp chill of the tap water until her hands became used to it. Afterwards she washed the cabbage and checked that the huge steak and kidney pudding she'd prepared and put on to cook before leaving the house hadn't boiled dry.

8

Methodically she made herself a cup of coffee, drinking it while she read the paper, studiously avoiding all the bad news. There was so much pain in the world, and she always felt helpless in the face of it all. Rain began to spatter in earnest against the windows and she sighed, knowing the men would come in cold and wet as well as hungry. Banking up the fires in the living room with wood and coal, she fed the Aga some more logs, expertly maintaining a steady heat, then dragged the vacuum cleaner from the cupboard and set about the house-work. When the sound of the farm's other two tractors growled into the courtyard an hour later, the table was set and the food ready. Her father was first in, as always.

'Hey up, lass, something smells good,' he said, and Bryn smiled. He'd said the same thing every day all his life – first to his mother, then to his wife, and now to his daughter.

'There's a fire in the living room, Dad. Why don't you warm up first, hmm?'

John Whittaker glanced at her, not fooled for a minute by her casual tone. So it was that obvious, was it? He nodded, both at her suggestion and his own thoughts. He shouldn't be surprised. Nobody could feel as ill as he did at times and not show it on his face. He walked stiffly through the kitchen and slumped thankfully into his favourite chair by the fire. He'd never felt so old be-fore. Wearily he rubbed his forehead then looked up as Bill and Sam, two of his older farm hands, moved to the sofa and sat down, stretching their bootless feet towards the hearth, bliss clearly outlined on their contented faces. John glanced away quickly. He hadn't told them yet. He felt guilty about that – a man had a right to know if his job was in question – but John hadn't the heart. Over sixty years ago his father had hired their fathers. He knew how hard the men, now both in their forties, would find it to get another job. Especially round here.

Damn the Government. And the EC too. What did Yorkshire farmers want with the Common Market, anyway? Whittakers had lived and managed this farm for over four hundred years, and done nicely enough, thank you. Now . . . John suddenly sat up straighter and surreptitiously pressed his hand against his chest. He winced as a spasm shot through him and glanced quickly at the two men, who thankfully hadn't noticed. He took a couple of slow, even breaths and the pain receded slightly. It was probably nothing. It felt like a bad case of indigestion, and there was nothing you could do about that. It was just a fact of life. Absently he began to rub his left arm, which felt slightly numb; he must have been leaning on it to get such pins and needles. He turned his gaze once more to the hypnotically flickering fire, his eyes troubled.

In the kitchen Bryn brewed a pot of tea and poured mugs out for Robbie and Ronnie Peters, the twenty-year-old twins who, along with Sam and Bill, comprised Ravenheights' staff, and then carried a tray of mugs into the living room. John looked up and smiled at his daughter, crow's feet appearing at the sides of his kind blue eyes. He accepted his mug and watched her hand out the others, his thoughts turning darker. What would happen to her, this youngest of his children, when he was gone and the farm was lost? For lost it was, no matter how much he and his lovely Bryony Rose might try and pretend otherwise.

John remembered the day she was born as clearly as if it were yesterday. He'd gone through it once before, when Katy had been born, pacing about this very room while the midwife kept him busy boiling kettles and searching for

10

more towels when he knew very well that every towel in the house was already upstairs. Hours had gone by, hours that were filled with daylight, and hours that were filled with darkness. Hours when Katy slept upstairs, despite her excitement about the imminent arrival of a baby brother or sister. And then the moment had come, and the midwife had called him upstairs, and there was Martha, his lovely Martha, sitting up in bed, pale and exhausted but smiling, the infant in her arms.

'Sorry, John,' she'd said, with patent insincerity. 'It's another girl.'

John shook his head now, wondering why on earth Martha had wanted to apologize, even teasingly, for producing the baby they would call Bryony Rose. She'd been his light and joy from the moment she'd come into the world. Not that Katy hadn't too, he amended quickly – and with some guilt, for he knew in his heart that it wasn't true. Katy was . . . well, Katy. But Bryony – Bryn, as nearly everyone called her except for himself – well, she was as different from her sister as chalk was from cheese. From the moment she could walk and talk it was apparent to everyone – Martha, Katy and later Hadrian – that Bryony Rose and her father were kindred spirits.

'All right, Dad?'

The soft voice brought him back to the present and he smiled at her automatically. 'Course, lass.'

His eyes sharpened as they looked at her more objectively, his worried mind racing ahead. If she was to cope on her own she'd have to find a husband, preferably one with a farm of his own. She'd wither and die in a city, this daughter of his who loved the country with every fibre of her being. But what chance did she have? Even he, who loved her blindly, could not deny that her figure wasn't the wafer-thin kind favoured by girls of today. He could not bring himself to admit that she was overweight; perhaps she just needed to lose a pound or two. But her hair was glorious – a rich, deep auburn which he knew those models that Katy ran around with down in London would kill for, and which was as natural as the water that flowed in the Ribble. And her skin was flawless – always had been; he could remember Katy complaining endlessly as a teenager that it was not fair that Bryn's skin should be so perfect. And as for her eyes . . .

John could remember the first time he'd seen those eyes. Walking to Martha's bed, he'd peered excitedly at the small bundle she'd held. He'd recognized the mass of conker-coloured hair immediately. Didn't Martha's own match it for glory? But when she'd pulled the sheet down, and the baby had opened her myopic eyes in startled awareness, John had felt the ground move beneath his feet. Surely all babies' eyes were blue? Katy's had been.

But the eyes that stared at him then were the same that watched him now, twenty-two years later, still slightly myopic without the ever-present glasses. If asked, John knew he would never be able to describe them accurately. The closest he could get would be to call them sherry. They were brown, but they were almost red too. And gold, deep, deep down. A red/brown/gold colour, with tawny flecks. They were at once both feline and gentle, doe-like and yet tigerish. He'd seen many a man do a double-take once he'd seen those eyes.

If only she weren't so big, he thought sadly. John loved big women. His Martha had been big, and no doubt that was where Bryony had inherited her large stature. She was nearly five feet eleven and moved with a statuesque grace that would have made Juno envious. But nowadays a lot of

12

men seemed to want girls who looked like whippets. Damn fools. Still, perhaps there was a man out there for her somewhere, if only she would go and look for him. But they both knew she preferred to stay at home, with him.

'Dinner's ready!' The call came from the kitchen and galvanized into eager action the two men who'd been sitting in almost total silence. Typical Yorkshire men, John thought, carefully manoeuvring himself out of the chair and following them. At sixty-two, John felt at least a score older. As he took his place at the head of the table he felt the letter he'd picked up that morning crackle in his shirt pocket, and dreaded the moment when he'd have to hand it over to Bryony.

The men watched her hoist the steamed meat pudding out of the huge saucepan on the Aga and place it on the centre of the table, their tastebuds already doing a jig. Without ceremony she untied the string around the muslin cloth, cut the suet pudding on top into six equal pieces and dished out the deliciously braised meat within on to the plain, white plates. Boiled potatoes and cabbage quickly followed. The meal was eaten in silence, with intense concentration and appreciation. The young twins especially wolfed down their food like starving dogs, looked on approvingly by the men and Bryn. Like her mother before her, Bryn liked to feed men well, and to watch them eat. In a world where people were always looking for more, Bryn knew how lucky she was to be so contented and secure.

'Yon Bryn cooks like her mother.' Sam spoke for the first time only after he'd pushed his empty plate away, and Bryn felt herself blushing.

Baked apples, stuffed with mincemeat and cooked in cider, followed, and, as the men trooped back out to the tractors and Bryony began to tackle the mound of washing-up, the rain finally began to clear. A stray ray of sunshine trickled its way into the kitchen. As it did so, John laid the letter gently on the draining board and looked his daughter in the eye.

She stared at it, recognizing the logo on the envelope. Germaine Leisure Corporation. How American it sounded. How hideous. 'Another letter,' she said quietly, and John nodded.

'Aye. Another one. I think you'd better read it.'

Bryn's lips, which formed a perfectly shaped Cupid's bow, firmed grimly. 'I'll read it later, Dad.'

John nodded hopelessly and zipped up his own fleece-lined anorak, stepping out into the courtyard with a tread much slower than the one he'd come in with. Bryn watched the tractors trundle out of the courtyard and listened to the silence settle once more. Tears blurred her vision, and she sniffed impatiently. 'Tears never solved a damned thing,' she could remember her mother saying stoically, the day the doctors had diagnosed her cancer. And Bryn couldn't remember seeing her mother cry, either, not even once in the five months before her death. Whittakers were made of strong stuff. Always had been. Always would be.

She made herself clean the kitchen from top to bottom before she finally sat at the table and opened the letter. It was addressed to Mr Bryn Whittaker. She always dealt with whatever correspondence needed to be done, since her father had always felt more at home with sheep than letters. She wrote well and clearly and wasn't surprised that the Germaine Corporation had mistaken her for a son, and not a daughter.

With a grimness that seemed to seep into her very

14

bones, she read the letter quickly. It was more of the same. Except that this time the offer to buy the farm had been raised by another thousand pounds, and Mr Germaine even offered to buy the flock – she checked the exact phrase – 'in order to facilitate the transaction'. Facilitate the transaction . . . She looked down at the signature she knew so well. Bold and straight, written in black ink, the name stared back at her. Kynaston Germaine. Angrily she scrumpled the letter into a tiny ball and threw it at the Aga, where it bounced and landed on Violet's back. The old dog raised her head and gave her a hurt look, then settled back with yet another long-suffering sigh.

Bryn leaned forward and hugged her round middle with arms that shook. How much longer could they hold out? The bank . . . the bank. Bryn grunted with anger. The damned bank, of course, wanted its loan repaid. It hadn't taken long for it to hear about the Germaine Corporation's offer. Of course not. Mr Kynaston Germaine would have seen to that, all right.

And lately . . . was it her imagination, or had her father seemed to . . . give up? At first, when the farm had started to make a loss about five years ago, he'd been sure they could turn it around. He'd refused to lay off any men, and they'd been loyal in return. She knew they hadn't had a pay-rise since. But with the threatened cut-back on sub-sidies issued recently by Westminster, and with new competition from Europe, they hadn't been able to cope. Even she knew it, although she'd never admit it out loud.

But she'd never sell to Mr Kynaston bloody Germaine, that was for sure!

She made herself a cup of tea, slamming around mugs

and milk bottles. At least Katy was well out of it, down there in London. Katy always had been the clever one – oh, not academically. Bryn knew that her own O and A-levels had irked Katy considerably, since she herself had never even bothered to sit her exams, having left school at Easter when she was sixteen. But Katy had been the one to go to London. And why not? She was so beautiful, after all.

Missing her sister as always, Bryn walked through to the living room and picked up the big, professional studio-shot of Katy that rested in pride of place on the Welsh dresser. It had been her first 'professional pic', as she'd called it. She'd been eighteen at the time and working in Otley as a receptionist at a hotel. One of their guests had been a photographer who had tried to chat her up. Katy was used to that, of course, Bryn thought with a smile. Men were always chatting her up. But this one had been almost honest; at least he *was* a photographer, and had taken this shot to prove it. Unlike Bryn, Katy had inherited their father's fair hair and blue eyes. Luckily she'd also inherited his wiry physique, giving her the dainty look of a sprite. Whenever her mother or father had read to Bryn the tale of Rapunzel or Sleeping Beauty, she had always pictured Katy, slender and reed-like, as the princess.

So when, at nineteen, she'd decided to move to London and try and become a model, Bryn hadn't been in the least surprised. Especially since Katy seemed to hate the farm and the loneliness of the countryside every bit as much as Bryn loved it. Martha had passed away when Bryn was twelve and Katy fifteen, so her stabilizing influence on her elder daughter had long since been forgotten. John had argued, instinctively disliking the thought of his little girl moving to the capital, but Katy had always had her own way. She could be quite sharp when she wanted to be, Bryn remembered now, staring down at the face that looked anything but.

Katy been in the big city now for six years, and although she never wrote, she sometimes phoned, and Bryn would listen for ages to the tales of her latest adventures. Sometimes she felt so proud of her big sister that she could burst. Fancy having a sister who was a professional model! Especially when she, Bryn, had turned out so unattractive. Ah, well. She pushed the thought aside and put down the photo. At least Katy was all right. Her world might be threatening to collapse, but Katy was safe. And so was Hadrian, their cousin, in York. Everyone, it seemed, was all right except herself.

Suddenly she found herself crying. Crying for her father, who was ill and defeated and trying so hard not to show it. Crying for Ravenheights, which might have its soul broken if this horrible Germaine man actually succeeded in stealing it from them and turning it into some sort of hideous *holiday* resort. And crying for herself too, because she was so ugly and fat and . . . *lost*.

Violet, alerted by the sounds of distress, came in and laid her grey muzzle in Bryn's lap, her anxious brown eyes fixed on her beloved mistress's face. After a minute or two, Bryn had herself back under control, and was looking at her problems more objectively. Her father had her to look after him, and so he'd be all right. He *would*. And, while Ravenheights had loyal people to protect it, the farm would be all right too. As for herself . . . well, she was fat, and always had been. So what was wrong with that? Unthinkingly she reached into the glass dish resting on the coffee table and unwrapped a sweet. Popping it into her mouth and chewing the juicy toffee vigorously, she instantly began to feel better.

'Come on, old gal, we'd best get on with feeding the chickens. That's if Dad's to have his fresh eggs for his tea.' Violet woofed softly, but Bryn noticed with a grin that the dog didn't follow her out into the cold, darkening afternoon air.

London

Katy Whittaker poured herself another drink. She drank a lot now. She had done ever since her first modelling job had led to nothing but other, smaller modelling jobs – although she always wrote home about how successful she was. To leave London was unthinkable. She simply couldn't face going back to the dreary farm and her cold, empty life there. So, she did what many women had done before her. She had found herself a man. A wealthy, married man.

But today he had come to her flat – or, more accurately, *his* flat, since he paid the rent – and told her it was all over. Just like that. She had only two days until the rent was due, and had no way of paying it. Then she was on her own. And Katy knew why, of course. She was not the only country girl 'modelling' in the big bad city. The bastard had found someone newer. Younger. Fresher.

Katy sniffled over her scotch, immersed in a drunken, deep self-pity. She would have to go home after all. Back to the farm. The thought made fresh tears course down her cheeks, her make-up running. She reached for her diary and poured out her latest tale of woe across its pages: the betrayal of her lover, the final loss of the chance to live her life in the city. Under her breath she cursed Sir Lionel

Stavendish, then, galvanized by her despair, rose abruptly, the diary falling forgotten on to the floor. She tore frantically through the house, yanking open drawers and pushing things haphazardly into a suitcase. She paused for a moment, the room swaying around her, then went into the bathroom, emptying the entire contents of her bathroom cabinet (which resembled a private pharmacy) into a large Harrods shopping bag. Then she went more methodically through the flat and collected every single item of value. But in her drunken haze she left the diary lying under the table.

She would miss her neighbour and only friend Lorna Vey, but the young solicitor was out at work, and Katy couldn't face her. She'd never approved of Sir Lionel. No, best to go now.

The catharsis suddenly over, Katy collapsed into a chair and cried her heart out.

Then she called her sister and told her she was coming home.

CHAPTER 2

Harrogate, Yorkshire

The stately silver-grey Rolls-Royce pulled up to a stretch of newly laid kerb, barely attracting any attention. Harrogate was, after all, *the* conference town of the north. The man who stepped out, however, and glanced towards his latest acquisition, attracted every female eye that happened to be on the street. Spring was nowhere yet in sight, but the man's silver-gold hair shone and gleamed as if he were standing in his own personal sun.

'Is she here yet?' The voice, undoubtedly American, cut through the sound of traffic and city life like an ice-pick through butter. It was not unduly loud, so much as distinctive.

'I think so. I can't imagine Janice not being on hand to lap up the praise.' The voice from the back of the car belonged to Michael Forrester, the Germaine Leisure Corporation's right-hand man in England.

'Good.' Kynaston Germaine walked purposefully through the ornate wrought-iron gates and stood on the newly laid gravel path, feet slightly apart, head to one side, impervious to the biting wind as he stared up at the building. At six feet four, lean and lightly muscled, he radiated power.

'It looks good,' Michael said unnecessarily as he joined

20

him. On first consideration, the last thing Harrogate needed was yet another hotel. But this, the Germanicus Hotel, could hardly be called 'just another' anything. The giant leisure corporation, Germaine, had accepted an award-winning architect's plans which had translated into a finished building that was as magnificent as promised. Only four storeys high and made out of local stone, it blended in seamlessly with the surrounding environment. The gardens had been just as carefully planned, and silver birch softened the surrounding walls, while newly laid lawns were already home to oval flower beds crammed with daffodils and tulips. The sixty rooms all had en-suite bathrooms and, in the deluxe quarters, a living area as well. Nothing had been stinted in its construction, and all the labour had been local. The thirty staff needed to provide five-star treatment were Yorkshire-born and bred.

'It looks good on the outside,' Kynaston Germaine agreed, his ice-blue eyes taking in every minute detail. 'Let's just hope our esteemed interior designer has done the same for the inside.' Michael quickly hid a grin. Janice Polmander was Britain's greatest interior designer — according to Janice Polmander. Fortunately for her, Kyn had done a tour of the other buildings she had worked on, and had agreed.

'Well, there's only one way to find out,' Kyn said briskly, his voice at once rueful and grim. If Janice had truly botched it, he wouldn't want to be in her shoes for all the money in the Germaine bank accounts.

Chipped marble pieces inlaid the concrete steps that led to the large double doors, and Kyn noticed their quality with detached satisfaction. Then, just as he was about to raise his hand, the doors opened with a flourish, and he found himself face to face with his interior designer. Janice

21

Polmander was something to behold. Nearly forty, she looked more like twenty-five. Black hair cut in a sharp, chic bob framed a face that was naturally pale and angular, like that of a cat. She had a personality to match her looks. Her self-confidence could hardly be distinguished from arrogance, and her sexual appetite was well known in the artistic community in which she travelled. So nobody had been surprised when she'd accepted Kynaston Germaine's offer with such alacrity. Being offered free rein in the design of a brand-new five-star hotel was enough to kill for anyway, but from the moment she had walked into Kynaston's office, her acceptance of the commission had never been in question. She'd taken one look at his face, and the superb body that went with it, and her insides had melted. Now, the work done, her eyes roamed over him possessively. She smiled widely, uncaring that she was keeping the owner of the hotel waiting on his own doorstep. She loved tall men, and anything unusual in a man immediately caught her eye. In Kynaston's case it was his hair – it was a wonderful silver colour which contrasted startlingly with his tanned face. And his eyes were like lasers – so icy a blue that in certain lights they looked almost silver.

'Janice. I hope this ambush doesn't mean that the hotel is a mess and you're trying to keep me from noticing?' Kynaston said, his voice now definitely drawling, and Janice felt angry red heat rush to her face. She flung the door open viciously. '*Voilà*,' she snapped, daring him to say one word against her genius. But he didn't have to. The floor was set with black and white hexagonal tiles, the reception desk made of the finest teak. A small but perfectly proportioned chandelier hung from the high-domed ceiling, sending rainbow colours spiralling across walls of deep cream. In narrow floor-to-ceiling vertical stripes, jade marble periodically patterned the expanses of plaster. Huge tubs of living greenery took up the theme, which was then reproduced in the jade-green sofas and chairs that littered the room in discreet groups. There were no pictures or ornamentation of any kind, but the curtains were velvet and floor-length and, of course, jade-green. It was at once simple, stark, beautiful and peaceful.

Kynaston nodded, ignoring Michael's gushing praise. 'We'll make a complete tour, starting with the dining room.'

Janice almost growled. Not a word of praise. Not a word of thanks. Not . . . Kynaston turned and looked at her, and the expression in his eyes stopped her thoughts dead in their tracks. There was something so knowing in them that she was, for the first time in her life, unsure of herself. Then, as she saw a small smile begin to turn up the corners of his impossibly kissable mouth, she almost laughed out loud. It was a thrill to meet a man who was her equal at last. She'd begun to doubt any existed.

The tour was slow, thorough and painstaking. He noticed every detail, from the lace pattern on the doilies in the restaurant to the toning colour of the swizzle-sticks in the bar. They progressed to the upper bedrooms, where the sheets in the deluxe suites were dazzling white satin. 'Only people with no taste sleep in coloured sheets,' Janice informed them arrogantly. She was especially proud of the way she'd decorated the bedrooms. Every floor had a colour scheme; the first was gold and cream, the second was blue and green, the third was grey and pink and the fourth was, as she put it, the celebrity floor, where the colours were jewel-bright and overwhelming, but in oh, such good taste. Every room was different.

23

They were in the last bedroom on the fourth floor, a brilliant concoction of sapphire-blue and dark gold. 'Well?' Janice finally snapped. 'You haven't said a word so far. Are you pleased or not?' She stood with arms akimbo, her breasts rising and falling beneath her jacket with every angry breath she took.

'Mike, take that two o'clock meeting for me in Leeds, will you?' Kyn said, so blandly that Janice almost missed it. Then Michael Forrester was suddenly gone and she realised that she was being neatly manoeuvred. They were alone, in a bedroom, in an empty hotel, and for the first time ever Janice did not feel in complete control. Nor did she care.

'You've done a good job, Janice,' Kyn said simply, and moved towards her. From anyone else such sparing praise would not have been acceptable, but for this man Janice was prepared to make an exception. She had waited so long! With a small sound she launched herself on tiptoe against him, instantly aware of the solidness of the body that gave not an inch as she clung to him, her arms around his neck, her feet leaving the floor, giving him no choice but to take her full weight. Her nipples tingled as her breasts were mashed against the solid wall of muscle under the Italian shirt and finest wool jacket.

Kynaston smiled beneath the greedily sucking mouth. A man would have had to be totally blind not to have read the red-hot signals this woman had been giving out ever since their first encounter, and the simple fact was that he'd had no female companionship since leaving America. Already his body was telling him in no uncertain terms to get on with it, and he neatly pivoted on his heels and laid her down on the geometrically patterned blue and yellow bedspread.

24

Kynaston had had a lot of success with women. Both his looks and his money had helped, of course, but they had only been the very delicious cherries on the cake. Kynaston understood women in a way that few men did. Perhaps it was because he'd raised his younger sister practically on his own, but he both liked, admired and respected women. And they sensed it. His affairs had been long-lasting and satisfying, both in bed and out. He was as happy talking to a woman as seducing her, as content to listen to his lover's opinions and thoughts as have her listen adoringly to him. And yet, despite all this, he'd never married. Sometimes he would wonder why, but mostly he was too busy to give it more than a passing thought. If the right woman came along, he was sure he would know. It was not that he was afraid of marriage or commitment. It was just that he'd never met that certain woman with whom he could fall in love. Now, though, happy to take advantage of a very rare 'one-night stand', he ran his hands down Janice's black-stockinged leg and felt her muscles quiver and jump under his warm fingers. Gently he slipped off her high-heeled shoes and let his fingers trail teasingly over her arches. Then his fingers splayed once more up her calves and ventured on to the creamy white thighs, expertly dealing with her garter and rolling the silky material down her legs.

He took his time. Staring at him with wide eyes darkened with want, Janice heard herself moaning. Impatiently she half-sat, hastily undoing the large brass buttons on her jacket and shucking it off. The pearly buttons on her white satin blouse almost popped as she wriggled out of her clothes like an exotic eel. Kynaston watched her with hooded eyes, appreciative but oddly detached. It was impossible to feel anything for a woman who so obviously felt nothing but lust herself. Her breasts were small and pert, with dark brown aureoles, and when she snatched for his head and dragged him down he offered no objections. Secure in his manhood, he had no problems with women who liked to lead in the bedroom, and Janice certainly knew what she wanted and was determined to get it. As his mouth filled with her nipple, he nipped just enough to make her jump and then his hands were on her, stroking from waist to armpit and then down, to her smooth flanks and between her legs.

Janice moaned, her hands finding their way under his jacket and pushing aside the buttons on his shirt to roam across the smooth, lightly haired chest, hard with muscle and bone. Impatient, desperate to have him inside her. She quickly dispatched his belt buckle and zipper with her red-painted nails. When her hands curled around him he moaned against her breast and obligingly cupped his hands around her surprisingly well-padded derriere, lifting her up to meet him. They came together in a mutually satisfactory blending that made Janice's eyes snap shut, even as her mouth fell open with a groan of pleasure.

Always, before, she'd felt this moment to be proof of her superiority. When a man was inside her, she was in control. *He* was her prisoner. But when she hooked her legs around Kyn's back, her naked body pressed against his still almost fully clothed one, she felt curiously vulnerable. She contracted her inner muscles, massaging and guiding his manhood, but she found that he was still the one dictating their rhythm, which was maddeningly slow and thorough.

Within minutes her pique at not being the one in charge was forgotten with her first, high cries of orgasmic ecstasy.

Later, when she was driving back to London, she felt

almost relieved that she would not be meeting Kynaston Germaine alone again. He was so . . . controlled, so . . . well . . . *strong*, in every sense of the word, that it would take a very special woman indeed to take him on.

When Kyn got back to his base in Leeds, Michael was waiting with the minutes of the meeting. It held no surprises. Planning permission for the domed park had been granted, but the local environmentalists were up in arms. 'Get Vince Colcort in on this. He should have all the green issues catered for.'

'Right,' Michael said, scribbling fiercely. He was immensely excited about Kyn's plans for Yorkshire. The Three Peaks Development Scheme was a three-point plan, cunning and yet simple in its execution. First, the Germanicus at Harrogate would provide the base for the planned holiday package Kyn was offering his customers. Secondly, the domed pleasure centre, where construction would start any day now that planning permission had gone through, would be a large complex built entirely under glass in the small valley in Wharfedale Kyn had selected, and provide everything from swimming and boating activities to tennis, squash and sauna/health facilities. A twenty-hole golf-course was already being sculpted out on the drawing-board, and would be within walking distance of the leisure dome. The third spearhead in the tourist attraction stakes was the dry ski run Kyn planned to build on the sight of Ravenheights farm, which would, it was hoped, lure non-skiers into learning the art, and from there lure them to Kyn's main base, Vermont, where he was the 'ski king', boasting hotels in all the top resorts. It was brilliant. Even his competitors had grudgingly admitted as much.

'What's the latest from Roger?'

Michael consulted the message he had taken not half an hour ago. Roger Gibb, who worked closely with Kyn exclusively in Vermont, hadn't sounded too happy. 'He wants you to call him back. He said to tell you that you were right.'

Quickly, Kyn punched out the numbers of his Vermont office. 'Roger? Kyn. You're sure?' he said briskly, without preamble.

'Yes,' Roger Gibb replied, just as shortly, used to his boss's crisp and efficient way of talking on the phone. 'It's not yet official, but old man Ventura has definitely approached our largest stockholders. Bradley for sure, and two others are making all the wrong denial noises.'

'Damn!' Ventura Industries was *the* biggest privately owned company in America. A colossus, it had its fingers in pies as diverse as oil and aircraft manufacture, leisure and tin-mining. It owned hotels and oil tankers. It was constantly moving, growing, shifting and expanding, under the control of Leslie Salvatore Ventura, its legendary head, who was always one step ahead of the competition, better financed, and better informed. No one quite knew how much Leslie Ventura was worth, but when you were thinking in terms of billions, putting a direct figure on it hardly seemed worth the effort.

'So they do want to expand their leisure enterprises.' Kyn spoke his thoughts aloud. 'I knew they would as soon as I heard the old man was selling off his steel monopolies. Damn!' The funny thing was, Kynaston had a lot in common with Ventura. They'd both started off dirt-poor and become self-made men of considerable wealth. They'd both lived, at one time or other, in the slums of

New York. And they both recognized the unbreakable bonds of family and tradition.

But Kynaston was only thirty-two and still only a multi-millionaire. And Germaine, unlike Ventura, was a public company. 'Damn the shareholders,' Kyn muttered. Oh, he still held fifty per cent of all the shares, but Ventura had the money to buy the other fifty per cent. And being equal partners with a behemoth like Ventura Industries was tantamount to being gobbled up like a tasty sprat. 'Who's in charge of the takeover bid, do you know?' he asked.

'Word has it that it's the son,' replied Roger.

Kyn nodded, his face tight with concentration and determination. 'That's good.'

Over the line, Roger Gibb laughed softly. 'I know you can take the son, but don't think the old man will stand by and let him screw it up. Everyone knows Keith wants out of Ventura and into SoHo. And everyone knows the old man won't let him.'

Kyn grunted, thinking rapidly. Keith was undoubtedly an artist of some talent, and, ironically enough, Kyn had one of his paintings in his own collection. Keith Ventura just as certainly had no head for business and even less backbone to survive in his father's shadow. But Leslie Ventura's son was his property, and at Ventura Industries he stayed. None of the Ventura family's internal squabblings would have meant anything to Kyn, except that Keith Ventura had been handed the task of taking over *his* company. 'No doubt the old man thinks junior can cut his teeth on us,' he said sharply, 'before going on to bigger and better things.'

Across the miles, Roger Gibb grinned wolfishly at his office wall. If the old man thought that, then he was in for one hell of a surprise. Giant or not, Roger didn't give much for Ventura's chances.

'All right, Roger. I want you to keep me informed. They won't move in too quickly for two reasons: first, Ventura is by nature a cautious man. And secondly, he wants Keith to do all the work. The last thing he'll expect is for us to bite back.'

'Right. Anything else?'

'No. I'll start Operation Biteback from over here,' Kyn said softly, and hung up. He moved to the window, his mind working rapidly. 'Mike, the opening ceremony for the Germanicus is the second of next month, right? So get the shareholders list faxed over, and invite everyone with a stake of one per cent or more in Germaine Leisure to the party. I want them to see how far we're going, and all without the help of Ventura Industries. Also, get on to the money men – I want to raise the payments on the shares to the maximum possible. Appealing to a shareholder's greed never fails.'

Michael nodded, his admiration for his boss growing. Other men, on hearing that Leslie Ventura was after them, would just give up, sell high and retire. But not Kyn. 'And what's the current status on that farm . . . Ravenheights? Have they agreed to sell yet?'

'No. But I'm sure it's only the son who's being so awkward about it,' Michael added hastily, not liking to admit his continued defeat on this matter. 'My man in Otley tells me the bank is ready to call in its loan, so it's only a matter of time,' he reassured Kyn.

'You offered to buy the livestock? Sheep, isn't it?'

'Yes. That was a good idea of yours,' Michael fawned. 'I haven't heard back yet, but I'm sure they'll see reason.'

30

'I'm sure they will,' Kyn murmured, but his thoughts were obviously elsewhere.

Michael watched him thoughtfully. In all the years he'd worked with Germaine, he'd never seen the tall American lose his temper or self-control once, not even when dealing with the most irascible of Harrogate's town council. 'I'm curious, Kyn. Have you always got your own way?'

Kyn turned from his contemplation of the city below, and Michael was stunned by the bleakness of his expression. His eyes appeared unusually out of focus, as if he were looking not at Michael, but at something else, far, far away.

'Not always,' he admitted finally, and it seemed to his employee that he'd gone pale under his tan. 'I was fourteen before I really knew how to get what I wanted. And a little older than that before I realised that you always have to pay for it.' He moved to the window and looked out at the grey city and the grey, rain-choked sky, his thoughts winging out across the Atlantic to America. Somewhere out there, Kyn knew, *he* was waiting and watching. And planning.

Demanding payment . . .

CHAPTER 3

New York

Marion Ventura Prescott shifted nervously in her seat as the judge sat down behind a darkly imposing mahogany desk. Judge Brenda C. Foulton looked first at her and then at Lance Prescott, her gimlet gaze so obviously unimpressed by both their counsels that Marion almost laughed out loud. It was her rapidly stretching nerves that made her want to giggle, of course. She wanted this *over* with.

'I take it the situation has not changed since last we met?' Brenda Foulton's voice, pure Mississippi, cut through the musty ambience like a meat-cleaver.

'No, Your Honour, it hasn't.' Bernard Menz, her lawyer, leapt straight in where angels would fear to tread, his tone almost hearty. 'Mr Prescott simply refuses to abide honourably by the pre-nuptial contract he signed on his marriage to my client.'

'Your Honour, it is still our contention that undue pressure was put on my client . . .' Lance's attorney, Ernest Vent, a small, imperious-looking individual, was waved to silence by the merest flick of Judge Foulton's hand. Brenda Foulton leaned forward, the gentle swishing of her black robes as she moved the only sound in the suddenly still room. Her steel-grey eyes swept over the

32

scene in front of her in a cynical but unbiased appraisal. Everyone knew who Marion Ventura Prescott was, of course: the only daughter of Leslie Ventura; it was hard to calculate her personal wealth. With various stocks and shares in the even more various Ventura companies, a penthouse suite at her father's luxurious hotel, the Ventura Towers, and another stately mansion in Connecticut, not to mention furs and jewels, she had to be worth somewhere in the region of fifty million. And she looked it, Brenda Foulton thought without envy, her eyes taking in the small, slender figure encased in Givenchy white linen, with a dark green silk cravat that complemented her pale skin. Lustrous sable-dark hair was now shaped in an elegant chignon, and pearl stud earrings were her only ornamentation. She looked the epitome of a New York heiress. Only the eyes didn't fit. They looked back at Brenda now, dark brown pools of apprehension that had that curious, flat look that only months of sleeplessness and dull ache could achieve. Yes, the eyes always told the real story.

Next, Judge Brenda Foulton glanced at her husband, who would within minutes be her ex-husband. Lance P. Prescott III, in his thousand-dollar-plus suit, with equally expensive haircut and accessories, looked, if anything, even more the part of a mega-rich New York socialite; in his case, it was a sham. Oh, the Prescotts had been wealthy enough in the past: generations of Prescotts had enjoyed the status of the select elite that had had its heyday at the turn of and in the early part of this century. Then the Wall Street Crash had robbed the Prescotts of everything except their prestigious ancestry and social standing. But the family still lived as they had in their heydey. And they managed it, of course, in just the same way that this, the latest Prescott prodigy, had done it. By marrying money.

'You spoke, I believe, Mr Vent, of having documented proof that . . .' Judge Foulton quickly checked her notes, her crisp voice giving away nothing of her thoughts '. . . ahh, yes, that "malicious and deliberate pressure" had been brought to bear on Mr Prescott by his father-in-law.' Brenda Foulton glanced at the lawyer, who confidently extracted a sheaf of papers from his briefcase. Marion glanced nervously at her own counsel, who shook his head with a confident smile.

'I have, Your Honour.' Vent handed the documents over with a flourish. 'As you will see, Your Honour, Mr Ventura practically threatened . . .'

'I can read, Mr Vent,' Brenda Foulton said tetchily, and Vent subsided with wry discretion.

Lance sat ramrod-straight and stared intently at the judge, the epitome of a gentleman-about-town. He was so perfect for the part he'd opted to play that it was no wonder her father had thought him ideal husband-material. He had the name; the Venturas had the money. How pleased the Prescott matriarch and Marion's father must have been the day their wedding announcement went out in the *New York Times*.

'This document seems to me to be a straightforward agreement of employment, Mr Vent.' Brenda Foulton's voice once more dragged Marion back to the present. 'I can see no reason why this document should have any bearing on the settlement in this case.'

'But Your Honour, Leslie Ventura was virtually blackmailing my client into signing that pre-nuptial agreement! His very employment at Ventura Pharmaceuticals depended on it.'

34

Brenda Foulton lowered her spectacles to the end of her nose and looked Vent straight in the eye. 'Your client, Mr Vent, was under no *obligation* to sign this document . . .' she rattled it imperiously '. . . unless he so chose. And, since it promised a high executive position at a correspondingly high salary, it is not surprising that he *did* so choose. He also *chose* to sign the pre-nuptial agreement. Mr Menz, is your client willing to abide by the stipulations set out in the contract?'

'Yes, Your Honour,' Bernard Menz said with alacrity. 'I have the banker's draft for $500,000 right here.' He extracted the cheque from his own briefcase and handed it to the judge. 'Together with the titles to the Dino Ferrari automobile also stipulated, and the deeds to Mrs Prescott's chalet in Stowe, Vermont, also as agreed.'

The judge took the papers, checked them carefully, then handed them on to Ernest Vent, who took them as if he were handling poison.

Judge Foulton turned her attention back to the two people most involved. They were both pale, but for patently different reasons. 'Since you have been unable to come to an amicable, mutually agreeable compromise between yourselves, your divorce petition is granted. On the matter of the settlement, I find for Mrs Marion Margaret Ventura Prescott. The pre-nuptial agreement stands. I am witness to the fact that it has been honoured, in accordance with the statutes of the State of New York. You are dismissed.'

Marion blinked numbly. It was only when Bernard Menz gently touched her elbow and winked down at her that she realised the nightmare was over. She rose shakily to her feet and moved to the green-baize-backed door, her knees like jelly. Outside, in the cool, marbled hall, she took a deep breath.

'Well, Ms Ventura, how does it feel to be a free woman again? And so cheaply, at that?' Bernard asked with a wry smile.

'Cheap as far as money is concerned,' she corrected grimly. 'It certainly didn't come cheap in any other way.' Briefly she remembered how Lance's bed-hopping had humiliated her, making her feel so unattractive and worthless as a woman. She remembered snickered comments, overheard at parties, about how Lance liked to spend Ventura money, but not time with his wife. She remembered the look of disappointment and disapproval on her father's face when she'd finally taken a hold on her life and informed him she that was going to seek a divorce. Yes, it had been a long, hard climb out of the pit she had dug for herself. But at last she was free.

'Your ex did put up a spirited fight,' said Bernard Menz. And who could blame him? Five hundred thousand dollars and a Ferrari wouldn't last Lance Prescott long. Not after his mother had taken out her share – and Bernard didn't doubt that she would. Moira Prescott had worked long and hard to ensure that her son was the man the Ventura 'Princess' married. 'I think Mr Prescott will have taken this setback rather badly,' he added, with true lawyerly understatement.

Marion laughed out loud. She couldn't help it. Lance, for all his angelic looks, was a devil she was well rid of. But in the end not even he had been able to stand up to Daddy's might. Marion suddenly sobered, her piquant face suddenly sad. 'Nobody stands up to Daddy,' she murmured, but her lawyer was too much of a gentleman to show that he'd heard.

Over his shoulder Marion saw Lance and his lawyer emerge from the judge's chambers. For a moment their eyes met, and Marion shivered and turned quickly away. 'Let's get out of here, Bernard. Since you did such a good job for me, I'll let you take me to lunch,' she added magnanimously, a twinkle in her eye.

'Delighted, Ms Ventura,' Bernard said, and meant it. Lance watched them go. His green eyes narrowed, his pupils shrinking to almost nothing. He looked like some particularly venomous snake, but when Ernest Vent turned to shake his hand in commiseration Lance's grip was firm, his corresponding smile almost pleasant. Nobody would have guessed, looking at the fair-headed, handsome young man with the perfect face, that he was seething with a hatred, bitterness, fear and frustration so strong that he could hardly focus properly on the white-clad figure leaving the courthouse.

Bitch. Bitch. *Bitch*!

Marion watched Bernard's car pull away with a small smile, then turned and nodded at the doorman who manned Ventura Towers. 'Chivers,' she said amicably, with a sunny smile.

'Mrs Prescott.'

'Ms Ventura now, please, Chivers,' she said gently, and walked into the foyer, where she took her private elevator to the penthouse. She draped her white sheepskin-lined flock coat across the nearest chair with a sigh. Long bottle-green velvet curtains framed windows that gave a breath-taking panoramic view of the Big Apple, while original works of art by Dali, Warhol and of course Keith Ventura held court on the walls. Orange tiger lilies were obviously 'in' this week, she noticed absently, for huge arrangements of them were strategically dotted around. Marion shucked off her shoes and went straight to the bathroom, where she filled the tub with freesia-scented foam and soaked for a good twenty minutes.

Slowly, very slowly, she began to relax. She was actually free of Lance and her mockery of a marriage. It was so wonderful she could hardly believe it. She sat up in the tub, her small pink-tipped breasts bobbing against the surface of moisturizing foam, and tried to remember just how she had felt on her wedding day. She'd been eighteen, so perhaps there was some excuse for her after all. And she'd been so well protected. No man ever got near Daddy's little girl, except, of course, men like Lance Prescott: men with pedigree and an ancestry that went back to the *Mayflower*. And even these blessed individuals were only allowed to meet the Ventura 'Princess', as the Press had taken to calling her, during strictly controlled social events. Consequently, she'd known nothing of men – absolutely nothing. Was it so surprising, then, that she'd been dazzled by Lance, who had performed his courtship rituals so well?

Reluctantly abandoning the cooling water, she wrapped herself in a fleecy towel and moved to one of the bathroom's many full-length mirrors. What she saw was a five-foot five-inch, twenty-four-year-old woman with bruised, dark eyes and damp dark hair curling around slender shoulders. 'Face it, Marion,' she said softly. 'You're the Ventura Princess and nothing more than that. Nothing more at all . . .' She had done nothing to earn her vast wealth – absolutely nothing. She hadn't, in fact, ever done a true day's work in her life. Chairing a few charity meetings and planting the odd tree in a park simply didn't count.

38

She turned abruptly and walked away from her reflection, going over to the built-in wardrobe that lined the entire length of one wall and pulling out the first hanger she encountered – a pale apricot Emanuel skirt, with an ultra-fashionable, simple cream blouse. Listlessly she dressed and brushed out hair tangled by the steam. She felt so tired. Even though the divorce was now behind her, she knew that there was still so much more to be done before she could call her life her own. But right now, right this minute, she was too exhausted to face up to yet another upheaval in her life. She moved to her bed, a huge, circular English-made piece that was rumoured to have belonged to Napoleon's Josephine, and lay face-down, burying her cool, make-up-free face against the white satin pillow. Today had been the most shattering of her life. Thank God it was over.

Five minutes later the telephone rang, the sharp, intrusive sound snatching her abruptly from the jaws of sleep. 'Yes?' she snapped crossly.

'Marion? Oh, I'm so glad you're there.' Marion recognized Carole Ballinger's voice immediately. She was her father's latest 'companion', a pleasant woman whose only son was currently running for the Senate. It was so unlike her to call that Marion found herself sitting up in bed, her heart missing a beat.

'Daddy?' The strangulated word feathered past her lips, but it was obviously too quiet for Carole to hear, because she carried on with barely a pause.

'Listen, Marion, I'm afraid something . . . very sad has happened. Keith has . . . well . . . he's been silly with some drugs. We're at the Pavilion – you know, the Manhattan Hospital? I think you'd better come over, Marion, dear. Your father is very upset.'

39

'Oh, no,' she whispered. 'I'll be right over.' Fortunately, taxis outside Ventura Towers were not hard to come by, and within minutes she was heading for the hospital. In the back, impervious to the cold March air, Marion gnawed on her lower lip. She knew Keith smoked grass, of course, but surely that was all? In her mind's eye she pictured her brother as she'd last seen him. It had been at his studio on the Lower East Side, which he'd managed to keep on in spite of Daddy's disapproval. He'd been sitting around the table with several of his artist cronies, baffling Marion with their talk of neo-impressionist new-wave punk art or some such thing. He'd been drinking cheap wine and was dressed in paint-smeared jeans. She knew how much he hated working at the office, how much he resented working with figures when he itched to work with paints. Had he turned to hard drugs in order to try and ease the pain, the sheer frustration he must have felt? Her heart lurched. Surely she would have known? She shook her head as the scenery sped past the window. It didn't matter. If he had got hooked on coke or crack or something, Daddy would help him. Modern clinics like the Betty Ford centre could do wonders nowadays.

As she paid the driver and hurried into the hospital reception area she was struck by a wave of guilt. Keith had always relied on her so much, and especially so since their mother had died. She was the only member of the family Keith felt he could talk to – all the other Ventura cousins and uncles and nephews worked in the firm and enjoyed it, each of them jockeying for a higher position, each venomously jealous of Keith's unassailable position as heir apparent.

'Oh, Keith,' she whispered, then quickly stiffened her

lips and backbone as she spotted Carole Ballinger beckoning her from the elevators.

'He's on the fifth floor,' she said quietly.

'This is Intensive Care,' Marion whispered, appalled, as the elevator opened out on to aseptic white corridors and rooms filled with terrifying machines. Suddenly, horrifyingly, she knew that it was worse, much worse than she'd imagined. Carole kept glancing at her anxiously as they made their way down the corridor. They turned a corner and stopped, both women wearing looks of utter dismay at the scene spread out before them like some ghastly panorama.

Outside a room, the door gaping wide open, Leslie Ventura was slumped against a wall, his shoulders heaving, great tearing sobs shuddering out of him. At sixty-four he was still a superbly fit man, carrying twelve stones of weight with ease on a six-foot figure. His full head of still dark hair, his healthily tanned skin and his usually imperious way of walking, sitting, standing and looking all combined to negate his years. Now though, he looked old. He looked defeated. He looked so helplessly out of control that Marion almost failed to recognize him. By his side was Maurice Gorman, the Ventura family doctor for over thirty years. 'I'm sorry, Les. Oh, God, I'm so sorry. There was just nothing we could do. The amount he'd taken . . . even if we'd got to him in time I don't think . . .'

Marion felt the corridor buck under her feet. She slipped sideways, cannoning into the wall, and pain shot through her shoulder. She felt it only momentarily. Keith was dead. He was gone. He was . . . gone. Quickly, Carole thrust a chair behind Marion's knees and gently but firmly pushed her down.

'He never suffered, Les,' Maurice's voice carried down

41

the corridor, and Marion grasped them like straws. Keith hated pain. He hated being ill.

'I've lost my son!' Leslie Ventura roared, the sound making Marion, Carole and a nurse just stepping out of a room behind them all jump. Maurice kept silent. He knew that Keith had been too knowledgeable about drugs not to know that the amount he had injected into himself must be lethal . . . 'What am I going to do without him?' Leslie asked, his face a mask of ravaged pain.

Searching for some crumb of comfort, Maurice gripped his heaving shoulder. 'You still have Marion.'

Leslie Ventura half moaned and half laughed. 'Marion is not a *son*,' he hissed, shrugging off the comforting hands. 'She is not my *heir*. Hell, today she got divorced, and she hasn't even given me a *grandson*!'

'You don't know what you're saying,' Maurice warned truthfully. 'It's the shock that's talking.' With considerable difficulty he prised his old friend away from the wall and led him gently along the corridor, away from the two women who had gone totally unnoticed.

Carole turned to Marion. Only then, looking into devastated, *terribly* hurt eyes, did she realise what her father's unthinking words must have meant to her. 'Oh, Marion,' she whispered, but Marion's eyes were fixed on the open doorway, where a nurse was gently pulling a sheet up over Keith Ventura's lifeless face.

She shook her head. What a waste. Oh, what a *waste*!

Marion turned and fled.

And for a long time Carole stood alone in the corridor, hoping that Leslie Ventura hadn't just lost his daughter as well as his son.

CHAPTER 4

Bryn suddenly slammed on the brakes and the tractor wheels ploughed up mud, making a few sheep that had come to meet her skitter away, bleating angrily. Inside the tractor cabin, she snatched the binoculars that were with her wherever she went and quickly directed them towards the swift flash of brown she had spotted up in the heavens. There! Over by Morreland marsh. It was! Her mouth curled into a wide, happy smile, revealing perfectly even, naturally white teeth. A hen harrier. Delighted, she watched the bird of prey circle lazily, wondering how many people casually glancing into the sky might think it was a common buzzard instead of one of Yorkshire's rarer birds.

Bryn leaned back in her seat with a sigh. It had been Hadrian who had awakened her interest in birds. Coming from York to the wide open moorlands as a boy, his new eyes had looked on in wonder at things Bryn had always taken for granted. Sighing once more with satisfaction, she put the tractor back into gear, slowly ambling her way towards the feeding troughs. She hurried through her task today, anxious to get home before Katy woke up. She frowned as she hauled hay and cut string. Katy had arrived in the early evening, and after the briefest of kisses for her sister and father had gone straight to bed. It was so unlike her that Bryn had spent the whole night tossing and turning with worry.

She was glad to get back to Ravenheights, and even more pleased to discover that Katy hadn't yet risen. Now *that* was more like her sister, Bryn thought with a grin, as she prepared a tray of tea and toast and carefully mounted the narrow wooden staircase. Halfway up the narrow stairwell the wall tended to bulge inwards, and she carefully negotiated the even narrower space, holding the tray carefully aloft.

Yesterday, she had frantically cleaned and aired Katy's old room, changing the sheets and bringing out the last of her mother's home-made pot-pourri to scent the old wardrobe and dresser. She'd cleaned the windows, put up the spare curtains that were a bright and breezy lilac, and hunted high and low for a matching-coloured lilac vase that she'd eventually found in the attic, and filled with snowdrops and crocus.

The landing floorboards creaked their usual warning of somebody passing, and Bryn tapped on her sister's door and walked straight in, feeling a wonderful sense of nostalgia. 'Out of bed, lazybones. There's sheep in them thar hills.'

'Oh, shut up!' Katy groaned, but grinned as she struggled out of the enfolding blankets. Bryn pulled the curtains with gusto, and white March sunlight flooded in. 'It's bloody freezing in here,' Katy complained. She'd forgotten about the lack of central heating at the farm. 'No wonder you're always wearing corduroys and thick sweaters.' She eyed her sister with a jaundiced impatience. She hadn't changed. 'Bryn, why don't you *diet*?' she said before she could stop herself, then felt instantly guilty as her sister blushed a painful red and obviously swallowed back a hard lump in her throat. 'Oh, forget I said that,' she said quickly. 'I'm just grumpy in the mornings, you know that.' But Katy was glad that she would always be the beautiful one, not an ugly duckling like her sister. Not even to herself would she admit that Bryn had an inner beauty of spirit that transcended physical allure.

Bryn grinned. 'Right. Eat your toast while it's hot. No honey or jam. See, I remembered.'

Katy sighed and, ignoring the toast, reached for the mug of tea, grimacing at its cumbersome heaviness. 'I'll have to bring my tea-set out of the car,' she said, and looked at her sister over the chipped mug rim. 'It's Spode. You know about that sort of thing. Is it any good?'

'Spode? Very good.'

'It's rimmed with gold too. Real gold, so Sir Lionel said.'

'Sir Lionel?' Bryn's eyes widened ever further, and suddenly Katy felt an almost overwhelming surge of love and guilt. She was such a bitch sometimes, but Bryn was always so full of love; she always wished the best for everybody. In London everyone tried to bring you down. That way there was one less person to scramble over on the quest to get the top.

'Oh, Bryn, I'm so glad to be home. London's horrible. Oh, I'm glad I went, and became a famous model and everything, but it's not home, is it?' Suddenly she was crying and for a second Bryn stared at her helplessly, totally astonished. She'd never, for a single instant, thought that Katy had been anything but deliriously happy in London, with her wonderful career and all the friends she talked about over the phone. Putting her sister's slopping mug of tea on to the table, she quickly

45

took Katy in her arms, holding her golden head against her amply padded chest.

'It's all right, Katy. Really it is. You're home now,' she crooned gently. With her cheek pressed against her sister's green woolly jumper, Katy laughed through her misery. Home. If only it were.

Stowe, Vermont, USA

'And this is why we must be ever-vigilant, ever-wary of developers waving the green flag. Thank you.' The applause that rang out in the small hotel's conference room was agreeably enthusiastic. Morgan smiled and nodded as several people in the first few rows got to their feet, clapping wildly.

'I'm sure you'll join me in thanking Mr Morgan of the Green Vermont Society for his informative and disturbing speech,' the local Green candidate for Stowe said into the microphone, and commenced a political speech of his own as Morgan made his way determinedly into the crowd, several hands reaching out to slap him on the back as he did so. He stopped and chatted to as many as possible, since all of them were potential converts to the Green Vermont Society, and, for Morgan, the Society was everything.

It was the stepping stone to destroying Kynaston Germaine.

A student buttonholed him, dragging a grey-haired companion (obviously his father), along with him. 'That was a great talk, Morgan. I'm glad somebody's making a stand against the greedy leisure companies.' He was all youthful enthusiasm.

Morgan forced himself to smile patiently. 'Do you live around here, Mr . . .?'

'Hank. No, worse luck. Dad and I are just spending a few weeks' vacation here.'

'Not staying at a Germaine Leisure hotel, I hope?' Morgan said quickly. Tonight his main argument had been against the new Germaine hotel due to open in the New Year.

The student shook his head emphatically. 'No way. Seems to me, though, that you must have your work cut out for you, taking on such a big company.'

Morgan smiled and shrugged, the movement causing his dark brown hair to ripple in the overhead lighting. His eyes gleamed like polished onyx. 'Somebody has to take on the big fish.'

Morgan was a good-looking man. Six feet tall, with wide-apart dark eyes, strong nose and jaw, he had a charisma that was undeniable. The student's father, the owner and editor of a small newspaper back in Maine, could easily see why he was such a popular speaker, and no doubt a big hit with the ladies. Their adoration had been obvious right the way through his lecture. He'd photograph well, too, his editor's experience assured him, and in his mind's eye he pictured Morgan's snapshot in the middle of a page. Perhaps it would be worth doing an interview. 'Hi, I'm Alfred Johns,' he introduced himself, since his son obviously wasn't going to. 'I own a small newspaper. Would you like to go on the record?' he queried, sensing a story.

'We need the help of the Press, of course,' Morgan said quietly. 'Otherwise the big corporations will continue to destroy our world until there's nothing left.'

'I understand your worries,' the newspaper man said, 'but I don't see what the Germaine Leisure corporation has done that's so terrible. Its hotel hasn't even opened yet, and – '

'But does Stowe need another hotel?' Morgan cut in hastily, before the other could finish. 'Hell no, what it needs is more trees, cleaner streets. Less waste, more recycling . . .'

'Sure, sure, but face it, Morgan. People are lazy. They don't really *care* what happens to the world, so long as their own private life is comfortable and pleasant,' Alfred Johns pointed out truthfully.

'That's what's wrong with the world,' his son hissed, his slightly long face flushing an angry red. 'That's why we need more societies like Morgan's here. Together, people *can* make a difference . . .'

'Oh, grow up, son,' Alfred snapped angrily. Why can't you be more like Tom? Now he . . .'

At this point, Morgan abruptly stopped listening. Hadn't another voice, at another time, said those exact same words? Only the name was different, of course . . . 'Why can't you be more like Kynaston . . .' How many times had he heard that? And from how many people? Teachers at school. 'Why can't you study harder, the way Kynaston does?' His own parents. 'Kynaston does his chores without complaining. Why can't you?' From his so-called friends. 'Come on, hit the ball, Morgan. Geez, Kynaston can hit it *yards* farther, and he's younger than you.' Kynaston. Always Kynaston. Sometimes Morgan wished he could gather all those people together under one roof and show them just exactly what their precious Kynaston had turned out like. He would give anything to point out to them how their hero had grabbed land, ruined it, destroyed it, how he had grown rich off the back-breaking work of other people – show those college teachers of his just how he had put to use all that education they'd so gladly given him. Show those same baseball-

48

playing boys just how hard they could work on one of Kynaston's construction sites, and how little wages they'd get compared to the great chairman's fat salary. Show his parents . . .

Morgan took a deep, painful breath. He could never show his parents anything now. Even if they were alive, they'd never believe him. Never trust him again. Not after that final betrayal. Even he, who had thought he knew Kynaston so well, had been totally unprepared for that final, breathtaking betrayal. He'd never believed Kynaston capable of such cruelty. How wrong could one man be? he thought, his lips twisting painfully. But no more. Now he was almost ready for Kynaston Germaine. Almost ready . . .

Suddenly he became aware of the two pairs of eyes watching him and abruptly, painfully, he snapped back to the present. 'Sorry, but I see so many fathers and sons fighting. It's the generation gap, I guess. Look, I have to go, I'm afraid. Perhaps we can get together some other time and discuss it further.' He muttered the platitude and wandered away, cursing the old fool under his breath.

He stopped as a tall, dark woman, dressed in a bright orange kaftan, took hold of his arm. 'I heard all that,' she said, her large, dark eyes caressing him. 'You're really into this whole green issue thing, aren't you?' she said softly.

Morgan nodded, the fanaticism slowly dying out of his eyes. 'Yeah.'

'You lived here all your life? Is that why you don't want to see any more hotels built? Like this latest Germaine Corporation building?'

She saw his shoulders tense, then he turned to her, his eyes darker than she'd expected. A shaft of desire ran through her. She liked strong men. Men who knew what

49

they wanted. Men who were *alive*, men who had a fire in their belly. And this one certainly had that.

'It's not just the hotel,' he said, his voice hardening. 'It's all the paraphernalia that goes with it. It's . . .' He stopped suddenly, and shook his head. A sheepish smile flickered across his face and was gone. 'Sorry. I get carried away, I know.'

The woman smiled. 'There's more to it that than that, though, isn't there, babe?' she pressed softly, and Morgan glanced at her quickly, surprised by the caressing, knowing tone of her voice.

'There is,' he admitted after a moment's thoughtful silence. 'I lost my farm to the Germaine Leisure Corporation a few years ago. A few? Did I say a few?' he laughed hollowly. 'It's more like ten, twenty years.' He shook his head, his eyes narrowing as they looked around the crowd, then moved to the window, and to the view outside. Already the winter season was all but over, and most of the winter visitors would be gone. But the Germaine Leisure Corporation went on. It already had hotels in Killington and Sugarbush, the top two resorts. Now the latest hotel was going up here.

He'd be glad when Kynaston came back home to Vermont. He didn't like him being in England, where he couldn't keep an eye on him.

'I'm sorry, babe,' the woman mumbled sadly, realising that a little loving comfort was the last thing on his mind. Pity. He sure was a handsome dude . . .

'So am I,' Morgan said softly, his eyes narrowing, the woman already forgotten. 'So am I.'

In the kitchen, Bryn stripped the excess fat off the last of the mutton and added it to the enormous pot. Katy watched her sister as she methodically peeled and chopped carrots, onions, parsnips and swedes and added them to the stew. She was restless already and she hadn't been home a full day. She'd be lucky if she could think of a single thing to put in her diary tonight. Her diary! Quickly she shot up from her chair and ran up the stairs, frantically searching her suitcases. But she had forgotten to pack it. Damn!

She crossed the landing and went into Bryn's room, quickly searching the dresser for the notepaper Bryn always kept in her top drawer. That would do. She needed something on which to jot down her thoughts or she'd go mad with boredom. Bryn had just finished mixing the dumplings when she came back down.

At twelve on the dot the men trooped in. Katy watched in amazement as the twins sat down, their shy eyes studiously avoiding looking at her, for everyone knew about Katy Whittaker who'd gone to London to be a model.

'You and I will have to sit at the counter,' Bryn said, carefully carrying two nearly overfilling bowls to the wooden cupboard tops by the sink. 'You don't mind, do you, Katy?'

Katy glanced at the bowl of meat, vegetables and fluffy dumplings and felt her stomach turn over. 'Nothing changes,' she said, and only when a quality in the silence suddenly wormed its way into her bitter, isolated little world did she realise she must have said it with all the despair and contempt she felt. Oh, hell! 'I mean,' she said hastily, grappling for a way out, 'that it's good to be home. London is a big and exciting place, but home is . . . well . . . home. And modelling isn't as glamorous as people think; there are always twenty of us going after one job, and the girls can be really bitchy.'

51

'Don't worry, Katy,' Bryn said gently. 'You're here now, with us. At Ravenheights. You'll be all right.'

Katy laughed, then put a hand to her mouth, realising it sounded almost hysterical. Dear old Bryn. Dear fat, ugly Bryn, who loved the sheep and the cold and the endless cricket stories. But Katy knew that Ravenheights could never be *her* home, *her* refuge. Bryn would never understand that. And because she never would, Katy did, for perhaps the first time in her life, an unselfish thing.

'I know. I can't tell you how glad I am to be back. I don't know what I'd do without you and Dad and this place. It's like a sanctuary.' Her voice trailed off, becoming flat and dull, her energy spent. 'A sanctuary.' A prison, more like.

John Whittaker's chair squeaked as he pushed himself away from the table and walked over to give his elder daughter an awkward hug. 'It's all right, lass. And you didn't do wrong, coming home when the world got a bit too rough on you. Eh, Bryony Rose?'

Bryn nodded, but, looking warmly at her father's sad face, she suddenly felt a shiver snake down her back. Something was wrong. Something was terribly wrong. But now was not the time to pursue it.

Katy seemed to cheer up a little after that, and even ate some stew, though Bryn noticed she didn't touch the meat or dumplings. The men, silent and awkward after the little emotional scene, ate more quickly than usual and left with quick goodbyes to Bryn and Katy.

Bryn waited until her father, always last out, was alone in the little hallway, putting on his wellingtons, then nipped out and caught his arm. 'Dad? What is it?'

'I don't get you, lass.'

'Dad!' Bryn said, her voice knowing, and John sighed.

He never had been able to keep anything from his younger daughter. Wordlessly he handed her a letter.

'Came this morning. I wanted to wait to tell you. Especially now, with Katy home and all. Ah, lass, I don't know what to say.'

His voice was breaking and he quickly turned and strode out into the yard, for a moment reminding her of the man he'd once been, the strong, unbeatable man she'd imagined him to be as child. She went back into the kitchen, glad that Katy had moved off into the living room – washing-up had always been her most hated chore.

Slowly Bryn opened the letter. It was from the bank. Through the polite, technical jargon, Bryn easily picked out the nitty gritty of the matter. They had one month to pay the bank what was owed them, or they would foreclose. Which meant they would have to sell to the Germaine Leisure Corporation or the bank would do it for them.

Bryn took a deep breath. She'd known this moment would come, of course, deep down. But she'd never *believed* it would. She couldn't lose Ravenheights. She couldn't. Especially now, when Katy needed it so much. Her sister had obviously had a hard time in London, and needed refuge. And she, Bryn, would fight tooth and nail to see that she had just that. Now, more than ever, she was determined to hang on to the farm. For Katy's sake as much as her own.

She'd have to go and see this Kynaston Germaine himself. Talk to him in person. *Explain*. Surely he'd understand?

CHAPTER 5

Marion stepped on to the sidewalk and looked up. The Ventura office building was modest by New York standards, standing only thirty storey high. But every floor was taken up with offices that dealt solely with Ventura Industries. Hundreds of offices, with thousands of people, running diverse companies that all sheltered under the Ventura umbrella.

She turned and watched as the black limousine pulled slowly away. From now on she'd take a taxi to work. Or walk – it was only a few blocks. There were to be no more easy rides for Marion Ventura. Inside, lights were on to dispel the dark March gloom, and for a second she felt a shiver of doubt, a sudden, unnerving loss of confidence, sneak up on her. On coming to this building before, she'd been the 'Princess', the daughter, the beautiful woman. Never before had she entered it as a Ventura, a real, honest-to-goodness Ventura, with business on her mind and commerce in her thoughts. Squaring her shoulders, she walked through the the familiar lobby and pretty-faced, expensively dressed women looked up at her from the reception desks and chorused, 'Good morning, Ms Ventura,' as she headed for the elevators. Marion smiled back, thinking how quickly word travelled. Ms Ventura. Not Mrs Prescott!

As the elevator doors slid open, however, some of her exhilaration left her. The top floor was reserved for the highest echelons of Ventura management, and here were the executives who had climbed to the top of their respective heaps. This was the place all the people working on the other twenty-nine floors were striving to reach. And she'd just walked in as if . . . as if she owned the place, she thought grimly, reminding herself that, in a way, she did. Her father owned this building. He owned the companies this building serviced. He paid the people this building employed. And she was his daughter. Nepotism. To the average American the word was anathema. To an Italian, however, it was a way of life, and an honourable one, at that. Who else would a man work for, sweat and toil for, except for his children?

And Leslie Ventura *had* worked hard. From slum boy to billionaire. And she was now his only child. She winced the thought away, for she always felt a raw edge of pain whenever she contemplated her lost brother. But Keith would have been the last one to want her to give up, if she really wanted something. He had often said, puzzling her considerably, that she was the strong one, she the one with the brains . . .

Realizing she was dawdling in the elevator, she quickly stepped out on to the smoky blue carpet and headed down the corridor. She passed real oak doors, bearing names she could remember from her childhood. Names of uncles and nephews. But there were names of outsiders too, top-notch men her father had filched from rival companies.

But it was to the second of the main offices, Keith's former office, that she headed. The largest rooms, of course, belonged to Leslie Ventura himself. And although her father hadn't set foot inside it since Keith had died, Marion didn't for one moment doubt that he would eventually take up the reigns of Ventura Industries again. But when? At the moment he was refusing even to think about it. That was one of the other reasons why Marion was here, to help her father snap out of his self-pitying grief.

Approaching the wide suite of offices that had once been her brother's, Marion heard a small but intense group of voices. Pushing open the outer door, she could see that Keith's secretary was absent, which was unusual so early in the morning, surely? Moving across to the inner door that was stood a little ajar, her attention became fixed on the conversation coming from within.

'I don't see where the problem lies.' She recognized her uncle Dino's voice at once. 'I am senior chairman of Ventura Mining, and that's long been acknowledged as Ventura's leading department.'

'That may be so, but that doesn't automatically mean you get this office,' Charles Ventnor, one of the outsiders, cut in, his cold, hard Canadian voice unmistakable.

Marion felt her throat go dry. They were arguing about who was going to get Keith's office, and he wasn't even buried yet.

After fleeing the hospital, her father's harsh words ricocheting in her head, she had walked for miles, at first just trying to comfort herself, but, eventually confronting herself instead. She knew, deep down, that her father's words had not been his own, that it had only been the shock speaking. Nevertheless, it had forced her to face facts. She was twenty-four years old, divorced, and rich. A recipe for disaster if ever there was one. Unless she took control of her life now and did what *she* wanted to for a change.

56

Her rebirth had started simply, by listing all the things she *could* do. She'd graduated with a top degree in business studies from Radcliffe, but had never used it. So, theoretically at least, she *could* run a business. Given time, and experience. She was also a Ventura. Still green, it was true, but then her father hadn't expected Keith to learn the business in five minutes. He'd been prepared to teach, to guide, to shape him over a number of years in order to become the future president of Ventura Industries.

Now it could be her future. And her father owed her. She'd done nothing with her life, except obey him. Never once had she even wondered what it was that *she* wanted to do. And now, here she was, contemplating taking over Ventura Industries. It seemed absurd and yet she was certain that she was right. Instinct told her she was doing what she must do. Now, standing outside the door and eavesdropping on her uncle's sickening conversation, she was even more convinced. *She* was the Ventura heir, and if she was to prove as much to her father she had to start as she meant to go on.

Taking a deep breath, she pushed open the door and stepped inside. Immediately all heads turned her way. Two recognized her as a relative, one as the boss's daughter. None of them recognized the new Ventura heir. 'Good morning, gentlemen,' Marion glanced around, smiling at the surprised faces. 'There doesn't seem to be anyone outside.'

'Oh. No, we asked Felicity to take a coffee break.' Francis Ventura, her cousin, was the first to recover.

'Ah, that explains it. Well . . .' Marion moved towards the large teak desk that dominated the room, and it was only then that they realised she was carrying a briefcase. In total silence they watched her walk to the leather swivel-chair and sit down. She could almost feel Keith's presence egging her on. How he would have loved to watch this. 'Well, gentlemen, to business. I would like to call an extraordinary meeting of staff for two o'clock this afternoon. Uncle Dino, I'm sure you can arrange that? Not everybody, of course, but a top representative from each company will be required.'

'Er . . . of course,' said Dino, staring at his niece as if she'd suddenly grown a second head. From her briefcase Marion extracted a folder which, had they but known it, was empty. She glanced up, looking surprised to see them still here. 'Perhaps, Frankie, you'd be a dear and ask Felicity to come back to the office? I shall need her if I'm to be prepared for this afternoon.'

Francis flushed. He hated being called Frankie. 'Certainly,' he said stiffly, and departed, not about to lower his considerable masculine dignity any further by waiting for further instructions. The other two stared at her for a moment more, but she was already searching the desk, checking Keith's diary and looking so intent that they doubted she was aware of their presence. They too moved reluctantly to the door, and as it closed she heard Charles's low, rumbling voice. 'I didn't know the old man was going to call a meeting.'

Marion wilted as the door closed, letting out her breath in a long, low whoosh. The first step of the journey had started. A moment later the door opened and Felicity Wrighton moved hesitantly towards the desk. Keith had liked her, and, meeting head-on the questioning, slightly puzzled blue eyes, Marion found herself liking her too. 'Hello, Felicity.'

'Hello, Mrs . . . Ms Ventura. I . . . I'm so sorry about

your brother. I'll miss him,' she added simply, but Marion was sure she meant it. She felt tears flood to her eyes and hastily swallowed back a hard, painful lump in her throat.

'Thank you, Felicity. I'll miss him too. And call me Marion.'

'Mr Ventura told me you wished to see me?' Her voice was businesslike now, and Marion was glad. Straightening almost imperceptibly, she nodded, little realising how much at home she looked in her brother's place. 'Yes, I do. I'd like you to get me a complete run-down on all Ventura companies, starting with the biggest and most profitable. I want a complete personnel list, and a copy of this year's quarterly profits, as well as their financial history. In the case of Ventura Mining, I want details of any new mining sites that are in any way controversial.'

Felicity blinked. 'That's a tall order, Ms Ventura.' For a second the two women's eyes met, and slowly Felicity began to smile. 'Yes, Ms . . . Marion. I'll begin right away. Do you want coffee?'

'I think I will. I've got a long morning ahead of me.'

Kynaston leaned forward, his eyes widening at the sight opening out in front of him. Heading deep into the countryside to check for himself the site of the covered park, he felt the full impact of the dale's charming beauty begin to hit him – the sheer vastness of green pastures, enclosed by mile upon mile of dry-stone walling. Quickly he made a note in his journal that the park boundaries should all be made of dry-stone walling. 'Slow down, Vince,' he muttered, then, 'Hell, what is *that*?' He looked in awe at the sight that suddenly appeared by his window.

'That's the Ribblehead viaduct, Mr Germaine. Quite something, eh?' his driver said proudly. Kynaston nodded. Indeed it was. Rows of elegant arches swept across the small valley, and in his mind's eye he could almost see a steam engine triumphantly trundling across it, the steam whistle blowing, steam chuffing out from under its iron wheels.

Kynaston sat back in the dark blue Daimler Sovereign, his face thoughtful as Vince began a happy monologue about local history. He was very good at listening. He did it often, and always reaped rewards for his patience. 'Course, that were built for the Settle-Carlisle railway, in Victorian times,' his driver pointed out.

Kynaston smiled. 'You seem very interested in the railway, Vince.'

'Most people are, I reckon. People who see the viaduct, anyways.'

'Yes,' Kynaston said softly, looking at it. Steam travel seemed to hold a fascination for everyone. He reached for the phone and dialled the office, getting through to Michael within moments. 'Mike, I want you to do some research for me on the Ribblehead viaduct. It might pay us to see if we can negotiate use of the lines around here. Then see if you can find any old steam trains on the market – they don't have to be in perfect condition, we can always repair and refurbish if necessary.'

'Oh, I get you. You're thinking nostalgia,' Mike's voice held a smile. 'You're right, of course. An old steam train would pay its way within a year.'

'Exactly. And you should see the countryside out here,' Kynaston murmured, taking a last glimpse at the viaduct through the back window. There wasn't a tourist around, American, Japanese or otherwise, who wouldn't pay plenty to ride through these glorious Yorkshire dales on a steam train. Quickly extracting his briefcase, he made a

60

brief note of it and jotted down a few more ideas. He talked as he did so.

'How are things on the dry-ski run progressing?'

'Fine, fine. We've just got that last parcel of land to buy up, but that'll be in the bag any minute now. I've had a word with the bank.'

'Fine,' Kynaston said vaguely. 'And the ski run material? Have they sent you a sample yet? Remember, I want the green to match exactly the prevailing colour of the grass in that valley. If anybody can see the slopes before they're right on top of them, there'll be hell to pay.'

'They say that's what's taking all the time. Dry-ski runs, apparently, are a standard colour.'

'Others, perhaps,' Kynaston said softly. 'Not mine.' He made another note, said goodbye and hung up.

'Here we are, Mr Germaine. Looks a right mess, don't it?'

Kynaston looked up at the cleared site of the latest Germaine venture, and nodded to himself. It did indeed, as his driver so succinctly put it, look a right mess. The ground was churned up where bulldozers had levelled off and cleared the land, and the beginnings of the access road looked like a raw, gaping wound on the landscape.

'You really gonna build one of them glass-domed things here, Mr Germaine?' Vince asked. He'd lived in the district for all of his forty-three years, and although he tried to look ahead and imagine a concealed, peaceful dome, he couldn't.

'Yes, I am,' Kynaston answered his question softly, watching the progress like a hawk. He glanced around at the wooded areas on all three sides. Yes, it was ideal.

Nestling in a little dell, it would make a perfect mini-environment. And he *could* picture what the finished park would look like.

Vince looked at the gaping wound on the landscape and sighed. Still, he knew that shouldn't complain. He'd been on the dole for nearly six months before Germaine Leisure hit town. Now at least he had a job for life, because when it was finished he'd been guaranteed a job working in the park as a gardener, which was his true vocation. He only hoped the American knew what he was doing. But he had to, didn't he? He was rich.

Marion didn't bother looking up when the door opened. 'Just put them on the desk, Felicity. I'll eat them later.' She turned the page of the huge computer printout which housed mind-boggling details of Ventura Paper.

'What the hell's going on?'

The voice whipped up her head and she found herself staring at her father. For a second her mind went blank. 'I'm sorry. I thought you were my secretary with the sandwiches.'

'*Your* secretary?' Leslie shut the door behind him and moved wearily to one of the large, comfortable chairs placed strategically in front of her desk. He slumped down and leaned back, looking at his daughter with a vaguely quizzical expression that she'd never seen before. His energy seemed to have deserted him, and it scared her. It scared her more than the thought of his wrath, which could be extremely loud and spectacular.

'Yes. Felicity,' she murmured, hastily scrabbling to-gether her defences.

'I know which secretary works in this office,' Leslie said drolly. 'What I don't know is what you're doing here. And what's all this about an extraordinary meeting for this afternoon?'

'I called it.'

'I assumed as much from Dino. He called me sounding almost hysterical.' For a moment a hint of amusement gleamed in his eyes but then it was gone as he suddenly seemed to focus. 'You're sitting in Keith's place.'

Marion went white, but she didn't move. She stared at her father, her eyes darkening with pain. 'I know,' she said softly. 'When I arrived, Charles, Dino and Frankie were arguing about who should get his office.'

This time it was Leslie Ventura's turn to go white. Then, almost against his will, he found himself smiling. 'So you decided just to walk in and settle the argument by taking it over yourself?'

'Yes. I settled it by just walking in and taking over,' she repeated, her voice both cool, amused, and a little sad.

Leslie lowered his eyes to the computer pages she was holding and read the first few lines upside down. 'Ventura Paper. Why are you reading that?'

'I've been reading about all of Ventura Industries' top companies. Or at least, as much as is humanly possible in . . .' she checked her small gold watch '. . . three hours and forty minutes.'

Leslie looked from the paper to his daughter's face, aware that something had altered about her. She looked tired, but it was her eyes that were different. They were older, much older than he remembered. Then it hit him. She had lost Keith too. And sometimes he'd wondered if she hadn't loved Keith more than any of them – more than he had, more even than Nadine, his wife and Keith's doting, over-protective mother. Suddenly the realization that his daughter had been suffering while he had done

63

nothing about it hit him like a bodyblow. Always before he'd protected his family. He'd had to admit defeat to the brain tumour that had taken his darling Nadine, and now to the drugs that had killed his son, though he'd already hired a private detective to find out who had been Keith's supplier, and when he did, he'd have the bastard locked away for life. But Marion . . . With a guilty start that felt like a knife in his heart he realised he hadn't given her a single thought in the last four days. She must be exhausted. And in pain.

'Marion, you shouldn't be here,' he said softly, then stopped abruptly, his mouth falling open as she unexpectedly rounded on him, launching herself to her feet, eyes flashing.

'Why? Because I'm not a man? Well, let me tell you something, Daddy: I may not be a man, but I *am* a Ventura.'

Leslie blinked, not prepared for the attack. 'What has that got to do with it?'

'Everything,' Marion said sharply, then abruptly sat back down again. 'Daddy, I want to work for my living,' she said softly. 'And where else should I work except here?'

He shook his head. 'Marion, you're not qualified!'

'I'm better qualified than Keith was,' she pointed out bluntly. 'I graduated with top honours, *top honours*, Daddy, from Radcliffe.'

'Look, it's just not possible,' he said roughly. 'This is still a man's world, and it still takes a man to do a man's job. You're just not thinking straight. Now, if – '

'On the contrary,' Marion broke in, all fear miraculously leaving her as she suddenly found strength, hitherto unsuspected, come flooding to her rescue. 'It's you who's

64

not thinking straight. You brought Keith into the company two years ago to learn the business. He didn't do very well, you and I both know it, simply because he wasn't suited to it. He didn't understand, or want to understand, how business works. I do. I'm qualified, but inexperienced, I freely admit it. But I won't be inexperienced for long. Not if you give me a chance to learn.'

Leslie looked at her, noting her defiantly angled chin and blazing eyes, and sighed heavily. 'This stupidity has to stop now, Marion,' he said coldly. 'High finance is no place for a woman, and if you were only thinking straight, instead of fantasizing about running Ventura, you'd know it. You're a beautiful young woman. You should be out enjoying life.'

'Oh, I intend to. But having a fruitful, challenging career is one of life's major pleasures. As you should know,' she added pointedly.

Leslie sighed angrily. He was too tired and too distracted to put up with Marion's madcap ideas now. 'Dammit, Marion, this has gone far enough,' he snapped, getting to his feet and walking to the door. 'There is no way you can take Keith's place. I'm going to call off this meeting and go back home. We'll talk later.'

'No, Daddy, we won't,' Marion said quietly, and watched her father stop dead in his tracks. Slowly he turned and looked at her, something in her voice penetrating deep into his subconscious. 'If you call off this meeting, Daddy, I'm leaving Ventura Industries and I'm going to find a job somewhere else. I'll start at the bottom if I have to, as others have done before me. But top honours don't go unnoticed, and I'll work hard. And I'll rise, and keep on rising, because I intend to be successful. And if you won't let it be here, at Ventura Industries, then it will just have to be at one of your competitors' companies.'

'Don't be so stupid,' Leslie snapped. 'Nobody will hire you.'

'You don't think so?' Marion asked sardonically. 'No rival company would hire the Ventura Princess? You're not thinking straight, Daddy,' she said softly, her eyes softening with concern. Always, but always, Leslie Ventura had been needle-sharp. The fact that he was so off the mark now made her more determined than ever to snap him back to normal. 'Just think of the wonderful publicity I would earn them, alone. The Ventura Princess working for someone else. I think I could get a job anywhere I wanted in this city, Daddy. Don't you?' she goaded softly.

Leslie stared at her, his mouth practically hanging open. This wasn't Marion. This stranger, this . . . this . . . cold-thinking, cold-talking woman wasn't his little girl. His cute, obedient, feminine little girl. 'You wouldn't,' he said, but even to his own ears he sounded unconvinced.

'Yes, Daddy, I would,' Marion corrected gently. 'But only if you make me. Only if you turn your back on me.'

'Marion!' He was truly appalled. 'I'd never turn my back on you. My God, you're my own flesh and blood . . .' he stuttered, stunned by the allegation.

'Then treat me like it,' she insisted softly. 'Go out there and approve that meeting. Introduce me, as you introduced Keith two years ago, as the new heir. I don't care what title you give me, or what jobs you give me, or what office you allot me. So long as you give me a *chance*. And an *equal* chance to the one you gave Keith.'

Leslie stared at her in silence. Marion stared back. The minutes stretched, and still they remained in angry stalemate, Leslie stood by the door, Marion sat behind her desk. Only she knew how much her knees were shaking, and how much it had cost her to speak to her father the way she had.

'I think,' Leslie said at last, his voice cold and heavy, 'that you're blackmailing me.'

'No, Daddy,' Marion said, tears in her eyes and in her voice. 'I'm standing up to you. Nobody's ever done it before, that's why you don't recognize it. Mummy never wanted to, Keith couldn't, and I wouldn't. But I am now.' She took a deep breath and looked him straight in the eye. 'The question is, Daddy,' she said softly, 'just what are you going to do about it?'

CHAPTER 6

Bryn forced herself to look in the mirror. The dress looked strange on her, but perhaps that was only because it was the first time she'd worn it in months. It was brown with black dots, and had four large padded buttons down the front. She'd found it in an Otley jumble sale. That had been over four years ago and it still fitted, so at least she wasn't gaining any more weight. She stared at her lumpy figure for a few seconds longer, then shrugged. Donning her one good pair of shoes, a hefty pair of brown suede lace-ups, she picked up her only handbag, another jumble sale purchase, and headed for the door. In the kitchen, Katy looked up, her eyes narrowing.

'What on earth are you wearing?'

Bryn flushed, wishing that Katy wouldn't undermine her already shaky confidence. If her sister only knew the importance of Bryn's journey, she would have been more helpful, but Bryn didn't have the heart to tell her. Throughout yesterday Bryn had been numb with shock. She'd thought she had more time, months, at least. But now, unless she could do something, they'd have to sell Ravenheights within just a few short weeks. It was an appalling thought, and one she just couldn't take in. This was her last hope, her one chance to keep the farm. She wanted to make a good impression on Kynaston Germaine, and having Katy tell her that that was impossible didn't help her any, even if she already knew, deep down, that her sister was right. Nervously she held out the skirt of the dress. 'It's the only dress I've got, Katy,' she half wailed, half laughed. 'Well, this and the skirt and blouse that used to be our school uniform.'

Katy shook her head in disbelief, and then, looking at her sister's fat, frumpy figure, she began to laugh. It was a dry, despairing bark of a laugh, and it sent chills once more running up and down Bryn's spine. There'd been a frightening change in Katy over the last few days. 'Katy, I don't have to go out today, you know. Why don't you come with me?'

'To Harrogate?' Katy scoffed. 'No, thanks. I'd rather stay here.'

Bryn bit her lip. Katy hadn't set foot outside the house since she'd arrived. It was almost as if she was afraid to go out. Before she'd left for London, Bryn could remember her sister spending hours on her make-up, soaking in the tub and rubbing cream into her skin. Now her hair was lank and unwashed, her face pale and drawn. She'd always 'chattered like a magpie', too, as their father put it. Now Katy hardly said anything. She just read the paper and bitched about the models featured inside, or watched Australian soaps on telly.

'All right,' Bryn finally sighed. She would have liked the company, but instinct told her not to nag. 'I've got everything ready for dinner, so all you have to do is keep the Aga stoked, and make sure the chicken pie doesn't burn. The spuds have been peeled and salted, so's the swede.'

Katy nodded. She hadn't a clue how to keep the Aga at a

steady temperature and she'd probably forget to turn on the vegetables. Serve 'em right. She looked up, surprised at finding herself alone. Bryn must have gone. Funny, she never heard her say goodbye. She sighed and reached into her handbag. Extracting one of her tranquillizers, she swallowed it dry. She really mustn't let such little things upset her.

Outside, Bryn gingerly started her sister's car and carefully reversed it out into the courtyard. It had been a long time since she'd driven anything but a tractor and she was very careful of the gears as she headed out on to the open road. She must do something about Katy, she thought anxiously. But what?

In Harrogate she parked in the town centre and buttoned her grey raincoat from chin to shin. The cold breeze froze her nose and ears to an ugly red, and she impatiently pulled a scarf from her pocket and tied it over her head. A policeman gave her directions to the hotel and within a few minutes she there. Feeling more and more sick with nerves, she stood in the driveway of the building and stared at it. There seemed to be a lot of activity. Reluctantly she walked up the crisp, gravel-lined road and paused outside the door. She felt about two inches high. Timidly she knocked on the hefty door, waiting for what seemed like aeons. Then she spotted a bell-pull and blushed beetroot, realizing nobody could possibly have heard her pathetic tapping. Feeling an idiot, she yanked on the pull and huddled further into her raincoat. A moment later the door opened, revealing a man dressed in a bottle-green uniform. 'Can I help you, miss? I'm afraid the hotel isn't open yet. You're not from the florists, are you?'

'No.' Bryn instantly recognized the man's accent as pure wolds. 'I was hoping to see Mr Germaine.'

'Do you have an appointment, miss? His office is in Leeds at the moment.'

'Leeds?' she echoed, dismayed. 'Oh, no. I've come practically all the way from Hawes,' she mumbled, her disappointment acute.

The doorman grinned. 'I thought I recognized the accent, miss. Look, tell you what. Mr Germaine *is* in town. I know for a fact he's going to the Exhibition Halls this afternoon. Why don't you . . .?'

'Jacoby? Is something the matter?' Michael Forrester appeared in the great hallway. 'Can I help you . . . er . . . madam.'

Bryn went red. 'No. I . . . well, I was hoping to see Mr Germaine, to discuss . . . well . . . some business matters.'

His eyebrow rose a notch. 'Business? I'm Mr Germaine's general manager, Michael Forrester. Perhaps I can be of help?' He sounded as disbelieving as he felt. What a great, unnattractive lump of woman. Lord, he hoped she didn't want to book a room.

Bryn breathed a sigh of relief, glad that she wouldn't have to screw up her courage all over again. 'Yes, perhaps you can help me. It's about Ravenheights Farm.'

'Ahh, yes. Please come this way.' Michael recognized the name of the farm immediately. He should – the damn thing had been the bane of his life the past few months.

Through the hall and to the right, she could make out a dining room buzzing with staff, vacuuming the carpets and brushing down the curtains. Silver and crystal lined the walls on a long trestle, ready to be set out on the tables once the tablecloths were positioned just right.

'We're having our grand opening ball tomorrow,' Michael explained the activity, and impatiently touched her elbow, before leading her to a small but cheerful-looking

71

office and beckoning her into a seat. 'Just let me get the file
. . . ah, here it is,' Michael returned to the desk with a
folder in his hand and opened it. 'Ah, yes. Our last offer
was raised by an extra thousand pounds. And a generous
offer for the stock, some . . . five hundred sheep. That's
quite a good number, isn't it?'

Bryn flushed, knowing when she was being patronized.
She didn't like this man with his false smile and hearty
voice one little bit. 'It's one of the finest flocks in the
dales,' she said defensively, becoming more and more
unsure of herself as she talked. 'I was hoping to explain
to Mr Germaine our circumstances. You see, Whittakers
have farmed that land for over five hundred years. We've
always lived at Ravenheights, and managed to make a good
living at it, too. It's only recently that we've hit problems,
but we can sort them out if only we could have a little more
time. I wanted to ask Mr Germaine if he would withdraw
his offer to buy the land. The bank, you see, are trying to
make us accept so we can repay their loan. If Mr Germaine
were to withdraw his offer, then the bank would let us stay
on, I know they would.' She knew she was smiling like a
nervous idiot, but was unable to stop herself.

Michael Forrester, who'd nodded and made comforting
noises throughout her rambling little speech, now sighed.
Of course he saw. Wasn't that why he had kept the
pressure on in the first place? Didn't this woman know
anything about business? 'The Germaine Corporation,
Miss . . . er, Whittaker?' he began with what he hoped
was a patient tone.

'Oh, sorry. I forgot to introduce myself. I'm Bryn
Whittaker.' She leaned forward and held out her hand,
and after a brief, startled pause Michael took it and shook
it. *This* was Bryn Whittaker?

72

'Yes, well, you see, Miss Whittaker, Mr Germaine has made a very generous offer for your father's land, and he's made it in all good faith. He needs the lower pastures you currently use to feed your sheep as a nursery slope for his new dry-ski run complex. I'm sure you understand that, given the amount of investment capital Mr Germaine has already spent, he cannot withdraw his offer simply to try and help you blackmail the bank?'

Bryn flinched back as if she'd just been stabbed. She went first red, then white. Slowly she stood up. 'I can see it's no good talking to you,' she said stiffly, wanting to both run away and really tear into him at the same time. One look at his mildly superior face had her biting her tongue to hold her temper in check. Like all easygoing people, Bryn seldom lost her temper, but when she did, she really did. She turned and marched to the door, yanked it open and walked blindly through the hall, not even noticing when the doorman leapt up from his chair to open the door for her.

In his office Michael shook his head. What an extraordinary woman. But at least that was the last they'd need ever see of her. Still, she'd obviously been upset. Thoughtfully he dictated a letter, offering another £100 to be put on the price of the flock. Perhaps that would help soften the blow.

Outside Bryn walked to her car, a fierce heat consuming her. She knew that that horrible man had been smirking at her behind his oh, so polite face, no doubt thinking how stupid she was, how fat, how *useless*. At the car, she leaned against its cold exterior and trembled. They would never let them keep Ravenheights, never, and she'd been dreaming ever to think they would. To Kynaston Germaine and his cronies it was nothing more than a bit of land they

73

wanted, to stick some horrible plastic on that people could ski down.

Realizing she was doing herself no favours getting so worked up, Bryn left the car and wandered into town, looking listlessly in shop windows, constantly fighting an absurd desire to burst into tears. Life wasn't fair, she thought, then had to laugh at the childishness of it. Of course life wasn't fair!

She found herself facing the Exhibition Halls. Subconscious accident or fate? Feeling that she had nothing more to lose, she crossed the road, paid her entrance fee and found herself in the midst of an outlandish modern art exhibition. The pictures she chose to decorate Ravenheights were all country scenes, and most of those had been painted in Giggleswick by old Fred Wainwright, a retired schoolteacher. Still, it was soothing and quiet and she slowly began to relax.

Suddenly her newly acquired peace died a cruel death as Michael Forrester entered and glanced around. Spotting his quarry, he headed quickly towards a corner she hadn't yet explored. Drawn by some masochistic instinct, she followed him.

'Hello, Kyn. I thought you might like to know that Dawson just called. We've got the green light for the golf course.' She recognized the manager's voice at once.

'Good.' The voice that answered, however, was as different from that fawning, squeaky voice as it was possible to be. Unable to resist it, Bryn carefully moved around to the edge of the wall and glanced around its corner into a little niche. Instantly she felt her gaze being pulled to the silver-gold head towering a foot and then some over his general manager's head. When he angled his head back, the better to view one of the pictures, she felt the room around her began to fade. Bryn had never seen a man taller than this one. Dressed in a dark grey suit, his back alone was the most beautiful thing she had ever seen. Starting with the unusual hair that glowed like fine white gold, his neck was long and healthily tanned, his shoulders wide but not disproportionately so. The length of his spine was impressive, making her fingers itch to trace his vertebrae. The narrowness of his waist was apparent even under the elegant grey jacket, and his long, long legs ended in elegantly shod black leather shoes.

Bryn felt her heart start to thump, and when it seemed he was about to turn fully around, she quickly moved back, leaning against the wall and staring blindly in front of her. She couldn't let him see her. She just couldn't. She didn't know why, but she was suddenly afraid. Terribly afraid. She began to sidle away, but the sight of a woman striding purposefully towards the end corner made her stop. She was a striking woman, with short dark hair and a small but perfect figure. She was dressed in a long scarlet skirt and a black, white and scarlet blouse.

'Kyn, darling. So glad to get your invite. Of course, I'd have killed you if you'd forgotten me.' The voice was pure, aristocratic London, and Bryn began to move more quickly, not wanting to know, not wanting to hear.

'As if I could ever forget you, Janice,' his voice answered, one that Bryn would have known belonged to him even if she'd never heard it before and had had to pick it out of a thousand others. 'You'll stay at the Germanicus, of course.'

'Where else?' A light, tinkling laugh followed, a laugh that hurt Bryn like a thousand knives. She froze on the spot as all three moved away from the little niche and into the main hall. If they see me, she thought hysterically, I'll probably die. But they didn't see her, and again her eyes were drawn to him, as if he held a magnet that attracted only her gaze. Kynaston Germaine's profile belonged on a coin. It was strong and perfect and, to her, seemed almost exquisitely cruel.

Long after they had gone, Bryn stayed where she was, unable to think what to do. Eventually, she pulled herself together and moved, stiff-legged, outside. For a moment she had to stop and think where she was, then she headed back to the car, keeping a wary eye out for people passing by. But none of them had silver-gold hair, and by the time she finally collapsed heavily into the driver's seat of her sister's car she had begun to feel more rational.

Anxious to leave the town, she drove east fast, and only when she was deeply into the dale and feeling safe again did she pull off on to the side of the deserted road and get out. Walking to a length of inevitable dry-stone walling, she leaned against it, staring out into the acres of green pasture in front of her. What on earth had happened to her back there? Oh, she knew she'd made a right mess of talking to that manager at the hotel. She'd been nervous and out of her element, and he'd been smug and superior. That smarted, but it was only her pride that was hurt.

· No, what frightened her was what had happened at the art exhibition. She knew she was shy, of course, and knew why. She was hardly anybody's idea of a pretty woman. But that didn't explain away her panic, her immediate and instinctive reaction to the man. A man who hadn't even seen her. A man who didn't even know she existed. Kynaston Germaine.

Bryn shuddered, and it had nothing to do with the cold wind. She could see again the brilliance of his hair as he turned his head to look at the painting. She could hear his voice. She could see him, *sense* him. She didn't understand it. Katy! Katy would know. But as she got back into the car Bryn already realised that she wouldn't be asking Katy what it all meant, because, deep down, she already knew. For the first time in her life she had felt desire. Want. Need. Attraction. And it had had to be for Kynaston Germaine. If she'd had the courage to think about it, she might have found it funny, in a bitter-sweet and ironic sort of way. But instinct stopped her from thinking, because it also told her something else. Something she didn't want to know.

There had been a sense of fate about her first encounter with Kynaston Germaine. A sense of inevitability. A sense of unalterable, unchangeable purpose. It was as if life had suddenly been wrenched right out of her control, and that was too horrendous a thought for anybody to contemplate. But especially herself, who had always needed to be safe, and who felt safe no longer.

When Bryn got back to the farm, she traipsed dispiritedly into the living room, catching Katy unawares. She'd been scribbling furiously on a sheet of paper, but she looked up when her sister came in and quickly stuffed the paper into her handbag. At any other time, Bryn would have been curious, but now she hadn't the energy.

'You're back early. I didn't expect you till teatime.'

'The day was not a success,' Bryn said drolly, feeling better just for doing something normal, like ribbing her sister. The day had taken on a nightmarish, unreal quality, and she was desperate to get back to mundanity.

'Oh, hard luck,' Katy offered automatically. The tran-quillizers had given her a nicely padded feel, as if she was moving through cotton wool. It was a pleasant feeling, and she found herself smiling as she made her sister some tea. 'Here you are. Drink this, you'll feel better.' She handed her sister the mug and took her place back by the fire.

The leaping flames licking against the logs reminded Bryn of the colour of his hair, and she quickly looked away. Outside the wind howled, but the walls were nearly a foot thick, and the two girls, for different reasons, felt comforted.

Katy wished Bryn would go away. She, who had always hated to be alone, now strangely craved it. As if sensing her sister's need, Bryn quickly finished off her cooling tea and got wearily to her feet. 'I'd better change the sheets. If we get another good drying day tomorrow it'll mean we won't have to have washing hanging up in the house. I hate that.' She was doing it again, she knew. Grappling for the normal. But she still felt like Alice after falling down the well into Wonderland. Except that it didn't seem so wonderful.

Katy watched her sister leave, then dived into her bag and grabbed her piece of paper. It was compulsive, this writing. She quickly read her last entry. 'It's only when I'm with other people that I get hurt. I want to stay alone. Stay free . . .' Lowering her head, Katy began to write once more, careful, when she was finished, to stuff the pages back in the envelope marked 'Private, Do Not Read' that she kept in her bag. Nobody must ever read what she wrote. Nobody.

Upstairs, Bryn started to strip her bed, then, still dressed in her raincoat and scarf, lay down instead and curled herself into a ball, staring dry-eyed at the walls. Within moments she was asleep . . .

She was thin and beautiful, and in a castle that had thick walls and low ceilings and overlooked a moor. The castle was besieged by soldiers wearing dark grey chain-mail. Her father was dead. Her sister was dead. Only she remained, in her room, her slender figure dressed in a long white gown. A bridal gown. She was afraid, for soon the leader of the conquering army would be at the doors, battering them down.

She went to the chapel to pray, and heard the battle cries of the men outside, and the walls shaking as the stronghold was breached. The candles flickered as the chapel door flew open and she turned, her waist-length hair flying out around her, as she'd seen Katy's hair do in a picture in a magazine once. A tall man, tall enough to touch the ceiling, a giant of a man, strode towards her. When he took his helmet off, fire shot out towards her, setting her alight. She could feel her hair burn, and when she looked down her lovely dress was turning an ugly brown and black dots were beginning to appear, like a plague.

She woke up crying and breathless, a strange, throbbing excitement deep inside making her curl up in shame and confusion.

Stowe, Vermont

Morgan looked up as a knock sounded on the door. Three short taps. He waited. They were in the garage of a local shopkeeper, and a wandering-lead lamp was hung up over the table, illuminating a map. There were two others with him, but nobody said a word. A tap came, then a pause, then three taps. Everyone relaxed. Morgan walked to the door and opened it a crack. 'Yes?'

'Deep Green.'

Morgan opened the door and stepped back, taking a quick look around at the darkening streets before closing the door. He turned back and looked at his visitor. He was a small, wiry-haired man, with a nervous energy that buzzed around him like a swarm of invisible flies. 'Hello, Greg,' Morgan said softly. 'It's been a long time. Glad to have you with us.'

'Glad to come,' Greg said, his small eyes shining brightly. 'You know you have only to say the word, Morgan. Any time,' he gushed nervously, wiping his hands on his shirt. There was something profoundly subservient in his voice that made the other two men in the room glance at each other uneasily.

'Come in, Greg. This is Claus Gruber.' He indicated a tall, blond, handsome man who nodded back once. 'And this is Bruno.' He did not give the man's last name. Greg nodded back, but barely glanced at them. Instead he turned back to Morgan and watched him like an adoring pet dog. Realizing the atmosphere had become tense, Morgan sat down, watching in silence as Greg did likewise. 'Gentlemen, Greg is a friend from way back. Way back,' he added softly, and saw that both the other two men understood at once. Their unease increased. 'He'll report only to me. And any and all matters relating to Greg's . . . area of expertise . . . will be dealt with solely by me. All right?' The other two relaxed slightly, glad they wouldn't have to have anything to do with their newest member. Not that Morgan could blame them. An escapee from a lunatic asylum, on the face of it, did not make an ideal comrade. Not that Morgan cared what they thought. While *their* motivating force might be environmentalism, for Morgan there was only 'The Plan'. The Plan that would destroy Germaine, and its chairman. Nothing must stand in the way of that.

'Now,' he began briskly, 'to business. Claus, you've applied for the job?'

The German nodded. '*Ja*. And been accepted, too.'

'Not surprising,' Morgan smiled, knowing flattery never hurt anybody. 'You're one of the damned finest skiers I've ever known.' Claus nodded, his handsome face not even cracking a smile. He'd been a ski instructor for five years now, and a member of Deep Green for three. He admired Morgan more than any other man alive, and if he wanted him to get a job at Germaine, teaching guests to ski, he had no objections. He was sure Morgan had his reasons.

Morgan did. 'During the Christmas break, Vanessa Germaine will be back home from college. She's an intermediate skier, and it's your job to improve her form.' He smiled slightly as he said it, and Claus smiled back. 'I want you to do more than help her on the *piste*, of course,' he continued softly. 'Vanessa is a lovely girl. Young – twenty. Just ripe for romance, and the pillow-talk that goes with it.' He thought of Vanessa as he'd last seen her. She'd been only two then, of course. With waist-length blonde hair and long, long lashes. She'd been pale as milk the last time he'd been allowed to look at her, and her small body had been racked with convulsions. All Kynaston's fault, he thought, his face for a moment looking savage. If Kynaston hadn't put his nose in where it didn't belong, Vanessa wouldn't have had to grow up in that damned slum. 'Vanessa . . .' he said softly, then glanced at Claus sharply. 'Vanessa's innocent,' he said, his voice hard. 'She has nothing to do with her brother's business and doesn't know what he does to earn all that money.'

'But she spends it well enough,' Bruno put in, the first time he'd yet spoken. He was a short man, but thickly built. His jowls were heavy, as were the bags under his

81

eyes. He spoke in a deep, short, barking voice that matched his appearance. He inevitably reminded anyone who met him of a bulldog.

Morgan grunted. 'Claus, once you're in her confidence, start opening her eyes to what her brother's doing to the land.'

Claus nodded. Not a bad assignment. Teach skiing, something he loved doing anyway. Take a lovely young girl to bed, also one of his favourite pastimes; and at the same time show her how her brother raped the environment. Yes, he could see where Morgan's plans were taking them. The sister would make a good spy for Deep Green. As always, he'd been right to trust Morgan. Claus didn't know how the little ferret of a man called Greg would fit in, and he didn't particularly want to find out. And as for Bruno . . . Claus looked at Bruno and smiled. A man like Bruno always had his uses. When Morgan dismissed him, the handsome German left quite happily. What he didn't know wouldn't hurt him.

But it would hurt someone, he was sure of that.

CHAPTER 7

'Katy, it's for you,' Bryn called, holding out the telephone.

'Thanks.' Katy took it with a sigh and leaned against the hall wall. 'Yeah?' Bryn heard the mail drop through the letter box and moved away.

'Hiya, Kate, how are things up in the sticks?'

'Maeve?' Katy recognized Maeve Finagal's voice even over the static and groaned softly. She'd been in London only a few months when she'd first come across Maeve Finagal's name. Some of the girls she'd been with on a sun-lotion ad were talking about the party Maeve was throwing at the latest, fanciest nightclub, and who'd been asked. She'd expected to hear a list of celebrities. Instead Veronique Finch, the most famous model in the ad, reeled off a list of unknown girls' names that had the others laughing and snickering. It had been left to Jayne Moore, an older and wiser model, to put Katy wise. Maeve ran a so-called modelling agency which mostly provided 'party companions' for big social affairs.

Even Katy had known what that meant. Entertainment for anyone who wanted it – girls with leather whips and handcuffs for those overtired politicians who needed to relax, a blonde, English-rose beauty for a seemingly never-ending string of Arab millionaires, and starlets willing to accommodate any showbiz maestro who felt bored and in need of company, in a desperate bid to get their foot through the showbiz door.

'You still there, kiddo?'

'What? Oh, yeah, sorry, Maeve,' Katy said, frowning. What the hell was Maeve Finagal calling her for, anyway?

'How're things going up there? Licking your wounds, huh?'

Katy laughed hollowly. So the word had got round that Sir Lionel had dumped her. It hadn't taken long, had it?

'Look, love, I was wondering when you plan on coming back down to the big, bad city?'

Katy sighed and ran a tired hand across her forehead. She needed to take a pill. Maeve always had made her nervous and unable to think straight. With sad regularity, Katy had watched her cull the ageing models from all the agencies, herding them into her little town house near Chelsea and pampering their ravaged egos, promising them the chance to snare a rich husband, or get that break into Hollywood.

'I don't know when I'm coming back,' Katy said at last, slowly and carefully, for a horrendous feeling was beginning to uncoil in her stomach. Deep in the back of her mind she began to realize exactly what it was that Maeve wanted of her.

'Well, when you do, remember who your *real* friends are. I heard you got the sack from Braer. Just because you couldn't work with that dishrag Andy. Well, who can? Bastards! They all think twenty-five is over the hill. Now, at Finagal's, we don't give up on models. Hell, our best girls are women, not silly little girls. They know a bit about life by the time they're twenty-five, and they know

84

the name of the game better. Mandy Martin certainly did. You remember Mandy, don't you, love?'

Katy did. Mandy Martin had landed herself some big producer from Hollywood, over in England to research a big studio's next blockbuster. But for every one Mandy there were a hundred other girls. Prostitutes. That was what they were, plain and simple. Katy shuddered.

'Well, give me a call soon, OK? I mean it.'

'OK,' Katy said automatically. It was easier to say what Maeve wanted to hear than to argue the point.

'Good. Finagal's will sign you up on contract the moment you say so. Oh, and don't worry about losing that little pad of yours. We'll soon fix you up with a nice little loft in Chelsea. I knew you were a sensible girl, Kate. I knew it as soon as I looked at you.'

Katy heard the jarring laughter end abruptly, and realised she'd slammed down the receiver. She stared at the phone for a long moment, her mind churning along with her stomach. So Maeve had known as soon as she'd seen her that she'd been potential fodder for Finagal's. Katy laughed, a dry, racking sound that, once started, she couldn't finish. All the time she'd lived in her little fancy pad, with her wealthy lover, doing her so-called glamorous job, thinking she was doing so well. All the time, Maeve Finagal had been just waiting to recruit her . . .

Katy walked like a sleepwalker through the hall, looking around her, wondering what she was going to do. Well, for a start she was going to take a pill. She picked up her handbag from the sofa and emptied two tranquillizers into her palm and took them, not noticing that her hand was shaking badly. Still feeling numb, she walked to the kitchen and stopped, unnoticed in the hallway, staring vacantly out of the kitchen window. Rain flung itself against the windows, and outside the lonely green pastures swept as far as the eye could see. She didn't see her father and sister sitting at the table talking. She was miles away. Miles and miles and miles away.

Bryn crumpled the paper into her hands, digging her fingernails into her palms, hurting herself as she tried to scrunch the white paper out of existence. 'The bastards!' she hissed, her voice cracking. 'More money for the flock,' she said, as if she couldn't believe it. 'As if an extra hundred pounds matters.'

John Whittaker winced and surreptitiously pressed his hand against his chest. It was hot in the kitchen, he suddenly realized, and he took several deep breaths. He had told the men that morning they they'd be laid off at the end of the month. It had been the hardest thing he'd ever done, but at least none of them had been surprised. He'd been the last to hold out, the last farmer to go to the wall. And although Sam and the others had taken it well, trying, for his sake, not to make too much of it, it had taken its toll on him. And now this. Suddenly it was hard to breathe and John swallowed back a rising sense of panic. Bryony looked ready to cry, and who could blame her? Perhaps now was the best time to tell her about how he'd spent *his* afternoon. 'Listen, lass. I went over to Clapham yesterday, to look at that cottage up for sale.'

'It's too dear,' she said, knowing what her father was thinking.

'It's a lovely spot, Bryony. A much smaller place, too – think of all the housework you'll save on.' He went on to praise the view, the village, the neighbours, the garden, but Bryn wasn't listening. Instead she was in the art gallery, staring at the back of the most beautiful man in the world.

86

'How could he do this to me?' she whispered, standing up so suddenly that her chair toppled and fell backwards. It was then that John Whittaker saw his elder daughter standing in the doorway. She was staring, blank-eyed out of the window, her face bearing obvious signs of shock.

Bryn marched to the door, flung it open and stepped out into the yard. He was having his big swanky party today too, she suddenly remembered. In her mind's eye she saw great baskets of flowers that must have cost a fortune, and crystal glasses, and polished silverware. Just the money he'd be spending on his party would probably be enough to pay back the damned bank loan. And what did he do? Bryn stood in the squall of rain, oblivious to the cold droplets falling on her face and penetrating the grey heavy jumper she was wearing. He wrote her a letter offering her another poxy hundred pounds for her sheep, that's what he did!

'Damn you!' Bryn screamed, then felt foolish. She glanced around, but luckily the wind had taken her defiant scream and carried it harmlessly across the dale. Suddenly she became utterly still as a breathtakingly daring idea leapt into her head. Her breathing became slower, and the smile that curled its way on to her face almost split it in two. Taking her bobble hat out of her trouser pocket, she rammed it on her hand and tucked her hair beneath it to keep it dry. In the far barn, she took down the old and dirty raincoat that perpetually hung there and paused to wipe her glasses free of rain with her handkerchief. Full of purpose now, she checked the old cattle-wagon. It was a 1960s model, and although everyone grumbled about its size, ugliness and general cussedness it had always saved them hiring out a truck to take the lambs to market. As usual, it refused to start, but as usual, with the help of a wrench and some oil, Bryn persuaded it to change its mind and go.

Inside, John looked up from the kettle and watched the truck trundle out of sight, his eyes worried. Bryony Rose was up to something, that was for sure. But it was not his younger daughter who concerned him now. 'Have some sugar in this cup, aye, lass?' He looked over his shoulder to where Katy sat at the table, leaning over it and ripping a paper tissue to shreds with her fingers. She looked at him blankly.

'Sure, Dad. Why not?' Why not? She might as well get fat, if she was going to be a prostitute.

John waited for the water to boil and leaned heavily against the sink. Wordlessly he opened the window, gratefully breathing in the cold, fresh air, hoping Katy wouldn't notice. She seemed to be in shock still. And who would have thought that she'd take losing the farm so badly? 'Listen, lass, we'll probably be moving to Clapham soon. There's a lovely cottage there. I'm sure you'll love it.'

Katy nodded. 'Yes, Dad.'

'You'll have your sister there, and me, of course. We'll make it a new home, you'll see. It'll be just as good as this one was. Here's your tea. Drink it up, now. I . . . I have to go and get those rams down from the upper quarter this afternoon; they reckon there's gonna be snow up there tonight. You'll be all right, won't you, Katy, lass?' he asked worriedly.

Katy blinked. 'Huh? Oh, yes, Dad. 'Course I will.'

He nodded, relieved that she was feeling better, and walked to the door, collecting the tractor keys as he went.

Katy wasn't sure how long she'd been alone. She thought it had been raining, but when she looked out of

88

the window it was to see bright sunshine. She put away her untouched cup of tea and moved slowly and painfully towards the living room. She was tired. So tired. Perhaps she'd take a nap. Except she couldn't take a nap without her sleeping pills. Try as she might, she always lay awake unless she took a pill. She trudged upstairs and got the phial of pills, then trudged back down again, sitting cross-legged in front of the fire and staring into it. She was going to end up like all those other hard-eyed, desperate women. No longer a big model, no longer a pretty young girl. She took out a pill and swallowed it. The log in the fire spat out a spark and she watched it burn a small black hole on the rug. She took another pill. Why wasn't she asleep yet? She sighed, looking around the room. There was the sofa that Mum had seemed to live on for the last few months of her life. Katy shuddered and looked away. She didn't want to think about her mother. Or the farm. Who ever would have thought they'd lose the farm? She smiled in spite of everything. It was probably the best thing that could have happened to Bryn. Now she'd be forced out into the big wide world at last.

She wished she had something to drink. She could do with a good glass of vodka. Except, of course, Bryn and Dad never kept anything in the house, except . . . 'Hah, Katy girl, your memory ain't as bad as all that,' she said aloud, her voice slurred, and got to her feet, blinking a little as the floor beneath her seemed to shift sideways. Under the stairs she squeezed past the bags of potatoes, her eyes squinting in the dark. Ah, there they were. Two brown crock wine jars, gathering dust, nestled against the back wall. Katy grimaced, grunting as she dragged the nearest one to her.

They were enormous and seemed to weigh a ton but she

hefted one by the handle and hugged it awkwardly in her arms, staggering back with it into the living room and almost dropping it in front of the fire. She grabbed a mug from the kitchen, glancing out of the window as she did so.

Good. There was no sign of anyone. She had difficulty getting the large cork out of the jar, but eventually it came free and the rich, pungent aroma of scrumpy escaped into the room. Clumsily, she poured a mugful of the pale amber liquid and raised the mug to the fire. 'To London,' she toasted, and laughed hollowly. After a good gulp, she gasped. She'd forgotten how potent scrumpy could be. 'That's good stuff, Dad,' she said respectfully, and took another mouthful.

Still not sleepy yet. She sighed and unscrewed the phial, tipping the pills out on to the rug and popping one in her mouth. She took another swallow of drink. She had to forget Maeve and London. It was all his fault, damn him. Lionel.

Realising she hadn't written anything in her diary today, she got her handbag and extracted the envelope marked 'Private' and a piece of paper and a pen. Leaving the envelope in her bag, she moved back to the rug and stretched out on it on her stomach. The pretty pink pills were lying in front of her and she took two more, swigging back a couple of mouthfuls of the extra-strong cider. Seeing that the mug was almost empty, she filled it again, then took the top off her pen and waved it in the air, looking down at the empty sheet of paper.

'It's all his fault,' she wrote, trying to stick to the pale blue lines but finding it impossible. 'So it is,' she said out loud, her voice slurred, and took another gulp of cider. Damned Lionel, jilting her, leaving her easy prey for Maeve. 'If it hadn't been for him, I would still have my pad . . .' She stopped. 'Pad' was what Maeve had called it, the snotty bitch. She blinked, tried to focus, and crossed it out, writing 'home' instead. She began to drift quite pleasantly, but suddenly she could hear Maeve again, telling her to 'sign on' with her. Turning to the paper once more, she continued to write in her diary. 'I don't want to go back to London.' Well that was true. If she went back she'd be a prostitute. She'd die of AIDS. The thought scared her.

She wrote 'I'd rather die,' and stopped. Was that true? She felt tears spurt on to her lashes and she rubbed her eyes angrily. Dammit, why wasn't she asleep yet? She reached out her hand and grabbed some more pills. She couldn't tell how many, but she crammed them into her mouth anyway. It took a lot of cider to wash them down.

She sighed and rolled on to her side, curling into a little ball. She'd sleep soon. And then she'd be safe.

'There it is,' Bryn said to Robbie Peters, pointing out the flash new hotel. She'd found Robbie in the pub in his village. He'd been surprised to see her, and when she told him what she was going to do he'd been *sorry* to see her. But she had been so angry, and so unlike the Bryn he'd always known, that he hadn't been able to say no to her. He was a shy lad, like his twin, and he wished now that his twin were here with him. He glanced nervously at the building. A man in a dark green uniform was guiding in a fancy low sports car. Robbie watched it enviously, then blinked nervously as the uniformed man turned and looked at them.

'Relax, Robbie, it's only the doorman,' Bryn said, recognizing the friendly man from the wolds. But she didn't suppose he'd be friendly for very long. She heard and felt the milling of the restless sheep behind her. With Robbie's help she'd managed to load twenty into the truck, all rams or ewes that had failed to conceive. 'Turn in here,' she pointed out the large entrance to Robbie. The wrought-iron gates still stood open from letting in the Ferrari, and Robbie swung the large truck obediently to the right. Bryn had a glimpse of the doorman staring at them open-mouthed as they went past, spitting up gravel as they went.

Robbie began to sweat. 'What do we do if he calls the police?' he asked nervously. He'd never been in trouble with the police before. His dad would kill him. Or he'd be proud of him. Robbie wasn't sure which. He only knew that, when Bryn had explained to him what she'd wanted to do, he'd felt elated. And he'd always liked Bryn, although, at the moment, he hardly recognized her. Oh, she looked the same, with her bobble hat and glasses pushed right up against her nose, but she seemed so totally different. She looked . . . well . . . strong, some-how.

'We won't be here long enough for that,' Bryn said comfortingly, but the truth was that she just didn't care. As soon as she'd had the idea of ruining Kynaston Germaine's fancy party, she hadn't cared about anything else. It was as if, once the fuse was lit, nothing would stop the dynamite from exploding. She could feel it now, getting closer, that glorious ignition of heat and energy. She could feel *him*, somewhere nearby.

The hotel was full of guests. She could hear the low rumbling noise of conversation inside as she jumped down out of the cab and walked around the back. The doorman was hurrying up the gravel path towards them, but Bryn ignored him. 'Come on, Robbie. Help me get this tailgate down.'

Inside the hotel, Kynaston moved away from a VIP with a nod and a thanks, and moved on to the reporter from the local newspaper. 'Hello. Glad you could make it. Food all right?' He listened to praise for the catering, smiling and answering questions, nodding to guests who caught his eye. It was going well. The 'big thirty', as Michael called the VIP guests, had arrived early and lunched at a sit-down feast in the dining room, joining the other guests as they arrived in the afternoon, to talk shop and speculate on their host.

The major shareholders of Germaine Leisure were, of course, fixated on the Earl and Countess of Vane, whom he'd invited for just such a purpose. That, of course, and the fact that the Earl, on the board of more companies than most people bothered to count, regularly organized conferences for those companies, and letting him get a first-hand experience of the Germanicus's facilities wouldn't hurt.

His eyes missed nothing. The buffet for the guests not privileged enough to have already dined was already half depleted, which meant people were eating well. And why not? Apart from the traditional cold cuts of meat, there were vegetarian dishes that even the most committed of vegans had never had the pleasure to try before. And for the more high-profile people there was caviar (six different kinds), lobster, pâtés and pasta. There were so many salads that the dining room looked green with them, and towering gateaux, calorie-laden chocolate mousse and exotic fruit cocktails awaited those who hadn't yet succeeded in stuffing themselves silly.

Wine ran the gamut from American red to French

white, from champagne to mead. He'd heard that someone had put on a bet that nobody could ask any of the six barman to pour or mix them a drink that they couldn't provide. So far, he'd been pleased to learn, nobody had won the money. Discreet chamber music was being played at the far end, with players from some of the most prestigious orchestras in the world. Now, he saw, there was quite a gathering of ardent classical music buffs, listening with rapt attention. Including a reporter for *The Times*, he noticed, gratified. Outside, a marquee had been erected in the gardens, and there the younger element had collected. Tents full of booze, five-star food and a local pop band who specialized in folk music was bound to go down well with yuppies. The gardens looked good, too, he noticed. A blaze of red tulips and purple primulas provided much-needed colour. He was relieved to see the sun shining – the marquee was waterproof, of course, but even so . . .

His thoughts crashed to a halt, his eyes widening, his mouth falling open. He stared as a sheep's head appeared in a patch of tulips and began to munch the flowers. He blinked, then stared again as a ram, complete with curled horns, gently shuffled against the back of some débutante's leg. She gave a muted shriek, and the ram happily picked up and began to eat the lettuce from the plate of salad she had dropped.

Kynaston moved. Summoning a waiter, he said crisply, 'Draw all the curtains and turn on the globes. All of them.' The man looked startled but did as ordered, and within moments the room was darkened and guests were looking on, amused and appreciative as the four huge silver-domed globes were turned on, rainbow lights flashing from their hundreds of reflective panels. Not that Kynaston noticed the success of his ploy. He was already outside. What he saw made him stare all over again. Sheep, at least twenty of them, milled around the guests, who were, for the most part, taking it in good part. Several men were laughing, and some of the women too.

'What the hell . . .? Mike? What's going on?'

He saw his harassed manager several feet away. He was desperately trying to shoo back a sheep from a bank manager's wife, who laughed more at the sight of Michael's dismayed face than because of the sheep. 'It's that damned woman. She's brought them here.' Michael was almost in tears. He couldn't believe it. The doorman had sought him out, frantically babbling about sheep, but he hadn't believed it until he'd seen it for himself.

'What woman?' Kynaston said impatiently.

'Round the front. Bryn Whittaker.'

'Whittaker? I thought that was all taken care of?'

'It is. Was. I thought it was, anyway. Ouch!' Michael winced as a ewe trod on his toe. 'Leave those damned primroses alone,' he yelled, his face going red with rage as a placid ewe began to make a meal of the flowers.

'Just what is this?' Kynaston said grimly, and, grabbing Michael by the arm, he moved him out of earshot of those within range. 'What's going on?'

Michael looked at his boss, his expression dismayed. 'I don't know. Some kind of protest, I imagine,' he admitted at last, looking crestfallen.

Kyn swore. 'Why didn't you tell me you were having trouble?'

'I didn't think I was!' Michael said huffily, then winced as Kyn's fingers dug in harder.

'Keep your voice down,' Kyn hissed. 'I've got the curtains drawn in there, but it's only a matter of time

95

before those inside get to hear about this. Including the reporters. Go in there and get all the spare staff you can muster. I want these damn sheep rounded up. Quickly!'

'Right,' Michael said, relieved when Kyn let him go. 'Er . . . where do we put them?'

Kyn ran a harassed hand through his hair. 'I don't know . . . the greenhouse is empty at the moment, or nearly so. Open it up and get the sheep in there.

Michael hurried away and Kyn looked at the people watching him. He looked at the sheep cutting up his newly laid, immaculate lawns and chewing placidly on his tulips, and began to laugh. He just couldn't help it. He hadn't seen anything so funny since the day he'd watched his grandfather try to catch a pig that had escaped on his farm. He shook his head and held out his hands in a graphic "why me?" gesture that had those guests still not sure whether to be amused or not grinning in sympathy. Then he noticed one ram come trotting around the corner and he moved quickly away, all but running now beside the side wall and skidding to a stop in the sweeping courtyard. A large, extremely old and unbelievably ugly lorry was just reversing down the drive. An overweight man dressed in scruffy corduroy trousers and wearing an old green bobble hat was guiding the driver down.

'Just one moment!'

Bryn's head whipped round. For a second she lost all power of movement as she watched him walking towards her. Part of the reason she'd come had been to assure herself that Kynaston Germaine meant nothing to her. Now, in that instant of seeing him again, she knew she'd been wrong. Very wrong. He was *more* than she remembered. Taller. His hair was more fiercely silver-gold, his walk more graceful. And his face . . . Bryn stared at his

96

face. He was so handsome. His eyes were like electric-blue ice that froze and burned her at the same time. She began to tremble. What had she done?

Kyn stopped a foot away from her. He saw a wide, heavy figure, covered in a foul-looking raincoat and heavy wellingtons. He saw a green woollen hat and rounded, angry-red cheeks. He saw an exquisite mouth and ugly, big black-framed glasses. And then he looked into her eyes. He'd never seen eyes like them before. They spat hate at him, and defiance, fear, pain, anger and something else. Something that made the angry words he'd been about to say slip totally out of his head. And the *colour* of those eyes – they reminded him of tiger's eyes. Ultra-feline, ultra-beautiful.

'You wanted our sheep so badly?' the woman finally spat, her voice broad Yorkshire, the tone pure defeated venom. 'Then you can have them!' Bryn turned and fled. She couldn't have stayed looking at that perfect, handsome face a moment longer. She was glad to see Robbie was waiting for her in the street, but when she climbed akwardly into the cab she was crying.

Robbie happily drove away with all the speed the ancient lorry could muster. Kyn watched it go, his face still a picture of stunned, confused surprise. Then he turned back as a large burst of laughter rocked the hotel. No doubt everyone was out there by now, watching the waiters trying to round up the sheep. But he no longer felt like laughing, and not just because his PR people would have their work cut out trying to minimize the damage, either.

He simply couldn't forget the sight of the most beautiful eyes in the world flooding with tears.

'Damn it, Michael,' he muttered under his breath. 'I

said tread easily around the farmers.' It was obvious the Englishman had blundered badly, and, as usual, it would be up to him to sort out the mess.

By the time they turned off towards the farm it was dark, and Bryn had stopped crying. Robbie, who wished now that he'd had the courage to take a peep and see how all the big nobs had taken it, was grinning with elation. Bryn stared out the window in silence. All *her* elation had vanished, along with her sense of justice, pride and righteous anger. It was as if they'd never been. She could only think of herself standing there, staring at him. What had he thought of her? She closed her eyes. What *had* he thought of her?

But as soon as they pulled up in front of the yard she knew there was something wrong, and all her self-pity fled. Her father was nowhere in sight. 'Isn't that Dr Bean's car?' Robbie said, pointing to a pale beige Volvo parked out front.

Bryn went cold. 'Dad!' she whispered, then screamed 'Dad!'

She charged to the kitchen door, stumbling through and coming to an abrupt halt. Her father sat at the kitchen table looking pale and lost, a mug of untouched tea in his hands. Beside him, Dr Bean looked up, his face lined and sad.

Bryn sighed in relief. 'Thank God. I thought . . .' She stopped. Her father was still staring into his mug of tea. He looked shattered. 'Dad?' she said, and waited as he slowly raised his head. His eyes, when they finally met hers, looked as bleak as the dales in January.

'Your sister's dead, Bryony Rose,' he said hollowly. 'Katy's dead.'

CHAPTER 8

New York

Lance Prescott put his empty martini glass on the bar and stared at it broodingly. Brezzie's, the latest 'in' bar, was already crowded. The Big Apple was a strange city for someone living in perpetual limbo, like Lance. Because of his pedigree, his name, his looks and his reputation as a stud, he moved in the top layer of the Big Apple cake. From the time he'd known what 'power dining' meant, Lance had been a part of the New York whirl – he'd negotiated the frenzied midday social crush at the top restaurants, commiserated with everyone who took losses on the Black Mondays, or Wednesdays, or Fridays. Most of his friends lived in Park Avenue, and he was adept at dodging most of the backstabbing and backbiting, while getting in a few good wounds of his own. He was a member of the best club, and, when there was a party, book launch, ball, art exhibition or theatre sensation, he was there. Always as somebody else's guest, of course.

And therein lay the problem. Oh, he was one of the 'Old Guard', and that afforded him a lot of mental comfort as well as practical help. In an insular world where the rich knew everybody else who was rich, it helped enormously not to be grouped with the 'New People', who were always suspect. In a world where everybody was out to screw everybody else, the 'Old Guard' stuck together – like glue. It was a pity, most people said, that Lance Prescott was poor, but at least he was one of *them*. His name was in the Social Register.

But he wasn't allowed to take a bite out of the cake. The poor 'Old Guard' could rely on their friends only so long as they knew how grateful they should be, and how far they could go. You could look, but mustn't touch.

'Another, Philip,' Lance's voice immediately attracted the attention of the head barman, who refreshed his drink without comment. Lance drank in brooding silence. He looked good when he brooded. His fair, almost angelic good looks took on a more interesting hue, and gave him a much-needed air of danger. And Grace Vancouver was in the mood for danger. She'd just left the salon, and her dark brown hair hung in a glossy curtain around her shoulders. She was twice-divorced, nearly forty, and permanently angry.

'Hello, poppet. I didn't expect to see you here so soon.'

Lance bit back a groan. 'Hello, Grace. What'll you have?'

'A Green Goddess, I think. To match my dress.'

Lance glanced at the emerald-green De La Renta, and smiled. 'Philip – a Green Goddess for the green goddess over here.'

'This place reminds me of a cattle market,' Grace said sullenly, and took a stool, crossing her legs and showing off lovely calves. Unfortunately the dress rode up, revealing not quite so lovely thighs.

'Does that make all the women here cows, Grace, darling?' Lance drawled, and Grace laughed heartily.

'I see marriage to the Princess hasn't dulled any of your delicious wit, darling. Just as well,' she purred, eyes narrowing, 'since you'll be needing it again. Got the latest walking purse picked out, have we?'

Lance smiled. Inside he could feel the anger begin to metamorphose into rage, but he kept it hidden. He was good at that. And why not? He'd had a whole lifetime's practice, after all. 'How about you, Grace? Could you afford me?'

Grace flushed at the direct hit. She'd got a good settlement from her first husband, an old Frenchman with a flourishing vineyard, but her second husband had been a mistake. The fool had gone bankrupt before she could divorce him. 'I'm afraid you're getting a little bit too old for me, darling,' she purred. 'I like my gigolos a *touch* younger. By the by, I hear your loving mama is giving a party Saturday night. Everyone's invited, so I hear. And of course we'll all come. Everyone's dying to see what your mother can really do.'

'Now that she has money, you mean?' Lance asked wryly.

'Ventura money, darling,' Grace corrected, scoring a direct hit of her own. 'Word has it that it won't last long. But not even Moira can get through millions so quickly, can she? Oh, it *is* millions, isn't it, darling? Everyone assumes you got that much at least.'

Lance smiled. He'd bet his last good watch, a Cartier, that everybody in town knew exactly, to the last dollar, how much he'd got from the divorce. 'Oh, at least millions,' Lance said, and laughed. Inside he could feel himself sinking. He'd been counting on that pre-nup being blown. He needed a base of at least five million dollars before he could feel safe. But Marion had blown it for him. The bitch! If only he hadn't had to sign that damned pre-nup. But the old man wouldn't have let his

101

little Princess marry without it. Oh, no. *Bastard*!

Grace laughed, wondering what was going on behind the bland, lying, handsome face. 'I hear that our little Princess is poised to take over the Ventura throne,' she said softly, her eyes fixed on his with all the concentration of a cat at a mousehole. She was not disappointed. She saw his pupils contract with shock.

'What?' Lance asked sharply, for the first time losing his equilibrium. Grace almost glowed with pleasure as she filled him in on all the latest news. 'It's such rotten luck for you, though, isn't it darling?' she concluded spitefully. 'Marion's going into the company now, I mean. If you could have held out a few months longer, wheedled your way into the company with her – well, who knows what divorce settlement you might have gotten then. Your lawyer could have claimed you helped make millions for dear wifey.'

Lance didn't need to be told the finer points of law by Grace Vancouver. 'Another Green Goddess, Grace?' he asked smoothly, then looked tellingly at her thighs. 'Or have you been having too many already? They're so full of calories, aren't they?'

When Lance got back to the flat later that night he walked straight to the phone and called his lawyer. 'I want you to appeal against the divorce ruling,' he said without preamble the moment Vent came on the line. 'I don't care what excuse you make – claim the judge was biased. Claim sexual discrimination, claim anything. But get my foot back in the door.' He hung up without waiting to hear Vent's reply. The rage continued to roil inside him. He had to get money. Money of his own. Money from that bitch he'd married. Somehow. Anyhow.

* * *

102

Marion yawned and glanced at her watch. Nearly one o'clock, but she wouldn't be stopping for lunch. Who could afford the time? She stood and stretched, only then aware that her neck was aching and her back was coming out in sympathy. 'Corporate crouch,' Felicity said, making Marion spin around. 'You've got what I call corporate crouch,' her secretary explained with a grin. 'It comes from leaning over a desk, head down, reading too many balance sheets.'

Marion laughed. She was still in Keith's old office, which seemed appropriate, since she'd inherited his old title. On the door was now a discreet, black on white plaque that bore the words 'Marion Ventura, Special Assistant to the President'.

Not that she felt very special. As Felicity went back to her own office, Marion moved to the window and looked out. Skycrapers and sky looked back at her. Down there was Wall Street and Madison Avenue, hundreds of shops, a giant, throbbing, commercial heart. And a large chunk of it belonged to Ventura.

She smiled, remembering the day she had walked into that extraordinary meeting. Everyone had been there, grouped around an enormous table. Fifty suits, with men in them. There was not one woman among them, Marion had noted angrily, except the two secretaries who were taking notes of the meeting. She could still see the looks on the men's faces when her father had introduced them to the new Special Assistant to the President. They had been shocked then. Later they were angry. Now, she knew, they were wary, for she was not buckling under the pressure her own father was heaping on her. Nobody had believed she'd last three days, let alone three weeks.

Taking her at her word, her father had thrown her in at

the deep end. For weeks now she had battled to understand the problems of the accounts departments, the personnel departments, the PR departments and the market research departments. Just when she'd shown she was beginning to grasp them, to the surprise of everybody her father had moved her on to study the sub-divisions, the networks, the integration of the companies that made up the whole. Marion knew what her father was doing, of course, but she wasn't going to give up. No way. She'd keep at it until she did understand the infrastructure of the company. At least the vast sums of money involved no longer scared her. But she felt as if she'd go stark staring mad if she had to look at another computer printout. Which was just what everyone was waiting for. It was unnerving and sad to know that everyone, including her own father, was waiting for her to fail. For a moment Marion wondered what it must be like to have a man she could rely on, like other women. A husband who'd cut his toenails in bed and leave the top off the toothpaste, but who'd always be there at night ready to cheer her on.

Suddenly she stood up and reached for her jacket. Today, she was going to have lunch. And to hell with them all! 'I'll be back at two,' she told Felicity, who raised surprised and then knowing eyes. 'If anyone calls, don't you dare tell them I'm out to lunch,' she added wryly. 'Tell them I'm . . . I'm at the docks, trying to track down what happens to Ventura Shipping invoices.'

Outside, spring had come at last. She bought a huge bunch of golden daffodils and an apple from a street vendor, and wandered over to the outskirts of Central Park. There she sat on a bench and ate her tangy apple, enjoying the the wonderful sensation of playing hooky.

She watched as a young couple came walking towards her, hand in hand. They had eyes only for each other. The girl was tall and stringy, and the boy was short and solid. He was black, she was white. They were dressed in jeans and leather jackets and they were so much in love that Marion had to look away.

She walked back to the office slowly, her mind on thoughts of love. She'd never been in love, she knew that now. Her brief infatuation with Lance had been nothing. She thought of the couple in the park. They'd go home, throw open the door, fall on the bed and tear each other's clothes off, eager to make love, eager to give and be given to, uncaring of anything save their desire. She couldn't imagine wanting to do that.

'There's been an urgent call for you from your lawyer, Marion,' Felicity said, the moment her boss walked through the door. 'He asked you to call him back as soon as you got in.'

'All right. Thanks, Felicity,' Marion murmured, handing over the flowers to her secretary. Back in the office she dialled absently. 'Ms Ventura,' she identified herself and was put through to Bernard immediately.

'Hello, Marion? I don't want you to worry unduly but Lance has . . .' Marion listened in silence as Bernard explained the ins and outs of appeals. When he'd finally come to a halt she was sitting tensely at the edge of her seat.

'How likely is it that the settlement will be overturned?'

'Extremely unlikely, Marion, don't worry. As I said, they're just whistling in the dark.'

'But I'm still divorced, right?'

'Right. Don't worry, you can go out and get married tomorrow if you like. I'll keep you informed on the developments as they arise. You won't be required to attend court, either, if that's what's worrying you.'

It wasn't. She was not worried about Lance; Bernard could easily handle him. But she was worried about herself. Bernard's words kept echoing around in her mind long after she hung up. 'You can go out and get married tomorrow.' But to whom? she thought grimly. All the men she knew were like Lance. None of them would say no to marrying the Ventura heiress, who was a mere Princess no longer.

Marion felt her smile wobble. She put a hand to her mouth and tried to swallow back the self-pity, but it wasn't easy. She was only twenty-four. She wanted to be in love. But how could she be in love, if there wasn't a man out there for her? She glanced out of the window, trying to picture the world and all the countries in it. All those men. Surely one of them, somewhere, could love *her* and not her money. Want *her*, not the power Ventura Industries represented. Someone who would cut his toenails in her bed and leave the top off her toothpaste, but who would always be on her side?

Hadrian Boulton pulled up into Ravenheights' courtyard and turned off the engine of his cheerful red Metro. For a long moment he stood looking at the farm, memories flooding back like a riptide. It hadn't changed. It looked as solid, as dark and imposing, as ever. Lights blazed from the kitchen, but there would be no cheerful sounds of talk and laughter, no delightful smell of bread or meat cooking. Not tonight.

He'd been ten when he'd first come to Ravenheights. His mother had been Joan Whittaker, younger sister of John, who had married a teacher at one of the comprehensives in York. They'd met at the Three Peaks Cycle Race, standing among the spectators, cheering on the local hero but politely admiring the visiting Swiss team. It hadn't been love at first sight, but it had been enough for them. Joan had left the farm and married her teacher, and they'd settled down to happy suburban life in York and five years after their marriage they'd had a son. In the fullness of time, Colin Boulton had been promoted to deputy headmaster, and things had ticked along nicely.

There had been nothing outstanding about Hadrian's childhood, either good or bad. He'd been a happy, easy-going boy, with a head for figures and a personality that was already developing with a healthy strength. The only blot on his horizon had been graduating from primary school to the comprehensive, because he knew he'd be ribbed about being a teacher's pet, although his father probably wouldn't have to take him for any actual classes: the school was big enough to avoid that awkwardness. But, as fate would have it, it proved not to matter. One Saturday morning, not long after his tenth birthday, Hadrian had stayed at home watching cartoons while his parents had gone out to do the week's shopping at a big superstore on the edge of town. They hadn't come back. Some drunken reveller of the night before had seen to that.

And so, abruptly, without even having been given the opportunity to say goodbye, Hadrian had been left alone. At least that was how he'd felt, even after his Uncle John and Aunt Martha had arrived from the country. He knew Uncle John only slightly – his parents and he had visited the farm sometimes, usually on a Sunday, as a day out, but the visits had been few and far between. Hadrian had enjoyed watching the sheep, and happily fed the chickens

107

and hunted for eggs with his favourite of his two cousins, Bryn, but he'd always been glad to get back to the city.

But suddenly, at the age of ten, it had had to change. Now, looking at the farm again, and looking back, Hadrian smiled. It hadn't been too hard. Oh, he'd been lost, those first few months. Distraught, angry, bitter, afraid. But Martha Whittaker had had the patience of a saint. When her husband had begun to wonder if the boy would ever settle down, ever stop picking fights at school, ever stop tormenting Katy, she'd say gently, 'Let it be,' and John, as always, had listened to his wife's advice.

Hadrian would come home from school with Bryn and walk into a kitchen smelling of bread and cake, rabbit stew or roast beef. He'd go to his room, wanting to be alone and determined to suffer. And Martha would coax him out with butterfly cakes with butter cream. She'd very wisely put him in charge of the chickens, and one gentle reminder that the poor hens were starving was enough to give him something else to think about besides his own pain. Silly as it sounded now, to his adult self, taking care of those flapping hens had been his salvation. Within a year he was happy again, at least in some measure. Oh, there were flies in the ointment, the biggest one being Katy Whittaker. She'd been jealous of the new addition to the family, calling him 'cuckoo' whenever nobody was around to hear, no doubt because she'd felt threatened by the new, male chick in the nest. She had always been getting him into trouble, telling tales and being generally spiteful and scornful. But Bryn had made up for it. Hadrian smiled now and got out of the car, locking it behind him out of habit. If Katy had been the fly, Bryn had been the ointment. It had been she who'd introduced him to the countryside, pointing out badger setts, naming flowers,

108

even, on one occasion, showing him how to tell if a fox had been around, not by tracks, but by scent. She had helped him at school, standing up for him when he came in for a little natural bullying. At ten, a girl was almost as strong as a boy, and a girl as big as Bryn . . .

Hadrian's reminiscing smile vanished as the door opened and he looked once more at his favourite cousin, who was more like a sister to him. He felt tears rise in his throat and he swallowed them back as instant guilt attacked him. She had done so much for him, this young woman. She had loved and accepted him with a generosity of spirit that, as he now well knew, was the very foundation of her character. And he should have been here to help her, just when she'd needed him the most. Oh, he knew that he couldn't have been expected to know what Katy would do, but deep down he felt that he'd let Bryn down badly. Again.

He'd left the farm when he was twenty. Martha had died, and Katy had gone to London, and he knew John had been hoping he'd want to take over the farm, but Hadrian had always known it was not for him. He missed York, and a life outside the insular farming community. And Bryn, bless her heart, had known and gently encouraged him to leave, assuring him that they could manage, just her father and her. Now, as he and his cousin stood watching one another, he could almost wish he had stayed.

'Hello, Bryn,' he said softly, and walked towards her. Bryn watched him in silence. His name was Boulton, but he had the Whittaker height – at least six feet of it. His hair was the dark brown of rich soil, his eyes the colour of a raincloud – a soft blue-grey that looked startling set against his naturally dark face. Dark eyebrows matched the dark stubble on his chin, and she remembered with a

109

tearful smile how he'd always had to shave every day. He'd complained about that regularly as a teenager. Her dad could get away with shaving only once a week.

She knew her thoughts were deliberately skittering about, like a butterfly that didn't dare to land. If they did, they'd remember Katy. Katy, alone. Katy dying. Katy . . .

'Hadrian,' she said softly. 'I've missed you.'

'I know,' he said, his voice full of regret. 'I never meant to stay away.'

Bryn nodded. 'I know,' she said softly, not a trace of censure in her voice. They stared at one another, and suddenly the old, familiar feeling was back. They were the two musketeers again, facing the world and the common foe.

She stepped off the porch doorstep and into his arms. 'Oh, Hadrian,' she said, her voice choking.

He felt her solid weight press against him and his arms came around her, hugging her, his eyes bright with unshed tears. 'It's all right, Bryn,' he murmured, his deep voice rumbling against her chest, his hands rubbing in comforting circles on her back. 'Everything's going to be all right.'

And in his warm, loving arms Bryn could almost believe him.

Almost.

CHAPTER 9

Morgan left the small suburban house belonging to the Green Vermont's official treasurer with a sense of relief. It had been a long day. He found touring schools to try and get the green message across to kids both boring and frustrating, since apathy was rife, and handing out leaflets on sidewalks always made him feel vulnerably exposed. Looking around nervously, Morgan glanced at every parked car. It paid to be careful. He knew Kynaston had not called off the army of private detectives he'd hired to track him down. A ten-minute walk took him twenty-five, but when he gave the secret knock on the battered blue garage door, he was sure no one had followed him. Greg let him in.

The garage was empty, but signs of occupancy were everywhere. Deep Green so far had only four members, but those four were worth a thousand of those that made up the 'respectable' face of the Society. The table in the centre of the garage was full of equipment – wires, metal tubing, boxes and a small, grey-blue lump of what looked like plasticine, but most definitely wasn't.

'How did it go?'

'Fine,' Morgan said wearily. He had more important matters to think about. 'Now, how's the *real* work going?'

Greg smiled. 'Fine. I told you, no problems.' He looked at his old friend, his monkey-like face a curious mixture of fond amusement and weary impatience. They had met at the hospital, of course. Morgan, tall, handsome Morgan, had attracted the small, wiry, ugly little man from Arkansas with all the ease that a magnet attracts metal filings. He'd been so strong, so *angry*, that Greg had instinctively known that Morgan was the man to follow. He'd told the tall Vermontian all about the little fires he set and all about the Navy, and the way they'd spent years training him before throwing him on to the scrap heap and wasting all those good taxpayers' money.

'Take it easy, Greg,' Morgan said softly. He'd become adept at watching Greg; keeping an eye on the volatile little man had become as natural as breathing. He knew all the signs. The little tic at the corner of the mouth. The wilder look in his eyes. 'We're not in the dungeon now, remember,' he said softly, using their special word for the hospital.

Greg instantly relaxed. 'No,' he said softly. 'I know we ain't. Thanks to you.'

Morgan smiled. 'You don't have to keep thanking me,' he said, glancing at the equipment scattered all over the table. 'You just keep on doing what you're doing,' he added softly.

Greg looked at him knowingly. 'You're thinking of *him*, ain't ya? I can always tell.'

Morgan glanced at Greg sharply, then looked away. In a rare moment of extreme weakness, he'd confided to Greg just what had been done to him, and who had done it. During those dark years, in those rare moments of lucidity when his body had begun to combat the old drugs, and before they'd noticed and started putting him on new drugs, the days had beens so *very* long. And he'd needed somebody to talk to. So he'd whispered in Greg's ears tales of Kynaston Germaine. Tales of horror. But he needn't worry that Greg would ever betray him. Greg worshiped him slavishly.

Moving to the roll of plans resting on the sideboard, Morgan opened them out. Inside were the blueprints of the new Germaine project currently being built on the outskirts of town. A beautiful, luxurious hotel for the idle rich. The way Kynaston was rich. But he hadn't always been that way. No, Kyn had known what it was like to live with cockroaches and despair. But Kyn had crawled out of that hole years ago, while he . . .

'I'm going to destroy him, Greg,' Morgan said softly. 'Slowly, so that he can feel every wound. Carefully. Bit by bit. I'm going to tear down all that that greedy, treacherous son of a bitch has built. I'm going to take it all away.' He glanced quickly at Greg. 'And you're going to help me. Aren't you?'

'Sure, Morgan, sure,' Greg said eagerly, the adrenalin rushing to his head, making veins pop out on his temples. He could see the building in flames. Lovely red, orange, yellow flames. Morgan nodded, his eyes looking beyond Greg to the brick wall behind him.

'I'll have you, Kyn,' he said softly. 'If it's the last thing I ever do.'

New York

In a city made up of skyscrapers, there was still the odd mansion or two shuffled in among the monsters – houses that had been built courtesy of generations of Vanderbilts, Astors, Rockefellers and Gettys. The Ventura Mansion was such a house. Set in six acres of exquisitely tended gardens, it had ivy clinging to almost every inch of its walls. Inside, every carpet was oriental; the sculptures were Brancusi, Moore or Rodin, the glass Lalique and the furniture by the English masters. Marion did not look out of place in all the splendour. The dress she was wearing was an apricot silk De Florentino, her shoes by Maud Frizon. And yet, for all that, she was just a girl, having dinner in her father's house.

Accepting the starter, a delicious French onion soup, she glanced yet again at the man sitting at the head of the table. He looked better than he had at Keith's funeral.

'Daddy . . . I . . . Thank you for inviting me over. I don't get to socialize much these days.'

'You shouldn't have divorced your husband,' Leslie said bluntly. 'Yours is the first divorce – '

'In the family for seventy-five years. Yes, I know, Daddy,' she interrupted angrily. 'I've heard it all before.'

'Don't take that tone of voice with me!' Leslie snapped, his whiplash voice making Marion jump. Knowing he was waiting for an apology, Marion found herself unable to give him one. Instead she looked at him steadily.

'My divorce is my business,' she said crisply.

Leslie flushed angrily, then shrugged, turning back to his food, his cold displeasure so apparent that even Carole felt herself shiver in the icy atmosphere. 'How are things at work, Marion?' she asked pleasantly, hoping to clear the air.

'Fine. No, actually, not so fine,' Marion admitted, taking advantage of the opening. 'It's very hard to try and take in everything at once.'

'You think there's no merit in learning how Ventura Industries is structured?' Leslie asked silkily, sensing criticism.

114

'Of course there is.' Marion quickly sensed the trap and sought to divert it. 'But I don't think going through mounds of paper and chasing accountants who do everything they can to be obstructive is the best way of going about it.'

'Is it getting on top of you already?' Leslie asked snidely.

Marion flushed angrily, but only when she had her temper totally under control did she speak. 'All I'm saying, Daddy, is that I can't be expected to learn all the intricacies of Ventura Industries by studying mounds of paper.'

Leslie leaned slowly back in his chair. She didn't know it, but he approved thoroughly of her self-control. Anyone who lost their temper had already lost the argument. Although he would never admit it, Leslie was pleased and, yes, a little surprised by the abilities Marion had displayed so far. She had understood more about Ventura's inner workings in the last month than Keith had picked up in a year. He was beginning to wonder if, perhaps, just *perhaps*, he had an heir after all.

'If you want to run Ventura Industries one day, Marion, you'll *have* to know all the ins and outs of every single company.' He stabbed his finger on the table as he talked, emphasising each word. 'You'll have to know what every single company is doing on any single day. You'll have to know who's in charge of what, when and where, and how every profit or loss has been made. You'll have to understand the nuts and bolts of every single piece of machinery in the Ventura corporation. I do.'

Marion nodded, a little paler now, but totally composed. She sensed they'd reached a turning point in their battle and it was crucial that she didn't falter now. 'I know you do, Daddy, but then, *you've* built the company up from scratch. You know all that you know because you've had fifty years to learn. When you started out you began with Ventura Real Estate, right?' Marion ploughed on, knowing that she had his full attention now and determined to make the most of it. Her very future depended on it.

Leslie nodded, his eyes narrowing, trying to figure out which way his daughter's mind was leaning.

'And you learned about it as you went along. You made mistakes, you learned by them, and you never made them again. You actually sold the real estate along with the salesmen you employed. You learned your market as you went along, you learned to read people and how to anticipate what they needed. It took three years, and only *then* did you start Ventura Mining. Be honest, Daddy. Have I shown myself to be a total idiot? Have I given up, as everyone expected me to? Or have I proved that I have the ability to do the job? I think I've proved to you and the rest of them at Ventura that I'm not in over my head, although you've done your best to push me under. But I can't learn the business from the top down. What I need now is to do what you did. Start with one thing. Be in charge of one thing and see it through. That way I learn a little of everything and what they mean in a practical way.'

'You have a point,' Leslie admitted, almost reluctantly. It had been so long since he'd started the company that he'd almost forgotten those early days, when he had indeed had to learn as he went along. He looked at his daughter, a new respect beginning to form deep down in his gut. 'But there's more to the job than just knowledge,' he warned, his voice deepening. 'The man . . . *person* who

116

sits in the chairman's seat has to have guts too. He has to make a hundred and one decisions that would make most people blanch. He has to sack people when times get tough, and not get a bleeding heart about it. He has to patrol the stock markets with a killer instinct that would make a shark feel envious. Do you understand what I'm saying, girl?' he snapped, watching her closely.

Marion nodded. She didn't approve of some of her father's business methods, and certainly wouldn't advocate them once she was chairman, but she had no intention of telling him that now. There would be time, later on, to show him that compassion and good business sense *could* go hand in hand.

Leslie's eyes narrowed suspiciously. He didn't for one moment believe that Marion agreed with his cut-throat philosophy. But dammit, it was a jungle out there, and her competitors would rip her to pieces unless she got tough. If she was to stand a chance, it was up to him to make sure she knew how to play the game. And the only way to play it was fast and dirty. He nodded.

Marion saw the slight movement and tensed. He was up to something. She could feel it.

'When Keith . . . before . . . he died,' Leslie forced the words out like venom-coated pebbles, 'I'd given him the task of taking over a company called the Germaine Leisure Corporation. Have you heard of it?'

Marion felt her heart trip with excitement. She'd done it! She'd convinced him. 'I think so, yes. They specialize mainly in the winter skiing trade, don't they?' They were building a new hotel in Stowe, where she had a winter villa. No, where *Lance* had a villa. It was part of his prenup.

'That's right,' Leslie said, surprised but pleased that she

117

was so observant. 'It's a small company by our standards; it has only a ten million annual turnover, but it's expanding rapidly. More important, it's already started to spread out into Europe. I want it. But be careful. Kynaston Germaine *is* a very clever man,' he said thoughtfully. 'You could learn a lot from him. But that's all the advice I'm going to give you. The rest is up to you.'

Marion stared at him, suddenly realising just how well he had set her up. 'You mean . . . you want me handle the takeover?' she asked quietly. 'A *hostile* takeover? You want me to . . . steal this man's company from him?'

'That's exactly what I mean,' Leslie Ventura said gruffly, forcing himself to ignore the shock in her eyes. 'You want to prove you're capable of taking over Ventura Industries? Bring me the Germaine Leisure Corporation.'

Bryn shivered at the edge of the large, gaping hole. It was raining, and so it should be. The flowers that lined the edge of the grave looked bruised but colourful, and suddenly the simile reminded her so much of Katy that she felt a sob rise up from her soul and shake her body. On either side of her, both her father and her cousin took an instinctive step closer to her. The vicar intoned the familiar words of supposed comfort, but Bryn couldn't take her eyes off the simple, wooden coffin. Katy.

She looked up at the grey sky, and the raindrops landed on her glasses, obscuring the view. She was glad. She didn't want to see her sister being lowered into the ground for ever. It was too hard. Too final. Too desperate. Because Katy had done it to *herself*. Katy had brought herself to this place, at this time. She had killed herself. But how could anyone feel so despairing, so without hope, that they'd want to do that to themselves? Bryn still didn't know. So she thought about something she did know. She thought about what she was going to do to Kynaston Germaine, the man who had forced Katy into killing herself. If it hadn't been for him, robbing them of everything they loved and cherished, Katy would still be alive. It was really *he* who had killed her sister . . . She could see him, even now. Tall, handsome, rich . . . so utterly desirable. *The bastard*! How she hated him.

The rain slackened its pace and eventually drizzled to a stop. The vicar shut his Bible and lowered his head. Everyone was quiet. Everyone was thinking of Katy. Except Bryn. She was thinking only of how to make Kynaston Germaine suffer. Suffer as her father was doing now. Suffer as Katy must have suffered in those dark hours before she took all those pills.

She didn't know how she would bring him to his knees. She only knew that she would.

Or die trying . . .

CHAPTER 10

Kynaston looked up as Michael Forrester flopped down into the chair opposite him. 'You've got the newspapers?'

Michael handed them over wordlessly. Kynaston leaned back in his chair to read the damage in more leisure, leaving Michael to sweat it out. When working, Kynaston dropped the impeccable front he usually presented to the world. Now his dark grey jacket was hung on the back of the chair, and his tie had disappeared. The top two buttons of his plain white shirt were undone, revealing a bronzed expanse of skin that was tight with muscle. His cuffs were rolled back, revealing a strong length of forearm, and a simple, plain watch with a neat leather strap. He reminded Michael of a young, golden lion – too young to be so rich and powerful. Michael wondered how Kynaston Germaine had done it.

'Well, it's not as bad as I expected, but not as good as we could have hoped for.' His employer's deep, pleasantly accented voice snapped Michael out of his envious thoughts, and when he looked up it was to find the American's ice-blue eyes trained on him.

'No. Well . . . we played it down as best we could.'

Kynaston smiled. Forrester looked acutely miserable, as well he should. The whole damned mess could have been avoided, if handled better. He checked the story in the *Journal* again, and glanced once more at the picture. It made his lips twitch, even though it poked fun at Germaine Leisure. The photographer had caught a particularly antsy ewe being chased by a waiter, at the same time rapidly chewing on a daffodil. In the background, well-dressed revellers looked on, obviously cracked up with laughter. The text was written in a light, humorous vein, but it nevertheless made the point that the sheep had been delivered in protest over the acquisition of Ravenheights Farm, at Cragsmoor, in the Three Peaks district. Any young journalist out to make a name for him or herself could make trouble. 'You've contacted the Whittakers?' Kyn asked abruptly, and Michael nodded.

'Yesterday. A man answered, but he seemed very abrupt.'

'John Whittaker?'

Michael shook his head. 'No. He said he was a relative. Apparently he was up from York to attend a funeral.'

Kyn frowned. 'There's been a death in the family? Not Bryn? The daughter?' he asked sharply.

'No. He said she was too upset to come to the phone. I asked if we could arrange a meeting, but I think I called at a bad time. In view of their bad news, I didn't want to push it.'

Kyn nodded. 'You did right.' He could remember the day of his own parents' funeral. Both had been killed in a freak subway accident on their way to their respective jobs. Kyn had just turned seventeen, and Vanessa was five. Suddenly they were alone in the city, not knowing how they were going to pay the next month's rent, or whether the authorities would take Vanessa away. The funeral had been held in one of the city's cold, cramped cemeteries, the service and flowers all the cheapest the funeral home offered.

Vanessa had cried for her mother as the coffins had been lowered. Kyn had been numb. Since the age of fourteen his relationship with his father had hardly been ideal, but he *had* been his dad. He'd had good memories of him too, mostly during those early years in Clearmont, before they'd had to leave the Vermont countryside and move to the city. As he'd stood there, holding a sobbing Vanessa in his young arms, he'd felt desolate. And apprehensive. It had seemed that the weight of the entire world had landed on his shoulders.

'You did right,' he said softly. 'A death in the family is a time to be alone. Give it a few weeks, then call them again.'

'By that time the sale will have gone through.'

Kyn looked up quickly, his manager's answer taking him by surprise. 'Already? When were the papers signed?'

Michael, looking into those narrowed, laser-bright eyes, felt his stomach turn over in fright. 'I think they went through six days ago. They would have been sent automatically after the bank made its final demand for repayment of their loan. I never thought to stop it. Let me check.'

Michael left and came back quickly. 'I was right – the papers *were* signed and returned. In . . .' he checked the legal document quickly 'five weeks' time, the property becomes legally ours.'

Kynaston took the document and read it. The signature at the bottom was that of John K. Whittaker. It was dated three days ago. Before or after they'd lost one of their family? Kyn wondered, a cold shiver running up his spine. He didn't like the look or the smell of this.

'I'll take over the land acquisitions personally,' he

122

notified his manager curtly. He watched Michael leave and then sighed. Damn! For a long time he sat and stared at the document that made him the legal owner of Ravenheights farm, outbuildings, stock and acreage. He shook his head as two eyes the colour of sherry stared back at him.

He remembered the day clearly when his family had had to leave his grandfather's farm in Clearmont. It had been a small, typical Vermont farm, and his grandfather had hated to see his youngest son leave. But in the 60s times changed abruptly. Once a reasonable living could be made by raising dairy cows on the rich meadowland, supplementing that income with crisp cider apples from the Germaine farm orchard, and selling pumpkins. In the springs of years past, when the maple sap was running, 'sugaring time' produced a great harvest of maple syrup, providing much needed cash. The price of gas had been cheap. The price of food had been cheaper still. But no more. The 60s had seen many farms go to the wall.

Kyn got to his feet and walked to the window, overlooking the rear gardens of the hotel, where the lawn still bore traces of sheep hoofprints.

He'd been nine when they had finally packed their few belongings and moved to New York. He'd hated the city from the moment he'd seen it from the back of his father's car. Grey and wreathed in smog, it had looked to him like some obscene monster, sprawling across the land. There were no mountains wearing caps of crisp white snow, no tree-studded hills that would turn glorious colours in the Fall. No white-spired churches, or twisting streets, no neat houses each set in its own garden, frothing with flowers. The skyscrapers in the distance became oppressive, the never-ending streets a painful maze of grey ugliness. He'd have done anything, *anything*, to get out of that place and back to Vermont. And so would *he*. Morgan.

He turned from the window and walked back to his desk and picked up the deeds to the farm called Ravenheights. Immediately two tiger's eyes looked back at him. Funny, he could recall practically no other details of the woman except that she was big and dressed like a disreputable scarecrow. But those eyes . . . Ah, those *eyes*. So beautiful, and so angry. And no wonder. He'd done to her exactly what he'd had done to himself. Abruptly, Kyn reached for the phone. 'Carpenter? This is Kynaston. Listen I want you to drive up to the Three Peaks district and make a list of all the farms there that are as close to the specs on Ravenheights, Cragsmoor, as you can find. No, I don't want to build, I want to buy. A farm as close to Ravenheights as you can get. Yes . . . yes, that's right. I've got a deal in mind.'

He hung up and glanced at the papers once again. He had to have Ravenheights' land, there was no getting around that, unless he was willing to scrap millions of dollars. But there were always alternatives.

Suddenly he was fourteen again, and waiting outside a red-brick building, shivering in his father's car. No, he thought grimly, there were not *always* alternatives. But there should be. And for Bryn Whittaker at least, there *would* be.

Suddenly, he began to feel better.

John Whittaker began to feel worse. Then he began to feel downright bad. So bad, in fact, that he stopped the tractor and turned off the engine, his hand shaking and numb. He leaned over the steering wheel, his mouth open, trying to draw in great gulps of air. It was no good. No matter how much he inhaled, he just couldn't seem to get enough air into his lungs. He opened the cabin door and half climbed, half fell out of the tractor. His feet landed square on the grassy turf, but to his dismay his legs refused to hold him, and he found himself on his hands and knees on the ground.

He looked straight ahead, trying not to panic. The view of the dale was glorious. The fields looked emerald with their spring coating of fresh grass, and high overhead a buzzard shrieked and wheeled. He felt hot. So hot. It began deep in his chest and moved up to his throat, making his breathing ever more tortured. No matter how much air he dragged into his lungs, it didn't seem to be enough. Suddenly his elbows gave out completely and he found himself face-first in the grass, which felt blessedly cool and damp against his flushed cheek. He could smell the good, clean scent of the earth and he thought of Martha. Martha, sitting up in bed, watching him get undressed, she already modestly clothed in her high-necked white nightdress. Martha, and her large, rounded breasts, against which he'd rested his head and slept for a good forty years of his life.

John could feel his heart thumping. It was too hard, too fast, too loud and suddenly there was pain. So much pain. He knew he had only a little time left. Minutes? Suddenly it didn't matter. He thought back on his life and there were no regrets. He'd married a good woman, one that he'd loved solidly for forty years. He'd had two lovely children, and then been privileged to take care of a lad as good as Hadrian.

Martha . . . He closed his eyes briefly. He'd soon be with Martha, after all. And Katy. Ahh, Katy. Perhaps soon he would be with Katy too. It hurt him so, that he'd failed her, and a sense of familiar guilt washed over him. The buzzard was directly overhead now. From his ground-eye view he could also see the sheep beginning to appear on the crest of the hill. No doubt they wondered why he had stopped here and not gone down to the racks with their feed.

Bryn.

The thought cut through everything – the feel of the damp ground penetrating his clothes, the heat that was now like a flame on his skin, the sound of his own harsh breathing, the pain in his chest and thoughts of the past.

Bryn. What was to become of Bryn?

John Whittaker closed his eyes, and from a distance that seemed far away, he felt his whole body began to shudder. Someone take care of Bryn, he prayed. Someone love her.

The shuddering stopped. The laboured sound of his own heartbeat stopped. The sheep made a circle around him, but after a while even their bleating, encouraging calls stopped. Only the harsh shrieks of the buzzard, circling high overhead, continued to rent the calm dales air.

Lance Prescott glanced once more in the mirror and straightened his already impeccable tie. Behind him, his mother watched his every move. She knew him so well – knew his every weakness and his greed, every impetus that drove him. And so she ought. She'd made him her life's work, after all.

In spite of humble origins, Moira had successfully chased and married Clive Prescott III, the epitome of the American east coast aristocrat, who'd lived well and thoughtfully died young. Now she was the admired and respected widow of one of the 'Old Guard'. She dressed conservatively, but well. She had taught herself how to play bridge and make the all-important social contacts. Her labour had paid off in dividends. But that had not been her only accomplishment. No, she had another iron in the fire. Lance.

Moira had not planned on having children when she'd married. Then, when she'd realised her true financial predicament, she'd thought again. A baby grew and got married. And, while a baby born to Clive Prescott III might not have any money, it would have something much more important: pedigree. And a pretty girl could have her pick of the new-wave millionaires when she also had that much coveted touch of 'class'. Moira, of course, had been disappointed again. She'd had a son. But there were compensations. A boy earned her the instant approval of both husband and society. After all, she had done her duty well by producing a Prescott heir. And she'd anxiously watched him grow, only relaxing when it became apparent that his baby good looks were going to stay with him into adulthood. She made sure he had the right clothes, went to the right schools, was friends with all the right boys. And, again, her work had paid off, just as she'd always known it would. She'd steered him towards Marion Ventura with all the skill of a cowboy on a cattle drive. She'd researched the Ventura Princess meticulously, making up a dossier that held everything from the girl's favourite colour to her favourite wine, and a planned calendar of where she dined, what parties and balls she was likely to attend, and even what her politics were. And all for nothing.

Her eyes sharpened on Lance as he yet again reached up to straighten his tie. 'It's perfect as it is,' she said sharply. 'Leave it alone. Our guests will be arriving soon.'

Lance bit back a heavy sigh. He'd be glad when the damned party was over. He despaired at the expense. He and his mother shared a joint bank account and, although he hated it, he could not get out of it. His money was her money, and Moira would have it no other way. 'Ah, the doorbell. Stand still!' she said sharply as Lance made to walk towards the bedroom door. 'The maid will answer. For heaven's sake, Lance, this is *my* party. Everything's to be done *right*,' she hissed. 'Quickly, now, we must be on hand to meet our guests.'

The first arrivals were Molly and Gerry Tinspin, notorious early arrivers. There followed in quick succession the cream of the New York 'Old Guard', all wearing their second-best jewellery and gowns, out of consideration for Moira, who was wearing her only Valentino original, and Clive's grandmother's jewellery. It was bad form to outshine the hostess, and really, everyone agreed, Moira *was* a good sport. Everyone knew the money from the Ventura divorce settlement wasn't much, but Moira was 'one of them', after all, and as such knew her responsibilities. After all the freebies the Prescotts had enjoyed over the years, it was only right that they should push the boat out once they got some money of their own. And to see their faith in Moira Prescott's stalwart personality being fully justified caused many of their guests a warm glow of satisfaction. So they ate the caviar and lobster, drank the Mouton-Rothschild and Moët et Chandon, duly admired all the inherited Prescott art, and let Moira bask in her moment of glory.

Lance didn't let her down. Somewhere in the crowd there had to be somebody rich. Somebody vulnerable. Someone like Marion, but without an all-powerful father. Lance hated to lose. He hated it because he was always doing it. He lost to everything and everyone, including his own mother. His mouth was dry with bitterness and a hatred and frustration so strong that not even a good gulp of exquisite pink Moët et Chandon champagne could wash it away.

Damn Marion. Damn New York. Damn his mother and all these people spending his money!

Lance wished he could do something, *anything*, that would show them all.

He didn't know just how soon he would get his wish.

CHAPTER 11

The day Bryn left Ravenheights, everyone came to see her off – Sam and Bill, the twins (Robbie giving her a bouquet of daffodils), and even Walter Gornwell and his six Yorkies had taken a detour from their usual morning walk, to come and see her go. She thanked him for his commiserations, then turned around and looked at the house. Ravenheights. It sat solid and square, dark and strong. Except now it looked different. Now it was empty. No fires burned in the grates. There was no dog sleeping by the Aga, because Violet had gone to Mrs Kennedy up the road. No daffodils sat on the kitchen table.

'Ready, Bryn?' Hadrian asked softly, his voice matching the look in his eyes. She nodded, and let him lead her to his car. She had only one suitcase of clothes, and a trunk full of books and photographs, her mother's favourite vase, and her father's collection of cricket memorabilia.

'Bye, lass. Good luck in the city,' Sam called as Bryn leaned back in the front seat and Hadrian closed the door. She smiled and waved, but she felt nothing. She felt as numb now as on the day of Bill's halting explanation of driving up the road to check for late lambs on the lower twenty and seeing John lying out in the field, and it was still with her now, the day after his funeral.

Hadrian looked across at her, opened his mouth to speak, then shut it again. What could he possibly say to comfort her? He turned the key in the ignition and smiled briefly at the little line-up that waved the car out of sight.

She watched her past life flash by from the car window. The little dell that had been her mother's favourite picnic spot. The tree that she, Hadrian and Katy had played on. She watched the sheep that were no longer hers call to their lambs and felt like crying, but knew she wouldn't. Or couldn't – she wasn't sure which. A part of her was aware of a great hole being ripped in her universe. Even if she wanted to, she could not ask Hadrian to turn the car around and go home, because she no longer had a home. She sighed, and noticed Hadrian look across at her quickly. Poor, dear Hadrian. He'd been so good to her the last two weeks. 'It's all right,' she said quietly. 'I'm not going to flood the car with tears.'

Hadrian looked back at the road, twisting and turning in familiar Yorkshire tradition. 'I wish you would,' he said even more quietly, but, although she heard him, Bryn said nothing. She knew he must be wondering what was going on. Apart from that first night after her father had died, when she'd sobbed out her grief into the pillow all night, she had neither cried nor talked about her recent losses. Nor did she talk about her future, and she was well aware that it worried him. He was more sensitive than most men, more able to understand the weaknesses and fears of people. Some mistook this gentleness in him for weakness, which was a big mistake. Hadrian had a frankness that was refreshing, but it covered a steely mind and a strength of character that was rock-like.

'You'll like York,' he said suddenly, knowing that the lower twenty was just coming up around the bend and wanting desperately to distract her. 'I know you don't think so now, but things *will* get better, in time. Believe me, I know.'

To his surprise, Bryn nodded. 'Yes,' she said simply, her eyes suddenly tiger-bright. 'I know they will.'

Hadrian felt the hairs on the back of his neck stand up on end. A cold shiver snaked its way down his spine and he found his foot pressing automatically on the accelerator. He couldn't have said why, but instinct warned him that things were going to get much worse before they ever got better.

'Bryn, you know I'll be here whenever you need me, don't you?'

She nodded. 'I know you will,' she said quietly, sincerely, then suddenly stiffened. 'Are you sure you don't mind my staying with you in your flat? If you want to bring a woman over, I can always stay the night in a bed-and-breakfast.'

'Don't be daft,' Hadrian said bluntly. 'Besides, there isn't anyone special in my life at the moment anyway.'

Bryn was surprised. Her cousin was good-looking, had a good job, and was one of the nicest, strongest men any woman could want. What was wrong with the female population of York?

Usually the sight of a city made her feel a mild sense of panic. But today, as York came into view, the numbness continued unchallenged. Only thoughts of Kynaston Germaine pierced it, bringing flooding tides of anger and hatred and, curiously, a sense of betrayal.

As they pulled up outside his flat, Bryn leaned across the gearstick and kissed Hadrian gently on the cheek. 'Thank you, Hadrian,' she said softly. 'I'm glad I'm not alone.'

Hadrian felt a quick wave of warmth wash over his cheek and almost laughed aloud. He hadn't blushed since he was a kid. Trust Bryn to be the one to start up the old habit. 'You're not alone, badger,' he said gruffly, using the old childish nickname. 'Not while you've got me.'

It was strange how life worked out, Hadrian thought. Fifteen years ago, he'd been orphaned and gone to live with Bryn, who had made his life bearable again. Now things were happening in exact reverse. He only hoped that he would be able to help her as much as she had helped him. But he wondered. There was something strange happening to Bryn, he was sure of it even though he couldn't quite grasp what it was. On the face of it she was coping remarkably well, and he was not surprised. While a lot of people mistook her shyness and generosity for weakness, Hadrian knew better. But there had been times during the last nightmare two weeks when he'd looked at her and caught an expression in her eyes that he'd never noticed before. It was a look of intense power, and of anger, and of such intense concentration that it had made him feel uneasy.

Bryn didn't want Hadrian to worry about her. She was going to be all right. She felt a small lurch in her chest, directly in the region of her heart, and for the first time fear pierced her shell. She *was* going to be all right, wasn't she? Then Kynaston Germaine leapt into her mind – tall, golden, beautiful – and the fear melted away. Oh, yes. She was going to be all right. It wasn't as if she didn't have plans. You couldn't be lost if you knew exactly where you were going. All she needed now was to find out how to get there. But she was confident she'd find a way. After all, she had nothing to lose any more, did she? She smiled. How free that made her. He'd already taken away her sister and father and her home. He could do nothing more to her, but she could do plenty to him. And she would. Oh, yes. Plenty.

The set of six spacious flats were part of a genteel house, on an elegant street of limes and chestnuts. The communal garden was small but neat and filled with flowers. Bryn looked at it appreciatively. It was a lovely house. Funny, she'd never noticed that before. She'd had Ravenheights then. Now, with the anchors of her past gone, she felt curiously free, and the thought shocked her. Katy had often said that their home was a millstone around her neck, holding her down and keeping her isolated, but she'd never understood what her sister had meant. Was it possible that Katy had been right?

'Come on, let's get inside and get the teapot busy,' Hadrian said with determined cheerfulness.

The flat was just as she remembered it. Two large bay windows overlooked a street that she no longer found grey and depressing. Instead she saw the window-box with its display of dwarf tulips. Then she looked slowly around the room itself. The carpet was bottle-green, the walls a pale aquamarine. The curtains, sofa, chairs and cushions were all shades of blue. It was like a peaceful underwater hideaway. 'Hadrian. About those things of Katy's – perhaps we should keep them for the flat.'

Hadrian shook his head. 'No, Bryn. Those are yours, and I think you *should* sell them, as you planned. Katy would be the first to sell them off if she'd needed cash.'

Bryn nodded. 'Yes, I know she would,' she said softly, and thought of the day she had gone through Katy's things. The clothes had been packed away reverently and sent to their mother's favourite charity. Katy's jewellery was now locked away in her own case, which had

134

previously only contained the three modest pieces her mother had left her. But the envelope marked 'Private' that she had found in Katy's handbag was now tucked away in the bottom of her suitcase, unopened. Katy had always guarded her privacy jealously when alive. Bryn just couldn't bring herself to do something she knew Katy would have hated now that she was dead.

'I'll go and get the luggage,' Hadrian said quickly. 'You know where the kitchen is, don't you, badger? Make us a cup of tea,' he added pleadingly, not so much because he wanted one, but to give her something else to do.

Bryn did as she was bid. The kitchen was everything that the kitchen at Ravenheights wasn't – small, modern and filled with gadgets. It took a while to find everything. By the time the tea was made, Hadrian was standing in the doorway, watching her. She was dressed in a brown dress with black dots, her long hair pulled back in a ponytail held by an elastic band. Fat padded her hips, thickened her waist and added an extra chin, but to Hadrian these things were almost invisible. He knew the woman inside, who was beautiful indeed, and knew too that she was hurting. She was also in trouble.

'There's no milk,' she said, handing him the mug of tea and sipping her own.

'That's OK.' Hadrian pulled her unresistingly into his arms. 'And you're going to be OK too.'

Bryn closed her eyes. It would be so easy to lean on Hadrian. He'd never let her down, never betray her. But who did she think had betrayed her? Confused, she looked up at Hadrian, resting her chin on his chest.

'Hadrian, I thought I saw your car . . . oops. Sorry. I didn't mean to interrupt.' The voice was bright and cheerful and cut the air like a kind knife. Bryn leapt

135

back, her face going red. Hadrian looked around, a broad grin spreading across his face. The woman who looked back at them was both puzzled and pretty. Five feet ten if she was an inch, she had short, curly blonde hair, wide blue eyes, a nose full of freckles, and a smile that was positively contagious.

'Lynnette, your timing is as impeccable as ever,' Hadrian teased, then looked at Bryn, who was backing off warily, as she always did around strangers. 'Lynnette, meet Bryn. Actually she's my cousin, but she's more like a sister to me,' he added, and saw the puzzlement leave Lynnette's pretty face. 'Bryn, this is Lynnette Granger, my next-door neighbour and the bane of my life,' he introduced cheekily.

'Nice to know I serve some useful function,' Lynnette said cheerfully, and walked across the kitchen, her hand thrust out. 'I'm pleased to meet you, Bryn. Actually, Hadrian *has* talked about you a lot.'

Bryn took the offered hand and shook it, and found herself smiling naturally back. 'Hello, Lynnette,' she said softly.

'Bryn. That's an unusual name.'

'It's short for Bryony.'

'Bryony? Now that's a much prettier name. If it belonged to me, I'd use it all the time.'

Bryn blinked. 'I never thought of it that way.'

'Do you mind if I call you Bryony instead of Bryn?'

'No. My . . . father always called me Bryony. Well, Bryony Rose, if I'd done something wrong.'

Hadrian looked from one woman to the other, a puzzled look in his eyes. Was it his imagination, or was something going on here? The two women seemed to have forged an instant bond. Bryn was aware of it too. There was some-

136

thing . . . *special* about Lynnette Granger. She wasn't sure why yet, but she just knew Lynnette was going to play a big part in her life.

'So, Hadrian Boulton, how come you did a moonlight flit?' Lynnette asked, and knew instantly that she'd said something wrong. Tension sprang into the air like an evil jack-in-the-box. Hadrian glanced at Bryn, who gave a very faint nod.

'I told you about the years I spent in the country, didn't I?' Hadrian began warily, his eyes watching Bryn for the first sign of pain. 'About living with Bryn and her sister, and my aunt and uncle.'

'You did,' Lynnette said quietly, and waited.

'Well, my other cousin Katy . . . Bryn's sister, died.'

'I phoned him and asked him to come over,' Bryn interrupted. He'd been the first person she'd thought of, which perhaps said more about Hadrian Boulton than anything else.

'Oh, I'm so sorry, Bryony,' Lynnette said. 'I lost a sister too. I was fourteen at the time, and Vivienne was only twenty. It was a brain haemorrhage. One second she was sitting at the table, studying, the next . . . she was gone.'

'Katy . . . Katy killed herself,' Bryn blurted out bluntly, managing at last to get the words past her tongue. Strange that they should be said to a stranger.

Lynnette looked shocked. Her pale complexion paled even further, and her wide eyes became even wider. 'Oh, lord. How awful. I'm so sorry. I don't know what to say.'

'Lynnette is a nurse,' Hadrian said quietly, explaining why she was so easy to talk to, and that she could be trusted.

'Actually, I'm also a dietician and a physiotherapist. I

went a little mad at nursing school,' Lynnette confessed wryly.

Hadrian shifted restlessly in the doorway. 'Bryn will be staying with me for a while, so you'll have another chick to be mother-hen to,' he said, confident that Lynnette knew him well enough to understand what he meant. She did, and she nodded in agreement. Bryn was obviously in deep shock and mourning, and Hadrian was anxious that she should have all the help she needed.

Bryn, needing a moment alone, made their neighbour a cup of tea. 'Here you go. Oh, I forgot to ask if you wanted sugar.'

'Thanks, I don't.'

Bryn glanced at Lynnette's svelte figure and smiled wryly. 'I didn't think so.'

Lynnette's eyes lit up, and a small smile hovered across her wide mouth. Inside Bryony Rose was a slim girl just waiting to get out. And Lynnette would see to it that she did. She'd have to be tactful, of course, but Lynnette knew all about that. Tact, firmness, kindness, compassion. 'So what do you think of the flat?' she asked cheerfully. 'Nice, isn't it?'

Bryn nodded. 'You should see Ravenheights . . .' She stopped abruptly as she remembered that Lynnette would never see Ravenheights. That not even *she* would ever see it again. Hadrian stiffened on the chair, and when Lynnette shot him her stare that demanded an answer, he shrugged helplessly. 'That's the farm. Or was. Bryn had to sell it.'

Lynnette's blue eyes darkened as she looked at the young girl hunched over her mug. 'You must be reeling,' she said softly. 'But where is your father, Bryony? Hadrian told me his uncle had lived on the farm all his life?' Again, the moment she spoke, Lynnette knew something was wrong. Good lord, what else had happened to this poor girl?

'My father died five days ago,' Bryn said starkly.

Lynnette swallowed back the lump in her throat but said nothing. Instead, she glanced at Hadrian. If she hadn't been happily married, she'd have snaffled her handsome neighbour up the moment she'd met him. As it was, a deep friendship had grown between them, and now she nodded at him, a silent communication passing between them. She would look after Bryony Rose. Her compassionate heart contracted as she thought about all that the poor girl must have gone through. Briony was obviously a country girl forcibly transplanted to the city. She'd lost everything she held dear. She was shy, and undeniably fat, but pretty, perhaps even beautiful underneath. And she needed, desperately needed, to make a new life for herself.

Lynnette nodded. Yes, that was the key. A new life. A new self. A new look. Her gaze became more clinical as she looked at Bryony Rose, and, sensing it, Bryn looked up.

'What are you thinking?' Bryn asked, for suddenly she knew it was vitally important. Instinct screamed it at her. Lynnette saw her fear and knew immediately that she had to take a straight, clear-cut path with this girl.

'I'm thinking how beautiful you could be,' she said, and saw the shock hit the younger girl like a tidal wave. Just as she'd thought. Bryony had always thought of herself as fat and ugly. Hadn't Hadrian said something once about the sister being a fashion model? That couldn't have helped. 'Bryony, you'd be a beautiful woman if only you lost some weight.' Seeing that Bryony didn't believe her, Lynnette marshalled her thoughts. 'Let's start with basics. Hair, according to all the beauty experts, is the most important thing of all, and yours is glorious and completely natural, am I right?'

Bryn reached for her ponytail and pulled it around, dipping her chin to stare at it. It was just her hair – thick, and with a tendency to get greasy if she didn't wash it every two days. She didn't see its glorious depth of colour.

'The next most important thing is the eyes,' Lynnette continued, and, kneeling in front of Bryony, reached up and removed the awful, black-rimmed, heavy glasses. Lynnette met the wary, hurt eyes and felt a frisson of pleasant shock sidle up her spine. Slowly, she shook her head. 'I've never seen eyes exactly like yours before. They're . . .'

'Brown,' said Bryony flatly.

'No, not just brown,' Lynnette denied. 'More orange. Tawny. Red even. Oh, I don't know how to describe them. Let's move on to something easier. Your bone-structure is basically sound. Once you've slimmed down, Bryony Rose, you'll have cheekbones again, and a good strong line of jaw. I'm no expert, I know, but I can already see you as you could be.'

She leaned back on her heels, her blue eyes wide and candid, and refusing to back down. Bryony felt the room suddenly move around her as she realised that Lynnette really *meant* every word she said. But could it possibly be true? If she were beautiful . . . Bryn's eyes suddenly became the eyes of a tiger. If she were beautiful, her chances of getting revenge on Kynaston Germaine would surely double. Triple. Slowly, she began to smile. And, this time, the smile *really* meant it.

Vince pulled the car up in front of Ravenheights farm, and in the back seat Kynaston felt his heart thump. He was not quite sure why. He didn't expect the meeting to be a particularly pleasant one, for both John and Bryn Whittaker were sure to be resentful. But he was confident he could persuade them to do the swop. The farm he'd located for them was thirty miles away and had roughly the same acreage as Ravenheights. He could foresee no real difficulties.

Then he took a good look at the house, and his eyes widened. This farmhouse was old and dignified, not at all like the more modern house that came with Duckworth farm. He might have gone through a time warp, he thought with a fascinated smile as he climbed out of the car and stood in the mud of the courtyard. The wind blew around the barns, creating an eerie whistling sound that raised the goosebumps on his forearms. It looked like a scene from *Wuthering Heights*.

The tithe barns, he knew, were rare and protected by law, so couldn't be pulled down. He watched, wide-eyed with wonder, as a barn owl flew out of one of the barn's ventilation holes and glided across the farm rooftop on silent, ghostly wings. He saw where an old well, long since covered in, had once been. But the house was deserted. Abandoned. And he felt a crushing sense of disappointment. It puzzled him until two sherry eyes, the colour of banked embers, leapt into the forefront of his mind. For a woman he'd barely met, she had certainly made an impression on him. So much so, that now he knew instinctively that she was absent from this place. He could sense it. Something had been taken from this place, and he could feel its pain.

Nevertheless, he walked to the window, the kitchen window as it turned out, and looked inside. He saw ancient tiled floors, original wooden beams, walls bulging

CHAPTER 12

The limousine ferried Marion straight on to the runway. The Lear jet was only one of a fleet, of course, and her father preferred to travel in his own extravagantly furbished DC10. The jet took off exactly on time and after a few moments she began to relax. She hated air travel, and she was glad of the mild tranquillizer she'd taken before leaving home. She was just drawing the curtain across her window when the steward appeared. He was not a tall man, but he was extremely handsome. 'Is the sun in your eyes, Ms Ventura?'

Marion smiled. 'No. It's cowardice, I'm afraid. Do you think you could draw all the curtains and put on the lights?'

The steward smiled. 'Of course. You can unfasten your safety belt now.'

Marion did so. 'How long before we reach Burlington?'

'Barely two hours, Ms Ventura. Can I do anything for you?'

Marion glanced up and their eyes clashed. Her heart picked up a quick beat, then slowly subsided. He too, seemed suddenly aware of the potential double-entendre in his words, but his reaction was entirely different. Marion saw consternation then downright fear leap into his eyes.

'I meant, tea, coffee, a glass of wine. Cocktail?'

Marion felt her stomach lurch. 'Thank you. A cup of coffee would be nice. Black, no sugar.' And just to make sure she'd done enough to reassure him, she lifted her briefcase on to the small table in front of her and extracted the first folder she found. She was still studiously reading it when the steward put the cup of coffee down beside her and left.

When he was gone, Marion slumped against the chair. He was *afraid* of her, she realized, and a sick feeling surged in the bottom of her stomach. He'd been terrified that she'd take offence, think he was coming on to her, and get him fired. She found herself swallowing back tears. The folder she had been studying, a biography of Kynaston Germaine's working career, was forgotten. She reached for her drink with hands that trembled slightly. Suddenly she gave a painfully wry bark of laughter. She terrified men! Or rather, her father's money did. Her father's power did. Her inheritance did. When it didn't make them salivate with anticipatory greed, that was. Marion closed her eyes wearily, fighting off depression.

Hadrian heard the sound of music coming from the flat even before he put the key in the lock. He was no longer surprised. When he walked into the living room, Lynnette and Bryn were lying in the middle of the floor, doing sit-ups. The first time he had come home to find them working out, his astonishment had made both women burst out laughing. Bryn had been wearing that ghastly brown and black polka-dotted dress and looking acutely miserable. Now she was dressed in a black leotard, her face red and flushed with exertion.

'That's it, Bryn. You're doing really well,' Lynnette

encouraged. 'Believe me, I know it's hard, but this is worth it. When you've slimmed down even more than you already have, your stomach muscles won't flop about if they've been tightened up like this. Good. Just two more.'

Hadrian sat down on the sofa, his eyes on his cousin. Bryn was red-face and sweating in obvious discomfort. She also looked more determined than he'd ever seen her before. Hadrian could see for himself that she had lost a lot of weight in just over a month. Already he could see that hourglass shape of a woman beginning to emerge. He was glad for her, but it also worried him, and he couldn't figure out why.

'Right. Let's take a little breather, then we'll do some bust exercises so that your breasts will be pert and upright, like this . . .' Lynnette's hands rose to her own ample, but well-shaped bust, and Hadrian hastily coughed. Loudly. Both women looked around, and Lynnette grinned, not one whit put out.

'Ladies. I must say, I didn't expect my flat to become an aerobics studio.'

'Oh. I'm sorry, I hadn't thought . . .' Bryn began, realising only then that they had neighbours to think about. At Ravenheights the nearest neighbour had been five miles away.

'He's teasing,' Lynnette interrupted, getting up with a lithe grace that Bryn could only envy as she hauled her own bulk into an upright position. Muscles twinged and complained, but Bryn ignored them. 'Let's have a drink,' Lynnette said. 'Remember my warning about dehydration?' She poured out two large glasses of mineral water.

Bryn nodded, while Hadrian looked on, his eyes thoughtful. He couldn't deny that Lynnette had worked wonders in the short time she'd known his cousin. Bryn had begun to lose that lost, haunted look, and once or twice he'd come home to find the two girls laughing together over a magazine, or just chatting happily over a glass of herb tea.

'How was work?' Bryn asked, waiting for her laboured breathing to return to normal. Was it her imagination or did it not take as long as usual?

'Work was fine. In fact – ' Hadrian rose to his feet, a big grin on his face ' – it was more than fine. It's official.' He worked at one of the best accountancy firms in the city. 'The partners have asked me to join them. I need to put my money where my mouth is of course, but I've saved up a good sum. Enough to go into Wright, Carter and Phipps, anyway. Or should I say Wright, Carter, Phipps and Boulton?'

'Hadrian, that's great!' Bryn cried, and gave him a huge hug.

'Congratulations,' said Lynnette. 'But was there any doubt? They'd crumble without you and you know it. Hadrian, admit it, you're a genius with figures.'

Bryn accepted a glass of mineral water with a slice of fresh lime and drank without a thought. Sweet, fattening drinks were a thing of the past. 'If you keep this up,' Hadrian said, pinching her drink, taking a swig, then handing it back, 'we won't recognize you.'

Lynnette laughed. 'That's more true than you'd think. You'd be surprise how much weight-loss alters a person's whole appearance.'

Bryn went cold, then hot. Was that true? Would nobody recognize her? She tuned out the other two, who were talking excitedly about Hadrian's new position, her thoughts becoming like concentrated ice. A man like

Kynaston Germaine was thorough – he had to be. He'd know by now about the deaths of her sister and father. He'd know – especially after that sheep incident – how angry she was at losing the farm. So when she showed up in his life again, although it was possible that he might not recognize *her*, he'd surely recognize her name. After all, Bryn Whittaker was hardly a common name.

'Bryn. What do you say?'

'What?' She blinked, looking at Hadrian. 'I'm sorry. I was miles away.'

'I said, why don't we go out tonight to celebrate? You, me, Lynnette and Phil.'

'Oh, yes. That'll be great. But I'll be having the salad.'

'I always thought you hated salads,' he teased, and winked at Lynnette, who grinned back. In fact, Lynnette had found it surprisingly easy to regulate Bryn's diet. It hadn't taken her long to realise that her main problem was too much fatty food, followed by comfort-binging on toffees and sweets.

'Dad always hated salads, you know that. He always called it rabbit food,' Bryn said with a smile. In fact, she now found dieting almost easy. But whether she did or not, it wouldn't have made a difference. She was determined to lose weight. But perhaps not stop there? Could she *really* change her whole appearance? Hadrian saw again that strange, tigerish gleam in her eyes, and frowned. He glanced at Lynnette, who for once didn't seem to notice anything amiss, but perhaps that was only because she didn't know Bryn the way he did. But something was wrong. He knew it. He could feel it. And, a nasty feeling deep in his gut told him that when she finally confided in him what it was, he was not going to like it.

Marion booked into the Chateau Lake Louise at two o'clock. By three-thirty, Morgan knew she was there. He had a range of 'green' spies that linked up into a network that would have made even the CIA envious. He wasn't worried. His immediate thought was that she was just another of the rich and famous taking a very late skiing holiday. But he'd have someone keep an eye on her and report back to him. Just in case.

Marion wasted no time in unpacking, but quickly rented some skis and headed for the slopes. Quickly she began to feel better than she had in days. Weeks. Months. There was something about the snow, the mountains, the freedom, that made all her cares and worries seem like nothing. As she skied to a halt at the base of Mount Mansfield, Ventura Industries was suddenly hundreds of miles away. No wonder Kynaston Germaine was building here. Instantly, Marion sobered. She still had work to do. It might be dirty, and seem unfair, but if she was to prove herself to her father it had to be done.

Bryn said very little during dinner at the restaurant that night, preferring to think and plan. Besides, what could she add to the evening's intelligent and amusing conversation? The only thing she could talk about was sheep! Afterwards, all four of them decided to stroll through town. They were walking down Stonegate, and stopped briefly outside one of the clothing stores. Bryn gazed in silence at the window display of the latest summer fashions, then said quietly, 'They're lovely.'

Lynnette smiled. 'It won't be long before you'll be buying some of those,' she said gently. With her strict diet and exercise, Lynnette knew, Bryn had already lost just over seventeen pounds. A lot of that had been water, of course, and progress would not now be so rapid, but even so, she confidently expected Bryony to lose, on average, just under a stone a month. And in five months' time it would still only be August. Bryn shrugged. 'Well . . . we'll see.'

Phil, Lynnette's husband, tactfully changed the subject. By the time they got back to Hadrian's car and drove home, the question of Bryn's new wardrobe was forgotten by everyone but Bryn. She would need good clothes; fashionable and expensive-looking clothes would be a must if she was to move in Kynaston's world and look a part of it. She would need other things too, of course, so she must sell everything of value she had. Her own things, and the things Katy had left. Her jewellery – everything except those three pieces belonging to her mother. She'd start on that tomorrow.

When they got back to the flat, they said a cheerful goodnight to the Grangers, and Bryn headed straight for the kitchen. Into her own mug of tea she put in a spoonful of the artificial sweetener that she now took instead of sugar. Hadrian was yawning happily when she handed him his mug. She knew looked at him nervously. 'Hadrian, how do you go about changing your name by deed poll?'

He blinked at her. 'I don't know. Why do you ask?'

'Because I want to change mine.'

Hadrian felt the cold shiver return to his spine. He knew something had been brewing. He just *knew* it. 'Why, Bryn. And what do you want to change it to?'

'Bryony Rose. I've been thinking . . . Bryony is my real first name, after all. And Rose is my own name as well. So it's not as if I'm really *changing* anything.'

149

'Except to get rid of the Whittaker,' Hadrian said bluntly, ignoring her wince. 'Why, Bryn? Are you . . . do you feel all right?' For the first time Hadrian wondered if his cousin had suffered some kind of nervous breakdown.

Bryn smiled, reading his mind, and it was a sad, tired smile that she gave him. 'I'm fine, Hadrian. But I haven't been totally honest with you. About . . . Katy.' Wordlessly, Bryn put down her mug, already getting out of the chair with more ease than she would have done only a week ago. Walking to her handbag, she extracted Katy's suicide note. 'Dad and I didn't show you this because . . . well, we were still trying to think it through ourselves. But now I think you should read it.'

Hadrian stared for a moment at the sheet of paper she was holding. He felt reluctant to take it. 'You didn't show this to the coroner, did you? Do you realise that's illegal?'

Bryn didn't flinch. 'Dad didn't want it read in the coroner's court. He felt guilty because he was the one who ran the farm into debt. Which meant Kynaston Germaine could take it away from us.'

'Germaine? What's he got to do with all this?' he asked sharply. Hadrian knew a little about the Germaine Leisure Corporation, through work. His company had bid, unsuccessfully, to handle some work for the company when it had become known that they were branching out into England.

'Everything,' Bryn said flatly. 'He's the reason Katy killed herself.'

Hadrian didn't like the flatness in her tone. His own reaction was disbelief. Reluctantly, very reluctantly, Hadrian took the note. The writing was Katy's – he would recognize her untidy scrawl anywhere. A cold film crept up over his skin as he read the few short sentences. He might not have loved Katy as he loved Bryn but even so . . . no human being deserved pain like this. And it seemed that Bryn was right. Katy had taken the loss of the farm far harder than he'd have thought possible. 'I don't know what to say, Bryn,' he said quietly, and she instinctively reached out to touch him. In that moment she decided that she would not ask for his help. It wasn't fair to ask him to go with her to America. But that did nothing to lessen her own resolve.

'I can't let him get away with it,' she said softly, almost to herself. 'Not about Katy, and not about Dad either.'

Hadrian looked up from the note, the cold film on his skin turning to ice. 'Bryn? What are you thinking?' he asked ominously, his voice lowering an octave.

Bryn took the note from his nerveless fingers and slipped it into her bag. Not trusting herself to face him yet, she walked to the window and looked out at the Minster, lit up in floodlights of gold. How odd that she'd never noticed it before. How beautiful it was, with its twin towers and spikes, its golden stone and tall, arched windows.

'Bryn?'

She turned, her eyes obscured behind her glasses, but Hadrian already knew they were tiger's eyes again. 'Bryn doesn't exist any more,' she said, her voice harder than he'd ever heard it. 'My name is Bryony Rose. First thing tomorrow I'm going to find out how to make it legal.'

Hadrian stood up. 'And then?'

'And then I'm going to diet and exercise like crazy.'

Hadrian took a step closer. 'And then?'

'Cut my hair. Lynnette says it's too long. It has no shape.'

151

'What else?'

'See if my eyes can take contact lenses.'

'I see. You want Bryony Rose to be totally different from Bryn Whittaker.'

'Yes. She *must* be different. Totally different.'

He was standing right in front of her now. His eyes were dark with concern, his heart deeply troubled. 'Why, Bryn?'

'Bryony.'

'Why, Bryony?'

She looked at him steadily. 'Bryn was a victim, Hadrian. I can't go on being a victim. I have to change. Besides, I want to be pretty. It's high time I became the woman I *could* be. And that has nothing to do with Kynaston Germaine,' she lied straight-faced, but felt a small blush creep across her cheeks. Luckily, Hadrian didn't seem to notice. He sighed, then nodded, his shoulders sagging. Reluctantly he said, 'You're going to take on Germaine, aren't you?' His voice was flat.

'Yes.'

'Do you really think revenge is so sweet?'

Bryony's eyes flashed, tiger-bright. 'Not revenge, Hadrian. Justice. Men like Kynaston Germaine think they can do anything they want and get away with it. Well, perhaps they can. Usually. But not this time. This time Kynaston hurt the wrong people. *My* people.' She tapped her chest with her thumb, then raised her chin and looked him straight in the eye. 'And I want to make sure he can't do it to anybody else. So I want to . . . check up on him. Dig into the company's background. See if there is some way we can . . . legally bring him to court, or sue, or even just get our story into the papers and warn other people about him.' She was lying, of course. She didn't really think they would find anything on paper in this country to bring Kynaston down. But, while she might need Hadrian's help to do some of the financial research, she would not drag him into the rest of the fight. It was going to get dirty. And dangerous too, she thought, knowing Kynaston Germaine as well as she did. And she wanted Hadrian safely out of the way in England when it all began to explode.

Hadrian nodded, less worried now that he knew he could help her, and look out for her. 'All right. I have some contacts. I'll see what I can find out.' She didn't need to remind him how much he owed to John and Martha Whittaker. Even Katy.

And he already knew how much he owed to Bryn Whittaker. And to Bryony Rose too, it seemed.

Whoever she might turn out to be.

CHAPTER 13

Morgan walked into the Trapp Family Lodge and easily found the Austrian tea-room. He was dressed in dark green trousers and a mint green and black sweater. With his dark hair combed back from his face and his tan topped up by the May sunshine, he looked devastating. Not surprisingly, he had no trouble being seated just where he wanted to be. Which was directly next to and opposite Marion Ventura's table. She had been in Stowe a month now, and Morgan was sure she was up to something. The skiing season was long over, yet still she remained. And there was a purposefulness about Marion Ventura that didn't quite equate with her image. Looking at her now, Morgan was aware of a typically male interest stirring in his body. Her eyes were dark and mysterious, and Morgan could feel her feminine, sexual allure with an appreciation that was genuine, but controlled. His mind was firmly on other things.

When the snow had gone, she should have done the same. Instead, her itinerary had been varied and interesting. It had begun with a strange two-day stay at practically every hotel in the town above three-star status. There had been a long, minute inspection of the tourist information office, before moving on to rent out a water canoe from the

Buccaneer Country Lodge. Only a week ago, she had checked into the Top Notch, Stowe's unique resort spa, that boasted heated pool, tennis and fine dining.

All this both intrigued and worried Morgan, and the information he'd received on the lady from his New York sources had done nothing to reassure him. She had just pushed ahead with a bitter divorce, and New York was said to be agog at her new role as President Elect of Ventura's. Once she'd learned the ropes. And it was the particular ropes she was learning that worried Morgan. It didn't bode well for a Green Vermont, and another avaricious corporation plundering his land was something he simply would not tolerate.

He made his move. Marion looked up to see a tall, handsome stranger smiling down at her. 'Hi.'

Marion smiled back automatically. 'Hi.'

'Do you mind if I join you for a moment?'

Marion hesitated. She felt instinctively afraid of the stranger and it was a new and an unsettling sensation. 'Well, I'm not . . .'

'I wanted to talk business. Honest injun,' Morgan held up his hands in a pacifying gesture, his smile widening. 'I represent the Green Vermont Society. I think you and I should get our heads together, don't you?'

Marion's eyes sharpened and Morgan felt a shaft of pleasure hit him deep in his groin. He'd always liked strong women – he was like Kyn in that respect. Strong, beautiful women.

'That sounds like an ecological group,' Marion said quietly.

'It is,' Morgan confirmed, sitting down unasked in the chair opposite her and lowering his lids a fraction. It made him look incredibly sexy.

Marion sipped some tea, giving herself time to think. On the one hand, it would be stupid and illogical not to get to know the local 'greens'. It made business sense, and besides, she herself agreed with a vast amount of green policy. But on the other hand . . . She glanced up once more at the stranger, her stomach tightening. He was a dangerous man, her instinct insisted. 'Well, I'm not sure what I can do for you, or your society, Mr . . .?'

'Morgan. Just Morgan.'

That cold, instinctive wariness that had gone hand in hand with her acute awareness of his masculinity now stepped up a notch. Why no last name? 'Well, as I said, I don't quite understand why you've picked me out. Unless you're recruiting?'

Morgan leaned forward, his movements slow and sinuous, like those of a snake, and she found herself leaning back in her chair, struggling for breath. When he smiled, it was the smile of a man who knew his own power. 'I would like nothing better than to have you join our group,' he purred. 'After all, converting Marion Ventura into a "green" would help solve an awful lot of global issues.'

Marion let out her breath on a burst of laughter. She blinked, desperately trying to find a foothold in this bizarre conversation. 'I wouldn't say that!'

'I would. Ventura is a giant. It pours huge quantities of waste into rivers. It gorges vast amounts of harmful gases into the atmosphere. It rips up forests of timber. It extracts billions of tons of the earth's minerals and riches. A green-minded person at the helm could help enormously.' Morgan didn't realise it, but his whole body, his face, even his voice, had changed. The hunting look in the eyes and the mockery in the voice had vanished. In its place was sincerity, stark and devastating. Although

156

Morgan was concentrating first and foremost on destroying Kyn, he still genuinely despised developers, any developers, with a passion.

Marion found herself staring at him, rapidly reassessing her first impression. 'You really mean it, don't you?' she breathed, her voice feathery with surprise.

Morgan blinked and leaned across the table. Before she could stop him, he took her hand in his. 'Of course I do.' Marion felt his fingers stroking the inside of her wrist, and the tiny shock-waves shot up her arm like little missiles.

She snatched her hand away, her eyes shooting angry sparks. She felt cold anger wash like a chilling wave over her. 'I hate to disappoint you, Morgan,' she said coldly. 'But I'm already a convert, and I've already decided to do something about Ventura's environmental record. You're not the only crusader, you know.'

'Some crusader,' Morgan drawled, caught off guard by her abrupt defences. 'I know what you've been up to. Sniffing out all the tourist goodies. Checking out the best hotels. Do you really think I'm not on to you, Ms Ventura?'

Marion's back went ice-cold. Had she really been so obvious? If this man knew, who else had guessed? Had she been too eager to learn all that had to be learned before going ahead with her plans? 'I don't know what you're talking about,' she said finally.

'No?' Morgan rocked back on the chair, hands curling around the armrests, imagining they were her breasts. 'Are you telling me that Ventura Holidays Inc. aren't interested in moving into the winter holiday markets? They are mostly summer-vacation-orientated at the moment, aren't they.'

They were. It had been one of the reasons her father had

been anxious to acquire a winter-based holiday operation. 'I still don't see why that should concern you or your society, Mr . . . oh, I forgot. You don't have a last name, do you? I wonder if the authorities would be interested in finding out what it is?' She had scored a direct hit. She could see it by the shock-waves that widened his pupils and shot his body upright in the chair. Slowly, Morgan stood and Marion moved one step back. He was much taller than she'd thought, and the air around them crackled with tension.

Then Morgan smiled again, though there was no hint of humour in his eyes dark depths. 'I expected as much from the Ventura Princess,' he drawled, watching her lips tighten in displeasure as he used the hated nickname. 'But the future President of Ventura industries should have more backbone. You *can* expect to encounter opposition, Ms Ventura. And if you build one of your Ventura monsters here, your royal highness, I can *guarantee* you opposition.'

Marion smiled. 'Perhaps you're not as well informed as you think you are,' she said softly, vastly relieved to find that Morgan was not as infallible as she had begun to think.

Morgan tensed. 'What do you mean?'

'I mean, Mr . . . Morgan – ' again she carefully used his lack of a last name as a psychological weapon against him ' – that I have no intention of building another hotel in Stowe. In fact, I rather think that it has more than enough, don't you?'

Morgan's eyes narrowed. This meeting was not going at all as he had planned. Marion Ventura was no pushover. Not at all. Perhaps he'd have to persuade her. 'Do you expect me to believe that? Do you really think we're so stupid?'

158

Marion flushed. 'I already told you, I agree with a vast amount of green issues. But there are other ways to acquire a winter-holiday company for Ventura other than by building . . .' She stopped abruptly, realizing too late that she had already said far too much. She picked up her bag and straightened her back, but she could see from the look on his face that she had made a bad blunder.

'You're planning a takeover,' he said softly, only then slowly straightening from the table.

'I never said that,' she snapped, her voice cold.

'Who?' he said sharply. He ran through a mental list of holiday companies, none of them sounding right. Ventura went for top-of-the-market. They wouldn't be interested in the rent-a-chalet market so beloved of middle classes America. No. They would go for the *crème de la crème*. And, in Stowe, that meant . . . 'Kynaston Germaine,' he said softly, seeing the dismay flicker into her lovely brown eyes before she could disguise it.

'I never said that,' Marion repeated herself helplessly. What a mess she was making of this! But her self-anger quickly disappeared as she forced herself to concentrate on the man in front of her, who had suddenly gone pale, almost as if she'd mortally wounded him. In his eyes there was a sudden shrinking and darkening that seemed to concentrate into something . . . mad. Without thinking about it, she took a step back, and then another.

Morgan shook his head, trying to clear it. 'No,' he said at last, his hands clenching and unclenching by his sides. She could not take over the Germaine Leisure Corporation. He would not let her. *He* must be the one to destroy Kynaston. *He* must be the one to take it away, to watch Kyn suffer. 'I can't let you do that,' Morgan warned,

159

staring fiercely at the woman who was trying to rob him of his golden, glittering prize.

Marion backed off another step. 'I have to go,' she said nervously, and, clutching her bag to her chest, she carefully walked around the table then headed for the door, walking so fast she was almost running.

Morgan watched her go, his body slowly relaxing, his mind settling into serenity as he faced the facts. It was simple really. He just had to stop her taking over Kyn's company. But how? Deep Green alone wasn't equipped to handle anything like this. He needed allies of a different ilk – allies who moved in the same circles as the Venturas. Big business people. People with their own axes to grind. People like Marion Ventura's bitter ex-husband, possibly . . .?

Morgan was not the only one thinking about Marion Ventura. In the office at the Germanicus, Kynaston pushed away the monthly figures for the hotel, his eyes thoughtful. The hotel was full, which was in itself very satisfying. The work at the domed park was continuing at break-neck speed and the dry-ski run in the Three Peaks district had been mapped out and was due to be laid at any moment. Even the work he'd had commissioned at Ravenheights farm was all but completed. He frowned as he thought of the sad and unexpected death of John Whittaker. Dammit, where was *she?* Bryn Whittaker. Should he find her and . . .? And what? He couldn't give her back her family. He shuddered, suddenly feeling cold. Would the image of those burning, sherry-coloured, tiger-bright eyes never go away? Tiredly he rubbed his neck. It was definitely time to go home – he missed Vermont badly, and a familiar restless longing to return to the mountains was nagging him once more. Forcing thoughts of Bryn Whittaker to the back of his mind, he reached across the desk for the latest wad of information from Roger Gibb and read it for the fourth time.

Marion Ventura had turned up in Stowe, the site of the latest Germaine hotel, and had been doing some very odd things. Gibb thought that she could only be on a scouting mission for Ventura Holidays Inc., and Kyn was forced to agree with his analysis. It was obvious that Marion Ventura was serious about going into the family business, and her presence in Stowe seemed to indicate that she was going about it by picking up exactly where her brother had left off. And that meant taking over Germaine Leisure. Reluctantly, he reached for the phone and booked a flight to New York.

'Now this is going to feel very strange at first,' the young man looming over Bryony warned her gently, his breath hot against her cheek. 'Obviously, anything to do with the eyes is very sensitive, but you'll soon get used to inserting contact lenses for yourself. Now, just relax . . .'

Half an hour later, Bryony left the opticians, having said goodbye to her old, heavy and ugly black-framed glasses for good. Yet another piece of the old Bryn Whittaker had been eradicated, and she smiled in triumph as she walked briskly back to the flat, where Lynnette was anxiously waiting.

'Let's have a look . . . Oh, Bryony, you look fabulous!' Happily, she dragged her friend in front of a mirror. 'Can't you see what it does for you? Before, half your face was hidden by those horrible black things. Now you can see where your cheekbones start and finish, and the top half of your nose is visible again – it's quite a good nose too, now

161

you can see it. Sort of . . . patrician. And your eyes . . . Bryony, they look fabulous.'

'The optician said that,' Bryony admitted, and blushed.

Lynnette nodded knowingly. 'And there'll be more compliments to come,' she prophesied. 'Lots more, I promise.' She hugged Bryony hard. 'Once you've lost another stone, we'll see about getting your hair cut. The hairdresser will have a better idea of what will suit you then.'

Bryony nodded. She could wait. After all, Kynaston Germaine wasn't going anywhere, was he?

CHAPTER 14

Hadrian sighed heavily as he passed the Roman sewer on Blake Street, driving carefully down York's narrowed, sometimes cobbled streets. By his side, Bryony glanced at him quickly. 'Is anything wrong?'

Hadrian shook his head and indicated left. 'No.'

Bryony never took her eyes off him. 'Come on, Hadrian,' she said reproachfully. 'You're talking to me now, remember?'

Hadrian felt a reluctant smile tug on the corners of his mouth. 'I swear you're a witch, Bryony Rose.'

She laughed softly, and glanced out of the window, looking at the beautiful city around her. The warm summer months had passed, and October had brought with it the usual flurry of falling copper leaves, reminding her that winter wasn't far away, and that the beginning of the winter skiing season in America was about to start . . .

Abruptly she pulled her thoughts up. She felt scared whenever she thought about the travel tickets she had bought secretly a few short days ago, and about just how quickly they would take her into Kynaston Germaine's territory. She'd never had secrets before, and she felt resentful that she had to keep lying to Hadrian now. But there was a deep hard lump near her heart that refused to be denied, and although she understood, in the deepest recesses of her mind, that she was walking dangerously closer and closer to an obsession that could destroy her, she was helpless to stop herself. Something inside her kept urging her on, whispering encouragement when she felt afraid, and scorn whenever her saner side told her to forgive and forget. But she couldn't forget. Not ever . . . She still found herself wanting to burst into tears at odd moments during the day. Little things brought it all back, like cricket scores on the radio. And she still couldn't look at pictures of women in magazines and not feel resentful that it wasn't Katy's face, nor ever could be again. She lay awake at nights, thinking of Kynaston Germaine, and all that she would do once she was in Stowe. Ironically enough, the money from Ravenheights had come through just a week ago, giving her a more than healthy bank balance. To destroy Germaine using the money he'd paid her was a delicious exercise in poetic justice. She only hoped that he'd appreciate it as much as she, when she finally told him all about it . . .

'Bryony,' Hadrian's voice snapped her out of it.

She looked at him, her face once again perfectly normal. 'You remind me of Violet when you frown like that,' Bryony said teasingly. 'Now *there* was a dog that could *growl*.'

Hadrian managed a laugh, remembering the old sheep-dog with affection. It was a good sign that Bryony could now talk more easily about the old days, wasn't it?

'Hadrian, stop the car.'

'What?' He looked at her quickly, a concerned frown creasing his handsome face. 'Aren't you feeling well?'

'I'm feeling fine. But you're not. What's wrong?'

Hadrian shrugged, spotted a parking space just coming

free and shot in before a sports car could get it first. Slowly he turned and looked at her. Bryony huddled in the seat as if trying to make herself invisible. 'You've no reason to feel self-conscious any more, you know,' he said softly. And it was true. The past four months had just about put the finishing touches to Bryony's new figure. Now her legs were long and shapely, with not a wobble of excess fat in sight. Her waist was certainly not wasp-like, but it was well-shaped and very evident. Her breasts were firm and upright, her shoulders, arms and neck showing a pleasingly faint line of bone.

'I could still do with losing some more weight,' Briony began dismissively, and almost jumped when Hadrian raised his hand quickly in a sharp gesture.

'No, you can't,' he said bitingly. 'That's just the point. Bryony; you've done enough. You can't be as slim as Katy, because Katy had a different bone-structure completely. If you lose any more weight you'll begin to look . . . forced.'

For a moment the silence in the car stretched uncomfortably, then she nodded. 'All right, Hadrian. Go on – you obviously want to say more.'

Hadrian sighed and ran a harassed hand through his thick hair. 'Look – Bryony. You look sensational as you are – you're a tall girl, with curves in all the right places. OK, so it's not fashionable at the moment to be curvy, but not everyone wants girls who are shaped like sticks. Didn't Lynnette say you were fit only yesterday? So there's no medical reason for you to continue starving yourself in the hopes of getting thinner, is there?'

'No, but . . .'

'But you want to be slimmer. Like a catwalk fashion model, right?' He heard the harshness in his voice but

165

didn't rein himself in. It was important that he get through to her on this. Very important. The spectre of slimming disease was never far away from his mind these days.

Bryony shifted on her seat and stared sightlessly out of the window. Hadrian was talking sense, she knew, but she was fighting the clock. Kynaston had been in the States for months and she needed to look her best, very quickly. 'Hadrian, you know I have to – I mean *want* to, look good,' she corrected herself hastily but he cut her off abruptly.

'You already look good, Bryony,' he said firmly. 'Don't all the wolf-whistles tell you that?' She blushed as she remembered the incident last Friday. She had been walking past a road crew, and every one of them had whistled at her.

'They were just teasing.'

'They meant it,' corrected Hadrian ruefully. 'And remember what the one with ginger hair said?'

Bryony nodded. 'He said that . . . it was nice to see a girl with a shape again.'

'Right. A girl with an hourglass figure was what he meant. Like women used to have in those 30s and 40s films. Girls like Rita Hayworth and Marilyn Monroe. Those girls weren't whippets, were they? And look at the way you walk now, Bryony. Remember all those nights when Lynnette was straightening your shoulders and making you keep your head up? You move with such grace that it doesn't matter if you're tall, not petite, or that you're shaped like Jane Russell and not Twiggy. You move . . . like . . .'

'A stately sailing ship instead of a nippy schooner?'

Hadrian laughed. He couldn't help it – it was just the sort of funny thing the old Bryn would say. 'If you like. Bryony, can't you get it through that thick head of yours

166

that you're no longer fat? You are *tall*. You are *voluptuous*. You are *not* fat. OK?'

Briony looked at him, realising that he was sincere. 'Do you really think I'm attractive?'

'Are you kidding? When a man walks down the street and every road-worker in sight wolf-whistles at the girl by his side, it makes him feel as if he's got Miss World on his arm.'

'That's laying it on a little too thick, kiddo.'

'OK. But only a little. Now, if you want to make it to the hairdresser's in time you'd better shift yourself.'

She gave a little yelp of alarm and leapt out of the car, sprinting across the road and heading for the hairdresser. She was wearing a plain navy blue trouser suit with white piping. Her long legs pumped easily as she crossed the street, the double-breasted jacket pulling against her own breasts as she moved, and he watched, amused, as every man in the street stopped to watch her go by. Her make-up-free face glowed with health, and her long, unshaped hair streamed out behind her. Apart from the new body shape, Hadrian thought with relief, she was still the old Bryn.

Bryony packed the barest essentials, knowing that once she was in America she'd have to shop for a whole new wardrobe. Fashionable outfits, things made out of silk and satin and lace. And evening dresses . . . She'd never, ever owned an evening dress. Or a cocktail dress for that matter. And the high-profile, dashing clothes she'd seen women wear on catwalks on television were totally beyond her field of experience. But she'd have to buy them if she was to move in Kynaston Germaine's world, and it was a daunting thought.

167

Packing done, she wrote Hadrian a brief note, saying only that she was going to take a holiday on some of the money from Ravenheights, and that she needed a little time to herself. If he sensed what she was planning, he'd never let her leave for the States alone. She checked her handbag and made sure that the new passport she'd got only a week ago, under her new legal name, was safely tucked into a side pocket, along with the tickets and her traveller's cheques.

She breathed deeply and, looking up, caught sight of her reflection in a mirror. Was she really up to this? Leaving the country? Leaving Hadrian behind, and all the warmth and comfort he represented? Was she up to taking on the wolf in his own territory? Over the last month Hadrian had done some extensive research on Kynaston Germaine, and she now knew all she possibly could about the man who was their enemy.

It had been surprising stuff. She could still recall her shock when she'd learned that Kynaston hadn't inherited a fortune at all, as she'd always assumed, but had made his own way after being born into a life of near poverty. He had never been married once, let alone the two or three times that she'd assumed. But most surprising of all was the fact that there'd never been a hint of scandal attached to either himself or his company. As they'd learned more and more about the size of his company, the enormous amount of his wealth, the influence and power he enjoyed, the more their task had seemed hopeless. Only Marion Ventura had given them hope.

Hadrian had come across her name on one of his many trips to Leeds. The financial world was a small one and getting smaller all the time, thanks to computers, phones and faxes. Gossip was rife about the new position of Leslie

Ventura's daughter. And a little digging had revealed Marion Ventura's recent visit to Stowe, where the latest Germaine Leisure hotel was currently being built.

Hadrian had been of invaluable help to her over the last month or so; she wouldn't have known where to start but for him. Hadrian was not merely an accountant, as she'd quickly come to realise. He'd taken courses in business studies, economics, banking and commerce. He knew all about takeovers and their politics. So when he'd told her that an even bigger conglomerate might try and take over Kyn's company, she knew she must have lit up like a Christmas tree. For days she'd pored over the Ventura papers, trying to see if there was an angle in there for her. Reluctantly, she'd come to the conclusion that there wasn't. She could hardly influence a giant company like Ventura. Still, it was heartening to know that there were others interested in giving Kynaston Germaine a body-blow of their own. If all else failed . . . if *she* failed . . . But she wouldn't. Her father was counting on her. Katy was relying on her. The old Bryn Whittaker, too, needed her to succeed. And she would. She still had a long way to go, but she'd learn. She'd buy the kind of clothes Kynaston's women wore, and she'd learn about make-up. She'd already taken a three-month course of elocution lessons, softening her broad accent. And she'd do anything else necessary. Anything at all to make him pay. To see him beg.

Again the cold, hard smile Hadrian would have recognized instantly flitted angrily across her face. She had, for the last two months, been taking regular and secret skiing lessons on a dry-ski slope, of all things, situated just outside Leeds. Another of life's little ironies.

She shivered suddenly, all her demon doubts rising and

clamouring in her mind. Sometimes, despair would take her over as her task seemed to become more and more impossible. There was so much she still had to do before she even stood a chance against him. But she'd do it. Oh, yes, she'd do it.

With a last sigh, hoping Hadrian wouldn't be too hurt by her leaving without saying goodbye, she checked outside to make sure Lynnette was nowhere in sight, then left. The door closed behind her with a small, but final, click.

Hadrian opened the door and saw the white envelope propped up on the sideboard immediately. Quickly he read the note. It was short, to the point, and didn't fool him for a minute. Quickly he pulled open the drawers, hesitating as he came across her files on Germaine. Most of them were gone. Only the stuff relating to Ventura was still there. Suddenly he remembered how she'd hoped to use Ventura to bring Germaine down. And now she was gone. 'Oh, Bryony,' he said softly, and shook his head. 'He'll eat you alive.'

He began to make a long, methodical list. He'd have to leave his job and arrange for his money to be transferred to a bank in New York. His passport was up to date, so that was no problem. He knew he had no way of finding Bryony, except through Ventura. If she contacted them . . . So that was where he had to concentrate his efforts. Like most big companies, they were constantly hiring new staff. He should be able to get a job there. He was extremely well qualified.

'I'm going to find you,' he assured himself quietly. 'Besides, I've got a feeling about New York . . .' He stopped, surprised by the words he'd spoken out loud.

Then, as he explored that strange thought more, he shook his head, feeling oddly perplexed. It was nothing he could trace, nothing tangible that he could hang on to. But he *did* feel that New York was going to change his life forever. That there was something there waiting for him. Something other than rescuing Bryony from her own folly.

In her penthouse at Ventura Towers, Marion stared out of the window. The city was huge, vast, grey and bustling. She'd never felt more alone. She sighed and turned, walking to her bathroom and running the hot steaming water. Adding a sprinkling of freesia-scented salts, she stripped off her office suit and climbed in, sighing as she did so. It felt so good. And perhaps the hot water would ease the tension that had been growing between her shoulderblades all day.

'Get a grip, Marion,' she murmured to herself, her voice echoing in all that tile and mirror. 'It's only dinner.' She smiled suddenly. Only dinner. Who was she kidding? It was dinner with Kynaston Germaine. And she didn't think he was going to be any too friendly.

CHAPTER 15

The head waiter at Chasens recognized Kynaston Germaine at once and greeted him effusively. Kynaston smiled back, remembering the ritual of high society dining, and treating the impeccably dressed man like an old friend. 'Thank you. Has my companion arrived yet?'

'No, sir.'

'In that case, I'll wait at the table.' Once the other diners at the top restaurant saw the highly flammable combination of Kynaston Germaine and Marion Ventura together . . . Kynaston smiled. He could almost imagine the shockwaves there'd be tomorrow morning, when the New York elite read the society pages.

Once seated, he ordered his favourite drink, Scotch malt whisky, and leaned back wearily. The city had bored him rigid within the first few days, but he had business to see to. For a whole month now he'd been stalking Marion Ventura, dogging her trail, talking to the shareholders she'd been talking to, ferreting out the information she wanted kept hidden, calling in all his IOU's, and recording her progress on charts. It was not much fun. Holding fifty per cent of the shares was normally an unassailable position, but Marion Ventura had already managed to purchase twenty-two per cent by carefully winkling out those in need of cash, and offering to buy shares in their own companies where cash-flow was a problem. She was both careful and clever, and extremely competent, and Kynaston was not about to underestimate her.

Outside, Marion stepped from the cab and paid the driver, feeling butterflies dancing the can-can in her stomach. She smoothed down her dress – a deep sapphire, heavy satin creation by Balenciaga. It was cut in a deep 'V' at the back, a more modest 'V' at the front. Around her throat was a choker of sapphires, diamonds and amber by Bulgari.

Kynaston stood the moment she approached his table. Her hair was swept up in an elegant chignon, her eyes huge and nervous in a small, piquant face. Kynaston felt a slight loosening of his taut muscles. He smiled and seated her. 'Ms Ventura. I'm grateful you agreed to meet me tonight.'

'Would you care for an aperitif, madame?' the waiter asked in French, and Marion answered in the same language, opting for a glass of chilled vermouth.

Kynaston smiled. 'Vermouth is an unusual choice. Or didn't you think I spoke French?'

Marion stared blankly at him. 'Why would I think that?'

Kynaston looked into her wide, innocent eyes and felt his tension loosen yet another notch. 'Sorry. I'm being overly sensitive again. Not belonging to the upper classes myself, I always imagine their displays of social superiority – like ordering in French – are designed to remind me of what an upstart peasant I really am.'

Marion felt herself flushing. 'I didn't mean that at all.'

'No,' Kynaston said softly. 'I know that now.'

Marion glanced away from his smiling eyes, a little out of her depth. Kynaston was a very attractive man, and she had an idea that she should feel much more wary than she did. But somehow his honesty had neutralized her much-needed aggressiveness. Kynaston was thinking much the same thing. He'd expected to be dining with some hard-hearted, spoilt little bitch, not a woman with eyes like a doe. The arrival of the waiter saved Marion from answering. She ordered melon, followed by salmon in a champagne sauce, not surprised when Kynaston ordered a simple steak and a knowledgeable selection of wines. 'So . . .' She fiddled absently with her empty wine glass. 'I must admit, I was surprised when you called.'

Kynaston shook his head. 'Let's not go this route, Marion,' he said quietly. 'You couldn't have been at all surprised.'

Marion blinked, took a moment to see if she felt intimidated by his direct approach, realised she didn't, and smiled ruefully. 'OK. No, perhaps I wasn't. But I must admit I haven't been looking forward to this much.'

Kynaston grinned. 'Other men might take that as an insult, but I'll let it pass.'

Marion blushed. It wasn't like her to speak without thinking first. 'I'm sorry, I didn't mean to imply anything personal. It's just that things, professionally, are a bit awkward for us at the moment.'

All around him, Kyn could feel the eyes and ears of the curious homing in on them, and he kept his voice determinedly low. 'That Swiss finishing school you must have gone to is showing,' he said softly. 'Things are not "awkward" for us, Ms Ventura. They're downright dangerous.'

'Call me Marion,' she said suddenly, her eyes sharpening. 'And it was a French finishing school.'

He noticed that she sat up a little straighter and inwardly nodded. Yes, she might have the eyes of a

174

doe, but she had the heart of a fox. 'OK. Call me Kyn.'

'All right, Kyn. Why don't we get down to business?'

'Why don't we?' he agreed quietly. 'So, tell me, Marion, what makes you think you have the right to take over my company?'

Marion felt the wind go right out of her. She hadn't expected such a simple, devastating question. 'I . . .' She stopped abruptly, knowing that now was not the time rush into speech. 'I think I have the right to take advantage of current business practices. You do the same all the time.'

Kynaston shook his head. 'Strike one. I've never taken over somebody else's company in my life. Try again.'

Marion flushed. 'Perhaps you're just not big enough?'

Kyn smiled. He wasn't sure why, but the tension was draining out of him further with every minute that passed. 'Perhaps Ventura is too big?' he countered smoothly. 'Has it forgotten how to forge new companies of its own? Perhaps it's got too fat and lazy, Marion.'

That, she knew, was a direct attack on her father. The trouble was, she had a sneaking suspicion he might be right. But she'd die before admitting it! 'Perhaps you're running scared?' she suggested, her small chin angling up belligerently.

Kyn looked at her, sensing a crossroads looming up in front of him. He didn't want a long, dragged-out battle with Ventura, but he was not afraid of it either. The question was – which way to go to avoid it? Abruptly he made up his mind. 'You're right,' he said softly. 'I am scared.'

Although his voice was quiet, Marion heard every word clearly, and she looked as shocked as she felt. This man, scared? Did he think she was a fool? 'I find that hard to believe,' she said at last, her voice stiff with suspicion.

Kyn shrugged. 'I don't see why. I started Germaine Leisure when I was nineteen, with a loan from a bank that thought it was doing me such a big favour. When the company started its whole staff consisted of one: me. I worked non-stop, snatching sleep where I could, when I could. I had a little sister to support, I'd sold everything I had except one good suit, one good pair of shoes and a watch. For six months I was half convinced we would both be thrown out on to the streets, and become just another pair of those poor derelicts you hand out change to whenever you go out shopping. So it's only natural I'd be afraid to lose it all, when it means so much to me.' His thoughts drifted back to those days. His voice had become even softer, and Marion found herself leaning forward to catch his words, her heart thudding heavily.

'It began with slums,' he said, surprising her totally. 'I bought a tenement from a slum landlord and did deals with the tenants – I provided the materials to do the building up, they provided the labour, free of charge. There were out-of-work plumbers in those buildings, Marion. Out-of-work carpenters, delivery men, construction workers. Within six months the place was habitable again – clean, decorated, decent. The lifts worked, there was no graffiti, no crumbling plaster. I sold the building, with the proper guarantees for the sitting tenants of course, at a profit that would be peanuts to Ventura Industries, but it was more money than I, or my father, had ever seen in a lifetime of work. With the money I made on that, I moved out of New York and bought my first hotel, a country inn in Connecticut. It had been run-down and left to slide, but I turned it around and sold it.

'By now I was employing staff – me, little Kyn Germaine, the ex-Vermont farm boy and slum-rat. I had a

176

secretary of my very own. I interviewed for maintenance staff. They all came looking for work, wearing despair like overalls, so much frenzied hope in their eyes it . . . hurt.' He said the word almost on a whisper, and again shook his head.

Marion began to feel a cold sweat break out on her back, knowing when a soul was being opened up to her.

'The girl I picked as my secretary came from a family of six, where only one other member had a job,' Kyn said simply, 'After I sold the inn, again for a good profit, I began Germaine Leisure as you know it today, and built my first hotel at Sugar Bush.' He looked at her, his eyes focusing sharply once more on the present. 'I *built* the hotel, Marion,' he stressed, hoping for both their sakes that he was getting through to her. 'And all the others like them. Tell me, if you come in and use your muscle and your money to take them over, will they be yours? I mean, will they *really* be yours?'

Marion leaned back in her chair, pushing her cold food away from her, her mind reeling. One part of her was grateful to him for explaining things to her. Another, more cynical part realised how good his tactics were. 'I think you're trying to make me feel guilty,' she said at last, and, because he'd succeeded, her voice was heavy and flat.

Kyn smiled crookedly. 'Of course I am. I'm fighting to keep my company – *my* company, Marion. The one I risked my own and my sister's future for. If necessary, I'll fight to the last inch to keep it. But I haven't lied to you. And I'm telling you straight, right now, that I'm going back to Stowe the day after tomorrow. Vermont is my home – I can't and don't want to live anywhere else. And while I'm there, naturally, I'm going to be making sure that my new hotel is the best there is and that Germaine

177

Leisure goes from strength to strength . . . with me at its helm.'

Marion took a deep, shaking breath. She couldn't tell him that his words had only reinforced her own doubts. She'd always wondered about the morality of what she was doing, but had pushed it aside, knowing that this was the test her father had set her. If she failed to produce Germaine Leisure, what would happen to all her dreams? All her promises to herself?

'Tell me, Marion,' Kynaston said gently. 'Don't you think you have it in you to create a hotel and leisure empire of your own? Even with all that Ventura money, all that Ventura clout? Or are you just being lazy?'

The challenge struck a chord deep inside her. 'But it's not as simple as that,' she said at last.

'I know,' Kyn said softly. 'But forget your father. It's *you* who must decide what to do next. You have to decide whether you agree with him or not. Whether to be an accomplice or strike out on your own, doing what you believe is right for the company. It's one thing to be feared,' he advised softly. 'It's something totally different to be respected. But whatever you do decide, Marion,' he continued earnestly, leaning across the table and taking her cold hands in his, 'you have to understand one thing. I'm not going to sit idly by and let you take what's mine. I can't.'

As her eyes met his, she was struck at once by the sincerity of them. They were no longer icy, but frank, and concerned. 'I don't want to hurt you, but if you insist on this takeover bid, that's probably what will happen.'

'Are you threatening me?' she asked, but surprisingly she felt no fear.

'No,' he corrected gently. 'I'm warning you.'

* * *

Bruno, sitting behind the wheel of a nondescript five-year-old Ford, watched carefully as the doors to the restaurant swung open. *He* came through it first – the Germaine man – looking every inch the rich businessman. The girl came through next, and Bruno sat up just a little straighter, his large, meaty hands tightening on the steering wheel. The newspaper clippings he'd collected ever since Morgan had given him his assignment had not done her justice. She was more beautiful in real life. They parted with a businesslike handshake. The Germaine man hailed a taxi with a single, simple lifting of his hand, and Bruno sneered as a yellow cab appeared like magic. The Ventura Princess, of course, stepped into a long, black limousine.

Bruno followed the limousine, but, as he'd expected, it led him straight back to the Ventura Tower. He pulled away and cruised until he spotted a phone booth that hadn't been vandalized. It was a bad neighbourhood and Bruno patted the small cut-throat razor in his shirt top pocket. It felt cold and comforting. Quickly, he dialled the unlisted number. 'Yes?' The voice was quiet and wary.

'Deep Green,' Bruno said, controlling his naturally loud, barking voice with considerable effort. 'The girl and Germaine have met.'

In Stowe, Morgan leaned slowly against a cellar wall, his face tight and angry. 'I see. I had hoped we wouldn't have to worry about the girl.'

'You needn't worry about her, chief,' Bruno said, a little surprised that such a tiny obstacle could concern his boss. 'I can take care of her.'

'Wait,' Morgan said quickly, knowing how impetuous Bruno could be, and how quickly he could move. 'We've got to be careful. The girl's father has a lot of money and clout.'

179

Bruno sighed heavily. 'So, what you want me to do?'

Morgan was a man who always felt comfortable with more than one card up his sleeve. He already had a good idea how to take care of the girl but if that didn't work out he'd need another way to go. 'Keep following her, and report everything back to me. I also want you to get me the blueprints for the office building. And, while you're at it, reconnoitre her apartment. See if there's any easy way in and out.'

Bruno nodded. 'You thinking of a raid?'

Morgan smiled. 'I'm thinking that New York is a very violent city and big fancy apartment buildings are very tempting to burglars.'

'And a lot of people get murdered by burglars,' Bruno added with a wolfish smile.

Over the miles, Morgan smiled. It was comforting to have such a man to call on, of course, but it was easy for Bruno to get out of hand. 'Perhaps. But I'd rather not have to risk killing her, and besides, I've got an idea how to get her out of the way and at the same time get money out of it. For the cause.'

Bruno laughed. Yes, that sounded like the chief. Always thinking. Always one step ahead. 'Right, chief.' As he drove back to Ventura, he planned. For a man who looked like a bulldog and growled like one, Bruno didn't share the limitations of the bulldog's intelligence. In fact, he was a very clever man. Unfortunately, his dumb-looking face fooled a lot of the people, a lot of the time.

Hadrian dragged his case off the carousel and headed out of the airport. It had been a long flight, and the last week had been a hectic one. He felt shattered. Getting a work permit hadn't been too hard, but the green card he needed had proved a little more elusive. He'd had to pull every string he had.

Taking the advice of friends who'd already visited New York, he'd booked rooms by telephone in a reasonable hotel at a reasonable price, and listlessly he gave the address to the cabbie. He perked up as they drove past the outskirts of Manhattan, but its famous skyscraper landscape was almost lost in a low grey blanket of cold October fog. So much for glamorous New York! He smiled, but his face felt stiff and tight. He rubbed his gritty eyes and yawned. He was almost asleep when the cab pulled up outside his hotel.

His room was small, clean, and looked out on to a wide, busy street. He forced himself to unpack before taking a bath and then, still feeling like something the cat had dragged in, he checked the phone book. The sheer number of listings for hotels made his eyes ache. No use trying to find Bryony that way. Besides, if he knew his cousin (and he was beginning to wonder) she wouldn't stay in New York long. She hated cities. No, she was long gone by now.

But Venturas' was here, and he had secured an interview with them for the day after tomorrow. They'd sounded impressed with his CV, and were always on the lookout for people with experience to help with their vast administration needs when it came to dealing with Europe. He was fairly hopeful of getting a position there. Whatever good it might do him.

CHAPTER 16

Stowe

Kyn stopped dead, staring at the woman walking up the path towards the club. Walking? Hardly the right word for the way she *glided* along the icy sidewalk. She was wearing a long grey coat in a military style that did nothing to detract from the feminine shape of her. He could see the long, exquisitely shaped lengths of her calves, encased in sheer silk stockings as she walked, tapering to a neatly turned ankle.

He found his eyes travelling upwards with an avidness that he had not felt for a long, long time. She unbuttoned the coat in anticipation of the warmth inside, and in profile he could see large, well-shaped breasts thrusting against a mint-green dress. She moved into the light spilling out of the club and her bell-shaped mass of thick dark hair swung gently with every step she took. Deep chestnut tints, obviously natural, glinted like rubies amidst the lush darkness.

Drawn like a magnet, he found himself following the woman inside. She was taller than he'd first thought, at least five feet ten or maybe even eleven. She took off her coat, revealing wide shoulders and long, slender arms. A slim waist gave way to powerful-looking hips and thighs, and he was back to her legs again. Kynaston felt like a

182

teenager with a mammoth crush and smiled ruefully. He circled the room carefully, keeping her in sight at all times. When she turned and took her seat, he saw her face for the first time. She was wearing sunglasses! The bizarreness of that gave way to another feeling altogether as his eyes slipped down to her lips. They were wide and perfectly shaped, and coloured a light plum. Her chin was firm and her cheekbones swept high on her face. She was not merely beautiful but eye-catching. He found himself hating those sunglasses that concealed her eyes from him. His mouth was so dry his tongue was sticking to the roof of his mouth. His heart was ticking away as if he'd just skied downhill for five miles. He simply *couldn't* look away from her. She ordered a drink. Lemonade. Kynaston blinked, but it was definitely lemonade.

Bryony lifted the long, cold glass to her lips and took a long, appreciate swallow. He watched her throat muscles ripple as she drank thirstily. No little sips, no affected little swallows. He found himself moving closer.

Bryony was tired. That day, she'd taken the Montrealer to Stowe, leaving the Big Apple behind with a sigh of relief. She'd stayed only long enough to buy her wardrobe and enlist the aid of a beautician to sell and teach her the use of cosmetics. Now she looked around the club, feeling vaguely self-conscious. She could see no other women on their own. This was her first night in Stowe, and she knew she had to be seen out and about. Men had to know she was there. And one man in particular. She only hoped she looked like a woman of the world. For once she'd set foot in Stowe she'd know she was in enemy country at last. Kynaston's country.

She'd taken a Vermont Transit bus into the centre of the town, not sure yet just how big the place was, and what was within walking distance. But she'd easily found accommodation at the Stoweflake Townhouses, a complex of beige-coloured bungalows with typically steep, dark brown roofs and a pleasant amount of garden per building.

She sighed heavily now, not knowing that ice-blue eyes watched the movement of her shoulders and breasts as she let out the long, mournful breath of air. Now that she was actually in Stowe, what was she going to do exactly? Always before, her plans had been vague. Find him. Seduce him. Destroy him. Easy. Except, now that she was here, she didn't know where to start. She'd spent the afternoon wandering aimlessly around town. The snow and sun had produced a glare that had quickly had her scurrying to buy sunglasses. Suddenly she realized she was still wearing them. She reached up to take them off, feeling like a fool, and then froze. Kynaston Germaine was standing not two feet away from her.

Her heart began to tumble over in her breast, forcing her to take a series of tiny, gasping breaths. He was dressed casually in plain white trousers and pale blue shirt, a knitted white sweater slung around his shoulders and casually tied by the sleeves across his collarbone. He moved with a fluid grace that Bryony remembered so well, and for a horrible moment she remained frozen in her seat, thinking back to that day in the art gallery in Harrogate, when she'd been so terrified he would turn and see her. But she was no longer that girl. Remember, you're Bryony Rose now, she thought feverishly. Everyone says you're beautiful. Everyone says you're stunning. It was a pity she didn't feel it. Truly lovely women, she'd noticed, seemed to wear an invisible cloak of confidence and assurance that was a million miles away from her own shyness and awkwardness.

184

His eyes found hers behind their protective covering of dark glass and she felt every muscle in her body jerk. Move, a voice screamed in her head. You're staring at him like an idiot. You're supposed to be cool, remember? Sophisticated. A woman of the world . . . for pity's sake, *move*! She reached for the menu standing upright on the table, and opened it. Her heart sounded like a gong to her own ears and her palms were clammy with fear and something else. Instantly she recognized it as that strange mixture of excitement, anger and desire she'd felt before whenever she'd seen him, and she almost groaned aloud. She'd hoped, as Bryony Rose, that the old feelings that had afflicted Bryn Whittaker would not affect her.

How wrong she'd been. Oh, God, what did she do now?

Kynaston could smell her perfume – a light, teasingly floral scent that tickled his nose and went straight to his head. He was at her table now, and a buzz of excitement he couldn't remember ever feeling before hummed along his bloodstream.

'Do you mind if I join you?'

Her chin snapped up. That voice! It was a voice she was never going to forget. Looking up into his face, a face that had haunted her dreams at night from the first moment she'd seen it, her first reaction was to give a sharp and dismissive 'no'. Then, just in time, her brain jump-started itself. One of her major worries had been how to initiate a first meeting and now here he was, doing it for her. Take advantage of it, her brain insisted cunningly, even as a more craven part of her whimpered at her to run away, to hide, before it was all too late. But a small shrug lifted her shoulders before she was aware of giving her muscles the order.

'If you want.' She looked around pointedly at the few

empty tables, but he either didn't notice or chose to ignore her obvious coolness. Instead he pulled out the second chair and folded his long frame into it, his legs under the table brushing against hers. Bryony could feel tiny electric shocks skitter across her skin and she jerked her legs away before she could stop herself. Damn! She should have raised one eyebrow in a cool, knowing way and then slowly withdrawn her legs – not acted like a scalded cat. Kynaston, surprised, saw her blush and felt the instinctive and rapid withdrawal of her leg. Her nervousness was strangely touching, and certainly uncommon. A woman as beautiful and unusual as this one must surely have had more than her fair share of masculine attention. Why then all the fuss over a simple, and genuine, accidental brushing of knees? 'I can recommend the local, traditional dishes here,' he said pleasantly, catching the eye of their waiter who quickly approached with another menu. 'Would you like me to order?'

'I have a mind of my own,' she snapped, instantly regretting her impetuous words. But in truth, his nearness was making it hard for her to breathe properly, let alone think straight!

'I'll remember that,' he said softly. Again, she had surprised him with her unusual reply. But he knew how to talk to women, and how to play the game. Until now, he'd assumed that all women knew how to play the game right back at him, but he was beginning to wonder. Why was she being so defensive? Quickly, his eyes shot to the third finger of her left hand. He was surprised, and a little alarmed, at the intensity of the relief he felt when he saw she wore no wedding ring. Impatient with himself and his unusual skittishness, he scanned the menu and ordered. Bryony quickly did the same. The waiter bowed and left.

'You're from Yorkshire, yes?'

Bryony's head snapped up. 'How . . . Ah, the accent.' She managed to sound, she hoped, amused and vaguely impressed. 'Is it so obvious?' What if he recognized her brogue?

'Not really,' Kynaston assured her, putting her mind at ease with his next words. 'It's just that I was in Yorkshire recently, and thought I recognized it.'

The last thing she wanted to talk about was Yorkshire! 'Oh?' she said nonchalantly, hoping that it came out just right – a touch bored, but ultra-polite. Kynaston's eyebrow shot up and a small smile tugged at the corner of his lips. He wasn't used to the cold shoulder from women, except of course, when they'd elected to play the 'hard-to-get' version of the game. It was a little old-fashioned nowadays, but some women still needed to play it. Somehow, though, he didn't think it applied here. She intrigued him. Something niggled at the back of his memory . . . what was it? Not the hair, he'd never seen that particular shade of chestnut before on any woman. And he knew he'd never have forgotten a woman with a shape like hers. The voice? Was it just that she reminded him of the beautiful dales of England's Yorkshire? For some reason the bleak farmhouse up in the Three Peaks district flashed into his mind – windswept, grey-stoned. Empty.

'Wine, sir?' The wine waiter interrupted his thoughts. and he ordered a Californian chardonnay. 'Madame?'

'I don't drink,' Bryony said shortly, her abruptness making even the waiter blink. Quickly, he retreated.

'Do you eat them for breakfast as well?' Kyn asked, amused, taking a long slow look at her. 'You scared the poor man silly.'

'Oh, I didn't?' she said at once, looking appalled.

187

'Hey, I was only teasing,' he said, finding himself wrong-footed yet again. What was it with this woman? He was acting like a teenager out on his first date.

The waiter returned. 'I'm sorry if I sounded a bit abrupt just now,' Bryony said, but the waiter didn't even pause in his pouring of Kynaston's wine. Perhaps it was not the done thing to talk to waiters, she thought, and groaned inwardly. Sophisticated? A woman of the world? She was pathetic!

Kynaston watched her, and in spite of the protection of the sunglasses she'd forgotten to remove, he read her reactions with ease. She was genuinely worried she'd hurt the man's feelings! A warm, tender sensation began to uncurl in his stomach and he found himself smiling gently. Bryony looked up, saw that he was laughing at her, and felt her hands curl into fists under the table. Quickly she looked away from him, a red rage rising perilously close to the surface. She hated him! Oh, how she hated him! She couldn't wait to see his smugness smashed, and his arrogance decimated.

The waiter left and she sighed deeply, taking a deep, shaky breath. 'That sounded mournful. Problems?'

'If I had, I'd hardly discuss them with a stranger.'

'Ah, of course. I was forgetting the natural English reticence.' Suddenly he stretched his hand across the table. 'My na . . . name's Kynaston Germaine.' The pause came when she reared back, as if he was going to hit her. His eyes narrowed as an odd sensation snaked down his back. There was something more going on here than he'd first thought. It wasn't just that she was shy. She wasn't just nervous either. There was something else going on inside her head. Something that instinct told him he should know about.

188

Bryony bit her lip as she noticed his eyes narrow suspiciously. She wanted to kick herself for being so stupid. If she was to take this man on at his own game and win she was going to have to do much, much better than this. She stretched out her hand, annoyed to see that it still trembled slightly. 'Bryony,' she said, then added reluctantly, 'Bryony Rose.' Her hand tingled at the touch of his fingers and she knew she couldn't stand it for much longer. She took her hand away quickly, but not quickly enough, she hoped, to be insulting about it.

'That's a beautiful name,' he said, almost thoughtfully, his hand feeling suddenly cold without hers in it.

'It's my own,' she snapped defensively.

He looked as surprised as he felt. 'I never thought otherwise. Should I have done?' he added softly.

She paled visibly. This was awful. She managed to shrug. 'People have said before it sounded like a made-up name. As if I was an actress or something.' She managed to give a genuine laugh at that. Her, an actress? She couldn't act her way out of a paper bag. Just look at the mess she was making of this! Dammit, pull yourself together, she told herself. Dad and Katy need you.

'I take it you're not. An actress,' he added, as she looked at him blankly. 'You can't blame people for thinking you might be. You're certainly beautiful enough to be.'

And with those words Bryn Whittaker was there. Bryony could feel her, deep inside. What would she have given to have heard him say that seven months ago, outside that ugly old sheep van, with all the sheep eating his flowers? She shook her head. No. Go away, Bryn. I can't cope with you now.

'So, if you're not an actress, what do you do?' he asked, genuinely interested. She was a fascinating enigma.

For a crazy second Bryony wondered what he'd do if she blurted out, 'I'm a sheep farmer.' It would be almost worth it just to see the look on his face. Instead she shrugged.

Kynaston's eyes narrowed. She was hiding something. That in itself was not unusual, of course. Women had their fair share of secrets, and why not? God knows, he had enough of his own . . . Like Morgan. The thought popped into his head like an evil genie, but he quickly pushed it aside again. It was not hard – not when he had this woman to figure out. And it would take some doing, of that he was sure. 'A woman of mystery, hmm? I've always wanted to meet one of those,' he said teasingly, his voice deliberately warm and falling a seductive notch. Bryony went hot, cold, then hot again.

'So, what brings you to Stowe, Bryony Rose?' Kynaston asked. The conversation was certainly hard going. He'd never met a woman who remained so stubbornly silent. It was just another mystery to add to her already growing pile. Like why was such a stunning woman so paradoxically shy? And why so hostile?

'Oh, I don't know,' she said vaguely. 'I wanted a change of air. A change of country. A change of pace.'

Kynaston nodded, his eyes thoughtful. He wished she'd take those damned sunglasses off. 'That explains why you came to America,' he probed carefully. 'But why Vermont? It's not the usual place the English immediately think of, is it? I'd have thought California, or New York?'

'I hate New York,' she said truthfully. 'I was only there a few days and that was long enough.'

'I know what you mean,' he grinned, relieved that at

190

last she'd something that was near-friendly and sponta-
neous. 'I can never wait to leave the place myself.' She
looked up at him, feeling a ridiculous sense of kindred
feeling, but immediately her eyes rested on his handsome,
treacherous face the smile fled. Kynaston instantly felt
the icy barricades come down once more, but he was not
about to give up. 'You haven't been in town long,' he
said, and added with deliberate softness 'I'd have noticed
if you had been.'

'I arrived this afternoon.'

'Then my luck is holding out,' he said enigmatically, but
his tone and smile were enough to convince her that he was
being charming. It was like a new language to her. What
was she supposed to say now? 'You have somewhere to
stay?'

'Yes, thank you,' she said politely.

Kynaston felt his teeth click together in annoyance.
This was like pulling teeth. 'There's plenty of accommodation available now, of course, but come November . . .'

'I've paid for two weeks. I'm not sure how long I'll be
staying,' she lied, and Kynaston felt his spirits nosedive.
The thought of her leaving in two weeks' time and
disappearing forever was definitely painful. He'd never
met a woman like her before and he'd never felt this
instantaneously attracted. He knew that it already went
further than the merely physical, and had the potential to
go far beyond the respect and friendship he usually shared
with all his lovers. No. This girl was special. In some way
he hadn't quite figured out yet, she was important to him
in a way nobody else ever had been, nor ever could be. It
was alarming and heady stuff. 'You ought to stick around
longer,' he advised carefully, his casual tone belying the
sudden tensing in his limbs. 'The leaves are really turning

191

now – this early snowfall is unusual and caught us all on the hop, but this next month or so is the best time to be in Vermont.'

'I thought you'd prefer the deep winter. That is when you hope to make all your money, isn't it?'

Kynaston's eyes narrowed. Suddenly he was alert. Bryony felt the change within him the instant it occurred, and she shivered, as if someone had just turned out her own personal sun. 'Why do you say that?' he asked bluntly.

Bryony stared back at him, her panicking mind scurrying to find a way to cover her blunder. She managed a half-smile. 'I recognized your name,' she blurted blindly. 'I think I walked past your hotel this afternoon,' she embellished 'Unless you've got nothing to do with Germaine Leisure?'

Kynaston smiled, but the alertness was still there. She could feel it, like the coiled tension of a cat at a mousehole. 'Yes, I own Germaine Leisure. How observant of you, to make the connection.' His voice was quiet, but as hard as rock. Suddenly Bryony was tired of it all. She was tired of being afraid, tired of being intimidated, tired of wanting him so much that she ached. She'd had enough for one day. She looked up at him, her mouth firm. 'I am clever,' she assured him arrogantly. 'I'm also tired, so I think I'll skip the dessert.'

She dropped some bills on to the table, turned and walked away without a backwards look. Let him think what he liked. She was too fraught to care. Her body felt as if had been hammered by the sexual kicks they'd received. His voice alone had made her shiver continuously.

Kynaston watched her go in silence. He had no trouble at all in believing that she was clever, very clever indeed.

But so was he. And whether she knew it or not, she had just thrown down the gauntlet by walking out on him, and he was just the man to pick it up. If she really *didn't* know how to play the game, he thought with a wolfish smile, she'd better learn. And quickly.

CHAPTER 17

Hadrian watched the most beautiful pair of legs he'd ever seen slowly emerge from the long black limousine. He'd been standing outside the Ventura building, cursing himself for being so early. Now, his eyes were glued to the emerging limbs. They were not long, but exquisitely shaped, and encased in sheer black stockings. His eyes skipped briefly over the high-heeled black shoes then up to the length of black skirt stretched across shapely thighs. A hand reached out to clutch the side of the door – long-fingered, with nails painted a pretty, shell-coloured pink.

Hadrian found himself taking a few steps forward. He was was wearing a new suit, which was business-perfect. Burgundy enamelled cufflinks and a plain silver-metal watch were his only adornments. Never had he been so glad that he'd taken so much trouble with his appearance.

The woman leaned back to collect something from the back seat, and, not wanting to be too obvious about his interest, Hadrian leaned against a phone booth, unaware of the many female glances being sent his way. Suddenly an amusing sight dragged his attention away from the most beautiful pair of legs in the world. A four-foot, six-inch man turned the corner, wearing a bright turquoise trouser suit and open-toed sandals. Attached to leads, ten Afghan hounds milled around him, their long blond coats shimmering in the sun, their tall heads almost hiding their owner.

At the same moment, legs transformed themselves into a whole woman and Hadrian's eyes flew to her face, his heart picking up a beat. A long neck led up to a small but perfect jawline, a straight but elegant nose, and a thick line of long, dark lashes. Her hair was pulled into a severe chignon at the back of her head, and gold stud earrings flashed in the smallest, loveliest ears Hadrian had ever seen. The woman began to cross the pavement, and Hadrian was a yard away from her when a plump middle-woman suddenly surged past him, pulled along by two large Alsatians. Red-faced and obviously worried, she cried helplessly, 'Boys, no! *No!*' But it was too late. The Afghans had seen them. Hadrian cursed inwardly as the sidewalk erupted into snarls, growls, barks and yelps.

Marion heard a low, ominous growling and turned just in time to see the comically dismayed face of a tiny, bald-headed man in turquoise being dragged towards her by a team of Afghans. Behind her she felt something soft and unbelievably strong push against her legs and she stumbled sideways. The large, handsome head of an Alsatian snarled around her knee.

She went white. She never had been overly fond of dogs, ever since, at the age of six, she'd been bitten by an extremely old and mean-tempered Jack Russell. Now, suddenly, she was surrounding by snapping jaws. The dogs seemed as huge as wolves. She bit back an instinctive cry of fear, and glanced around wildly for a means of escape.

'No, Jip. Down, Fifi. Madam, kindly control your dogs!'

'My dogs? I only have two. Yours are nothing but bullies.'

One female Alsatian had discovered a particularly handsome Afghan, and what they were doing was definitely not fighting. Marion almost laughed. Almost, but not quite. One Afghan, misjudging his lunge for the growling male Alsatian, cannoned into her leg, his teeth retreating just at the last minute. Even so, Marion felt the touch of its teeth, and gave a fearful cry. It was all happening in a matter of seconds, but already Hadrian was moving. He'd seen the stark fear on her face, her eyes wide pools of deep brown terror.

'Hold on. I'm coming.'

Marion jerked her head in the direction of the voice, surprised that anyone could be heard above the din created by the frenzied dogs. Striding towards her, and nudging aside the huge dogs as if they were no more than chihuahuas, was a tall man with the most handsome, strong and yet gentle face she'd ever seen. When he held out his hand to her, she took it without thinking. But although his strong grip urged her forward, she found she couldn't move. Two Afghans were standing pressed against her, front and back. Right in front of her an Alsatian bit an Afghan on her silky ear.

World War Three broke out. Marion shut her eyes as flashes of white snarling fangs lashed around her. It was like something out of a nightmare. One part of her mind insisted on seeing the funny side – the silly little man in his turquoise suit was screaming at the red-faced woman. But another six-year-old, terrified part of her made her moan in fear.

Hadrian, who loved all animals, knew that all she had to do was firmly nudge the dogs aside and they'd let her pass

– after all, they had no interest in her. But she was obviously paralysed with fear. Quickly but gently kneeing a dog aside, he reached her and lifted her in his arms, high above the snarling mass of dogs. She weighed so little – in spite of the high heels she still only came up to his shoulders.

Marion clung blindly to the man holding her, her eyes still tightly shut. She heard herself giggle, and quickly turned and pressed her face and lips against the shoulder of her rescuer. She breathed in a faint but pleasing scent of pine and tangy soap. It had none of the cloying, expensive fragrance she was so used to men of her acquaintance wearing.

When they were clear, her eyes slowly opened and met his. They were not blue, but the colour of thunder-clouds, or a pigeon's back. Attractive crow's feet fanned out at their corners, and she caught sight of her own pale pink nails curled around his white collar. The sight of them, resting against his dark brown hair at the nape of his strong, lightly tanned neck, made her stomach dip, as if she'd just ridden a rollercoaster from top to bottom. Hadrian kept walking. He didn't want to put her down at all, but knew that he must. Eventually he knew he could hold on to her no longer, and slowly, with evident reluctance, he let her legs slip out of his arms. With equally obvious reluctance, Marion put her feet on the concrete, and found her knees were shaking. But whether from the fright the dogs had given her, or for very different reasons – all having to do with the man smiling down at her now – she wasn't sure. 'Thank you,' she said, with heart felt sincerity. 'I was really frightened.'

'They wouldn't have hurt you,' he said, his voice an

octave deeper and huskier than normal. 'They weren't really interested in you at all.'

Marion blinked, fascinated by his voice. She'd never heard anything like it, and it was not just the strange accent. It was deep but gentle, full of warmth and life. It was like warm honey, soothing her jagged nerve-endings and helping her heartbeat return to normal. 'I know that,' she agreed wryly, 'in here,' and she tapped her forehead. 'But in here . . .' Marion pressed her palm to her heart and shook her head.

Hadrian laughed. 'I'm sorry. I'm not laughing at you, honestly. But that . . .' He turned to look at the scene, still going on behind them, and laughed again.

Marion loved the sound of it. It was so natural. She too began to laugh. Belately realized she must look a mess. Her hand shot up to tuck a stray curl of hair back into her chignon, and she straightened her rumpled skirt furtively,

'Are you all right now?' Hadrian asked, concerned once more.

Marion's heart sank. He was going to go – just walk away and leave her. Anxiously, she searched for an excuse to make him stay. 'Well, actually I still feel a bit shaky. I think I could do with a coffee – all that wicked caffeine . . .' she stopped, realising she was babbling like an idiot.

Hadrian grinned. 'All that wicked caffeine will probably do you the world of good. Come on, let's search out a cup. That is, if you know of a good café round here.'

Marion did. Of course. Within minutes they were seated in a discreet little bistro that served delicious cappuccino. Hadrian listened to her order it in perfect Italian and found himself nodding. With her black hair and eyes, he'd guessed she had Latin blood in her ancestry somewhere. 'So, do you make a habit of rescuing maidens in distress?'

she asked, and was amazed at the light, flirtatious teasing in her tone.

'Oh, yes,' Hadrian said earnestly, his face solemn. 'At least three a day. Five on a really good day.'

Marion laughed. 'I can't get over your accent. What is it? Eastern Europe?'

'Good grief, no,' Hadrian laughed. 'I'm a Yorkshireman, born and bred. That's in the north of England.'

Marion mock-scowled at him. 'I know where it is,' she said huffily, but her eyes were twinkling. 'I'm not a complete Philistine.'

'Promise?' Hadrian said softly, and heard her draw her breath in sharply. Quickly he leaned back a little in the chair, cursing himself for being so obvious. So . . . what would an American call it? *Tacky*. 'So . . .?' he began.

'Are you . . .?' she said. They both broke off, glanced at each other, then laughed. The waiter placed their cups in front of them, and tactfully retreated.

'Sorry. You first,' he urged, and reached for his cup. The light caught one of his burgundy enamelled cufflinks and Marion glanced it, surprised by the colour. Most of the men she knew wore diamonds in their sleeves. She smiled, wondering why she was so delighted by his unusual choice.

'I was just going to say,' she said with a shy smile, 'are you over here on holiday?'

Hadrian shook his head. 'No, I . . .' Suddenly he remembered his interview and he glanced quickly at his watch. He almost wilted in relief – he still had twenty minutes to go. But that meant he'd have to leave her soon, and his heart fell. 'I'm over here to work,' he said, realizing she was still watching him, waiting for a reply. 'Hopefully.

If I can find a job. I've got an interview in twenty minutes.'

Marion's heart sank. So soon. How on earth was she going to make sure they met again? And she did want them to meet again – so badly that it should have shocked her, but somehow didn't. 'We'd better drink up, then,' she said miserably, and raised her own cup to her lips. For once the excellent frothing coffee seemed tasteless.

'It's OK. I only have to go around the corner,' he said, and groaned inwardly. He was hardly making sparkling conversation.

'Oh, good,' She brightened so visibly that he felt his spirits instantly lift. It was an eerie sensation – as if he were an eagle enslaved on thermals of her own making. 'So, tell me all about Yorkshire. Is it very beautiful?'

Hadrian smiled. 'It is. Very. In the summer the dry-stone walling turns to gold. There are miles and miles of it. And dales full of sheep and century-old oaks. And streams that flow from Scotland.'

Marion swallowed something hard in her throat. 'Oh, lord,' she whispered. 'I want to go there right now.'

'And York itself,' Hadrian said, his voice softening. 'The Minster is the most beautiful building in all the world. And the narrow, cobbled streets are the most haunted in Britain.'

'Ghosts,' she said softly, and shivered. He laughed softly and without thinking reached across for her hand. She felt his warm fingers close around hers and sighed deeply. Hadrian glanced down and saw the time.

'Oh, damn,' he said. 'I've got to go.'

Marion blinked and took a deep breath. Slowly she withdrew her hand, but it hurt to do so. Hadrian got to his feet, frantically seeking out a way to get her phone number with at least a modicum of finesse. In silence they walked out into the street, both automatically turning in the same direction.

'So, what made you leave Yorkshire?' Marion asked, walking as slowly as she dared, impossibly glad that he did the same.

'Oh . . . I lost my family,' Hadrian said, not wanting to lie, but knowing he must be careful. 'There's only my cousin left, but she's more like a sister. I suppose a change of scene for both of us appealed, so we flew over just a few days ago.'

'I'm sorry,' Marion said. 'I know how it feels to lose someone close to you. My brother died nearly six months ago. I still miss him.' Wordlessly, Hadrian reached out for her hand, and Marion slipped her fingers into his, feeling as if they belonged there. She had never been able to talk to anybody as freely as she could with this man. It truly did feel as if she'd known him for years. At the same time, everything about him was new and excitingly alien to her. His accent, his choice of accessories, his mind, his humour, his unbelievable warmth. She could feel the solid strength of his personality like a tangible force. She'd never known anyone like him. Not even the most shark-like of her father's business associates seemed to have one tenth of his quiet strength.

'People tell me this city changes completely in winter,' Hadrian said, seeing the Ventura building coming slowly nearer. Although the interview seemed totally unimportant now, there was still Bryn to think of. 'They say it's a hard, cold place to be. I don't think I fancy facing it alone.'

Marion's heart leapt. Was that a hint? 'I thought you said your cousin was here?'

'Yes, but she's in . . . Vermont,' Hadrian improvised,

wondering if he'd guessed right. 'She's lived in the countryside all her life, and couldn't stand the city,' he carried on, knowing that much at least was true.

'But you prefer the Big Apple?' she asked, unaccountably glad. This city was her home, and she knew she'd have felt oddly cheated, if he didn't love it as much as she.

'Yes. It has . . . I don't know. A certain modern grandeur. The same way that the crags on the moors have an ancient splendour, this place has the same magic, but on a different level.'

She smiled. 'I know what you mean,' she said, but she was looking at him as she spoke. And how far she had to look up. She hadn't realized he was quite so tall. They walked slowly, close together. Neither of them noticed the Ford behind them, crawling in the slow lane.

'But they also tell me it's the hardest city in the world to conquer,' Hadrian continued thoughtfully. 'And unless I can secure a job . . . my work permit . . .' He let his words trail off, in case she thought he was whingeing.

'You'll find something,' she said, her voice both strong and slightly angry.

He laughed, touched by her fierce assurance. 'I hope so. Well, I'll soon find out. This is my first port of call.' He nodded behind him and Marion turned. And saw the Ventura building. 'Here?' she said, her voice rising in surprise.

Hadrian glanced quickly at her, caught by a strange tone in her voice. 'Yes, here. Why? Isn't it a solid company? I'd heard it was one of the biggest.'

'Yes. It is,' she said, recovering from the surprise. After all, why should she be unnerved by this latest twist? Ventura was always hiring. 'It's *the* biggest independent company in the world. What sort of job are you going for?'

'One in the accountancy department.'

'You're an accountant?' she said, her voice openly surprised. She stared at him, half smiling, half shocked.

Hadrian grinned abashedly. 'Do you have something against accountants, lady?' he growled in mock anger. 'I'll have you know I was a partner in my old firm, a most, let me repeat, *most* respected establishment in York.' His voice was mock-pompous, which was so at odds with his young, ruggedly handsome face that Marion found herself bursting into girlish laughter, something that she hadn't done in years.

She remembered her own unsuccessful days in the accounts division and shuddered. 'Don't apologize. I have the greatest of respect for accountants,' she assured him, 'believe me.'

'Look, I . . . well, I was wondering if maybe you'd take pity on a poor Yorkshireman and show me some of the sights one day. Or perhaps lunch or dinner?'

'I'd love to,' Marion said, almost before he'd had the chance to finish. 'Here, my card.'

The old Ford pulled into the kerb. Quickly Bruno reached for his camera and took several snapshots of Marion Ventura and the man with her. Marion grinned, and suddenly disappeared into the building. Intrigued, Hadrian quickly followed her into the impressive foyer. Her eyes were sparkling with life and laughter. Apart from her beauty, she didn't resemble at all the pale, frightened girl he'd rescued from the dogs just half an hour ago. 'If you don't have any interviews tomorrow, why don't we make a day of it?' she asked. 'I'll give you the grand tour from the Statue of Liberty to Broadway.'

'You're on,' Hadrian said, and glanced down at the card 'Marion Ven . . .' he stopped, blinked at the name on the card, and slowly looked up at her. '*You're* Marion Ventura?' he said at last, and she nodded slowly, suddenly afraid. He sounded so . . . odd all at once.

'Yes. It's funny that we've spent all this time together and not known each other's name, isn't it?' she said nervously, all the words coming out in a jumbled rush.

'Yes,' Hadrian agreed hollowly, staring at her helplessly. 'Odd,' he added grimly.

'And you are . . .?' Marion pressed, half-teasing, half-afraid. Something had gone wrong, and she didn't know what it was.

'Oh, sorry. I'm Hadrian Boulton,' he said, and, before he had a chance to think about it, thrust out his hand. Delighted, Marion took it with another burst of soft laughter.

'A bit late,' she grinned, 'but how do you do?'

Hadrian managed to smile, but inside his spirits dived. He'd always known, deep down, that he didn't want to work at Ventura just to *find* Bryony. He wanted to *help* her, in any way he could. Hadn't he always wondered if he could somehow use Ventura to topple Germaine? And this woman was a perfect doorway into the company. But only if he manipulated her. Guided her towards taking over Germaine Leisure. Used her. And then, when it was all over, and Bryony was safe at last, just walk away . . .

'Hello, Marion Ventura,' he said, and his voice was thick and harsh. Oh, God. Why you? Why did it have to be you?

Morgan stepped off the Greyhound bus and looked around the New York streets carefully. Only when he was sure he was not being followed by one of Kyn's private

204

eyes did he meet up with Bruno, quickly and quietly. 'Well?'

Wordlessly, Bruno handed over the blueprints of the Ventura building. Morgan looked them over. It would need careful planning. But he was good at that. Very good. 'You've been following the girl?'

'Day and night.' Bruno related the story of the dogs while Morgan listened. 'I got pictures of him too.'

Morgan nodded, and left the car without a word. Ten minutes later he was looking up at the genteel home that belonged to Lance and Moira Prescott. He nodded thoughfully, then left for the Old Gold club, one of Lance Prescott's favourite haunts. Morgan was most anxious to meet with him. Although Prescott might not realise it, they had business to discuss. Big business.

CHAPTER 18

Bryony rented a car and headed into the hills. Apart from the fact that she felt as if she was sitting in the passenger seat, she felt reasonably confident of her driving skills. She knew just where she was going, but regularly consulted the open map by her side. Coldstream Farm was just three miles out of town, situated on the base of Mount Mansfield. No doubt that was why Kynaston was so keen to buy. What she needed to know now was, just why was the improbably named Mr Elijah P. Ellsworthy unwilling to sell?

She'd been exploring the town yesterday, and had stopped in at the Trapp Family Lodge for lunch. It had been there that she'd overheard, quite by chance, two waitresses disussing Old Man Ellsworthy and his farm. The conversation might have passed her by except for the fact that Kynaston's name was mentioned. One waitress bemoaned the fact that he hardly ever came into the Tea Rooms, the other, older one was more concerned about how he was hounding the old farmer for his land.

That had made Bryony sit up and take notice.

The countryside was glorious – maple trees were not all that common in Yorkshire, but here they grew in abundance, their leaves turning from green to yellow, pale pink, copper or vibrant red. With her window down she could hear unfamiliar American robins singing on the fence-posts she passed. A simple white pointed arrow indicated a single-lane, neatly tarmacked road, and Bryony found herself almost standing on the brakes in order to make the turn. When she reached it, the farm was nothing like Ravenheights, though she felt a strange sense of *déjà vu* as she pulled up in front of the white-painted wooden and stone building. A dog barked from the porch, no black and white collie like Violet, but a dun-coloured bloodhound, all mournful eyes and drooping jowls.

Bryony smiled, stepped out of the car – and froze. Through the opening door came the twin barrels of a shotgun. An old man emerged from behind it, his pale brown eyes blinking at the sight of the woman standing by the car. She was tall, and with hair that looked like the colour of oak leaves in fall. She had large, well-shaped breasts, a well-defined waist, and rounded, pleasing hips. Her legs seemed to go on forever.

Elijah P. Ellsworthy lowered the gun to point to the wooden porch floor, muttered, 'Shaddup,' to the still baying bloodhound, and stepped further away from the house. With a shock of white hair and his deeply tanned and weathered skin, he looked the epitome of a man who'd worked hard and outdoors for all of his life. Bryony recognized her father in this man.

'Mr Ellsworthy?' she asked tentatively, stepping forward with one eye on the now lowered shotgun, another on the dog.

'Yop.' The old man watched her approach. Not only did she have the figure of a real woman, she was dressed like one too. None of those jeans or leggings. This girl (anyone under forty was a girl to Elijah P. Ellsworthy) was wearing a simple but elegant warm winter frock of gold, copper and primrose-yellow. She moved like a real woman too, he noticed, having fond memories of sitting in the cinema with Betty Hartington, watching Rita Hayworth sail across the screen in a smooth, silent, dignified glide, just as this girl was doing now.

'I'm very sorry to bother you, Mr Ellsworthy, or visit you without calling first, but I wasn't quite certain that you'd agree to see me. It's about Mr Germaine.'

'Ahh.' The sound was half-grunt, half regretful sigh. 'He sent you over to try and butter me up, aye? Well, at least he's got taste,' the old man grunted, a twinkle suddenly appearing in his eyes. 'I'll gi' him that.'

Bryony found herself grinning stupidly. Quickly she changed it to a scowl. 'I think you've misunderstood me, Mr Ellsworthy. I'm not here on Mr Germaine's behalf, but on my own. It's . . . well, rather complicated. Would you mind very much telling me why you don't want to sell to Mr Germaine?'

'I 'ud. That's my business,' he said bluntly, his head moving to one side. 'It's also my business to offer 'ospitality to young ladies that come a' calling. I'se just made a pitcher of lemonade. Would yuh like some?'

Bryony smiled. 'Yes please. I've never tried real home-made lemonade before. We don't make it much in England.'

'Huh,' Elijah Ellsworthy grunted, which Bryony took to be an expression of sympathy. She mounted the steps warily, but the bloodhound just snuffled loudly and wetly over her shoes and let her go by. Inside, Bryony looked around her with interested eyes. The beaming was obviously original and made of good solid oak. The chimney was original brick, not the thousand-a-minute kind produced nowadays. A good sturdy stone surround and hearth took up almost the entire length of one wall. 'Sit yerself down.' Elijah suddenly loomed up with two glasses of tall, cloudy-looking liquid and thrust it out at her. She just managed to take it before it spilt.

'Thank you. I was just admiring your fireplace.'

'I s'pose you young ladies are used to gas fires nowadays.'

Bryony grinned. 'Hardly. Back on my farm in Yorkshire I used to cook on an old Aga. It preferred hardwoods, if you wanted to keep it an even temperature.'

'Oak?' Elijah asked, seating himself in one quick, seemingly uncoordinated movement into a low, over-stuffed chair.

'Yes.' Without waiting to be asked, Bryony seated herself opposite him, missing the appreciative look the old man cast over her as she decorously arranged her skirt over her knees. 'Firs were fine, provided they were well dried.'

The old man nodded. 'Well, yuh either are a farm girl, or you've done some research well. Whaddya want?'

Bryony blinked. 'Well . . . I want to know why you won't sell to Mr Germaine,' she answered bluntly. She was beginning to get a measure of the man now, and although she instinctively felt his bark was worse than his bite, she was sure that he was a man who cherished honesty above everything else.

'I told yuh. That's my business.'

'Well, it could be mine. If you wanted to sell, but not to Mr Germaine, I might be able to make you an offer. Or help you negotiate for what you want with Germaine Leisure. Whichever you preferred.'

Elijah's eyes narrowed to near invisible slits. Nervously

she took a gulp of lemonade. It was tangy, cool and delicious, and she found herself taking three good swallows. 'That's lovely. Do you think I could have the recipe?'

'Yop.' Bryony waited, but he said nothing more. Nervously, she found herself pitying any Germaine employees sent to try and deal with this man. Then she smiled.

'What's funny?' Elijah growled.

Bryony shrugged. 'Nothing really. It's just that I can just see you sending Kynaston Germaine away with a flea in his ear.'

Elijah grinned. 'I didn't quite manage to do that. He's a tough feller. Strange, too. Not at all what I expected. Not a slick city feller. I 'eard he was Vermont-born and bred. Which makes it worse . . . you're a woman all right.'

Bryony blinked. Although getting used to his bluntness, he still managed to lose her with that one. 'Pardon?'

Elijah's eyes crinkled. 'A woman, through and through. Look like one and act like one. My Betty had the same way about her. I'd say I wussn't gonna do something, and then she'd laugh and wheedle, and afore I knew it I was doing just what I said I wussn't.'

Bryony smiled. 'I'm sorry. Well, no, actually I'm not.'

Elijah grinned. 'In that case I might as well tell yuh what yuh want to know and save us both some time. I inherited this farm from my pa. Maple syrup, cattle, a few horses. I got by. Betty and me had two boys. One died in 'Nam, the other in a car wreck.' He spoke in short sentences without a trace of emotion, but Bryony wasn't fooled. He'd suffered. 'My Betty's gone, and I don't have any kin to leave the old place to,' Elijah continued rapidly. 'I can't run the place on my own any longer – gettin' too old. I was just comin' round to thinkin' I should sell to that

Germaine feller after all. But he builds them big fancy places for the rich and stupid. And I just don't wanna see the old place go that way. Satisfied now?' He stuck out his neck, just like a tortoise.

Bryony smiled gently. 'Yes. You see, I thought it must be something like that. So I've been thinking . . . There's a way we can both get what we want.'

Elijah glanced at her sharply. He liked her already, for he was a man who read characters quickly and accurately, and made up his mind more or less right away whether he took to a person or not. But it weren't good for a woman to be as angry as this one was. 'What you got agin' that Germaine feller, Miss . . .?'

'I'm sorry. I'm Bryony Rose,' she held out her hand. 'And that is *my* business,' she said firmly. She met his unblinking eyes for a long, long second, then slowly he smiled.

'Fair enough. Let's 'ear this plan o' yours.'

Bryony nodded. '*I* want to buy this place from you, Mr Ellsworthy.'

'You got the money?' he asked bluntly.

'I have. I used to have a farm too. In Yorkshire,' her voice nearly broke. Looking up at him, she shook her head. 'Will you sell to me?'

Elijah slowly leaned back, his eyes narrowing. 'Now why should I do that?'

Bryony smiled. 'Because I can guarantee that you'll still be able to live on at your farm after you've sold it to me. Not only that, but any building done here will have your seal of approval. We might even be able to keep the farm working, which means hiring help. With you as overseer, of course.'

Elijah P. Ellsworthy smiled. That was a lot of promises.

211

Too many, some might have said, to be taken seriously. But, looking into her eyes, Elijah found himself trusting her. 'Hell, I gotta sell to sum'mon,' he grumbled. 'Might as well be to you.'

Lance walked into the club and nodded to the barman. He slipped on to his favourite stool and ordered a Manhattan. Somebody sat beside him, and, casually turning his head, Lance saw a complete stranger. 'Hi. New here?'

'Yes. Would you like a drink, Lance?'

Lance was not surprised that this man knew his name, but a faint prickling at the back of his neck warned him that he was dangerous. 'Thanks. I'll have another Manhattan.'

Morgan ordered the drinks, having a second pint for himself.

'We haven't met before,' Lance said, probing carefully. His nose scented something good.

'No. But we have a mutual interest. Marion Ventura.'

Lance's face turned sour and bitter, and Morgan smiled.

'I don't care who the bitch goes to bed with,' Lance said, and made to move away. With a swift, totally impersonal movement, Morgan grabbed his shoulder.

'I don't either. I'm not talking about screwing the lady. At least, not in the physical sense . . .'

Lance moved back squarely on to his stool. He took his fresh Manhattan and sipped it. The last attempt to wring money from his divorce had been shot down in flames only last week. His mother had already used up her half of the settlement, and his own was dwindling fast. He was having an affair with Gina Knight, the youngest daughter of a textile millionaire, but he didn't think anything was going to come of it. She was already casting eyes at some famous

212

Grand Prix racing driver, and her father was notoriously stingy with money anyway.

He turned slowly and looked Morgan in the eye. 'What have you got against Marion?' he asked curiously.

'Nothing. She just happens to be in my way,' Morgan said matter-of-factly.

In spite of himself, Lance shivered. Morgan smiled again. Prescott was so weak he might as well have worn a neon sign taped to his forehead stating as much. On the other hand, he was also greedy. And angry. Always a useful combination.

'And what exactly do you intend to do about that?' Lance asked warily. He was torn between a desire to get up and run and an equally strong desire to stay and listen. He hated Marion so much himself, he was fascinated by anyone else who might also feel the same way.

'I intend to take her out of my way,' Morgan said patiently, as if he was dealing with a backward ten-year-old. 'And make me and you rich in the process,' he added silkily.

Lance's eyes widened. 'Say again?'

'I said,' Morgan repeated quietly, repeating each word very carefully, 'I intend to make us rich.'

Lance's heart leapt. How beautiful those words were. 'How?'

'By getting Leslie Ventura to give us thirty million dollars.'

Lance stared at the stranger. Was he just a loony after all? 'That's a lot of money,' he said at last, his voice coming out in a rasp. 'But why should Leslie Ventura pay us thirty million bucks?'

Morgan smiled. Lance was so stupid. So malleable. He himself was always strong. Always too careful for anyone

213

to take advantage of *him*. Then, suddenly, Kynaston's face flashed across his mind. He was twelve years old, and his nose was running with blood. 'I'll kill you, Morgan,' he'd screamed, his face puckered with rage, not a trace of fear in his eyes. 'One day, I'll get you.' And he had, hadn't he?

Morgan abruptly reached for his lager. He took a long, soothing swallow, and when he turned back to Lance Prescott his face was totally blank. 'Are you interested, or not?'

'In thirty million? Of course I'm interested. What do you want me to do?' Lance asked nervously.

Morgan shrugged in boredom. 'It won't be hard. Just make a phone call.'

'That's all? Why? What have you got in mind?'

Morgan smiled wolfishly. 'It's simple. We're going to kidnap Marion Ventura.'

Heading back into town the sun was directly in her eyes, so Bryony quickly donned her sunglasses. At Kyn's new hotel the doors were locked, so she went around the back.

Kynaston, working at his desk, saw the sudden shadow fall across it and he spun around, leaping to his feet. Bryony, alarmed by the suddenness of his movement, sprang back and for a second they stared at each other through the expanse of glass, each of them wide-eyed with surprise. Kynaston recovered first. He opened the window wide and leaned out. Instantly Bryony felt his nearness attack her body. It started with a rapid increase in her heartbeat, then tingles shot up and down her spine. Her nose picked up the scent of his crisp, clean aftershave and body scent, and her knees went weak. 'Hello,' she greeted him breathlessly.

'Hello, Bryony Rose,' Kynaston said softly, his eyes

drinking her in. His eyes narrowed on her sunglasses and he sighed. Damn the woman, would she never take them off?

'Just Bryony,' she said sharply. Only her father had called her Bryony Rose.

'Then you must call me Kyn.'

'All right. Kyn.' She managed to force out the short, hard syllable as if it were a pebble in her throat.

'Come in. I'll get you a coffee.' He took a step back, intending to go around and open the front the door. A slight scraping noise behind him made him turn around. Bryony, taking him at his word, was climbing in through the window. Her dress rode up to her thigh, revealing a long line of exquistely shaped leg. Pale, creamy skin, naked of any stockings or tights, found it easy to reach the floor, and she ducked her head under and through with a grace that, half a year ago, would have been impossible for her.

He was staring at her. 'What?' she demanded belligerently.

'Nothing. I just thought you'd prefer to use the door.'

She flushed. She was so used to clambering about in barns and sheds, she hadn't thought. 'Oh. Well, why bother going all that way? I'm perfectly capable of climbing in through a window,' she snapped, humiliation making her angry.

Kyn smiled. 'So I can see,' he said softly, trying to imagine any other woman clambering in through a window, and failing. They'd all be worried about snagging their nylons, or mussing their hair. But not this woman. Not Bryony. 'Please, sit down. How do you like your coffee?'

'Milk, one sugar, please.' She wasn't about to ask him if

215

he had artificial sweetener. She wasn't *that* gauche. Kyn nodded. It fit. Any other woman would ask for it black, determined to watch their figure. The paranoia women had about their shape irked him. It was as if they felt that they were their looks and nothing else. As if their brain didn't count, or their personality didn't do anything for their attractiveness.

She sat in the low chair facing his desk and he handed her the coffee. Having been given no other choice, he took his regular chair behind the desk. His eyes moved regretfully to the low-slung, comfortable sofa behind her. 'I have a business proposition to make, Mr . . . Kyn,' she said quickly, desperately trying to regulate her breathing. It was hard when he was so close. His tie was missing, and his shirt sleeves were rolled back. She could see the firm, tanned flesh at his throat and on his arms, with their light smattering of silver-coloured hairs gleaming in the sunlight. His jacket was missing too, and the shirt he was wearing did nothing to hide the firm muscles on his upper arms and chest. His hair looked slightly tousled too, as if he'd just got out of bed, and her stomach did a strange flip at the thought.

'Oh?' Kynaston was disappointed. He'd have to persuade her that she had no need to make up excuses to see him. It would be a delightful chore, assuring her of his interest. He leaned back in his chair, a wickedly enigmatic smile on his lips. 'Just what did you have in mind, Bryony?'

'Coldstream Farm,' she said bluntly, and had the satisfaction of watching him stiffen in his chair and the smile disappear. Ahh, that was better. He didn't feel so superior now, did he?

'What do you know about that?' he asked, instantly

216

wary. The Coldstream Farm purchase was not vitally important, but it was genuine business. Just what was going on now? Once again, Kynaston felt totally wrong-footed by this woman. No one else, male or female, had been able to so consistently surprise him, and it was unnerving.

'You wanted to purchase the property from Elijah P. Ellsworthy, I understand.'

'You understand right,' he agreed warily.

'But he was unwilling?' Her voice was utterly business-like. It was not at all like the voice he'd dreamed about last night. That voice had been saying very different things, in a very different way.

'He made his feelings plain,' he said wryly. 'Along with a double-barrelled shotgun.'

Before she could stop herself, Bryony grinned. 'It is big, isn't it?' she said almost fondly. 'So's his dog.'

'The dribbling hound from hell,' Kyn said drolly. Then his eyes sharpened. 'You've been out there?'

'Of course. As I said, I have a business proposition.'

Kynaston smiled, but the smile didn't reach his eyes. There was something so intent about her that it instantly sent alarm bells buzzing in his head. Oh, she wanted him, that he knew, but then he wanted her even more, so that was hardly reassuring. He couldn't quite put his finger on it, but something warned him to be careful, when all he really wanted to do was take her in his arms and kiss that tormenting mouth of hers right off her lovely face. His eyes moved to her lips, and Bryony, very much aware of his every glance, felt her tongue flicker out to lick lips that had gone painfully dry. She thought she heard him make some sort of sound, but then he twisted round abruptly in his chair and leaned forward, his hands locking together.

'All right, Bryony,' he agreed, knowing that he had to keep her in his life somehow, be she potential lover or enemy. And if that meant doing business with her, so be it. 'What was this proposition of yours?'

Bryony smiled, feeling pure triumph wash over her. 'To buy my farm, of course.'

He stared at her, a faint puzzled frown knitting his brows. '*Your* farm?'

'Yes. My farm. Mr Ellsworthy sold it to me this morning.' That was not strictly true. But she and Elijah had shaken hands on the deal, and that, she suspected, was far more binding than any signed papers.

Kynaston managed to keep the shock he felt from appearing on his face. 'Really? That was very . . . clever of you.'

Bryony felt a shaft of dismay sink into her breast. He was so cool. So unfazed. 'I assume you still want the property?' He nodded. 'Good. Then perhaps we can discuss a possible purchasing price?' she smiled. Of course, she had no intention of selling it to him. She was going to write to Marion Ventura personally to-night, outlining the farm, the land, and its ideal situation for a brand new Ventura leisure complex. And if Venturas' didn't want it, she'd hold on to it herself. Anything, but sell it to *him*!

'Good idea. Why don't we have dinner tonight and discuss it?' he asked, his eyes like rays of electric-blue ice. How the hell had she persuaded the old man to sell to her? What did she hope to gain. *What was she really after*?

'Oh. Yes, of course. Thank you,' Bryony stuttered, caught off guard. This was not going according to plan. She'd expected him to be angry, or at least miffed.

Kynaston grinned wryly. It was hardly the most enthusiastic of acceptances. They both rose, and when he moved towards her she took a step back, her wonderfully full breasts rising and falling in agitation. He could almost smell the scent of mutual, intoxicating attraction being released into the air by hidden animal hormones, and his loins tightened in reaction. She caught her breath audibly. He was right. She *was* attracted to him. She wanted him, every bit as much as he wanted her. Was she just inexperienced, was that it? In spite of looking the way she did, was her sexual experience limited, making her nervous and unsure how to act?

His own breathing caught at the thought, and a strange, totally alien feeling landed deep in his chest. 'Bryony, I . . . I look forward to tonight. Very much.' He had to be careful now. Any wrong move on his part might scare her away.

'Oh. Er . . . yes, so do I.' She smiled vaguely and backed away towards the door. Once outside, she all but ran to her car. Her whole body was shaking in reaction.

'I'll call for you at eight,' he called after her. 'You're at the Stoweflake Townhouses, right? Bungalow five?'

'Yes. Eight o'clock is fine,' she agreed. Anything to get out of there and away from his presence. But deep inside she was elated. He was interested in her after all. She'd done it! She'd made him feel attracted to her! It was more, much more, than she'd ever dared hope for during all those long months of dieting and exercising. But she'd done it. He *wanted* her.

Suddenly her jubilation fled. Tonight they were going out on their first date. Logically, she had to build on what had already begun. Make him want her more. Even . . . even . . . She shook her head. No. No, she couldn't bear it if he touched her.

CHAPTER 19

Bryony stood in front of the mirror and looked herself over. Since accepting Kynaston's dinner invitation, she'd typed up her report for Marion Ventura and posted it express, which had left her very little time to get ready. She had taken a quick shower and thoroughly shampooed and conditioned her hair, spending barely ten minutes on her make-up. Luckily she only had three suitable evening dresses to choose from, or else she might have panicked!

The dress she'd chosen was of pale lilac, shot through with tiny threads of silver. It was of a light, floating material she couldn't for the life of her name, but it made the full skirt billow around her legs whenever she moved. The top of the dress consisted of two wide swathes of material that criss-crossed her breasts and tied behind her neck, leaving two, thin, trailing ribbons to fall down her bare back, where the dress hugged her waist before flaring out into the skirt. With it she wore her mother's silver and amethyst bracelet on one of her bare arms, and her matching silver and amethyst-drop earrings. She'd just managed to arrange her hair in an elegant french pleat when the doorbell rung.

On her feet were low silver pumps, and she picked up

221

her one good evening bag – a dark silver-grey bag that Lynnette had bought her, which reminded Bryony of chain-mail.

She looked good, her brain insisted. Chic. Sophisticated. If only her stomach didn't churn like a cement-mixer!

The doorbell pierced the room again. Pulling herself together, she forced herself to walk serenely to the door. After all, it was going to be all right. She had an entrée into his world and life, and he was obviously taking the bait. Everything was going her way.

The moment she opened the door, he knew who she was. He found himself staring into eyes that he would never forget. The setting sun caressed her face, its orange light enhancing the echoing orange light in her eyes as she smiled coolly at him, her eyes at last naked of concealing sunglasses.

Kynaston felt every muscle in his body tense, as if he'd turned a corner and found a crouching tiger right in his path. His blood began to pound in his veins, his quickening heart-beat pumping it into his arteries at a giddying speed. At the same time, everything masculine in him quivered to attention. She was so beautiful, shimmering gold, silver and lilac in the sunlight. He had to keep blinking, just to keep his eyes focused on her. Bryn Whittaker.

'What . . .?' Even as he spoke, his brain leapt into action, stopping him from stammering out the obvious questions. Bryn Whittaker was at best an unknown quantity, at worst an enemy. It could not be coincidence that they had met again, and certainly nothing like a coincidence that she had managed to secure for herself a place in his life. Aware that she was still waiting for him to speak, he cleared his throat. 'What a constant surprise you're turning out to be, Miss Rose,' he murmured, alone aware of the deeply painful irony of his words. Dimly he felt his heart begin to sink, leaving him with a sickening feeling of soul-deep disappointment. What exactly was her game? He didn't know, but he was sure he wasn't going to like it. And nobody, not even this woman, was going to make a fool out of him.

Bryony felt the air around her turn cold. He was looking at her in a way she'd never known before, and was it her imagination, or were his eyes like blue lasers of ice tonight? He was dressed in a black evening suit that was devastating with his colouring, and she felt her breath catch.

Kynaston was already beginning to fit the puzzling pieces of the jigsaw together, his astute mind working overtime. 'I thought we'd try Charlie B's tonight – they've got some fresh squid in and a new folk singer everyone's been raving over.'

Bryony thought about squid, which, given the state of her stomach, was not the cleverest thing she'd ever done, then hastily moved on to folk singers. He was still watching her like a hawk, and she found her feet strangely reluctant to leave her doorstep. Somewhere, far in the back of her mind, a tiny voice was screaming at her to head for the hills, find herself a nice quiet spot, and bury herself there. But her eyes were locked on his – ice-blue and tiger-bright, clashing like ancient, age-old adversaries. And something else. Something more. Something heady . . . Bryony took a harsh breath as, deep inside her womb, something stirred, stretching like a lazy cat after a long sleep. A fierce warmth invaded her lower body, making her knees feel weak. It travelled upwards, stiffening her nipples behind their flimsy covering, rushing up her neck, flushing her cheeks.

Kynaston watched, fascinated, as her nipples suddenly strained against her dress, and an answering savage kick landed in his loins. Quickly he turned away. He had to think. 'Your carriage awaits,' he said drolly, indicating the low sports car waiting on the road.

Pull yourself together, girl, Bryony snapped at herself. But it was hard. He looked so dangerous tonight. His face was shuttered, his eyes blank. It was so unlike the other times they'd met. Then he'd seemed more friendly, almost teasing.

The sports car was low, smelled of real leather and wood, and felt very small. When he got in beside her, she could feel his knee brush against hers and she quickly stretched her long legs out in front of her as far as they would go.

'Seat-belt,' he said quietly, and watched as she buckled up, his eyes moving from her ringless hands to the line of the belt across her breast, and up to her face. She looked pinched and nervous, as well she might, he thought grimly. Yes, all the pieces were fitting into place. No wonder she jumped whenever he was near her – she probably couldn't stand even to have him breathe the same air. The thought, rather than give him a rueful satisfaction, made a hot lance of pain shoot across his chest.

Bryony heard the car growl into life, and a moment later the G-forces pressed her back against the comfortable seat as they roared away from the kerb. She couldn't help but notice the fluid way he changed gear, the movement of muscle in his thigh as he pressed down on the pedals, and her body flamed. When he pulled up outside Charlie B's, she didn't wait for him to open the door for her but stumbled out on to the pavement, gasping in great lungfuls of air.

Kynaston watched her, his eyes narrowing. Was it as bad as that for her? After finding Ravenheights deserted, he'd had Michael make a few general enquiries. He'd learned of her sister's suicide, and then, sadly, the loss of her father soon afterwards. Deeply concerned, he'd had both deaths thoroughly investigated. What he'd learned about the sister's lifetstyle in London had both surprised and depressed him. Learning of John Whittaker's heart troubles had angered him. A man with a bad heart shouldn't have been struggling to keep a farm going in the first place. He'd have bet his last dollar that Bryn Whittaker had had no idea of the true state of her father's illness.

Now, looking at her struggling for control, watching her walk up to him with that slightly swaying, utterly sexy walk of hers and smiling at him so winningly, he wondered how she managed it. She'd obviously put herself on a killer diet. Contact lenses instead of glasses. The hair . . . he hadn't ever seen her hair, he realised now, his eyes moving to the sophisticated french pleat the rich colour of conkers. He didn't think she'd had it dyed – her arching eyebrows were the same colour and . . . Abruptly, he dragged his thoughts to a halt. What the hell was he doing, musing about her hair, when she was obviously out for his blood? And there could be no other explanation, of that he was sure. She probably blamed him for her father's death and certainly for the loss of her home. He remembered eyes full of tears and hate and pain as she'd driven off in that ridiculous sheep truck.

The eyes watching him now were smiling. Full of lies.

Full of deceit. And so very beautiful. She'd played him well, he had to admit. Even with anger threatening to choke him, he had to admit that. Suddenly he smiled. It would do her good to remember that two could play that game. 'I hope you're hungry,' he said, taking her arm into his. Where her side pressed against his, he felt her flesh quiver, and his smile widened. 'Because I am. Very hungry,' he added, almost on a whisper, ducking his head so that his lips were only a scant inch from one, small ear. She trembled.

Inside the restaurant, Bryony began to relax. She ordered her meal, and listened as he selected the wines. When the rich red Bordeaux came, he filled her glass.

'I don't drink,' she demurred softly.

'Oh?' His eyebrow shot up in surprise. 'I still find that very hard to believe. Women of today . . .' He let the suggestion trail off, his eyes as hard as diamonds as they watched her squirm. Let her get out of that one.

Bryony flushed. Damn, she should have known the women he knew would all be first class wine aficionados. Grimly she reached for her glass and took a tentative sip. It did little for her. 'It's very . . . strong,' she ventured, and Kynaston smiled. There was something both cruel and slightly shame-faced about it, and Bryony felt her heart stall alarmingly in her breast. Again she sensed that something was dreadfully wrong, but what? She hadn't made any mistakes, of that she was sure. Was he growing tired of and bored with her already?

Kynaston raised the glass to his lips and drank. What was she thinking? No doubt she was congratulating herself on being so clever, and who could blame her? He'd let her walk all over him, leading him like a bull with a ring through his nose.

But no more. The first few battles of the war might have gone to her, but she'd lost the element of surprise now. A slight frown gathered over his eyes. She was no match for him. It was going to be a hard lesson for her to learn, and something warned him like a niggling toothache that it was going to be just as hard for him to teach it to her.

'Drink up,' he urged abruptly, not liking the direction in which his mind was turning. 'There's a particularly delicious Cabernet to come.' An enemy was an enemy. Morgan had taught him that. And a beautiful woman was always particularly dangerous. He'd have to remember that, too.

Bryony reluctantly took another sip of the horrible liquid, doing her best to look as if she was enjoying it. The evening had started off badly. It was going to get worse.

Their first course came, and Bryony stared in dismay at Kynaston's plate. It was covered with . . . she stared at it, sure she was wrong, but she wasn't. Snails. Big, huge, enormous snails. She watched as he picked up a small, silver pick and expertly and delicately skewered a garlic-scented piece of flesh out of a shell. Quickly she looked away, this time taking a sip of her wine without any trouble. Her own plate of melon, passion fruit and chinese gooseberries went untouched. 'Humm . . .' Kynaston drawled, his eyes half-closed with pleasure. '*Escargots*. French cuisine will always be the best, don't you agree, Bryony?' he asked softly, his eyes glinting wickedly as they watched every nuance of expression crossing her face.

'Oh. Yes, of course,' she agreed hastily.

'You must try this. It's delicious,' Kynaston carried on,

227

his voice soft and tender as he speared a piece of dark meat on to his silver stick. Bryony watched, horrified, as he leaned over the table with it, his eyes half-closed in pleasure, offering her the morsel with an indulgent smile.

It should have made her heart sing. The candlelight was romantic, their little corner-table even more so. Most touching of all, he was feeding her from his own plate, just like in the movies. It was just what she'd hoped for. But when she glanced at the silver stick and its grisly offering, her stomach did a double somersault.

Kyn watched her predicament with a loving smile. She'd obviously gone to so much trouble to become a sophisticated woman of the world. The accent had been toned down, the walk, the clothes, the make-up, all pointed to a complete change in her lifestyle. It was the least he could do, he thought savagely, to continue her education. And a lesson in fine cuisine would surely help her new persona along no end.

She didn't notice the ice-hard gleam in his eyes as she slowly, reluctantly, leaned across the table. Nor did she see him catch his breath as she slowly opened her lips and felt the moist morsel slip into her mouth. She bit down, quickly, once, twice, three times and swallowed, the whole procedure over with in a second. She shuddered graphically and quickly reached for her wine glass and took a good, hefty, gulp.

For an agonized moment she waited, sure she was going to do something totally ignominious like be sick, right there and then. But her stomach was made of stern stuff. She sighed in relief and opened her eyes. Quickly Kynaston looked down at his own plate, unable to keep the smile off his face.

He indicated to a waiter they'd finished and drained

his wine glass. His strong fingers held the delicate stem with such finesse that she wondered if his fingers would be so adept on her body. Instantly, her whole being went into shock. Where had that thought come from? She could almost see, in the deepest, darkest part of her mind, his hands on her breasts, his fingers touching, stroking . . .

The wine waiter brought another bottle of fine vintage, and the the next course came. Her own was whole trout with crab sauce. His was a dish of white, slippery, disgusting-looking squid. Bryony almost got up and fled there and then. Only stubbornness and pride kept her seated.

'So, Bryony. What part of Yorkshire do you come from?' he asked, annoyed that the touch of her gaze alone was enough to make him break out in a fine, exquisite sweat.

'Leeds,' she lied abruptly.

He smiled and nodded. 'Ahh. Leeds.' If she'd visited that city more than three times, he'd eat her dress. The thought of chewing that lilac concoction right off her body made his loins surge with heat. He breathed in deeply, glad that the long tablecloth hid his reaction from her. The lying, conniving, bloodthirsty little witch. God, she was beautiful.

He picked up his fork with an angry jerking movement and tasted the excellent squid. He glanced at her quickly, noting how she speared a delicate morsel of pale pink trout and quickly ate it. No doubt to chase away the taste of snails. He quickly hid his savage grin of satisfaction, and carefully speared a piece of white flesh on to his fork. 'If you liked the *escargot*,' he murmured, and watched her head shoot up like a wary deer, such patent dismay crossing her lovely face that he had to fight hard not to laugh out loud, 'you're going to adore what they do with squid here,' he finished lovingly.

Bryony fought a brief but savage urge to tell him exactly what *she'd* like him to do with his precious squid, and bit her lip. Hard. Again he leaned across the table, his expression one of indulgence and smouldering sexuality, as if they were already lovers. She longed to smash his face in with the nearest blunt object, but instead she opened her mouth obediently and felt the seafood slither on to her tongue.

At least it wasn't octopus. The thought slipped into her mind before she could stop it, and she made a small, desperate sound. Quickly she sat back, the movement forcing the squid to the back of her throat, and reflex took over. She swallowed it. Whole. As it went down, so did a gigantic shudder. Kynaston watched, fascinated, as the spectacular ripple of muscular reaction made her wonderful breasts move beneath the clinging lilac chiffon. Quickly he looked down at his plate as she shot him a look that would have slain him on the spot, had he been foolish enough to meet it. He took a sip of wine, his lips pulling into a wide grin as he did so.

Bryony felt a ridiculous urge to burst into tears come and slowly go. Angrily she reached for her glass of new wine and took a hearty swig. This wine went down better than the first. It felt warm and honey-like in her throat, but exploded like gelignite in her stomach.

'How much do you know about the real estate game, Bryony?' Kynaston asked quietly, and she looked at him sharply. Her eyes looked a little glazed now, but underneath the hardness was still there, he noticed angrily. Someone really had to take her in hand . . . The thought of taking her in his hands made his loins harden even further.

'I know enough, Mr Germaine,' she said, her voice hard. 'And what I don't, I can learn very quickly.'

'We agreed you'd call me Kyn, remember?' he reminded softly, running his forefinger gently across the back of her hand. He saw her instinctive movement to pull her hand away, and then saw her change her mind. His lips pulled briefly into a tight, thin line. She just didn't know when to quit, did she? Then he was smiling again and Bryony blinked helplessly. She had the distressing feeling that things were running away from her. With an effort, she gathered her battered self-confidence together.

'I'm sure you are a quick learner, Bryony,' he said softly, just a hint of savagery beneath the smooth-as-honey words. 'You're also very beautiful. But then, you know that, don't you?' he added gruffly.

Bryony's flush turned into a fully-fledged blush. 'Th-thank you,' she said, and wondered where the stutter had come from. Lord, she was going to make a mess of this. Quickly she reached for her wine glass and took another sip. 'This ish very good,' she said, and blinked. Had she slurred a word then? 'So, let's talk about Coldstream Farm,' she said, bravely trying to get back on track. 'I take it you're prepared to make me an offer?'

Kynaston nodded. 'I am.' His voice was low and intimate. 'But there's plenty of time yet to talk about boring old business,' he promised, his smile utterly charming. His forefinger moved from her hand to slip under and stroke the delicate contours of her wrist. She shivered as tiny tingles shot up her arm. Against her dress, her sensitized nipples rubbed against the dress material every time she breathed. She tried to stop breathing, but it didn't work. 'You're a very sensual woman, Bryony,' he said softly, wondering just how drunk she was. She looked up at him quickly, her eyes widening, reminding him of a myopic owl. She looked bewildered, almost stunned. A voice told him he should be ashamed of himself, taking advantage of her this way. Another, harder voice insisted she was getting everything that was coming to her. If she wanted to play in the big league, with the big boys . . .

'Me?' she laughed. Bryn Whittaker, sensual? 'No.'

Kynaston tensed, touched by something deeply sad in her voice. 'But you are,' he insisted, taking her hand. This was what she'd wanted, wasn't it? To get her beautiful, sharp little hooks into him. Well, let her think she'd succeeded. And hasn't she? a small, laughing little voice piped up somewhere and was ruthlessly crushed.

But, far from looking satisfied, she looked stricken. Bryony felt the touch of his lips on the inside of her palm, and everything changed. She knew it, but fought against it like a wild thing. 'Don't,' she said, her voice choked with hatred and self-loathing. 'I . . . I . . . can't.'

Kynaston tensed, sensing her confusion. 'You can't what?' he urged softly, all the savage anger in him draining away.

Bryony shook her head. 'I . . . I . . . lord, I think I'm drunk. Will you take me home pleash . . . please?'

For a second, Kyn wanted to shake her. Why didn't she give it up? 'Yes, I think it's time we called it a night,' he agreed brusquely.

Once outside in the cold night air, she nearly took a nosedive down the steps. Only the quick, strong hand that Kynaston slipped under her elbow stopped her from landing in the gutter. 'I'm sorry,' she said, her voice as tiny as that of a field mouse. 'I don't usually . . .

232

act like this.' In the moonlight he saw tears glisten in her eyes.

His jaw tight, he guided her to the car and drove her home, a small, tiny tic fluttering in his cheek. He wanted her so badly it actually made his whole body ache. He helped her out, holding on to her as she swayed slightly. At the front entrance, he reached for her bag, extracted the key, and pushed open the door. 'Goodnight, Bryony,' he said, his voice carefully devoid of all emotion and she looked at him blankly, desperately trying to concentrate. Wasn't he supposed to kiss her? 'Goodnight, Kyn,' she said and leaned forward, putting one steadying hand on to his chest and lifting her lips obediently for his touch.

'Bryony,' he said warningly, but she was too quick. Clumsily she aimed her mouth at his, crossed her fingers, and sucked. Her lips, whether guided by destiny, instinct or subconscious design, landed square on his own. Without thinking, his arms came around her, holding her against him, her tall length a perfect match for his height, her generous breasts pressed against his chest. Urgently he opened her lips beneath his and their tongues met. She made a brief surprised sound, half-pulled away, and then thrust against him again. His fingers splayed out over her bare back and his eyes shut, closing out the world. For a long, long moment they kissed, each oblivious to the reality that awaited them.

Bryony found the taste of his lips and kiss more heady than any wine. Her heartbeat roared in her ears, but she clung to him, unable to pull away, unable even to think a single coherent thought. Suddenly, Kynaston thrust her aside. She felt the cold rush of air hit her like a battering ram and her eyes flew open. Sanity, sobriety and reality returned. For a long, long second their eyes remained

233

CHAPTER 20

Marion, waiting in a cab outside the office building, checked her watch for the tenth time. She was due to meet up with Hadrian Boulton for their sightseeing tour, but was half convinced the handsome Englishman wouldn't show up. Her anxiety made her laugh. Did one tour of the Big Apple constitute the beginnings of a relationship? She hoped so. Oh, how she hoped so. She was like a teenager waiting for her first date to arrive. It was all so silly. And wonderful. Suddenly, she saw him. He loped along with the tall, easy gait that some men had, his thick, dark hair waving in the breeze. His eyes were scanning the pavement anxiously, and Marion saw, with a tender pang, the way his shoulders drooped when he saw she wasn't there.

She paid off the cabbie and hurried towards him. 'Hadrian . . .' she called quickly, noticing with a great surge of satisfaction the way a wide smile split his handsome face.

'Hello. I thought you might have forgotten me,' he teased.

'No chance,' she said, without thinking, then laughed. It was true, so why try and pretend otherwise?

'You look wonderful,' he said softly.

'Thanks. So do you.'

Hadrian grinned. 'Well, now the mutual admiration society has formally opened for business, where do we go from here, New York girl?'

'Where else?' She cocked her head to one side, reached for his arm and tucked it happily under her own. 'The Statue of Liberty, of course. You can't start a tour of the Big Apple without it.'

'True. A French statue is the obvious choice to begin to explore the American psyche.'

'You're not supposed to mention that!'

'OK. The Statue of Liberty is as American as apple pie. Except apple pie is a traditional dish from England.'

'Hadrian . . .' she said, elongating his name warningly, and suddenly they were both laughing.

'OK. Pax, pax.' He held up his hands. 'I'll be good,' he promised, then, as their eyes met and their breath caught, he added softly, 'if I can.' Marion opened her mouth to make some flip retort right back, then realised flippancy was the last thing on her mind. Or his, it seemed, for slowly his hand came out to cover hers resting on his forearm, and she felt a warm, delicious flutter climb up her arm.

From his nondescript Ford, Bruno watched them, his small brown eyes noting their every move.

The statue was everything it was supposed to be, Hadrian mused, staring up at it a quarter of an hour later, but his eyes kept straying to the woman at his side. Marion noticed, and her heart contracted. 'Don't tell me there's a resemblance,' she warned playfully, her voice nevertheless husky, 'because I know there isn't.'

'Not in looks, perhaps,' Hadrian conceded enigmatically, then raised a mocking eyebrow as she cocked her head to look up at him, her eyes dancing with laughing suspicion.

'Beware of cryptic Englishman bearing dodgy compliments,' she murmured.

'Oh, definitely. We English are a perfidious lot. I learned that in history lessons at school!'

She grinned. It evoked images of him as a saucy-faced young boy, and she found herself longing to know everything about him. 'Tell me about school,' she urged softly.

'You first.'

'I went to Miss Fortnum's School for Young Ladies,' she said primly, but her eyes wouldn't stop dancing.

Hadrian grinned. 'I think Cragsmoor Primary is a slightly different proposition,' he finally admitted. 'It was a single stone building set right on the edge of the dale . . .'

For two hours they wandered the streets of New York, exchanging life histories. Marion listened, fascinated, sad and pleased, as he explained how he was orphaned, left York for Ravenheights, and found a new family. When it came to her turn, she listened to the story of her life through different ears, and it didn't sound good.

'I always had money,' she said at last, 'even as a little girl. It alienated me from so much of life.' They were walking down Broadway, the signs for the latest hit shows hanging up all around them.

'You can't be blamed for your childhood, Marion,' Hadrian said softly, sensing her sudden melancholia. 'Money and ethics are for adults, but kids are kids the whole world over.'

Marion looked up at him, into his open, beautiful grey eyes, and smiled. 'I know you're right. But when I grew up

I was supposed to develop a character and backbone of my own.'

Hadrian saw the sad, almost self-disgusted look in her eyes, and shook his head. 'I find it very hard to believe you did anything so very terrible,' he teased. 'What did you do? Rob a bank? Oh, I forgot. Your father owns one, doesn't he? There wouldn't be any fun in that. It would be like scrumping apples from your own tree.'

'Scrumping?'

'Mm, an old English pastime. You find the nearest fruit tree, wait till dark, check for dogs, then shinny up and pinch a bagful. There's nothing quite like it.'

Marion laughed. 'You idiot! Come on, all this talk of apples and plums has made me hungry. I'm starving.'

'In that case, let me treat you to dinner,' Hadrian offered gallantly, and promptly walked up to the nearest hot-dog vendor and ordered two whoppers, handing her the greasy, paper-wrapped dog, smothered with onions and mustard.

Marion grinned wryly. 'You're all heart,' she muttered.

'Now, now,' he chided and took a healthy bite. 'Mmm. At least this *is* American,' he said, smacking his lips loudly. 'Oh, no, I forgot. The frankfurter sausage is a German dish.'

'Pest,' Marion rebuked, but took a bite of her own hot-dog, a little surprised to find it so delicious. 'Hey, this is good,' she said, then laughed as Hadrian did a quick, ostentatious double-take.

'Don't tell me you don't eat at least one of these a day? And you a New York girl too. Tut tut. For shame.'

'Oh stop it,' she said, delighted. 'Now where was I?'

'About to tell me of your nefarious ways as a teenager.'

'Oh. Right,' she said, sounding less then enthusiastic.

238

'Come on, give,' he urged. 'I dare you. I double dare you.'

'Double dare?' she said archly. 'OK. You asked for it. I got married at eighteen. Not because I was in love, but just because Daddy wanted me to. There. Now, isn't that shameful?' she challenged, but although she was still smiling, her eyes were darker than he'd ever remembered seeing them.

Hadrian, his sprits nose-diving after her first stark statement, began to recover. 'Hum. Well, let's see. You were eighteen? Well, who can be held responsible for what they did at that age? When I was eighteen I was convinced I was in love with the pub-keeper's wife. Now, tell me how you felt when you were *twenty*, and I'll know more.'

Marion grinned. 'At twenty I wanted a divorce. I just recently managed to get one.'

Hadrian almost wilted in relief, but he managed to suppress the mile-wide grin that threatened to break across his face. 'See?' he said smugly. 'What did I tell you. You're perfectly normal. Or at least, as normal as I am.'

Marion laughed. 'That's not saying much!' Then, as he made to grab her, growling threateningly, she backed off, hands held up in surrender. 'OK, OK. But you did walk right into it. Most men call me.' She looked at him coquettishly out of the sides of her eyes, feeling so incredibly light-hearted and somehow *safe* that she never even stopped to consider how childishly she might be acting. 'Let's see . . . beautiful, of course, but also . . . vivacious,' she ticked them off on her fingers, 'clever, sophisticated, charming, exciting and . . . oh, yes. Freddy Berringer-Hoight called me sparkling.'

'Sounds as if he's getting you confused with wine,'

Hadrian said dismissively. 'Eat your hot-dog.' Marion did so. Nothing had ever tasted better. They finished with Broadway and Hadrian hailed yet another taxi. 'Now where?'

'The Empire State,' Marion said, both to Hadrian and the driver. 'This is the grand tour, remember?' In the back seat, she felt his leg press gently against hers. She could feel the tension of the last six months drain away with every minute spent in his company. She looked at him tenderly. Hadrian, with his laughter and warmth, his odd, soothing accent, and solid, desirable body. Not daring to think too much about his desirable body just yet, she concentrated on being just warm and happy.

'I suppose there are bigger buildings,' Hadrian mused, unaware of her thoughts. 'But King Kong didn't climb them, so they hardly count. Oh. I forgot. King Kong was a Hollywoodian.'

'You beast!' she yelped, and thumped him with all her might on his arm. She might have been battering solid marble, she thought mutinously as his face broke into laughter, and her fist started to tingle. 'Ouch,' she muttered, and blew on her clenched hand.

'Poor baby,' he commiserated. 'Here, let me kiss it better.' Suddenly, the laughter was gone. Hadrian found his thumb stroking her hand, which trembled in his own. The driver, the cab, New York disappeared. 'Marion,' he said huskily and kissed her knuckles – one by one. His senses picked up every tiny speck of information about her – the way her pupils contracted as he leaned towards her, the soft, floral scent of her perfume. He heard the small, quick intake of her breath before the pounding of his own heart took over.

Bruno, right on the taxi's tail, saw through the rear

window the intimate gesture and snorted. Hand-kissing? Was this guy French or what? He supposed he'd better find out. Damn it. When was he going to get some action?

'This is as close as I can get,' the taxi driver said, startling them both. Quickly, Hadrian pulled away and glanced out. He shook his head, and smiled ruefully at himself. Marion caught the smile, even as he leaned over to pay the driver, and it made her spirits soar back up into the stratosphere.

So he was as affected by what had just happened as she was. Suddenly, as they entered the crowded elevators that would take them to the roof of the most famous building in New York, she wished they were anywhere else. Anywhere quiet and deserted. Her apartment, for instance . . .

The wind was the first thing Hadrian noticed as he stepped out on to the roof. Then, as they approached the wide steel barriers and nets, the view. Marion looked at the city that was her home with new eyes as Hadrian happily queued to use one of the telescopes. When it was his turn he stuck in his coin and swung it around. 'That's some view you've got, New York city girl,' he said at last after an awestruck silence, then beckoned her to his side. She didn't need asking twice. 'Here. Show me where you live,' he said, his voice husky now. 'I want to see it.'

Marion smiled tremulously. 'Why don't we go there next? I want to change my clothes anyway,' she added hastily. 'I though I'd take you out on a cruise around the harbour.'

Hadrian's eyes were on her, soft and gentle, and she didn't care how aggressive she might have sounded, or how silly. Somehow, with this man, she could never be misunderstood, or judged. It was a new feeling for a girl who'd always been the Ventura Princess. Quickly, she

241

picked out her father's hotel with the telescope and he moved to look, standing so close to her that she couldn't resist leaning against him. In unspoken understanding, he looped a hand gently around her waist.

'If you see any bi-planes come buzzing around,' he muttered from behind the telescope, glad that she couldn't see how his loins were hardening or his chest heaving for breath, 'tell them King Kong went that-a-way.' He pointed to his left, and Marion began to laugh.

'You're a clown.'

'I know,' he said. 'But your accounts department must think I'm a competent clown. They offered me the job.' He turned her in his arms and looked at her carefully, his eyes for once, totally serious. 'Do you mind?' he asked softly.

For a second she wondered what he was talking about. She opened her mouth to laugh and say that of course she didn't. Then, with that uncanny and growing way in which they were beginning to read each other's minds, she realised what he meant. He'd be working for her. As an accountant. A long, long, way down the ladder from Special Assistant to the President, and heir apparent. No doubt her father would not approve of her seeing a lowly accountant and her friends would think she'd gone mad. Suddenly, she laughed. What the hell did she care what they thought? What did the world matter at all? What did her father's approval matter when she felt like this? For the first time ever, she felt alive. Like a woman. Like someone who might, just might, get a shot at love after all. Deep in her heart, she knew she was already in love with Hadrian. It was as if, in a single morning of fun and silliness, he'd somehow managed to perform a miracle and wipe out every last niggling thing that had made her

242

feel so down before. And now that she'd had a taste of how life could be, she'd never let them grind her down ever again. 'No, Hadrian,' she said at last. 'I don't mind at all.'

Hadrian felt his breath leave him in a long, slow, sigh. 'I was hoping you'd say that,' he admitted with a rueful grin. Then, more gently, 'Do you still want to stop by your apartment and change?'

Marion knew the question meant more than the sum part of its words. She knew she could back off, slow things down, and he'd let her. With him, there was no sense of saying one thing, and meaning another. 'I want to show you the decadent place where I live,' she made up her mind quickly. 'Just so you'll know the worst right from the beginning.'

Hadrian's smile faltered. He already knew the worst, but how was he going to tell her? She looked so trusting, she *was* so open and honest that he felt like Judas. He had not expected to fall in love at first sight, and he knew that that was exactly what he'd gone and done. This girl already held his happiness in the palm of her lovely hand. 'Come on, then,' he said softly at last, taking her hand in his, his thumb tenderly rubbing against the inside of her palm. 'And I promise not to laugh at your million-dollar Picassos or get upset over all your Ming vases.'

'That's so magnanimous of you.'

'I thought so.'

As they got into the crowded elevator, Marion felt his hand close around hers. In the packed little box, she squeezed his hand back. They were still holding hands when they emerged.

Bruno pulled the car forward, almost level with them. Just then a yellow cab appeared around the corner. The girl saw it and raised her arm, about to take a step off the

243

kerb. Suddenly his heart leapt. Morgan wanted the girl out of the way, didn't he? What if she had an accident? Hit-and-runs happened all the time, so there was no reason for Leslie Ventura to be unduly suspicious. Only a bare half-second had passed, and the girl was now leaning right over the kerb, waving furiously. The man beside her was laughing and making some joky comment. It was now or never. Bruno rammed his foot on the accelerator, and the Ford engine, surprised by the sudden demand for power, roared noisily.

Hadrian heard the sound and whipped his head around in surprise. He saw a large car, a flash of colour he didn't have time to assimilate, and his mouth opened to give a cry of warning. Without even thinking about what he was doing, he screamed her name and launched himself towards her. Marion heard his voice, distorted with fear, just a second after hearing a noisy engine. She half-turned and saw the car bearing down on her. Then strong hands were around her waist, and she felt her feet being lifted off the ground. She had a dazed sensation of immense strength, and then the car was upon her, the front tyre only inches from her leg. She was yanked backwards. The car roared away, and she fell back, her body landing on a soft cushion that turned out to be Hadrian Boulton. He let out his breath in a whoosh as Marion's elbow dug into his ribs. Dimly, he heard the tooting of angry horns as the car shot off into the traffic. Marion lay still for a moment and then she twisted around awkwardly, looking down at him. Passers-by gave them a wide berth.

'You OK?' she asked, her voice breathy. 'I forget how crazy New York drivers are.'

Hadrian managed a weak grin, but the fear still clenched

244

his insides with a cold, hard fist. 'Another second, another inch and . . . *maniac*!' he finally yelled at the street, but the car was long gone.

Marion shivered. 'I know.' Slowly she leaned her cheek against his coat lapel, and heard the strong beating of his heart. They lay like that for several moments on the sidewalk, oblivious to the people watching them. His arm looped around her shoulders and held her close.

Kynaston picked up the dossier on Bryn Whittaker and Ravenheights, and read it again. But no matter how many times he re-read it, the facts remained the same. The loss of the farm had been inevitable. Even if he hadn't made an offer for the Whittaker's land, the banks would have foreclosed anyway.

But there would be no convincing Bryony of that. She held him firmly responsible for her losses, of that he was sure. Why else would she alter her whole appearance, change her name, and track him down? It was like being stalked by a tigress, except that, instead of fear, he felt something else totally. It was as hot and sharp as fear, but much more pleasant. Much more insidious. It was intoxicating. Hell, *she* was intoxicating. A stunning mixture of innocent and avenging fury. Beauty and danger. It was almost addictive . . . With a sigh he tossed the document back on to his desk and forced his mind to think straight. It was hopeless. No man could be expected to be immune to a woman as beautiful and angry as Bryony Rose. She was a challenge that was as old as desire itself. And therein lay the danger. Only a fool let a tigress snap at his heels, no matter how beautiful she was, or how wild. Or how much he wanted her . . .

It was no good putting it off. The insanity had to end

before one of them got hurt. He punched out her phone number.

'Hello?'

'Bryony. We have to talk,' he said crisply. 'About Coldstream Farm and my offer for it.' Who knew, perhaps if he offered her enough she might think of it as compensation, and take the money and run. Yeah, and I'm Mary Poppins, a little voice sniggered in the back of his head.

'Oh. Oh, yes, of course,' she said, her voice hesitant and a little dismayed. 'Are you at the hotel? I'll be right over. Give me ten minutes.'

As soon as she arrived, he led her to the office, his face blank. 'Before you say anything, I want to apologize for last night,' she plunged right in. He looked particularly handsome today, the usual business suit replaced by casual jeans and a white polo-neck sweater. She could almost believe he was just a normal human being, instead of the cold, calculating business machine she knew him to be. 'I'm afraid the wine went straight to my head,' she continued awkwardly, and slumped into a chair. Her head ached with its first hangover, and vague memories of last night made her uneasy. Had she made a complete fool of herself?

She looked so beautiful, so cunning, so naïve and so dangerous that Kynaston didn't know where to start. 'Bryony . . . Is there anything you want to tell me?' he asked, as surprised as she by the words. 'I mean . . . is there anything . . . personal, that you feel I should know?' Why did he feel obliged to give her a chance? He must be getting soft!

Bryony went hot, then cold. She shook her head. 'No. No, I don't think so. Besides, what would anything

246

personal have to do with my selling you the farm?' she asked, deciding that attack was the best form of defence. 'Oh, by the way, I do have a second party interested in the farm,' she exaggerated, watching him closely for signs of a reaction. If *he* wanted the land, it stood to reason that Ventura's would want it too.

'I'm sure you have,' he said, his voice cold. All right. He'd given her a chance to bow out gracefully, but she was determined to play hard ball. OK. So he'd let her. He was interested to see just how far she'd go. Give her just enough rope, and then . . . 'OK, Bryony. I'll contact my bank and lawyers, get some figures rolling. I'll call you when I have a deal ready.'

She smiled. She was going to enjoy stringing him along, dangling the farm in front of him, and then snatching it away again. It was wonderful to have him right where she wanted him. 'OK. I'll wait to hear from you. But, as I said, there are other interested parties . . .'

He didn't take the bait. He showed her out, even smiled as he said goodbye then went back to his desk. He still felt guilty about Ravenheights, even though he knew it wasn't his fault. For a long, long while he sat staring vacantly into space. He'd offer her a fortune for the farm, but he knew in his heart she wouldn't take it.

For better or worse, they were locked together in combat. And she would lose. There was just no way she could possibly win, not when he held all the aces.

The thought, far from exhilarating him, made him feel curiously depressed.

CHAPTER 21

'I think your doorman is watching us,' Hadrian whispered as they walked across the lobby and headed for an elevator.

Marion grinned. 'I'm not surprised. This is the first time I've brought a man back to my apartment.'

'Very nice,' Hadrian said as they stepped into the elevator. The carpet underfoot was inch-thick, the walls actually wallpapered in a Laura Ashley-type flowered sprig pattern. 'It's a bit small, though,' he mused, looking around. 'I don't see the bedroom.'

'You're a nutcase,' she said, a delighted grin spreading across her face. 'This is only the elevator.' Her eyes twinkled. She hadn't had so much silly fun since she'd been a child. 'This goes straight to the penthouse, and only people who have a key can use it.'

'Ahh. Does this mean no one can get on it once you've pushed the button?'

'Yes.' She strung the word out archly, wondering what he was up to now. Hadrian laughed and wagged a finger under her nose. 'You should see the suspicious look on your face.'

'I can't imagine why,' she said drolly. 'I'm trapped in an elevator with a world-class teaseaholic.'

'True. It sounds a bit like one of those shlocky titles of a B-picture horror movie, doesn't it?' She was still laughing over that one when they walked into her penthouse.

'Dah-dah!' she said, giving a slight half-bow. 'Marion Ventura's penthouse suite, as featured in all the best home and lifestyle magazines. Except that it isn't, because I won't let their reporters and gaggle of photographers in.'

'Naturally not,' Hadrian said, his feet sinking into the white carpet. 'But I thought it was a fogey of photographers?'

'Or perhaps a *filet* of photographers?' she offered. 'We're being terribly silly.'

'I know. Let me look around this den of money and vice in peace, so that I can enjoy it. If you want to do something useful, you can make me a cup of tea.'

'Yes, O master,' she drawled, hands on hips, looking so ferocious that he wanted to kiss the scowl right off her eyebrows. She turned and stomped to the kitchen, doing her level best to hide her grin from him. Hadrian looked around, a touch uneasy. This was a long way from his life in York. He walked to a table and stared at the floral decoration sitting on it. Bird of paradise flowers and tropical orchids. 'Good grief almighty,' he said and when she poked her head around curiously. 'Do you feel safe living with all these triffids?'

Marion grinned. 'Don't worry. If they eat me alive, my father will sue the florists.'

Hadrian grunted around his grin, and moved on. A selection of paintings caught his eye. Modern scenes, of a New York he both recognized and failed to recognize, caught his imagination. They were bleak and yet full of life, ostentatious and yet sensitive. From the kitchen, Marion watched him in silence, her gaze feasting on the

249

expressions that crossed his expressive face. It felt strange having a man in her 'private space', but it also felt incredibly right. He brought the room alive. 'Those are my brother's,' she said at last, when he'd inspected the last one.

'He was good,' he said gently. And meant it.

'Thank you,' Marion said, tears clogging her eyes. Over the years, many people had complimented Keith's work, but somehow Hadrian Boulton's simple and sincere judgement meant the most.

As her eyes clouded over, he walked towards her. 'How's that tea coming, woman?' he asked gruffly, towering over her.

'You know, I'd better buy a whole new set of shoes with a higher heel,' she said musingly. 'Otherwise, I'm going to get a permanent crick in my neck looking up to you.'

'I could always go around like this,' he offered, bending at the knee and doing a passable Groucho Marx walk.

'In which case I don't think I'd want to be seen in public with you,' she growled, backing away into the extensively equipped, high-tech kitchen.

'Coward,' he mocked, then slowly straightened up, looking around him with eyes growing as wide as an owl's. 'I've just walked into NASA,' he said, letting his mouth fall open. 'What time does the shuttle take off?'

'Five-thirty. It goes out the skylight.'

'Handy for flame-barbecuing spare ribs.'

'Very.'

'So. Where's my tea?' he asked, watching her closely as he added, 'My cousin, Bryony Rose, would have had it made by now.' But she showed no reaction to the name at all. So Bryony hadn't contacted her yet.

Marion hung her head. 'I don't have any tea,' she admitted mock-ashamed.

Hadrian stared at her. 'No tea? *No tea*?' he asked, his voice aghast.

Marion giggled. 'Nope. You do have a choice of sixteen different kinds of coffee, though.'

'I don't believe this,' Hadrian said and began opening cupboards. Most of them were bare. Finally he turned back to her, caught her out trying to hide a highly amused expression, and shook his head. 'This may be a silly question, but what do you live on?'

'I eat out a lot. All right, every day, then. I lunch at the company with Daddy, and at night I either order in – '

'Pizza, I bet,' he interrupted grouchily.

'Or go out.'

Hadrian leaned back against a pink marble-topped counter and heaved a woebegone sigh. 'Are you trying to tell me you can't cook?' he asked forlornly.

She grinned widely and shrugged. 'Sorry.'

He raised his eyes mournfully to the ceiling and held out his two hands in mute appeal. 'Where did I go wrong?' he asked, his lower lip actually trembling.

'This is the 90s, buster,' Marion said crisply, wondering just *how* he did that. She tried making her own lower lip wobble, but failed miserably. 'Can *you* cook?'

Hadrian grinned and pointed a finger at her. 'Hah! Got you. Yes, I can cook – very well, I might add. In fact . . .' He glanced at his watch. 'Yes, we've got time. What say we forget about the cruise around the island, and I cook you a proper dinner right here, in NASA?'

She knew he was acting the clown to put her at her ease. His thoughtfulness was so unusual in a man, and so touching, that she wanted to cry and kiss him at the same

251

time. The thought made her lips tingle. 'OK, you're on. I must warn you though,' she said coyly, 'I'm used to eating at the best restaurants in town. French, Italian, Greek . . .'

'Greek, shmeek,' he grunted, grabbing a notepad and pen and beginning to scribble furiously. 'What you need inside you is some good, honest down-to-earth Yorkshire cooking, like Ma-Martha used to make.'

'Ma-Martha. You mean your aunt?'

Hadrian looked up from his shopping list, his eyes going incredibly soft. 'Mmm. After a while she became like a mother to me, but I couldn't quite bring myself to call her that. It smacked too much of disloyalty to my real mother. But I didn't think it fair to her to call her "aunt" either. She certainly never loved me any less than she did Katy or Bry . . . Bryony.'

'Ma-Martha. It goes together nicely,' Marion agreed softly, and for a second their eyes met, clung, then, almost shyly, moved away again.

'Right,' Hadrian said briskly. 'Nothing is more traditional than good old roast beef with Yorkshire pudding. With it you've just got to have roast potatoes and parsnips. What greens do you like?'

Marion hung her head. 'None. I usually do without veggies.'

'All your teeth will fall out and your hair will go purple,' he said matter-of-factly. 'I'll do you Brussels sprouts and you'll eat 'em.'

'Oh, no. Not Brussels sprouts,' she begged, and was still begging him when they alighted from a cab at her local market.

'Control yourself, woman,' he warned her as he collected a trolley. 'Be good, and I'll let you drive.'

Leslie Ventura walked to his daughter's office and opened the door. '*Ciao, bambina* . . .' He stopped as he realised Marion was not in. That was unusual. He was about to leave when he noticed the large brown envelope on her desk, obviously only just delivered. It was marked 'Burlington, Vermont'.

Obviously something to do with the Germaine takeover. He slit the envelope open without hesitating, removed the papers and quickly digested the contents. He nodded to himself and smiled. Everything seemed to be coming right for him today. The deal sounded good. He didn't know this . . . he checked the name. Bryony Rose. But if the property she owned was as ideal as it sounded, it would be a good addition to the Germaine Leisure deal, once the company was his. Expansion was one of his favourite words. Quickly he penned a telegrammed reply to Bryony Rose and gave it to his own secretary to send. That done, he went on his way to the executive dining room, humming as he went.

Marion accepted the trolley and wondered what Hadrian would say if she told him she'd never been in a supermarket before. 'Hey, these wheels all want to go in a different direction,' she said, struggling to get the trolley moving down the aisle. Hadrian grinned at her. She looked as out of place in the aisles of dog food and baked beans as a camellia in a field full of cowslips.

'Here, let me,' he drawled, wild-west style, and gave the trolley a good yank. 'It still takes a man to do a man's job.'

'Chauvinist,' she hissed. 'And that's the worst James Stewart impersonation I've heard in years.'

They managed to get their shopping done amid a lot of bantering. He finally relented about the Brussels sprouts

253

and bought leeks and spinach instead. If the doorman had been boggle-eyed before at the sight of Ms Ventura and a man entering her private elevator, he was doubly so when they arrived back with a couple of shopping bags full of groceries arguing about who was going to make the gravy.

From his car, now painted a dirty kind of grey, Bruno watched them re-enter the building. He was feeling guilty about missing her. He still didn't know how he could have failed to kill her. He hoped Morgan wouldn't get to hear about it. Bruno suspected he'd been hasty, and the urge to make up for his mistake was almost overwhelming. But how did he get into her flat? The doorman was too young and alert to be a pushover. He had to have an angle. But what?

'I think you've ruined my reputation,' Marion commented, as Hadrian began to unpack the groceries in the kitchen

'Yours?' he said archly. 'What about mine?'

She made them both a long, cold drink, and sat sipping hers in happy silence as she watched him work. A lock of dark, earth-brown hair kept falling over his forehead as he bent over the table, making her long to run a finger through it, pushing it back. What would he do if she did? She took another hasty swallow of her drink.

'There. All done. The meat will need a couple of hours, so we've got a little time to kill.'

She swallowed hard again. 'What do you suggest?'

She'd meant that to come out as a teasing challenge, but suddenly, as he looked at her oddly, she realised it hadn't sounded that way at all. Again, she didn't feel in the least embarrassed. In fact, as if in perfect accord with her feelings, Hadrian smiled, perhaps a little sadly.

'I know what I'd like to do,' he said, all teasing gone. 'But it's too soon. Much too soon.'

Marion felt the air around her turn still. 'Is it?' she asked, the question not quite rhetorical.

Hadrian felt every muscle in his body quiver to attention. 'Marion,' he said, took a step towards her, then stopped. 'We've only known each other two days. Not quite that.'

'I know.'

'We don't know the first thing about each other.'

'Don't we?' she asked softly. 'I think we know each other well,' she disagreed quietly. And because her lips were beginning to feel paper-dry she wetted them with her tongue.

Hadrian watched the flickering pink movements and snatched in a breath of air. 'Marion, I think we should be careful.'

Marion smiled tremulously. Something was happening to her, she could feel it. She was feeling reckless, when always before she'd been cautious. And yet she was not afraid. How could she be, when Hadrian was with her? Hadrian shook his head. 'Marion . . . come and sit down with me. I want to talk to you. I mean, really talk.' She felt his hand slip over hers, and a delicious tremor shot up her arm, flirted with her nipples, then nose-dived into her womb. A hot, wonderful ache began to spread in her abdomen, but at the same time her mind became crystal-clear. He looked so serious suddenly, almost concerned. Her heart got in on the act, and began to throb in a tender pain that was not at all unpleasant. He was putting her first again, and she liked it. In fact, she could get seriously used to it . . .

The intercom buzzed and both of them jumped. 'Oh,

damn,' Marion said and reluctantly punched the button on the wall. Hadrian heard a muffled voice, but he took no notice. He was too busy watching her. 'All right. Send him up.'

'Visitors?' Hadrian asked, his heart sinking.

'No. Just a delivery. You didn't think I'd let anyone up here who was going to take more than a minute of my time away from you, did you?' she asked softly, her voice sultry, her eyes wickedly knowing.

Hadrian gulped, then laughed. 'Witch.' She blew him a kiss just as the doorbell rang. She opened the door to a huge bunch of flowers. Behind the mammoth bunch of lilies, gladioli, sprays of japonica and frothy white baby's-breath, a voice barked, 'Delivery for Ms Ventura.'

'Thank you.' She reached for the flowers and took them. The delivery man hesitated and she realised she hadn't remembered to bring a tip. 'Just a moment.'

Neither Marion nor Hadrian noticed the man take a little step inside. He was also wearing a plain blue cap, pulled low on his forehead hiding the dark brown eyes that flitted rapidly over every inch of the apartment that he could see. Bruno looked to the windows first, then the fire escape. Quickly he turned his head and looked at the deadbolts on the door beside him, and finally the make and serial number of the alarm box fitted discreetly over the doorjamb. The woman returned with a twenty-dollar bill. He took it with a grunt and left. It had all taken less than a minute, but he'd seen all he needed to report on the penthouse security. Morgan would be pleased. Marion closed the door with a quick snap, eager to get back to Hadrian. She didn't notice that the flowers, unusually, had no card attached.

Hadrian pulled her gently down beside him and looked

her straight in the eye. 'I think we should . . . get a few things straight. Don't you?'

Marion took a deep breath and nodded.

'All right,' Hadrian let out his own breath on a long sigh. 'Honesty can be tough on the nerves sometimes, but . . . well, here goes. We've only just met but . . . I think I'm already half-way in love with you.'

'Only half?' she asked, her heart soaring.

Hadrian put a finger to her lovely lips. 'This is no time for jokes, Marion.'

'Who's joking? I'm already totally in love with you,' she confessed huskily.

'Don't say that!' he said harshly, her trusting words rubbing his conscience raw. When she flinched, he groaned. 'It's just . . . oh, dammit, Marion, you're so vulnerable. Don't you see?'

Marion shook her head. 'I don't feel vulnerable. In fact,' she shrugged lightly, 'I've never felt stronger.'

Hadrian sighed. 'Marion, you're a very rich woman. And I'm not a very rich man. Hell, I'm not even a moderately wealthy man.'

'So?'

It was hard to tell who was most surprised by her one, quick, simple word. All her life, Marion had lived in a world paranoid about money. But – and it was a huge, ocean-wide, grand-canyon sized 'but' – Marion knew it wasn't like that for her and her Yorkshireman. She knew, as surely as she knew the sun was hot and the earth was round, that Hadrian didn't give a damn about her money. Genuinely didn't care.

Hadrian, for his part, stared at her. She'd simply floored him. 'So . . . people will assume that *you've* flipped your lid and *I've* hit the jackpot.'

'I know they will,' she admitted quietly.

'Don't try and tell me that you don't care,' Hadrian said softly, gently running a finger across her cheek, loving the way her eyes half-closed as he did so and the way she turned to press her cheek more firmly into his palm. 'It doesn't work that way, sweetheart,' he said ruefully, his voice husky. 'What people think can hurt, and often does. And the Press will put their oar in. There'll be nasty little hints and sneers. And then there's your father . . .'

He stopped as she opened big brown eyes. 'Yes,' she said calmly. 'Daddy will be . . . surprised.'

'Daddy will be furious,' Hadrian corrected drolly, and suddenly they were laughing. Slowly Marion began to get serious again, and she shook her head, still smiling.

'So. What are we going to do?' she asked simply.

'Put in the roast potatoes,' Hadrian said, and abruptly moved back into the kitchen. She followed him, knowing he was trying to slow things down again for her sake. But for only the second time in her life, she knew exactly what she wanted. And that was for Hadrian and herself to have the chance they deserved. The chance that they were entitled to. When he turned around, she was leaning her elbows on the counter-top, her chin cupped firmly in her palm. 'I'm not going to live my life the way other people want me to any more,' she said, her voice both quiet and determined. 'I'm not going back that route, Hadrian,' she warned him, shaking her head. 'I won't.'

'Bully for you,' he said gruffly. There was both respect and admiration in his words, and Marion heard them clearly.

'Then you'll help me,' she said softly. 'Or should I say, join me?'

Hadrian looked puzzled. 'How do you mean?'

'I mean,' she said gently, 'will you let me love you without worrying about all that other baggage?'

For a moment, everything stood still. Time, noise, thought, feeling. It was just two pairs of eyes, meeting, talking, understanding. Then he felt himself breathe and saw her move – just a slight angling of her head, and they were back in the real world again. Together.

'Yes,' he said simply. 'But only on one condition.'

Marion tensed. 'What's that?'

'That you'll let me love you back.'

'Granted.'

'You're so magnanimous.'

'I try to be.'

'Come here.'

'Why? So you can kiss me?'

'No,' he shook his head. 'So I can show you how to cook leeks properly.'

'Oh. Well, in that case . . .' She walked towards him, but when she was in range he quickly swept her into his arms, his mouth swooping down on hers. Marion felt again the powerful strength of his arms lifting her from the floor, the hard length of his powerful chest and the sturdy width of his thighs pressed against her own. She opened her lips quickly and willingly as he lowered his head to hers, and their lips met with an explosion that rocketed them both into the heavens. He could feel and taste every minute microscopic cell of her lips beneath his own, the cushioned sweetness of her flesh, the tiny ridges on her lower lip, the warm, sweet moisture that opened to his invading tongue. He breathed in the the scent of her and it made him giddy. Her tongue met his, lovingly clashing, passionately dancing. Hadrian held her tigh-ter. He held her so tight she thought he'd never let her go, and she was glad. But he did let her go – albeit long, lovely, lingering minutes later. Flushed, dazed, incredibly happy, he let her slide back to the floor, where she looked up at him, her own flushed, dazed and incredibly happy face so open and trusting that he wanted to cry. He'd have to find Bryony and explain . . .

'I love you, Hadrian,' she said huskily, and he gently pulled her close to him, her cheek nestled against his chest. She sighed, deeply and contentedly. Over the top of her head, Hadrian stared at the wall. He saw nothing but problems lying ahead. How did he tell Bryony that she had lost her one and only ally? How was he going to cope with this new feeling called love? He'd had no practice at it . . . And how was he going to fit into her world? For he surely couldn't ask her to fit into his. And in spite of her brave words, they would still have to run the gauntlet of the world's disapproval.

And her father. Leslie Ventura. Already he was looming, like a vast, chilling shadow, threatening to block out the sun. The road ahead looked mighty, mighty bumpy.

'We must be mad,' he groaned happily, and against his chest, Marion laughed.

'So?'

CHAPTER 22

Virgin snow. It was all Bryony had heard her fellow tourists talk about for the last few days. The pistes were all right, well-maintained and safe and all that, people said magnanimously, but to ski where no other skiers had left their mark . . . well, that was the ultimate thrill. So, that morning, Bryony took a chair-lift to one of the higher peaks to see for herself. She'd already bought the best pair of skis she could find, a couple of poles, a good pair of sun-goggles, and of course a padded coat and thick, warm ski-suit in a pretty cherry-pink colour. But she felt nervous, sure that people could tell at a glance that she was new to all this, some upstart impostor pretending to be one of the 'beautiful' people.

But, as she followed the line of dedicated skiers up Mount Mansfield, past the advanced runs on Nosedive, Hayride and Chin Clip, she began to relax. Nobody took the slightest bit of notice of her; they were all too busy chatting excitedly, relishing the sport to come. The mountains looked glorious. Soon she, too, began to catch their mood. Below, *far* below, Bryony noted a bit queasily, Stowe lay surrounded by trees still bearing the very last traces of the famous New England autumnal colours.

As she followed the rest of the skiers out into the cold

air, the sun bounced off snow so white it made her teeth ache. Quickly she put her goggles over her eyes, and promptly wondered what the hell she was doing up here. With a confidence that dismayed her, her fellow travellers quickly abandoned her, rushing off down pistes that made her stomach rise to her throat just to look down.

She laughed at herself, unable to help it, and then gasped, swinging around as an amused voice said, right next to her left ear, 'Bitten off more than you can chew, Bryony Rose?'

Kynaston watched her turn quickly towards him, her hair flying out to land across her reddening cheeks. He watched, fascinated, as the strands clung to her skin and she angrily pulled them away, angling her chin up the few extra inches needed to look him in the eye. 'I don't know what you mean.'

Kyn smiled. 'No? I thought you seemed to be a bit nervous, but if you're OK with the run . . .' He dug his poles into the snow and began to push away.

'No!' she said quickly, then could have kicked herself – *hard* – as he turned and looked back, flashing his teeth at her in a grin that was so smug she longed to wipe it right off his face. He himself looked so competent, of course, in a dark blue ski-suit and bright orange coat. He moved with a grace that she had never thought existed in men, and she could imagine the laser-blue eyes behind the darkened goggles glinting with laughter directed at her. They were alone, and although she knew the next cable car would probably be full of fellow tourists, she still felt as abandoned and vulnerable as a beached fish.

'Something wrong?' he asked, his voice neutral. But his lips were twitching again, and she just *knew* he was aware of her plight. It made her gloved hands clench into tight fists of sheer impotent rage. Damn him, she would not give him the satisfaction! He was just waiting for her to ask for his help. Well, dammit, she'd die first. Desperately she grappled for a way to salvage her pride. 'I was wondering if you'd come up with a figure yet. For the farm,' she added, her voice cool and businesslike.

Kynaston shook his head. 'Not yet,' he admitted cheerfully. 'Are you coming?' he added, pointing down the long, twisting, neck-breaking length of snow. His lips were twitching again.

Bryony looked down the mountain and remembered the gently sloping dry-ski slope she'd practised on. Then she looked away from the steep path of snow in front of her and back to his face. 'In a moment. You go ahead,' she added hastily. 'I want to take a few minutes to enjoy the view. After all, this is what I came to Vermont for.'

'Sure it is,' Kynaston said sardonically, and pushed away, his legs moving from side to side in quick, supple swathes. He'd actually left her! She couldn't believe it. God, what did she do now? The cable car came to a halt behind her and several people got off. Immediately she relaxed, mentally telling herself off for being such a rabbit. All she had to do was ride right back down again.

Hundreds of yards below, behind the dark green fir trees that marked the bend in the piste, she saw a flash of orange. It was perfectly stationary, and instinct told her immediately what it meant. Kynaston was watching and waiting. She could almost hear his mocking laughter echoing up the hills. He'd laugh himself sick to see her get back in the car and ride down again. Bryony found herself walking away from the car. Dammit, she would not give him the pleasure of humiliating her. Besides, she was supposed to be the kind of woman who *could* tackle a ski-run like this with her eyes closed.

Determinedly she put on her skis. They felt alien on her feet. She took a deep breath, deliberately recalling all her lessons. She could do it. But it had seemed easy then, on the run back in Yorkshire. Here, she'd have to 'traverse' to get down: go diagonally from side to side, slow the speed right down. And he was still there, waiting for her pass, just waiting for her to fall on her backside and make a fool of herself.

'Hey, Colin. Over here. Jack Mensing said there was virgin snow over this way. Come on, let's check it out.' The voice came from a kid who couldn't have been more than fifteen. His friend, of similar age, followed. Once more she was alone on the mountain and dithering like an idiot. She could just imagine Kynaston coming back with his knowing eyes and exaggerated helpfulness as he assisted her down the rest of the piste. Dammit, she wouldn't give him the pleasure. She just wouldn't. Without pausing to think, she followed the tracks of the two teenagers who were now nowhere to be seen. Within minutes, the well-marked piste was out of sight as stands of trees came between her and the lines of comforting green flags. She began to descend.

Carefully, making extra use of her poles, she knew she must look awkward and clumsy, but for once her 'style' wasn't half as important as getting down in one piece! She snowploughed like crazy to keep her speed down to a crawl. It would take her hours to get to the bottom, but she didn't care. Far below she could hear the two teenage boys hooting and hollering, having a whale of a time, and she smiled grimly. Her calves were beginning to ache. Unbelievably, sweat began to run down her forehead, even though the gasps of air she took into her lungs were icy. She kept her eyes fixed to the two sets of ski-trails in front of her. Once, about ten minutes into her run, she suddenly realised that if the boys didn't know where they were going it was possible they might all three of them get lost and freeze to death before the rescue teams found them. It was a sobering thought.

She slipped, fell on her backside, and got up again. From his position fifty feet or so behind her, Kynaston shook his head. He had indeed been waiting for her, knowing he couldn't leave her alone. She'd obviously only had the barest minimum of practice, and if she was foolish enough to tackle the difficult piste she'd need all the help she could get. He'd breathed a sigh of relief when she'd headed back for the cable cars, but relief had quickly turned to alarm when she'd done a sudden about-face and disappeared from sight. It had taken him five nerve-racking minutes to pick up her tracks, and his mouth had set in a grim line that was still on his face now as he'd realised she'd gone off-piste. He'd wanted to strangle her for being so stupid, and even now his hands curled around his poles, wishing they were her lovely neck.

Bryony got up, brushed the snow off her behind and pushed off again. Kynaston laughed softly to himself, even as his anger simmered. Her style was chronic, but he had to admire her grit. Her legs must be aching like crazy by now. If she only knew just how far she still was from the bottom, Kyn thought, his laughter turning into a wide grin, she'd probably just sit right down and cry. The thought was a pleasing one.

Suddenly he heard a low, ominous grumble. The unseasonably early and heavy snow had been worrying the mountain patrol for some time now, he knew. Already he'd heard several small detonations at night, set by the ski patrol to dislodge potentially dangerous overhangs of snow. His experienced eyes instantly sought and found the shifting of snow, only a few hundred yards up and to his right. It was shifting their way at a frightening rate. Those on the piste, of course, were safe enough, protected as they were by stands of fir. But here there was nothing between them and it. Quickly he pushed off with his poles and within a second was beside her. Bryony, panting hard, had heard nothing except her own breathing and heart-beat, but suddenly a flash of orange right next to her made her lose concentration and she began to fall. In a flash, his hand shot out and grabbed her arm, keeping her upright. 'What the hell . . .?' she began angrily.

'Avalanche,' Kynaston yelled, the single word killing her angry diatribe in mid-sentence and turning her blood to ice. She began to look around, but his hand on her arm kept her moving forward. She just had time to make out a vague, ominous shifting of what looked like white mist above and behind her, before Kyn shouted at her to look where she was going. Now she too was aware of the low, rumbling noise, and could actually feel the ground vibrat-ing beneath her skis. Her heart leapt into her throat. Her fingers curled tenaciously around her poles, but her knees turned to jelly.

'Come on,' Kyn yelled, still pulling her forward, careful to keep their skis well apart. She found herself moving faster and faster. 'I'm not good enough for this,' she yelled, and by her side he nodded. 'I know,' he yelled back grimly. 'But you're going to have to be.'

Bryony said nothing. There was nothing she could say.

'Follow me, watch me, do what I do,' Kyn shouted,

pulling a little ahead of her. She saw at once that he could easily go twice, three times as fast as he was. Her brain just had enough time to briefly register the fact that he could have left her and ensured the safety of his own life, before instinct took over. She saw that he was crouching lower than she was, and did the same. She traversed where he did, keeping her knees together more as he was doing and leaning at a more acute angle. Every second or so, he looked over his shoulder to make sure she was still with him, his eyes moving above her, checking the path of the avalanche. Was it wishful thinking or was it slowing a little? He concentrated on his skiing, keeping his movements fairly short, knowing she could never keep up if he went any faster. He looked back, a groan of relief feathering past his lips. The avalance was slowing, petering out. He was sure now that it would not reach them, or, if it did, that it would have sufficiently thinned and slowed to present no danger to their lives. He knew he should yell over his shoulder and tell her, but he didn't. Anger once more replaced fear. The silly little idiot could have gotten herself killed moving off-piste the way she had. The thought of the rescue forces digging her cold and lifeless body out of the snow made him so angry he wanted to scream at her for her recklessness. He knew *he* would have been able to outrun it. But she . . . Hell, she could have been dead by now. Looking over his shoulder once more, he could see that her face was white behind the wind-whipped redness staining her cheeks. Good. He hoped she was terrified.

Bryony could feel her leg muscles begin to scream in protest, and it seemed as if Kynaston was moving even faster, making the traverses further and further apart, building up speed. She wasn't sure how much longer she could keep this up. Several times she nearly fell, but panic, luck, instinct or the grace of God, kept her on her feet. How much longer? Dear God, how much longer?

Eventually Kyn's rage began to cool. He looked over his shoulder yet again, and saw that the movement of snow had stopped altogether. He began to ease off, then slow, then stop. She shot past him. He blinked, realised she was going too fast to stop easily, and swore graphically. She belonged on the nursery slopes! He dug in his poles and took off after her. Bryony, taken by surprise by what seemed to her to be his sudden stop, began to snow-plough, but she was going much too fast. Again a flash of orange flashed into her peripheral vision, and Kyn was there. 'Like this,' he yelled, moving once more in front of her, showing her how to slow down without breaking her neck.

She followed his example with tears streaming down her face, whether from exertion, fear or relief she didn't know. Eventually, when they'd slowed enough, Kyn stopped and placed himself firmly in front of her, catching her in his arms as she cannoned into him. They landed in the soft virgin snow with a combined 'whoomp.' For a second Bryony lay, half on top of him and half in the snow, hardly daring to believe she was still alive. 'The av-avalanche,' she gasped, panting in short, sharp bursts.

Kynaston stared up at the sky and an overhanging branch of pine. He too was breathing hard. 'We've out-run it,' he said tonelessly.

Bryony closed her eyes, her cheek cushioned against his chest. She began to shake. 'I thought I was going to die.'

Kyn snarled. There was no other word to describe the sudden, angry sound he made and suddenly Bryony felt herself being catapulted from his comforting chest and being forced onto her back in the snow. Kyn's face reared over her. Angrily he yanked the goggles from his face and then did the same to hers, leaning so close their noses were almost touching. She flinched, as if his eyes really were electric-blue lasers that could dissect her at a glance.

'You very damn nearly did,' he snarled, his lips curling back from his strong, white teeth. His hands on her shoulders began to shake her back and forth, his own upper body moving up and down in unison as her head snapped up and down, hitting the snow and making tiny clumps of it fly into the air. 'Don't you realise how dangerous it is to snow off-piste? Especially for bloody *amateurs*!' He shouted the last word so loudly that it made her wince.

Wordlessly she looked up at him. She didn't know that her eyes were wide and enormous, almost orange with fear and shock, and shining with tears. She wasn't aware that her lips trembled as she stared up at him, or that they had fallen open in surprise. She only knew that he had saved her life. That he hadn't abandoned her on the mountain, even though her own stupidity had surely put them both in danger.

'Kynaston, I . . .' Her words feathered into nothingness. Suddenly he was leaning closer, but not out of anger. His eyes were like the sky above her now, a bright, jewel-like blue and full of an emotion she couldn't begin to name. 'Kynaston,' she said again, but then his lips were on hers. They felt warm and life-giving, and she found her arms snaking up over his shoulders, her gloved hands digging into the muscles beneath his padded coat. Her head left the snow as she strained upwards, wanting the kiss to deepen and go on for ever. There was a fire being lit deep inside her, and it burned so hot she was sure it must be melting the snow all around them. Kyn moaned as his lips opened beneath hers, forcing her own apart. Bryony sighed tremulously as his tongue darted into her mouth, and a small ricocheting explosion shuddered from the tips of her toes to the last strand of hair on the top of her head. The fire was burning like a volcano now. Surely it would melt all the snow on the mountain, leaving Stowe itself awash in the flood of ice-water?

She could feel her nipples harden, excited by the pressing weight of his chest even through all the layers of clothing that separated them. His body pushed her down, down into the snow, and she could feel the hardened length of his manhood pressing against her. Her thighs began to tremble, and her legs fell apart. Instinctively she clung to his strong shoulders, pushing herself up, up, up, so that her breasts were crushed against his chest and her lips were locked against his. Her eyes were closed against the bright sunny day around them. She pushed his fair, silky-soft hair away from his temples with one gloved hand and cupped the back of his strong neck with the other.

Kynaston shuddered. Just her touch, and not even one made with her bare fingers, seemed to scorch him, hardening his body, sending his blood racing to his head and other, more urgently needy parts of his body. With a muttered oath he pulled his head back and took a deep gulp of air. He opened his eyes and forced his elbows to straighten, levering himself away from her. Reluctantly her arms fell away from him and landed listlessly in the snow, either side of her. She looked up at him as he half turned and sat beside her, a shaky hand running through his hair.

'I'm sorry,' she said, and then wondered what she was

apologizing for – putting them in danger, or kissing him. 'I didn't know you were following me,' she added. Then, after another small silence, 'I didn't *ask* you to,' she pointed out, struggling to get to her feet. It was hard. Her legs felt like water. He sighed tellingly, got expertly to his own skis, then held out his hand. She looked at it, and shook her head. 'I can get up on my own, thanks,' she muttered, and he watched in grim silence as she struggled and strained to do just that. She was hardly full of gratitude now, was she? he thought wryly.

'We still have a good mile to go to the bottom,' he said, wearily. His lips, that only moments ago had felt hot and full against her mouth, were now perfectly straight and forbidding. 'I'll get us back on to the piste and we'll take the first car down we can find.' His voice too was emotionless. It was as if what had just happened had never actually happened at all. But then, she though grimly, it probably wasn't any big deal to him. He kissed beautiful women all the time. OK. She could be cool, too.

'Thank you,' she said stiffly. Then, remembering just how much she really *did* have to thank him for, she added more softly, 'For everything. You could have left me back there . . .'

Kyn smiled grimly. No doubt that was what she'd have expected from him. She must be as puzzled as hell right now, trying to figure out why he hadn't. 'That's all right. Look, there's more to Vermont than just skiing, you know,' he added, his tone deliberately warming. 'And I don't think you should take to the mountains again for a while. Why don't I take you out for the day tomorrow and show you some of the less stressful sights?' he asked, enjoying her dilemma.

Bryony wanted to refuse. Every atom of her screamed

271

at her to say no. But she couldn't afford to look a gift horse like that in the mouth. 'Thank you. I look forward to that.'

Kyn nodded. He had to hand it to her – she recovered fast. 'I'll pick you up at nine, tomorrow morning.'

Lance Prescott had been pursuing the daughter of a textile magnate for some weeks now and was very aware that his future rested on his prowess tonight. He had the lights turned low, and handed her a chilled glass of champagne. From there it was but a step to his bedroom, and he undressed her with care, ignoring the over-large stomach and thighs. Luckily, she turned the lights out and pulled him quickly into her. When he felt her begin to buck and thrash beneath him he quickened the pace even further. So when the doorbell rang he almost shot off the bed in surprise. He smiled, muttered he'd be back soon and all but ran to the door. He kept the chain firmly on.

'Let me in,' Morgan hissed through the gap, pushing so hard that Lance heard the chain crack. Frightened, he unclasped it and stepped back. 'Would that be Gina Knight in there?' Morgan asked, his voice pitched loud enough to be heard through the closed door. 'I know she's loaded, Lance, old chap,' he said jovially, his voice rising a notch higher. 'Does she know just how desperate you are for cash?'

Lance stared at him, dismayed. 'You bastard,' he said helplessly, and watched a minute later as his meal-ticket marched past him and disappeared forever. When she was gone, he looked back at Morgan. 'I could kill you for that,' Lance said, his voice bitter. But they both knew he wouldn't. He wouldn't dare.

Morgan smiled. 'I couldn't have you coming into

millions, Lance, now, could I?' he asked reasonably. 'Otherwise you wouldn't need or want the millions Leslie Ventura is going to pay us to get his darling little girl back.'

CHAPTER 23

Hadrian looked around the empty room. In one corner stood a sink and a cooker. A large single window over-looked the street below. The walls were an unbecoming shade of dark blue, and the paint was peeling. 'I'll take it,' he said to the agent, who smiled happily.

'Long-term lease or three-monthly, Mr Boulton? Natu-rally, a long-term lease is a more financially rewarding investment.'

'Naturally,' Hadrian said drily, but took the three-month lease, which he signed there and then. The agent handed over the keys and left. With a sigh, Hadrian checked his new home. The water in the taps ran on command, and when he picked up the telephone, lying on the floor, there was a reassuring dialling tone in his ear. Quickly, he punched out a number he now knew off by heart and waited. 'Hello. It's me.'

'Hi, me.' Her voice was warm and caressing, and he found himself shivering pleasantly.

'You took your time,' he grumbled warmly. He'd come to meet the realtor right from work – his first full day at Ventura – and his mind was still buzzing with facts and figures.

'You got me out of my bath, you rat.'

Facts and figures quickly took a hike as he imagined her, warm and rosy from the bath, standing in the middle of her big penthouse suite with only a bathtowel wrapped around her, soapsuds sliding down her lovely shoulders and gliding between her breasts. 'That's not fair,' he said softly. 'I get to picture you in all your soap-and-water glory, and the only thing *I'm* doing is standing in an empty apartment with a couple of taps, a telephone and peeling paint for company.'

'You got a pad?' Marion squealed. 'How'd you manage it so soon?'

'I settled for elegant squalor,' he said laughingly, looking around. 'I don't suppose I could persuade you to pick up a few gallons of pastel paint from a DIY shop and come over and help me paint the walls, could I?'

'Could you?' the warm voice purred. 'Give me half an hour and I'll be right over. What's your favourite colour?'

Hadrian blinked. 'Huh . . . pale yellow, I suppose. Why?'

'You want your apartment painted yellow?' Marion asked, her voice shocked. 'Oh, well, there's no accounting for taste. See you in a little while.'

Hadrian gave her the address and hung up, still grinning. She was full of surprises. He made himself a cup of tea with some relief, and thought about the hectic day he'd just had at Ventura. Surviving the crush in the elevators, he'd managed to find his way to the accounts department, a vast area of floor-space dotted with square, glassed cubicles. Herb Lawrence, his boss, had quickly put him to work on a vast pile of EC-related accounts, but he wasn't complaining. Within hours he was getting used to the vast amounts of money that flowed through the Ventura books.

Now he explored his new home, a small, square, empty piece of space, and shook his head. Was she really going to arrive with a gallon of paint? Marion Ventura, the Ventura Princess?

He walked once more to the window and looked out. The lights of Manhattan were twinkling on, illuminating vast towers of offices and apartments while, up in the sky, the stars fought to compete. Suddenly, Bryony flashed into his mind. No doubt where she was the stars could bask in all their well-deserved glory. The air was probably crisp and clean, and, if anything, she would pity him his view. For he now knew where she was. Marion had been complaining to him about how her father had arbitrarily put in a bid on a farm in Vermont, and it had been easy – so very easy – he thought guiltily, to pump her for more information and discover that Bryony Rose had bought the property. No doubt she was trying to sell it in order to boost Ventura's interest in acquiring Germaine Leisure. Hadrian wasn't sure whether to be glad or sorry that Marion didn't want to take over Germaine Leisure but build a company of her own from scratch. He didn't want to have to choose between the two women he loved. At least he knew where Bryony was now: Stowe. But was she all right?

He frowned, wondering why he suddenly felt so uneasy. Bryony was a beautiful woman now. If she'd made contact with Kynaston Germaine (and surely she had), who knew what damage he might do to her? But it would be no good trying to change her mind and get her to leave Vermont, that Hadrian knew instinctively. She was too determined to see Germaine pay for what he'd done. Too angry. Too obsessed. Perhaps that would save her, Hadrian thought, his eyes bleak as he looked up into the night sky. Yes, perhaps, after all, it was Germaine himself who was in trouble. He hoped so. 'Be careful, Bryn,' he muttered, his happiness of only moments ago suddenly reduced to ashes in the pit of his stomach. 'For pity's sake, be careful.'

Bryony stood to one side as Kyn brushed past her and flicked a switch. 'Home, sweet home,' he said drily, shutting the door carefully behind him.

They'd spent the day sightseeing, and she'd done her best to be witty and charming. She'd let him take her arm to lead her along the icy streets, and never once flinched when he'd touched her. Their dinner had been intimate, the gondola ride they'd taken afterwards spectacular. But why, oh why had she accepted his offer of a nightcap at his home, which had turned out to be a large log cabin on the very outskirts of town? She was playing with fire, and she knew it.

'It's some home,' she heard herself saying, and looked around. One wall was devoted to a huge brick fireplace, and Kyn walked quickly towards it. As he thrust some well-dried pine logs into the embers, it quickly caught.

His sister's college flag hung on the same wall that housed a painting by Rubens. Angry for some reason with that silly white and dark blue silk flag, she turned away. The furniture looked dark and solid and domestic. She'd expected fancy French that showed off his wealth. Picture-windows looked out over the town, and she gravitated towards them. Kyn, who'd been watching every move she made, began to walk in the same direction, but, getting there ahead of her, he pulled the drapes across. Bryony stopped dead.

'You don't like the view?' she asked, licking lips that had gone suddenly dry.

'I love the view, that's why I bought this place,' he corrected softly. 'But I don't share my fellow countrymen's habit of leaving the curtains open and all the lights on at night. I prefer my privacy.'

Bryony looked at him. Was he deliberately trying to scare her? Being alone, in a man's home, was the sort of thing a woman like he supposed her to be would take in her stride. So why did she have this feeling as if he was . . . testing her in some way? Deliberately baiting her? Seeing how far she would go?

'I think we settled on hot chocolate, didn't we?' Kyn asked softly, and Bryony nodded, breathing a sigh of relief at being on her own for a few minutes. But when he came back with the mugs, he chose the long, low leather couch facing the fire. He saw the look of near-panic in her eyes, and smiled grimly. 'Are you going to stand there all night? Sofas are for sitting on, you know. That's why somebody invented them.'

She nodded glumly and took the few steps necessary, sitting down next to him. Kyn looked across at her taut, grim profile and sighed. She was so obviously miserable that he felt a cold, hard rage build inside him. This was all *her* idea, after all. Slowly he half turned and raised his hand. Out of her peripheral vision she saw the movement and every nerve in her body tensed. Kyn saw the tiny movement, and his lips twisted grimly. How long, he wondered, before she bolted? 'You know, you really do have lovely hair,' he said softly, and lifted a long, heavy lock in his hand. As he did so his knuckles gently brushed past her earlobe, and she shivered, taking a deep, compulsive breath.

'Thank you,' she managed to reply huskily.

'And lovely skin,' he added, rubbing the backs of his

278

fingers downwards, over her cheek and downy soft skin. 'It really is like an English rose – pale pinky-cream, velvet and soft. But then,' he turned more fully on the sofa, letting his bended knee brush against hers 'you must already know that. Men, lots of men, must have told you so.'

He wondered, with a shock wave that rippled right the way through him, if there really *had* been any men at all. Living way out in that lonely Yorkshire countryside, she'd hardly have been swamped with suitors. The tantalizing thought that she might still be a virgin sent tiny ripples through him. His fingers trembled against her cheek and he reluctantly lowered them. What had started out as a cat-and-mouse game was suddenly no longer even cruelly amusing. She was convinced she was the cat, using all her feline wiles against him, getting ready to sink her lovely teeth into his hide, while all the time he was sure *he* was the cat, on to her little game and already several steps ahead of her. Now he wasn't so sure. She had a nasty habit of pulling the rug out from under him. The fact that she did it without even trying was enough to make him break out in a cold sweat.

'This is lovely chocolate,' she said, and took a hasty sip.

'I'm glad you like it,' he said wryly. Why was he worrying about her? Why did he care . . .?

'I do. Like it. Very much,' Bryony insisted, and wished she'd shut up. She was babbling again.

'Good,' he said, his voice once more lowering intimately. 'I love doing things that you like,' he added, letting his hand stray across to her own. He felt the pulse in her wrist leap under his caressing fingers. 'But then, I don't suppose that comes as any surprise to you, does it, Bryony Rose?'

Bryony's head snapped up to meet his, and she wished it hadn't. How had she ever thought his eyes were icy? They were hot – laser-hot, burning, penetrating, melting . . . 'I . . . don't know what you mean,' she managed to choke out.

Kynaston smiled. She probably didn't – but she would. Oh, yes. She would. 'I mean, a woman who looks the way you do, a woman as beautiful as yourself, must take it for granted by now that men do what you want them to.'

Her heart began to pound. But wasn't this what she wanted? Hadn't she always imagined Kynaston Germaine falling in love with her? Wanting her? Hadn't she secretly thrilled and longed to have him in the thralls of that age-old power that women had enjoyed over men since time began? 'I hadn't noticed,' she said, managing to laugh lightly as she spoke. That's it. Flirt, tease, take control . . .

Kyn's eyes narrowed. 'You surprise me. Take me, for instance. You want me to want you, and I do. So much so, it almost hurts. But that's what you wanted as well, isn't it?'

She swallowed hard, leaning back against the side of the sofa as he leaned closer. 'I . . . yes, that's what I want,' she admitted in a rush of defiance, her voice strong and suddenly demanding. Quickly she looked up at him, catching, she was sure, a look of sudden surprise in his eyes. Then, hardly aware of what she was doing, she pressed herself against him, running her hand up his chest, her fingertips tingling as they collided with one hardening male nipple, before carrying on over the smooth, fascinatingly strong shoulders and to the nape of his neck. His hair curled around her fingers, cool and clean and silky.

Kyn stiffened at her unexpected manoeuvre then reacted to her words and actions with a compelling male instinct that he'd never felt so strongly before. His loins hardened as an electric jolt shot through his body, taking him completely off-guard. Snake-like, his arms curled around her, one curling around her waist and dragging her forward, the other moving behind her shoulders, turning her around and squarely against him. Bryony just had time to gasp as her breasts were crushed against the steel cage of his ribs and then she closed her eyes as his lips moved down to seal themselves against hers.

Blood pounded in her head as his tongue demanded entry into her mouth, and when she found herself obeying the silent, imperious order she moaned softly against the hard superiority of his lips as their tongues met and duelled. She felt the full force of his desire clash with her own, and the explosion of passion that erupted like adrenalin into her blood had the moan turning into a small cry. His hands splayed across her back, and she could feel every imprint of his fingers against her spine through the thin material of her dress. She shuddered as heat spread from them, burning right through her and coming out the other side, making her nipples burst into flame. She could feel the hard little buttons of flesh move against him, every tiny movement of their bodies magnified a hundred times so that she felt as if she was nothing more than a mass of exposed nerve-endings. Suddenly she felt herself sliding down, and then the ceiling was above her, and so was he. His lips were still fastened on hers, but she could feel the downward brush of his hair against her face, and the whole length of his body lying flat against hers as he lay atop her on the couch. But his weight didn't crush, instead it intensified the burning ache that was beginning to clamour for attention deep and low in her stomach. She felt her vaginal muscles clench in sudden, instinctive want, and a warm, wet honey began to melt at the top of her legs. She could feel the steely strength in his thighs through his trousers, and her own thighs began to tremble and fall apart. Bewildered by the violent and instinctive reaction taking place in her body, she whimpered against his mouth, and his kiss immediately gentled. He opened his eyes, and they were laser-bright, but somehow gentler. Slowly, he began to lift his lips from hers, but almost at once they were back again, but gentler, softer, quicker. She sighed as he traced the contours of her lips, then moved across to her cheeks. She gulped in a breath of badly needed air, and her hands, clutching his shoulders, began to move in slow, circling caresses. The ache inside her didn't abate, but it too gentled, spreading all over her body, making her bones feel like warm, thick, liquid. His lips found her ears; his teeth nibbled on her lobes, and then suddenly his tongue darted into her ear, making the ache spear outwards, like a sudden pulse of electricity. She moaned and jerked at the unexpectedness of it, and Kyn's hands held her down gently, firmly, lovingly. Slowly his hands left her waist and, as his lips moved down and around, blazing a fiery path of kissing nibbling heat to her throat, his hands moved upwards, over the quivering slope of her stomach and higher. Her back arched as his hands moved up over her breasts, her nipples stabbing into his palms as he caressed her.

He thrilled at the fullness of her breasts in his hands, heavy and warm and infinitely desirable. He moaned against her throat, his fingers fumbling urgently with the buttons, every sense and instinct in him demanding that he have access to her bare skin. His mouth pulsed in anticipation of sucking those wonderful buds against his

282

tongue, and Bryony heard the sound of his desire as if from a long way away.

At least he was feeling the same desire that she did. At least she was not alone in this stunning new world. Except, a small voice taunted with a sudden chilling coldness from the depths of her fevered mind, it isn't a new world for him, is it? He's done this countless times with other women – like that woman from the art gallery in York, all chic, dark hair and scarlet cloak. Bryony stiffened. 'No. No, wait . . . I'm not . . . ready.' Kyn suddenly froze. Slowly, as if with great difficulty, he raised his head, then raised his upper body away from her on elbows that shook slightly. He drew in ragged, deep breaths, his chest rising and falling with the effort. His eyes, she noticed with an incredible joy that almost dynamited her mind into smithereens, looked, for the first time since she'd known him, cloudy and hazy, almost unfocused.

'What are you talking about?' he finally rasped, gathering his scattered wits together. He'd been lost in her, he realised a moment later, his eyes snapping back into the electric, icy blue alertness that was becoming as familiar to her as the sound of her own breathing. 'What game are you playing now, Bryony?' he asked, his voice low and ominous and rasping with the stubborn remains of desire that still pulsed dully in his bloodstream.

Bryony shook her head. She was in danger of blowing it, and all because she'd panicked. 'I . . . I don't mean I don't want you . . .' she attempted to assure him, trying at the same time to remember what Lynnette had said about men having fragile egos. 'It's just that I'm . . . not ready. You know . . . prepared. Protection, that kind of thing,' she added awkwardly, not knowing whether to laugh or cry when he slowly straightened up and away from her, getting to his feet and running a weary, harassed hand through his hair.

Quickly she scrambled off the sofa, tugging her rumpled clothes back into position. In spite of the roaring log fire, she felt cold. It was as if he'd taken all the warmth with him when he'd left her. She chewed nervously on her lower lip, staring at his back. He looked tense and angry.

'I'm sorry,' she said, her voice small and getting quickly lost in the vast silence of the room.

Kyn shook his head. 'I'm not.'

Bryony went hot, then cold. 'What do you mean? Don't you . . . want me any more?'

Kyn's lips twisted wryly. Not want her? When his body was screaming for release and fulfilment? When his mind was still whirling like a crazy carousel? No woman had made him want her more. That was the trouble.

'Come on, I'll take you home,' he said wearily. He had some heavy thinking to do.

CHAPTER 24

'I think I prefer you with a yellow nose.'

'What?' Marion spun round, paint roller in one hand, eyes wide. She was wearing a pair of denim dungarees over a plain white T-shirt, her hair was caught up in a tiny ponytail. She had paint all over her nose. Hadrian had never seen her looking more beautiful. 'Your yellow nose. I like it.'

'Oh, wonderful,' she grumbled, her eyes twinkling. 'Perhaps it'll start a whole new fashion trend.'

Hadrian cocked his head to one side and narrowed his eyes. 'Perhaps green would go better with that outfit you're wearing. What do you think, O setter of trends?'

'I think you'd better get on with your half of the wall, or I'll be finished first. Then what will you do?'

'Go away and sulk, probably. Either that, or take the roller off you and ravish you in a corner.'

'Oh. Well, that's all right then,' she said and turned back to the wall. It was, Marion thought with a smile, strangely satisfying to decorate an apartment. When she'd first seen the place a week before, she'd been angry. It seemed so unfair that he had to live like this, when she could give him so much more. But she knew better than to offer to buy him a bigger place. Besides, he'd genuinely

285

wanted her artistic input on how to do the place up. It was the first time anyone had ever asked her for her help before. From that moment on, Project Apartment had taken control.

The walls had needed to be stripped and sandpapered, and the skirting boards done. The floorboards, they both agreed, would look wonderful polished. Marion, who'd never done a single day's physical labour in her life, found herself at ten o'clock most nights on her hands and knees, scrubbing floorboards. If her father had been able to see her, no doubt he'd have keeled over in shock. She chipped nails, her knees ached, her back ached, her neck ached and as for her arms . . .

Of course, none of it had mattered, just as it didn't matter now that she had a primrose-yellow nose. Hadrian was right there with her, complaining that his neck, back and arms ached more than hers did. It didn't matter because every night, after the work was done, they'd sit on the two beanbags she'd bought, that were the flat's only furniture, and share coffee out of the one single mug they had, and talk and laugh and hold hands and kiss until midnight. Marion couldn't remember being happier. Broken nails notwithstanding.

'There. Finished,' Hadrian's voice cut across her reverie and she looked over, a chagrined frown crossing her smooth, dark brows. She glanced at his smooth, still wet and shining expanse of wall and almost growled.

'You must have cheated.'

'Rubbish,' he said crisply. He threw his dark, wonderfully handsome head back. 'You're just a sore loser, that's all.'

'Do you want to have a pint of paint thrown at you?'

'See. Sore loser,' he grinned, then, when she turned to

round on him, he laughed, hands held out in a gesture of appeasement. 'OK, OK. I'll make us some coffee. Perhaps the caffeine will calm you down. What a grouch!'

He made mumbling, uncomplimentary comments all the time he worked in the small kitchen. As she dipped the roller in the tray of paint for the last time and watched the last bit of unattractive plaster disappear behind the layer of paint, she smiled. Finished at last!

Her day at the office had been a particularly hard one. Since her illuminating and disturbing talk with Kynaston Germaine she'd had her team begin a detailed analysis of what it would take to build their own hotels from scratch. It had turned out to be an enormous undertaking. She was beginning to see what Kynaston had meant when he'd talked of building a company out of your own sweat. But she was getting there.

'You look like a cat who's just found a canary in her dish of cream,' Hadrian said, taking a sip out of the mug and then handing it to her. She accepted the mug and took a hefty swallow of coffee. It tasted good, even though she knew it was the cheap, instant stuff. 'I was just thinking what a great job I did on this hell-hole,' she said, looking around.

'How modest you are. But, now that I come to think of it . . .' He too looked around. The light-coloured walls made the whole room look twice as large as before. All it needed was furniture. He smiled. 'What say we get this sheeting up and the rugs down?'

'You're on,' she said, catching his sudden excitement. They'd chosen the rugs together on Saturday morning at a local flea-market. They were second-hand but still in good condition, and Hadrian had immediately liked the dark blue, white and yellow pattern of big lotus flowers. Marion had been less sure, but, as they placed the two, large rectangle rugs on the floor, finally agreeing on the best locations for them, she realized Hadrian's instinct had been right. The dark blue added depth to the room, while the white and yellow in the pattern perfectly matched the paintwork. 'We'll have to be careful about the furniture,' Marion said thoughtfully, her eyes still on the rugs. 'And give me that coffee before you drink it all, you pig.'

'I always suspected you had eyes in the back of your head,' he grumbled, but handed over the half-empty mug of cooling coffee. Marion drained it, then glanced at him.

'Will you come with me to pick out a bed?' he asked suggestively, giving her a leer. If things worked out, and he made his home here in New York permanent, he might even stretch to a sofa and a table or two. Then he felt the happiness slowly evaporate, as it always did when he contemplated the future. So much depended on Bryony. And on Marion. And on himself. And on what Ventura Industries did. Hadrian shook his head. Let's face it, he told himself ruefully, your future is so unsure, it makes the stock-market look positively stable!

'What's up?' Marion asked softly, moving over to him and leaning her cheek against his back, her arms coming round to drape loosely across his waist. 'You looked so sad suddenly.'

She had caught that look on his face once or twice before, and it always worried her. Even though she knew that their worst hurdle – her immense wealth – had already been cleared, and she believed him when he said there was no one else, she knew that there was *something*. She wished she knew what. She had a feeling it was important. Behind her cheek, she felt his spinal muscles shudder. Surprised, she raised her head and stared up at his tense shoulderblades. 'Are you cold? I thought the heating in this place was fairly good.'

'It is,' Hadrian agreed huskily. 'Why do you ask?'

'I felt you shiver.'

'Ahh . . . and the fact that you're pressed against me and driving me crazy couldn't possibly have anything to do with that, I suppose?' he asked, his voice husky now and almost breathless. Suddenly Marion became intensely aware of her nipples tingling to life against the smooth expanse of his back beneath his thin cotton shirt, and of her hands on his waist, pressing close to the top of his belt. If she moved her fingers down just a few inches . . . Suddenly, her fingertips began to tingle in anticipation.

She was suddenly aware of how much she wanted Hadrian. Not just a man. Not just sex. But Hadrian. She longed to touch every inch of him, and see if he had any moles, or scars. She wanted to taste him to see if he tasted the same everywhere. She wanted to hear his voice doing other things than speaking words – she wanted to hear him give a tiny moan, a loud sigh, a lingering, longing groan of want and desire. She wanted him inside her, filling her, pleasuring her . . . Slowly she drew away and, as she did so, he turned to face her. From the look on his face, she knew, just knew, that he was thinking the same. 'Marion.' The word was more than her name – it was a question, a celebration, a love poem.

'Come on,' she said softly and took his hand, incredibly touched to feel it tremble slightly in her own. She knew how strong his hands were – she'd seen them bend nails, work floorboards loose and hammer them back again. And yet in her small hands they trembled, and impulsively she lifted one to her mouth and began to kiss the backs of the knuckles, her eyes never leaving his. She saw his pupils dilate, his mouth fall slightly open, and heard the breath whistle in between his parted lips. 'I think,' she said softly, her eyes both tender and burning with volcanic heat, 'that it's time we christened those rugs of yours properly.'

Hadrian swallowed hard. He knew he should say something – this moment was too precious, too meaningful not to. But no worlds would come. Instead, he turned her hands over in his and bent to kiss one palm, loving the way her fingers curled up compulsively and lightly grazed his cheeks, loving even more the way she shuddered in delight at the contact.

Slowly, they sank down on to one rug, their lips meeting in a long, lingering kiss that held the promise of a lifetime together. Hadrian slowly undid the copper-coloured buttons of the dungarees at her shoulders, smoothing the fabric down to her waist. Against the white T-shirt her nipples thrust upwards, crying out for his touch, and when he spread one large hand over her breast, she arched her back, a small, inarticulate cry escaping her lips. 'Marion . . .' he said her name again, just for the pleasure of saying it, then kissed her again, unable to resist her soft, red, parted lips. Quickly his tongue darted into her mouth, and, when he felt her own tongue on his, his whole body shook.

She reached for his other hand and brought it up to her other breast, uncaring that now he was laying his whole weight against her. As if realising it, he moved slightly to his side, taking her with him, and as her eyes shot open and looked into his she saw love, for the first time:

Oh, she knew her father loved her, and she knew her mother and Keith had loved her. But she'd never seen love before, in somebody's eyes. Not the way she could see it now. And suddenly she knew why people killed for love.

290

Why people died for love. Why poets wrote about nothing else. Why nothing else mattered as much as that look in his eyes. Her heart leapt as she realised that he must surely see the same answering look in her own eyes, for she knew that she'd never loved anyone as she loved this man. 'Hadrian . . . Oh, Hadrian, I love you,' she whispered as his lips left hers, leaving them feeling bereft and cold.

'I love you too,' he whispered intently.

She felt hot tears slide out of the corners of her eyes, and then he was lifting her up, hugging her, holding her against him, rocking her like a child. But she was no child, and her body clamoured for him. Her heart had just given itself away, her soul had just joined his, and her body was not going to be left out. Quickly her fingers fumbled with the buttons on his shirt, tearing them apart and then slipping inside, splaying over his chest, exploring the mat of dark, fine, silky hairs on his chest before finding his hard male nipples.

Hadrian groaned as her fingers pinched and soothed, then her hands were on his shoulders, shoving the shirt away, pulling it down his arms. Her lips went to his ears, then down his neck, then across his shoulders, finding the small, sensitive indents as if radar-targeted. He shuddered, tiny tingles spreading all the way down his spine and lodging in his loins, which were hardening uncomfortably against his jeans.

Not to be oudone, he quickly tugged the bottom of her T-shirt upwards and she lifted her arms obediently as he pulled it up and off her. For a moment he could only gaze in silence at her beauty. Her breasts were not large, but they were exquisitely shaped, with upturned tips of a rose pink that was totally irresistible. With a harsh groan that thrilled her to the tips of her toes, he ducked his head and sucked one nipple into his mouth, letting his teeth graze the hard button of flesh before his tongue closed around it, laving it lovingly.

Marion cried out and fell against him, losing all strength in her body. She threw her head back, and quickly his lips left her breast and rose upwards, kissing the long, aching line of her throat. Slowly he let her fall backwards on to the rug and then followed her down, leaning over her and cupping one breast in one hand and returning his lips to the other.

Marion closed her eyes against the newly painted, pristine white ceiling. Her breaths came in deep, ragged gasps, and when she felt him pulling down the trousers of her dungarees she lifted her bottom up to help him, thrilling to the feel of his hands curling around her bare calves. When his lips closed over her big toe her eyes shot momentarily open before slowly closing again. With infinite care, patience and enjoyment he blazed a trail over her delicate arches, then around her ankle, then up to the bend in the back of her knee. He felt her leg muscles jerk spasmodically and then he was moving up, higher, to the plain white briefs that covered her most intimate possession. When his lips licked against them, Marion shuddered. Reaching down, she quickly pulled the last remaining garment from her body and tossed it away as if she hated it. Hadrian felt honoured by the strength of her desire and so grateful for her trusting passion that he felt tears shimmering across his vision. Slowly he lowered his lips to her hot, wet, waiting womanhood and began to lick her delicately, finding her clitoris slowly and then nibbling gently, carefully holding her thighs apart and down as she began to buck and moan in desire as a great tidal wave of pleasure washed over her. Quickly he drew off his own clothes, his penis springing to throbbing, upright, relieved attention the moment it was set free. Marion reached for him gently, wanting to feel him in her hands. She was amazed by the hard strength of his desire, and by the silky, velvety feel of his skin. Holding his eyes with her own, she reached lower, delicately cupping his silky flesh in her hand, seeing the desire hit him and send a warming red flush to his cheeks. His jaw stiffened even as his mouth fell open, and when his eyes closed in helpless desire, she leaned forward and kissed him feverishly, first his mouth, then his nose, then his closed eyes. Lance had never let her touch him, and now she understood why. He hadn't wanted her, or cared whether she wanted him. But Hadrian both wanted and loved her, and as she had felt so right about opening herself and her body to him, so he also felt safe putting himself in her hands. It was a moment of complete trust and understanding, as well as passion, and it made silent tears of happiness slide down her own, flushed cheeks. Then his eyes opened, and they were on fire, and suddenly they were kissing, and Marion was pulling him down against her, opening her legs and guiding him urgently into her. Hadrian thrust instinctively, crying out as her hot, tight muscles sheathed him and her legs twined around his calves, holding him a willing prisoner inside her.

Marion too cried out, bucking as he filled her. He was so big it felt as if she could feel him in every part of her. Slowly, he began to move, his thrusts slow and deep, and so unlike Lance's perfunctory and quick movements as to be in a different league. Together they felt every movement, savoured every nuance of touch, delighted in every quickening of the rhythm. 'Hadrian!' she cried out as first one orgasm, then another rocketed though her. She wasn't

293

aware of her nails raking his back as their bodies bucked and thrashed in a passion that only love understood, and when he felt his own control begin to slip away from him, he too cried out her name.

It was a long time before they slowly parted and lay back, exhausted, against the rug. Even then, their fingers were locked and their arms were pressed side by side as they looked up at the ceiling they had painted together only yesterday. 'I've never made love before,' Marion said, then wondered if he understood. 'I mean . . .'

'I know what you mean,' Hadrian murmured softly and truthfully. 'And I don't think I've ever made love before either. Not like that.' For a moment they lay in silence, sharing a contentment so perfect it was almost magical. Then, slowly, she turned on her side and looked at him, tracing his profile with one, small finger. 'Don't ever leave me. Please,' she said, a sudden lance of fear making her shiver.

'I won't,' he promised. 'I couldn't, even if I wanted to.'

'And you won't love anybody else.'

'No. Nobody else.'

Marion nodded. She wasn't sure why she was asking all this of him, when she already knew, deep in her soul, that Hadrian would never hurt her. But something, far away but buried deep inside herself, was still afraid. It had something to do with that strange, sad look that sometimes came into his eyes.

Hadrian thought of Bryony, all alone and struggling with Kynaston Germaine and her own demons. He thought of what he could do to help her, and all that he still owed her. And it scared him. For to help Bryony he had to use Marion. The thought made him shudder. Wordlessly, he reached across and cradled Marion's small body against his own, and felt her nestle against him, sighing happily. If she'd looked up, she'd have seen that look was back in his eyes . . .

Outside, Bruno scribbled in his notebook. He knew the man's name now, and that he worked at Ventura. And he knew all about the apartment he'd just brought. After a few minutes, Bruno stopped writing and looked up at the building, counting along until he found he Englishman's windows, ablaze with light. There was no doorman here. No state-of-the-art security system. He'd have to mention it to Morgan.

In his study at his mansion, Leslie Ventura was reading through a thick file with incredible speed. It was a copy of the one his daughter was working on. As he'd long since suspected, the file was not a takeover plan of Germaine Leisure, nor anything like it. It was a blueprint for a brand new hotel to add to his existing leisure company. Leslie sighed. The work was competent, the principle sound. Her research was thorough and her ideas were solid. But it wasn't what he'd asked her to do.

He sighed deeply. He should have known that having a woman in charge of Ventura Industries would simply never work. They lacked the killer instinct. One dinner with Kynaston Germaine and she'd folded. A man would have gone straight for the jugular. As he had. His agent had confirmed that Coldstream Farm was indeed a sound proposition, and he'd cabled Bryony Rose an offer for it. He intended to advertize the place as a taste of the 'True Vermont'. The ranch horses could pull sleighs. The cattle could provide milk, if he could persuade the wholesalers to take his excess stock. The hens would provide fresh eggs.

It was a city-bound executive's dream. Just the kind of thing he would add to Germaine Leisure, once it was his.

Leslie sighed again. He'd have to take the project away from her. Give her a job more suitable for her talents. Head of PR, perhaps? Carole called down and asked him to come to bed.

'Coming,' he called, his eyes resting briefly on the report. 'I just had some business to see to, but it's all done now.'

CHAPTER 25

Lance jumped nervously as the doorbell rang and looked down the empty corridor when Morgan brushed past him. Thankfully, there was no one in sight. 'I don't like meeting here,' he complained petulantly. 'Shouldn't we have met in some crowded, public place?'

'To discuss kidnap plans? I hardly think so.'

Lance flushed. Morgan hefted a well-used briefcase on to the low, glass-topped coffee table. 'Got any coffee?'

Lance jerked. He felt badly off-balance. 'Sure. Colombian or Costa Rican?'

Morgan smiled. 'I'll leave the important decisions to you,' he said drolly, and again Lance flushed. Nevertheless, he stalked to the kitchen and made the coffee. He had no choice.

After Morgan had wrecked his chances with Gina Knight, Lance had been deeply depressed. At this rate it wouldn't be long before his friends started to desert him. And the only way to get rid of Morgan was to do what he wanted. And perhaps Morgan really *was* clever enough actually to pull the kidnapping plot off. The thought of getting money out of Marion and the Venturas after all they'd put him through was undeniably sweet.

Morgan was studying the blueprints of the Ventura

office building when Lance returned with the coffee. 'I hear your ex has found herself a new man,' Morgan said casually, watching Lance's face with all the attention of a hawk. 'Some Englishman or other. A big, handsome man, by all accounts.'

Lance stiffened, and Morgan's smile widened. Good. He was eaten alive with anger and jealousy. Bruno's information was turning out to be useful after all. 'So . . . are you ready to listen?' Morgan asked, but one look at Lance's suddenly bright and avid eyes told him the answer. 'Now, here's what I had in mind . . .'

When Morgan left Lance Prescott's flat an hour later there was a spring in his step. He'd planned a little surprise for Kynaston too, to coincide with the hotel's grand opening in January. Revenge would be sweet. He could still remember all the injections, all the pills. The basket-weaving. The model-making. The hours spent watching afternoon soaps. The talks with shrinks. The shock-therapy. Yes, revenge would be sweet.

He took the subway and used the back alleys to get to his seedy hotel and his dingy single room. He sat down on his sagging bed wearily. He'd be glad to get back to Vermont, now that Lance Prescott had been successfully hooked. He lay back on the bed and stared up at the cracked, dirty ceiling. He didn't mind the squalor now. Funny how it had once infuriated him. It had been to escape the squalor of their New York slum his father insisted on calling their 'home' that had made him try and get out in the first place, giving Kyn the perfect opportunity to get rid of him.

Morgan laughed bitterly. His plan had been a good one, too. It would have worked. Vanessa would have been allright. Trust Kyn to panic. If he hadn't, everything

298

would have been great. The authorities would have been forced to move them to better accommodation, but, if not, he'd had a back-up plan to go to the Press. They were always looking out for human interest stories. Hell, they might even have been able to take on the city and win enough compensation to get back to Vermont.

But Kyn had had to ruin it all, going to the cops.

Still, Morgan knew that his own time was coming – that it was going to be *his* turn to do the destroying and make all the money. Soon. *Very* soon.

Kynaston reached for the binoculars once more, the setting already perfect for what he had in mind. It should be. He'd been watching her all morning.

The last week in November had brought with it an unusually high amount of snowfall, and already Stowe was alive with tourists, gondolas and ski-lifts packed with happy, red faces.

He dug his ski poles expertly into the snow and moved off, his skis making crisp, clean tracks in the snow. He was on Spruce Peak, where mostly beginners and intermediates chose to begin their holiday. He smiled as the cherry-red figure made yet another successful run. He was proud of her. Most people, after nearly dying in an avalanche, wouldn't have the courage to take to skis again, at least not for some time. But not his lovely, stubborn Bryony. She'd been out the next chance she got, practising for all she was worth. She didn't even have an instructor with her.

He headed towards her, skiing gracefully and without any conscious effort. Bryony, her eyes fixed to the front of her skis, wasn't aware of his presence until a shadow fell over her, and she jerked to a less than graceful halt. 'You'll have to watch out, I'm . . .' Her voice faltered and trailed

299

off as he lowered his darkened goggles and she found herself staring into eyes as pale a blue as the sky above her.

'You never give up, do you?' he said softly.

Bryony looked him straight in the eye. 'No. Never. And I'd better get back to pract . . . ising!' She landed in the snow with a whump.

'Are you OK?' he asked, laughing and bending down to help her up. With his hands under her armpits he lifted her easily, and when she turned to look at him she was smiling ruefully.

'I'm fine.' Except, suddenly, she wasn't. His hands were still under her armpits, and their skis had crossed as he'd moved closer. She could feel her body leaning towards his, and, with the awkward skis attached to her feet, she suddenly couldn't halt the movement. Briefly his hands tightened on hers then relaxed, and she reached out to clutch his shoulders to steady herself. 'I don't think I'm safe to be let loose,' she said, her heart hammering in her breast, her mouth going suddenly dry.

'I wouldn't say that. You just need an instructor, that's all, and I'm more than willing to teach you a lesson. In skiing, I mean,' he added softly as her head whipped up, her eyes narrowing suspiciously.

'Oh, that's not necessary,' she said quickly, the dismay so evident in her voice that he wanted to laugh out loud, and at the same time take her by her lovely, padded shoulders and shake her until her teeth rattled. 'I really don't mind just learning by trial and error.'

'That's a very painful way of doing things, Bryony,' he said softly, and reaching over he lifted her chin with one finger until their eyes were locked together. 'Didn't the avalanche teach you that much?' For a second they remained absolutely still, then he slowly withdrew his hands from her arms and moved back, leaving her feeling suddenly bereft. Shaking her head, she took a deep breath, and the sound of her sigh sent tingles shooting through him. Unbidden, his eyes roamed hungrily over her. She looked good. Even through the thickly padded suit he could see the swelling curves of her breasts, and his hands tingled as they remembered their perfect, heavy, hot weight in his palms. He swallowed hard.

Bryony's nipples stood to attention the moment his eyes touched her there. She bit her lip to prevent the small moan in her throat from escaping, and she swallowed hard. Think, dammit! a warning voice screamed in the back of her head.

'I was wondering if you've come to a decision about Coldstream Farm yet,' she said, clearing her throat and digging her poles into the snow. 'I can't wait forever,' she added, her voice dropping an octave, and, giving him a quick glance of mocking eyes, she pushed off down the shallow piste. She grinned when she heard him mutter a soft curse. He had to follow her, of course. They both knew that, and her smile turned into soft, delighted laughter. She was actually having fun, she realised with a little tremor of shock. She was in Stowe in winter, on the pistes and dressed in bright red. It was so far from Ravenheights, her old brown clothes and the nullifying routine of her old life that it was almost impossible to tally the two together and believe she and the old Bryn Whittaker were the same person. Then, out of her peripheral vision, she saw him moving with her, his own dark blue ski-suit never leaving the corner of her eye, and suddenly it wasn't hard at all. This was still Kynaston Germaine beside her. And she still had a lot to do.

With growing expertise she came to a neat halt and

turned to look at him, about to say something sophisticated, but her heart leaped into her throat as he pulled up
beside her, his lean body bending close to hers, his
flashing blue eyes shooting sparks of anger and desire.
Frantically she tried to stem the unwanted shivers of
pleasure coursing through her body.

'What are you thinking, I wonder?' he asked softly, and
before she could make any move to stop him he leaned
forward and gently lifted the goggles away from her face.
'That's better. You've got such beautiful eyes, I . . . they
take my breath away every time I see them,' he said softly.

'I was thinking . . .' she swallowed hard, and tried
again. 'I was thinking that if you don't make an offer
on the farm soon I'll have to sell it to someone else,' she
determinedly dragged the bait under his nose again. 'I
need to make a profit, after all,' she added chidingly.

Kyn smiled viciously. She wanted him to beg for that
land, wanted it so badly that he could feel it emanating
from her. The tension stood out in the tendons of her
lovely throat, and she was tuned so tight she was quivering
like a bowstring. Perhaps it was time to see just what she
was made of. His smile turned sweet. 'Oh, I don't know
that I want it after all,' he said nonchalantly, watching her
closely as she gave a small gasp of shock. 'Not now that
I've bought that parcel of land adjoining the hotel . . .
Funny thing about that,' he mused. 'The previous owner
died four months ago, and it took a while for probate to go
through. I had it all set up to buy from the heir the
moment the legalities were through. I just got back from
signing the papers this morning. So you see, I'm not sure I
need any more land at the moment.'

'Thanks for telling me,' she said stiffly. Damn. Damn!
Suddenly, her eyes sharpened. Just why was he telling her

all this now? Surely he didn't suspect. No, he couldn't, she reassured herself hastily. He was just playing a game of one upmanship. And two could do that. 'Well, that certainly makes it easier to accept another buyer now. They . . . he,' she deliberately stumbled over her supposed mistake, 'is very keen to buy. I'll call New York tomorrow, then, shall I?'

This time it was Kyn who stiffened. Knowing Bryony, she was easily clever enough to realise that selling to a rival leisure company would hurt him the most. Damn, she was a vicious little cat, he thought, his stomach clenching as excitement shivered through him. He forced himself to shrug and smile. She smiled back, her eyes glittering like those of a tiger. Yes, she'd make a wonderful tigress, he thought, a powerful lance of sexual desire suddenly shaking him to the core. All teeth and claws, and beautiful, bright, pagan eyes . . . Oh God, how he wanted her! He heard his breath catch in his throat, the sound raw and unmistakable, and Bryony felt her vagina contract in sudden, abrupt reaction. Her knees turned weak and her nipples thrust savagely upwards, making her own breath catch and lodge in her lungs.

Suddenly Kyn moved forward, crossing his skis over hers, very cleverly pinning her to the spot. She made an instinctive backward movement, but since her legs couldn't move there was nowhere for her to go. She windmilled her hands briefly to get back her balance, and his hands shot out, grasping her hard by the shoulders and pulling her, almost brutally, into his waiting arms. His lips were on hers a moment later, his hands holding her arms firmly to her side, as if he expected her to struggle. But struggling was the last thing on her mind. She'd wanted him to do this for days. It was as if no time at all had passed since they'd lain together on his couch, their bodies clamouring for release. She parted her lips willingly, her whole body quivering at the moist, erotic, welcome invasion of his tongue. She moaned behind his lips, yearning to press herself into his arms, to feel her tingling nipples rub against him, for her trembling legs to lean against his as her whole body turned liquid, but the long, awkward skis kept them apart.

'Kyn . . .' she breathed his name as he slowly lifted his head.

'No more games, Bryony,' he said, the words half plea, half demand. Still dazed and unable to think clearly, she numbly shook her head and followed his lead.

'No. No more games.'

'You'll have dinner with me tonight?'

'Yes.' His eyes bored into hers, and she suddenly felt naked. What was he thinking? What was *she* thinking? For a weird, eerie second she didn't know. Then she forced her brain to work. Obviously he still wanted her, and she was just agreeing to play up to that, wasn't she? She had to gain access to his files at the new hotel somehow, and before it opened to the public. And to do that she had to gain more of his trust. That was all there was to it. Simple, really. Except . . . except her heart was thundering in her chest, and a hot, dizzying pulse was throbbing in her blood.

'Good,' he said softly, but when she looked up at him his eyes had lost that tender, almost bemused look, and they were once again icy blue lasers. 'I'll pick you up at seven tonight,' he said forcefully. 'All right?'

'Lovely.' She watched him ski away until he was out of sight, nibbling her lower lip all the while. Time was passing. She had to do something, soon. From now on, she had to make things happen by herself. And tonight was just the beginning. Tonight . . . when they'd be alone together. Inexperienced she might be, but she knew what had just happened between them. And Kynaston Germaine was not the kind of man who would be prepared to wait for long; she'd just have to accept that. Then she remembered the way she'd responded to his touch, and a hot flush spread over her. It wouldn't be hard, would it? a mocking little voice whispered at the back of her mind. It wouldn't be hard at all to 'force' herself to accept his lovemaking. She shook her head, angry at herself. She had to do more than just . . . seduce him. She had to do something constructive. Think! she urged herself, making her careful way back to the ski-rental shop and handing over her skis. There had to be others who weren't in his back pocket; others besides the Venturas who might be able to help her.

Quickly she changed and headed for the library. There had to be someone who would be interested in any flaws in the oh, so white Germaine Leisure Corporation.

There was. It was called the Green Vermont Society.

CHAPTER 26

Hadrian drove his recently purchased second-hand Subaru into the curving arch of driveway and switched off the engine. Beside him, Marion chewed nervously on her lip. She had plucked up the courage this morning to tell her father about Hadrian, and, as expected, she'd been ordered to bring him to dinner. Now, as they got out of the car, she glanced at him, trying to gauge his reaction to the Ventura Mansion. But Hadrian came from a country that knew a thing or two about imposing houses, and he gave it a jaundiced eye. 'Not bad,' he said finally, and Marion burst into laughter. Two seconds ago she'd been terrified of this upcoming ordeal; now she felt as light-hearted as a helium balloon. Suddenly the door opened and Jacobs, the family butler, stood in the light streaming from the doorway. 'Good evening, Ms Ventura. Sir.'

Hadrian looked across at Marion, winked, and held out his hand, which she happily took. Together, they walked into the lion's den.

'Don't let go of my hand or I'll get lost,' Hadrian whispered loudly as they headed for her father's favourite study, and again Marion giggled. But by the time they'd reached a large oak door, her face was once more pinched with worry. Silently he squeezed her hand.

'I know it's silly,' she said. 'But I can't help feeling . . . I don't know. That disaster lies just around the corner.'

'That's what I like about you,' Hadrian said, his voice briskly pragmatic. 'Your unfailing optimism.' She grinned, shook her head, took a deep breath and opened the door. Hadrian followed her in.

If it had been anyone else, Carole Ballinger immediately thought, a young man entering behind Marion Ventura would have looked exactly like a lapdog following its mistress. But although Marion was still every inch the Ventura Princess, she saw at once, with a pleased, age-old feminine wisdom, that the man with her was no mere prince consort. No yes-man. From the chair opposite her, Leslie Ventura slowly got to his feet. Hadrian's eyes moved the few necessary degrees and the two men were looking at one another. Marion found herself holding her breath.

Leslie looked every inch the owner of Ventura Industries. His suit was exorbitantly expensive, his slicked-back hair still youthfully dark and vibrant. His discreet tie-pin, cufflinks and watch would have cost more than three years of Hadrian's present salary. Leslie knew it. Hadrian also knew it, but didn't care. 'Mr Ventura,' he said, his voice both pleasant and neutral. 'I've been looking forward to meeting you.' He did not add 'sir', but, strangely enough, Leslie didn't feel it had been omitted as an insult.

He moved across the vast expanse of hand-knotted Arabian carpet and held out his hand. 'Mr Boulton, I presume,' he said, his reproving glance sliding briefly to Marion, who had forgotten to do the introductions. Hadrian felt his hand being clamped by a vice. He could return the killer grip, but that would only lead to whitened knuckles, painful cramps and a pointless exercise in

307

masculine point-scoring. Instead he applied the exact same pressure he'd always done, and looked Leslie Ventura straight in the eye. It was easy to do. Leslie, who was used to men having to look up at him, found, if anything, that Hadrian was an inch taller than he.

Marion found herself holding her breath again. For a long, long while the two men stood eyeball to eyeball. Eventually, Leslie let go and took a step back. 'This is Mrs Ballinger. Carole, Hadrian Boulton.'

Hadrian smiled at the beautiful, mature woman walking towards him. 'Mrs Ballinger.'

'Call me Carole.'

'Call me Hadrian.'

'Hadrian. That's an unusual name.'

'I was named, I think, after the Roman emperor. The one who built the wall.'

Carole laughed. 'I'm not surprised,' she said, and gave Marion a look that spoke volumes.

Leslie coughed. 'Why don't you sit down, Mr Boulton. Brandy?'

'Call me Hadrian, please. And I'd prefer lager, if you have it.'

Leslie blinked. 'I think we have lager somewhere. I'll get Jacobs on to it.'

Marion glanced at her father as he walked to the wall and pulled the bell cord. Then she looked at Hadrian, who raised one eyebrow at her and smiled gently. Jacobs came, went, and came back with a glass of lager. Hadrian, now sitting in one of a nest of leather chairs grouped around an original Adams fireplace, took it. 'Thank you.' The butler looked momentarily surprised. When he was gone, Leslie took a chair opposite him, and took a swallow of his own brand.

'There's no need to keep thanking a servant, Mr Boulton,' he began, his voice more condescendingly kind than hostile. 'They don't expect it.'

Hadrian looked across at him. In contrast to Leslie's thousand-dollar Italian silk suit, he was wearing a pair of dark green corduroy trousers and a cream polo-neck sweater from Woolworth's. 'Perhaps not,' he conceded quietly. 'But I was raised to say "please" and "thank you", and it's a habit I don't intend to grow out of.'

Leslie, to his enormous surprise, felt immediately uncomfortable. For the first time in many, many, years, he felt like a crude oaf. 'I . . . have no argument with good manners,' he said, his voice clipped. 'I was just trying to put you wise to the etiquette of the situation.'

Hadrian smiled. 'Thank you. But I only follow etiquette when I agree with it.'

Leslie smiled. Like a crocodile. 'So do I. And although etiquette dictates that I should indulge in polite chit-chat with you just now, quite frankly I am concerned about my daughter and I would like a few assurances from you.'

'Daddy,' Marion said quickly. 'I didn't ask Hadrian here so you could give him the third degree.'

'Then you should have known better, Marion,' Leslie said, his voice lowering ominously.

Marion took a deep breath. This was not going well. If only Hadrian wouldn't be so unbending. If only he'd . . . Marion brought herself up short. If only he'd what? Play up to her father, the way everyone else did? Compromise himself a little? She shuddered. No. No! She was glad he wouldn't back down. Glad he wouldn't be intimidated and made to feel small. She looked across at him with pride in her eyes, and, catching the movement of her lovely head, he looked back at her. And winked. Quite outrageously.

Carole grinned into her sherry, Leslie went a dull shade of red. 'So, Mr Boulton . . .'

'Hadrian, please.'

'Hadrian,' Leslie gritted. But when the Englishman turned calmly to look at him, one eyebrow slightly raised, he found he'd forgotten what he'd been about to say. It infuriated him. He was used to being the biggest fish, in the biggest pond. But now, in the space of just a few unbelievable minutes, he felt as if he'd met his match. With an accountant, of all things. 'So . . . Hadrian,' he purred. 'How do you like working for me?'

The sheer put-down arrogance of the question made even Carole's teeth grind together. She knew why he was doing it, of course. He was not used to self-possessed men who could give as good as they got. Marion paled with fury, and instinctively both women looked at Hadrian. Who was smiling.

'I find it very interesting and very satisfying, Mr Ventura,' he said, no trace of anger in his voice. 'And I seem to be doing well. I was promoted today.'

Leslie smiled grimly. 'Yes. I know.' He had, in fact, grilled Herb mercilessly, not sure whether to be pleased or angry that his daughter's boyfriend seemed to be such a big hit with the head of accounts.

'I dare say,' Hadrian agreed, his voice deadpan.

Leslie waited. It was one of his favourite tricks. Prolong the silence, and the other man broke. Except this one wasn't going to. He knew that instinctively about half a minute into the taut silence. Marion shifted in her chair. She had the feeling she should do something, but she didn't know what.

'Your move to America surprised me,' Leslie said at last. 'You were doing very well in York. You were about to

310

become partner in a well-respected and old firm. You had a home, but no girlfriend. Why was that?'

Marion hissed in her breath. 'You've had your damned private detectives out spying again, haven't you?' she demanded, her voice forcing its way past her gritted teeth.

'Of course I have,' Leslie snapped back. 'You're my only daughter. And when you calmly tell me you're seeing some total stranger, what do you expect?'

'I expect you to be happy for me,' Marion said, her voice wavering just a little. 'Daddy, can't you just be happy for me?' she pleaded.

Leslie swallowed hard. 'Of course I could. If I was sure you were . . .'

'What?' she snapped. 'Going out with the "right sort"? Tell me, Daddy, what is the right sort?'

'An American, for a start,' he snapped back.

'I thought you were Italian, Mr Ventura?' Hadrian's voice, mildly curious, cut into the father-daughter deadlock.

Leslie's head whipped around. 'I am. Or rather my father was. I was born here, in New York.'

'Ahhh,' Hadrian said. 'I see.'

Leslie flushed. 'I'm not prejudiced against Englishmen, Mr Boulton,' he snapped back, not liking one bit being forced on to the defensive.

'You just don't want your daughter marrying one?'

'No. I don't,' Leslie said flatly.

'I rather think that's up to her. Don't you?' Hadrian asked, fighting to keep his temper. Damn, this was hard work. He'd always known Leslie Ventura was going to be a major stumbling block, but he'd always assumed that the man could be reasoned with. Now he wasn't so sure.

Leslie took a deep, calming breath. 'Yes. Of course it is

311

up to her,' he finally agreed, and everyone heard Marion's audible sigh of relief. 'But it is up to me how much money I give her. Or what job I allow her to do.'

So that's the way it is, Hadrian thought wearily. No doubt Leslie Ventura had him pegged as a gold-digger.

'What has that got to do with it?' Marion asked exasperatedly. Hadrian glanced at her, surprised that, with her quick intelligence, she hadn't caught on. Then he realised why she hadn't, and a sudden, powerful wave of love washed over him. She hadn't even contemplated the possibility that he was after her money.

'I could just kiss your toes silly,' he told her softly, and Marion gaped at him. In her Maud Frizon, ultra-expensive pumps, her toes curled. She smiled. She loved him to kiss her toes, as they'd discovered only a few weeks ago.

'Could you?' she asked softly, her eyes glowing.

Leslie coughed angrily. The intimacy of the Englishman's words made him want to reach across and throttle the man. How dared he make love to his daughter right under his nose, damn him? 'I wonder how long you will stay around if Marion ceases to be my heir?' Leslie asked, his voice like ice in the room.

'Not for long,' Hadrian said. Everyone's jaw dropped.

Marion looked at him. Uncertainly she said, 'You wouldn't?'

'Of course not,' Hadrian said softly. 'If you weren't his heir, you'd want to be your own boss. I doubt we could do it here in New York. Not with . . .' he glanced at Leslie '. . . things as they are. But we could do it somewhere else. York, perhaps. Or on the west coast, if you want to stay over here.'

Marion's eyes glowed with pleasure. He'd said so little, and yet so much. To begin with, he'd acknowledged her independence and strength. And he'd said 'we'. That one word that meant so much. Nor was he asking her to sever her family and national ties for the sake of love. Yet she'd have done so, had he asked her. Just because he'd do anything for her.

'That sounds very sweet,' Leslie chewed out the last word as if it were foul-tasting bubble gum. 'But I doubt the reality of the situation would measure up.'

Hadrian's eyes left Marion's and returned to her father. He sighed deeply. 'I don't want us to be adversaries, Mr Ventura,' he said, adding quietly as Leslie began to smile smugly, 'for Marion's sake.'

'For your own sake, you mean,' Leslie corrected grimly.

'No,' Hadrian said softly. 'You have nothing that I want.'

Leslie laughed in sheer disbelief. 'No? I have millions of dollars. Hundreds of millions. Hell, thousands of millions. You don't want that?'

Hadrian smiled. 'You can only live in one house at a time, Mr Ventura. Wear one suit at a time. Eat one meal at a time. Drive one car at a time. I can provide all that for myself and Marion. *Marion* can provide all that for herself – she's clever, and talented, and strong. We really don't need your thousands of millions of dollars, Mr Ventura.' He spoke quietly, never once raising his voice, and Carole and Marion listened to him, spellbound. He means it, Carole thought. He really *means* it. Marion swallowed back tears of pride and happiness. Oh, God, how she loved him.

'Do you really expect me to believe that?' Leslie asked, his face going a dull, ugly shade of red, as it always did whenever he was really angry. Or afraid. Suddenly, he wasn't sure which emotion was uppermost now. Looking

313

into the Englishman's clear, unafraid eyes, he felt, for the first time ever, totally at a loss.

'No,' Hadrian said heavily. 'No, I don't suppose you can believe it. And that is a great pity.'

'Save your pity for yourself, Boulton,' Leslie snarled back, his volatile Italian temper finally erupting. 'And save some for my daughter as well. Because of your meddling and greed, I'm now forced to sack her from her position as my Special Assistant.' Even as he said it, he felt ashamed. Ashamed for putting the blame on Hadrian Boulton when he'd already decided Marion must be demoted. It made him feel small in his own eyes, and that made his rage even more acute. 'I want you out of my house,' he roared, getting to his feet. He was shaking from top to bottom.

Marion leapt to her feet. 'Daddy! If Hadrian leaves this house now, then so do I. And neither of us will ever come back.'

Carole shot to her feet, her mouth falling open in dismay, but no words came out.

'You do that, and you can walk out of Ventura Industries as well.' Leslie said the first thing that came into his head. He simply could not believe his little girl would choose the Englishman over him. 'I had planned on offering you head of PR . . .'

'You can *stuff* the head of PR,' Marion all but screamed.

'With sage and onion, or garlic and herbs?' Hadrian asked, and Carole Ballinger, her nerves giving way, burst into semi-hysterical laughter. Marion stared at him, her lips beginning to twitch. She wanted to cry and laugh at the same time. She couldn't leave like this. It was too . . . *unnecessary*.

'Daddy,' she began, her voice pleading, but Leslie had had enough. The Englishman was laughing at him, he could feel it. He wanted to kill him. He turned abruptly away, leaning his two clenched fists against the fireplace and staring deeply into the flames.

Hadrian looked at his tense back and felt defeated. He had handled this all wrong. But what had been the alternative? To let the man walk all over him. What kind of life would it have been for Marion and himself then? And how did she feel now? She loved her father, that he knew. He looked at her and she saw immediately the defeat and fear in his eyes and ran over to him, slipping her arms around his waist, reaching up to cup his face in her hands. 'I love you,' she said softly. 'Let's go.'

Hadrian nodded. He glanced at Carole, who was looking at them sadly, and wordlessly shook his head. He glanced once more at the tense, hostile back still turned towards them, then turned away with a sigh. Slipping his hands around Marion's waist, he walked them out of the room. When the door closed behind them, Leslie straightened up. He moved and felt like an old man. 'Have they gone?' he asked, his voice as dead as charcoal.

'Yes,' Carole said dully. 'They've gone.'

'Fine,' Leslie said heavily. 'I never want her name mentioned in this house again.'

Carole turned to face him as he turned heavily away from the fireplace. 'You're a fool,' she said bluntly. 'Not only have you lost your son, you've just lost your daughter too. You don't *really* think she'll come back, do you?'

Leslie stared at her, taken aback. It was the first time Carole had spoken to him so sharply. 'I had no choice. You saw what he was like,' he muttered defensively.

'Oh, yes,' Carole said. 'I saw. He was strong. Too strong to bow and scrape to you, and that hurt, didn't it? He was clever, too. Too clever to let you manipulate and humiliate

315

him. And that made you angry. But what makes you a fool is that you failed to see how much Hadrian Boulton loves your daughter. And she loves him. That's why you'll never see her again unless *you* do something about it. And quickly,' she warned him sharply. And, turning on her heel, she left.

Leslie stared at the closed door, his face frozen in shock, expecting it to open at any moment and for Marion to come back. Or Carole. Or even the Englishman. But the door didn't open. And the big mansion suddenly felt very, very empty.

Marion walked into the penthouse and kicked off her shoes with a sigh. Hadrian watched her and smiled. 'Your father does take it out of you, doesn't he.'

Marion sighed angrily. 'I don't want to talk about him. Not ever again. He's out of our lives for good.'

'No, he isn't,' Hadrian said gently. 'It may take some time, but we'll bring him around.' He watched her wilt with relief and grimaced. He only hoped he was right. 'So,' he said briskly. 'To work. What are our assets?' For the next hour they tallied up their working capital, which was considerable. Marion's jewellery alone came to over a million dollars. 'So. We have a hefty working capital, and I can handle the accounts part of it all,' Hadrian said, rubbing the back of his neck tiredly. 'The question now is . . . where do we direct it?'

Marion sighed. 'I don't know. I'm a little scared now we're on our own. What if I can't cope?'

'We'll go on the dole,' Hadrian said flatly, determined not to let her sink into despair or pessimism. 'Now, think, woman. What have you been working on? What do you know most about, and how can we turn it to our advantage?'

316

'A new leisure company,' she said immediately, and gave a yelp of triumph. 'I know! We could buy that farm in Stowe and use it for ourselves,' she enthused. 'Of course, we'd have to have the buildings renovated. And we'd have to expand quickly. Buy sites in other locales – Europe, for sure. Lech, Gstaad, those sort of places. But we could do it,' she enthused, her eyes glowing with renewed vigour. She didn't notice the look of dismay on Hadrian's face. Instead she quickly gathered the Coldstream Farm papers together. In her enthusiasm, she didn't recognize the name of the owner as that of Hadrian's cousin. 'I have to get down to some serious thinking,' she laughed up at him. Dragging the leisure portfolio towards her, she began to make rapid notes. Within moments she was lost in the world of high finance.

Hadrian drove numbly back to his flat and let himself in. So, it had finally come, then, he thought grimly. The moment he'd dreaded. He had to choose between Marion and Bryony. He'd managed to track down the address where Bryony was staying in Stowe. But she needed to sell to Leslie Ventura in order to bring down Germaine. Could he really pick up the phone and ask her to sell the farm to them, instead? But if he didn't, what would happen to Marion, and their new start together? They badly needed that farm too . . .

He sat down heavily and stared at the telephone. He stared at it for a long time before he finally picked it up.

CHAPTER 27

Bryony pushed open the door and switched on the light. 'Well, this is home. For the moment, anyway.'

Kynaston looked around. There were no photographs on the shelves. No sentimental-value-only knick-knacks; nothing.

'You want coffee, chocolate, or something stronger?' she asked, slipping off her blue frock-coat. His eyes strayed towards her, unable to look away. Her dress shimmered pale gold in the light. Cut low and straight across the top, it revealed the tops of the creamy orbs of her breasts. Her hair cascaded over her naked shoulders like chestnut silk. Her lips were gently red and totally kissable. And those incredible sherry eyes . . . He realised with a start that she was waiting for him to reply, watching him with a slightly puzzled expression.

'I'll have coffee, if it's not too much trouble.'

'Nothing's too much trouble for you,' she purred, and turned to the kitchen. He grimaced ruefully. She'd been flirting with him all evening. Stroking his hand on the table-top. Gazing at him through the candlelight. If it hadn't been affecting him like a force ten hurricane all night, it would have been laughable. As a seductress, her inexperience should have made her hopeless. Except that he'd wanted to be seduced. He murmured a curse under his breath. Again he looked around. The room held no clues at all to the personality of the real Bryony Rose Whittaker. So why did he feel as if he knew her as well as he knew his own soul?

'Milk, one sugar, right?'

He turned and accepted the mug she handed over. 'Hum . . . Delicious . . .' he purred, letting his voice drop suggestively and holding her gaze with his own. If she wanted to play seductress, why not give her a helping hand? The air around them became suddenly electric-still, crackling, waiting to dish out the volts. She took a small step towards him, her lips parting just slightly . . . and the telephone rang.

She jumped. 'I'd better answer it,' she said apologetically, thinking it was the man from the Green Vermont Society calling her back. It wasn't.

'Hello? Bryony Rose?'

She recognized the voice immediately, of course. So warm and familiar and so very, very good to hear. Unknowingly her face softened incredibly, and Kynaston, on the verge of looking away, suddenly found himself staring at her. 'Hadrian?' she said. 'How did you know where to find me?'

'It wasn't too hard to guess what you were up to,' Hadrian's voice said gently and she felt herself blush guiltily.

'I know. I'm sorry I left without saying goodbye but I thought the note I left would stop you worrying.'

'It didn't. I left for New York as soon as I could. But I'll be in Stowe tomorrow.'

'Oh, that's wonderful. Tell me when your train gets

319

here and I'll meet you at the station. 'I've missed you,' she said softly.

'I've missed you too,' he said gruffly. 'And Bryony . . . I'm bringing someone with me. Someone . . . I hope will agree to marry me when I pluck up the nerve to ask her.'

'Marry you?' Bryony breathed, stunned, and sank down onto the nearest chair. A few yards away, Kynaston stiffened. Some of the colour drained away beneath his healthy tan, and the mug of coffee in his hand began to shake.

'Yes. I . . . I really love her, Bryony Rose,' Hadrian said, his voice sounding oddly strained. She frowned, sensing instinctively that Hadrian was uncomfortable and worried. 'There's something else. I wanted to wait until I got into town and spoke to you face to face, but I have a problem and I don't think I have the time,' he said, his voice sounding more and more strained with each word he uttered. 'Tell me, has Leslie Ventura made an offer for the farm you bought?'

'How did you know?' she gasped. 'Yes, he has. I'm holding on to it. I wanted to wait . . .' and make Kynaston Germaine miserable, is what she had intented to say, but just in time realised that he was still in the room. She glanced at him, her whole body going cold at the look in his eyes. They looked silver and almost murderous. She blinked and looked away again.

'Good,' Hadrian said briskly, and with relief. 'Bryony, I want you to hold off selling the farm until I get there with Marion. Marion Ventura,' he added, his voice softening on the name, and suddenly she knew who he was in love with.

'Oh, Hadrian,' she said, her voice confused and happy and angry and frightened.

'I know,' he said simply. 'Bryony, I have to explain things. They're very difficult and complicated and . . . I need your help. I know that's not fair, and that I should be the one helping you. Believe me, that's what I came to America to do. That's why I got a job at Ventura. But things . . . got out of control. Can you understand?'

Bryony glanced across at Kynaston. He was staring out the window, his face in taut profile. He looked impossibly handsome, and pulsing with some kind of animal anger. Her nipples tightened, thrusting against the satin of her dress, and her knees began to impersonate jelly. She nodded. 'Oh, yes. Yes, Hadrian, I understand.'

She heard him sigh in relief. 'You'll wait until we get there, then?'

'Of course I'll wait for you,' she said gently.

'I love you, Bryn Whittaker,' Hadrian said softly.

'I love you too,' she whispered, but not quite softly enough for Kynaston not to have heard. 'Bye. See you tomorrow.' She hung up.

Kynaston stared into his coffee. The thought of another man making love to her, listening to her voice say 'I love you' made him want to commit murder. Hers. He slowly stood up, and as he did so, she saw his keys fall out of his jacket pocket on to the chair. 'You've lost your –'

'Who was that on the phone?' His voice cracked like a whip. Suddenly, Bryony sensed the raw fury emanating from him and felt a sudden shaft of joy lance through her. He was jealous!

She shrugged. 'Oh, someone I know from back home.'

'Is he your lover?' he asked bluntly, and she gasped.

'That's none of your business!'

Kynaston smiled, a hard, cold, mocking smile. 'It isn't? I rather thought it was. But, if you say it isn't, then I guess

I've been reading my signals wrong. So I'll say goodnight. Or rather, goodbye.' His voice was Arctic-cold. He turned to walk to the door and Bryony could see her revenge going with him.

'No, wait.' She ran towards him.

Kynaston stopped. Ahh. He didn't think she'd be able to let go of her hate. At the moment it was the only thing he had going for him. 'I want to kill you for what you've done to me,' he gritted angrily, spinning suddenly on his heel and reaching out for her. She barely had time to draw breath before his lips were on hers, hot and crushing, his tongue darting into her unprepared mouth and making her collapse against him with a small sighing moan. Instantly his hands moved around her, one on the small of her back, the other on the back of her head, holding her lips locked on to his. Slowly his hand moved up from her back to her bare shoulders, his fingers caressing the sensitive hollows between her shoulderblades, stroking and exploring, sending line after line of tingles down her back and to her breasts.

Slowly he lifted his head from hers, his eyes glittering like electric ice. 'Was he your lover, Bryony Rose?'

Bryony shook her head, no thought of tormenting him even entering her head. 'No. No.'

He believed her. He couldn't have said why, but he just knew she spoke the truth, and the relief made his eyes flare into flame once more. Again he dipped his head to kiss her, this time his hand cupping one breast in his palm as his other hand encircled her, clamping the length of her body to his. Bryony groaned, her nipple bursting into hardened life under his questing fingers, her back bending slightly against the pressure of his arm. Hadrian was forgotten. Hate was forgotten. Justice and revenge never existed.

There was only his mouth on hers, his hands on her body.

Finally he straightened, satisfied. He felt light-headed with relief, then suddenly cold, as if he'd been drunk and had a gallon of ice-water thrown over him. He loved her. And not only that, he was *in love* with her. And she wanted to cut out his heart and serve it up on a silver platter. He backed away just a step, his eyes narrowing. He had to think. Get out of her dangerous, magnetic orbit before he burned up like a meteor, and think, dammit. 'Goodnight, Bryony Rose,' he said softly. 'I'll see you tomorrow.'

He turned and left. She stared blankly at the door for a second, then turned back, spotting his keys on the chair. She'd forgotten them. A cool, calm voice that she found herself hating began to clamour inside her head. Grimly she removed the key labelled 'Hotel Office', then opened the door and ran after him.

He took them. 'Thanks. You'd better get back in. It's freezing out here tonight,' he added, a wry note in his voice. Freezing didn't quite cut it for what he felt deep in his marrow. She nodded and went back inside, like a marionette being pulled by invisible strings. Slowly, she picked up the key. She would search his office. Find some evidence that she could use against him. The Green Vermont Society would help. They'd been most interested when she'd called on them that morning. If she could find proof of environmentally damaging policies by Germaine Leisure, it would be a start. She lifted the key to her mouth, where his lips had so recently touched hers. It felt cold. Slowly she slid down the wooden door, tears rolling down her face.

Vanessa Germaine stepped off the Montrealer and dumped her suitcase on the station platform. She was tall, just twenty, and pretty with long, fair hair and blue eyes.

'You look cold, *fraülein*. You need a lift?'

The accent was German and she spun around, just a little nervously, in its direction. A car had pulled up at the kerb, and leaning out of the window was one of the most handsome men she'd ever seen. Blond, square-jawed, blue-eyed.

'Thank you, no,' she said cautiously.

The Adonis smiled wryly. 'I understand. Perhaps we shall meet in better circumstances later, *fraülein*,' Claus said, running his eyes over her. 'I'm an instructor here,' he offered the information casually. 'Please feel free to look me up. My name is Claus. Everyone knows me here,' he added, and waved cheerily as pulled away.

Vanessa waved back, vowing to look him up. This looked as if it had the makings of a wonderful Christmas vacation!

It was six-thirty in the morning, the first day of December, when Bryony let herself into Kynaston's office and began searching it. She walked to the nearest filing cabinet. It was locked. Heaving a sigh, she went to his desk, searching for a key. 'Damn, where is it?'

'Where's what?'

She jumped out of her skin at the sound of his mocking voice and when he flicked the switch, flooding the room with light, she was already backing away from him, her mind slowly kicking back into life. 'What are you doing here so early?' she finally managed to ask, as he walked through the doorway and closed the door behind him with a soft, ominous, click. 'How did you know I'd be here?' Her voice wavered weakly.

He smiled bleakly. 'When you gave me back my keys, minus one, I had a fair idea.'

Bryony let out a long, shallow, panicky breath. 'I suppose you're wondering what I'm doing here, then?' she asked, desperately stalling for time. An excuse. There had to be a reasonable, valid excuse, if only she could think of it.

But Kynaston once again surprised her. 'No. I know full well what you're doing here.' He carried a folder to his desk and slumped into a chair. It had been a long, hard night. 'You're looking for something incriminating. Something . . . what? Illegal perhaps? Potentially scandalous. Something to feed to the Press?'

Bryony's mouth fell open. 'How did you know?'

Kynaston smiled. 'Oh, Bryony Rose. Or Bryn Whittaker, I suppose I should say . . .' He paused, watching her go deathly pale. 'Oh, yes, I know who you are.'

'When?' she croaked.

'From the first moment I saw your eyes,' he said matter-of-factly. He wouldn't have thought it was possible, but she paled even further. 'So soon?' she whispered, appalled.

He nodded. 'So soon,' he agreed simply.

'So all this time . . .' She trailed off.

'Yes.' He nodded grimly, but when he leaned across the desk towards her, it was not punishing her that was on his mind. 'I know you blame me for losing Ravenheights,' he began gently, 'but if you could see what I've done with the place . . .'

'It's not just Ravenheights,' she said quickly, not liking the way her heart leapt with treacherous hope. She so *wanted* to believe him. 'My father . . .' she began, desperately summoning up all the old bitterness.

He held up his hand. 'I know about your father,' he said,

325

surprising her even more. And with that he slowly pushed the folder over the desk towards her.

She stared at it as if were a coiled cobra. 'What's that?'

'Read it. Or are you afraid to?' he asked gently.

Angrily she grabbed the folder. It was all there. The slow, inexorable slide to ruin for Ravenheights that had nothing to do with Germaine Leisure. More horrifically, the slow disintegration of John Whittaker's health. He'd had the heart condition that finally killed him for years. *Years*! She felt something hot on her face and realized it was her tears. Silently she closed the folder. She felt arms move around her and turned her face into a warm, hard shoulder. 'He never told me,' she cried, her voice choked with pain and guilt. 'If I'd known, I'd have m-made him leave Rav-Ravenheights,' she sobbed.

'I know. I know you would have,' he murmured against her hair, kissing her temples gently. 'It wasn't your fault, Bryony, believe me. But I had to make you understand. If we're to stand any chance at all, you have to see things as they really were. I love you, Bryony Rose Whittaker,' he said into her wide, shocked, beautiful tiger eyes.

'But Katy . . .' she said, and stopped. Katy. The loss of Ravenheights and her father might not be his fault, but Katy . . . Katy had needed a home, and this man had taken it away. Now Katy was dead . . .

Kynaston sighed, holding her close, his eyes closed. It felt so good to just hold her and not to have to worry constantly about her ulterior motives, or his own strategy. Last night he'd come to the conclusion that love, no matter how complicated or unwelcome, was something so rare that it deserved a chance to live and grow. Besides, he knew he had to save her from herself, before her hatred consumed and destroyed her.

Bryony slowly sniffed away her tears, and said tentatively 'You love me? Really?'

He smiled and nodded. 'Yes. I really, really love you.'

Slowly, Bryony closed her eyes. She was too tired, too numb, too shocked to think straight now. He loved her. But what could that matter? How could she *let* it matter? She had to remember her promise to Katy. Oh, but he *loved* her! The pain of it made her shudder.

'It's all right now, Bryony Rose,' he said softly, holding her close. 'It'll be all right, I promise,' he vowed.

Grimly, full of misery, she nodded. Yes, she believed his promise, because she believed *in* promises. She'd made one of her own on her sister's grave. And promises had to be kept. No matter what the cost.

CHAPTER 28

Lance felt a trickle of sweat run down his face as he reached for the phone, picked it up and dialled Marion's penthouse number. On the other end of the line he heard the phone ring, and acid bile rose in his throat. And yet, through the fear, there was also excitement. It was happening at last. At this very moment, Morgan and the others were at the office building. He glanced at his watch. It was eleven-thirty p.m. Lance swallowed hard. The phone rang for the fourth time. What if she wasn't in?

'Hello?' The weary voice made Lance almost drop the phone.

'Hi. Marion? It's me. Lance.'

There was a long, long pause. Then, 'What do you want, Lance?'

He could hear the impatience in her tone, and his handsome lips curled into a sneer. 'You could sound more hospitable, darling,' he drawled. 'Especially since I'm ringing for the sole purpose of doing you a favour.'

On the other end of the line, Marion smiled grimly. That would be the day. She and Hadrian were leaving for Stowe tomorrow. The sooner her father realised she was serious, the sooner they could reconcile again. With hours of work still facing her, the last thing she needed was

Lance. 'The day you do me a favour, Lance, is the day I'll tap-dance naked at the Lord Mayor's Banquet.'

Lance laughed. Sarcastic bitch. But she'd learn. Oh, yes, she'd learn. But first he had to do his bit. He lowered his voice in an attempt to make it cajoling. 'Oh, come on, Marion. Can't we put the past behind us? There's no point in us remaining at loggerheads. And today I heard something on the grapevine about a cartel that's going to try and scupper Ventura Paper. Apparently . . .'

'Tell it to my father, Lance,' Marion cut in abruptly. 'I no longer work for Ventura. I've already sent in my pass.'

'You did what?' Lance whispered, his face going pale, the sweat now pouring down his face in a torrent. But she had to go to the office! Morgan was waiting for her there.

'But thanks for the tip, Lance,' Marion said thoughtfully. After all, if Lance could try and bury the hatchet, she didn't want to be the one to hold on to a grudge. 'I'm sure my father will appreciate it. I have to go now. I'm leaving New York tomorrow and I still have to pack.'

'Wait!' Lance screeched, but the dialling tone was already buzzing in his ear. Slowly he forced himself to calm down. Morgan was not the kind to give up. That Lance knew, only too well. There would be a next time. Of that he was sure.

The phone rang and Bryony shot across the room. 'Yes?'

'Hello, Bryony Rose.'

Bryony felt the blood in her veins roar off in top gear, shooting red-hot sparks the length of her body. She swallowed. 'Hello, Kyn.'

'Is . . . everything all right?' he asked, the hesitation in his voice making stupid tears of guilt and anger leap into her eyes. Slowly, she collapsed into a chair. She'd been up

329

all night, going over and over what had happened yesterday. Did he really love her, or was he just playing another of his games? He could easily have got rid of her. But he'd said, 'I love you,' instead. Words the old Bryn Whittaker had never expected any man to say to her. But what was the use? Because of him, she'd lost Katy. She could still remember her suicide note as if it was burned into her mind. And her funeral. Her promise to her poor, broken sister . . .

'Bryony?' he prompted anxiously.

'Yes. Yes, of course I'm all right. I just . . . didn't sleep very well.' Well, that at least was true. She hadn't. In the end, it had been sheer logic that came to her rescue. Kynaston loved her. She couldn't think why, but he did. Which meant that she could now destroy him, and Katy would be avenged. So why did she feel so damned miserable?

'I know what you mean,' he said, his voice warm and gentle. 'I hardly slept either. I was wondering if we could have dinner tonight? My sister is dying to meet you.'

'Of course. Vanessa.' He wanted her to meet his family. Suddenly the net around her seemed to tighten. He really did love her. Oh, God . . . Bryony's stomach took a nosedive. Her heart decided on going in the opposite direction and shot straight to her throat. It took her several swallows to get it back down again. 'Oh . . . Well, I'll see you tonight, then.'

'OK, sweetheart. I'll pick you up at seven.' If he was disappointed in her lukewarm response to his words he didn't show it. Bryony hung up and trudged back to the dinner table. She felt old and bitter.

She stopped by the window as a taxi pulled up at the

bottom of the road, and her battered heart lifted as she saw a familiar tall figure emerge. A moment later a smaller, chic figure emerged from inside the taxi, and Bryony strained her eyes to try and get a better look. She could see the woman gesturing at the townhouses.

'Is this where we're staying?' Marion asked, but Hadrian shook his head. 'No. I haven't got that sorted out yet.'

Marion looked at him, puzzled, but he was already picking up their cases. Bryony saw the small, dark-haired woman shrug and begin to follow. Marion Ventura. Bryony sighed deeply, gave up a quick prayer that this first meeting would not be a disaster, and walked to the door and opened it.

'Bryn,' Hadrian said happily, picking her up and swinging her around. 'I'm so damned glad to see you. You look . . . wonderful!' he added, only then taking in the changes in her. The new hair. The confident make-up.

Bryony beamed at him, instantly transported back home to Yorkshire and Ravenheights. Her face glowed. 'It's so good to see you too,' she said, and kissed him. It was what they'd always called a 'Bryn Special' – a big, wet, sloppy kiss, given more in fun than affection, although today it had elements of both.

Marion stood and stared. What she saw was a gorgeous woman with breasts to die for hugging and kissing *her* man. She had the most beautiful hair Marion had ever seen, and the fact that it was natural made Marion want to scratch her eyes out. Straightening her shoulders, Marion moved forward. She'd deal with Hadrian later. When she'd dealt with this . . . this . . . praying mantis. She opened her mouth to order the creature to let him go when Hadrian turned around, his face wreathed in smiles.

'Marion, darling, I want you to meet my cousin Bryony Rose. You remember I told you all about her?'

Marion skidded to a halt on the slippery paving stones, her thousand-dollar sheepskin-lined suede boots just managing to get a grip. She did the same. 'Bryony?' she queried, feeling both sick with relief and sick with mortification at the same time. Abruptly she wiped the outrage and anger off her face. 'This is your sister in all but name?' she nevertheless wanted the matter definitely spelt out, and Hadrian grinned.

'That's right. We grew up at Ravenheights together.'

Marion nodded. Hadrian had described his cousin-cum-honorary-sister as fat and plain and wearing glasses. Hah! 'I *am* glad to meet you, Bryony,' Marion said, her tone of voice silently adding, 'even if it didn't seem like it.' 'Hadrian has told me a lot about you.'

Bryony grinned. 'Which is more than I can say about you. Hadrian called me last night and just sprung you on me. Well, come in. You can't stand out in the snow all day.'

There was nothing sarcastic in the voice. Nothing hostile. And nothing possessive either. Marion immediately relaxed.

Within minutes, they were drinking hot chocolate laced with rum and tucking into a delicious salad lunch. 'Have you ever thought of being a model, Bryony?' Marion asked, spearing a lettuce leaf and chewing thoughtfully while Bryony laughed.

'No way. And if you'd seen me a year ago, you'd know why.'

Marion blinked. So Hadrian had been telling the truth. And . . . she looked closer. Was the taller woman wearing contact lenses? She thought so, but not coloured ones.

332

Those incredible eyes were actually all her own as well. Marion sighed. 'I wish I had your figure.'

Hadrian choked on his coffee. The two women looked at him, then at each other, and burst out laughing.

Bryony liked her. She'd been terrified that she wouldn't, that she and the super-rich Marion Ventura would take an instant dislike to each other and she'd lose Hadrian forever. But that was not how it was going to be, she knew that instinctively. Marion's eyes were dark, warm, full of laughter and humanity. Yes, Bryony liked her. Catching Hadrian's eye, she silently conveyed the message to him, and Hadrian smiled happily back.

Later they moved to the living room, congregating naturally around the fire. It was then that Hadrian brought up Coldstream Farm, explaining everything to her. 'So you see, the Farm could be just the start we need.'

'Naturally we'd pay you a fair price for it,' Marion assured her, glancing at Hadrian, who was staring at his feet, looking miserable. It surprised her so much that her enthusiasm ground to a complete halt.

Bryony too looked at Hadrian and knew at once the reason for his gloom. She also was thinking of Kynaston. But if she sold the farm to Marion Ventura and her own cousin, how could he read anything hostile into that? She was not selling to Leslie.

'Is something wrong?' Marion asked, aware of a taut silence between the cousins that hadn't been there a little while ago.

'No. Nothing's wrong,' Bryony said quickly. 'But there will be a few provisos to the sale.' She explained about Elijah Ellsworthy and her promises to him.

'That's fine,' Marion said. 'We'll need a good estate manager.'

Hadrian stirred. 'Bryn, you don't have to . . .'

'It's all right,' she said quickly. 'I have my own reasons for wanting it like this. I'll . . . tell you about it some time,' she added, aware that Marion was watching them, a small puzzled frown creasing her dark brows.

Hadrian smiled. 'Bryony, I don't know how to thank you.'

'You don't have to, idiot,' she said, all her old affection back in her voice. Hadrian grinned in relief, then looked at the woman he loved.

'Well, we've got some work ahead of us. Fancy a ride out to see your new farm?'

Marion laughed. 'Our new leisure complex, you mean.'

Bryony saw them off, her spirits once more sinking. She still had Kynaston to worry about, and had a hard task ahead of her. To prove to Kyn that she loved him. Except, she realised with a blinding flash of self-knowledge, it wouldn't be so hard after all. Because she *did* love him. She loved the man who had killed her sister.

Vanessa's jaw dropped. The woman who stood in the doorway of her townhouse was . . . was . . . incredible! Her hair seemed to glow like embers from a fire. The face was dominated by the most unusual eyes Vanessa had ever seen. Her figure was like something out of 1940s Hollywood and her dress did nothing to hide the curves. Not that it was flagrant – far from it. It was made of demure white velvet, with a halter neck that left shoulders and arms completely bare.

'Hello, sweetheart,' Kyn said, reaching up and gently kissing the vision. 'This is my little sister, Vanessa.'

Vanessa found herself holding her breath. A woman this beautiful could only be a bitch.

Bryony smiled. 'Hello, Vanessa. I'm really glad you could come tonight. I've been looking forward to meeting you.'

Vanessa blinked. The accent was strange – not at all the hoity-toity English accent she'd expected from watching re-run after re-run of *Brideshead Revisited*. Nor was there a trace of that superior 'woman in charge meeting the little sister' tone either.

Kyn looked from one to the other. 'I can see I'm going to get ganged up on this evening.'

'Of course,' Bryony said, raising one eyebrow archly. 'That's a woman's role in life. Keeping the men firmly under here.' She raised her thumb and winked at Vanessa.

Vanessa laughed. 'Will you give me lessons?'

'Just watch and learn,' Bryony advised, feeling as brittle as a vase with a crack in it. She'd learned only hours ago of her love for this man. Now she was teasing him as if she hadn't a care in the world.

They ate at the Trapp Family Lodge, and the more Vanessa learned about Bryony, the more she liked her. It was as plain as the nose on her face that Bryony was in love with her brother, although at times she seemed a little strained. They'd be talking and laughing, and suddenly she or Kyn would say something and Bryony would get this momentarily frozen look.

As they drank their coffee, Kyn told her about their near-miss with the avalanche. 'Really?' Vanessa said, going pale. 'You must have been scared silly,' she said to Bryony. 'I know I would have been.'

Bryony smiled. 'I was. But Kyn was with me so it wasn't so bad.' She stopped suddenly, getting one of those frozen looks. Kyn reached across and took Bryony's hand, the gesture at once comforting and intimate.

Vanessa sighed romantically. 'I know what you mean. If Claus had been with me I don't suppose I'd be so scared.'

'Claus?' Kyn said, one eyebrow rising, and Vanessa went red.

'Claus is a ski instructor. We were on the slopes this afternoon. He's a hunk,' she said, and winked at Bryony.

'Miss Rose?' Bryony blinked at the sound of the rich, deep voice and looked up at one of the most maturely handsome men she'd ever seen.

She nodded. 'Yes?'

'I'm Leslie Ventura.' The man gave a small, continental half-bow. Bryony shot a quick, alarmed glance at Kyn, who was watching them, stiff and alert.

'How do you do. What can I do for you, Mr Ventura?' she asked. 'I'm sorry. This is Vanessa and Kynaston Germaine.'

For a moment the two men looked at one another like two tigers meeting in the jungle. Leslie kissed Vanessa's hand then turned once more to Bryony Rose. 'I was hoping to discuss our business, but I can see you are dining with friends.'

'Our business? Oh, you mean Coldstream Farm. I'm sorry, Mr Ventura, but I have already sold the farm. To my cousin and your daughter, I believe. Marion is your daughter?'

Leslie frowned. 'Yes. Then your cousin is . . .'

'Hadrian Boulton. Yes,' she said, her lovely eyes never flickering an inch.

'I see,' he said, his face shuttered and tight. 'Then I am too late,' he said heavily.

Bryony shook her head. 'I hope not, Mr Ventura. Your daughter spoke of you very fondly.'

Leslie smiled stiffly, but was not about to take advice.

336

Especially from a cousin of the hated Hadrian Boulton. He executed another half-bow, gave Kynaston one more long, considering look, and left.

'Wow,' Vanessa said. 'What a hunk.'

Bryony grinned at the description, then caught Kynaston looking at her. 'You sold to your cousin?' he asked gently.

Bryony nodded. 'He and Marion are . . . an item.'

Slowly Kynaston leaned back in the chair, a slow, happy smile coming over his face. He was glad she'd taken the farm out of the picture. Now there was nothing standing in their way. Unless the private detective he'd hired to research Katy Whittaker came up with anything.

He hadn't liked the way Bryony had clammed up over Katy. He sensed a mystery, and, being on such shaky ground already, he didn't want any surprises. But he'd never even met Katy Whittaker, so he wasn't expecting it to come to anything.

Still, better safe than sorry.

He didn't know yet just how sorry he was going to be.

CHAPTER 29

Morgan was furious. Both Leslie and Marion Ventura were in Stowe, of all places! He paced the garage restlessly. Bruno was in one corner picking his teeth with a wicked-looking stiletto, and Greg was in another, playing around with a timer that he was forever re-tuning. Morgan felt like screaming.

There was a tap at the door, followed by a pause, then three more taps. It was the German.

Claus looked around, feeling uneasy. He knew something had gone badly wrong for Morgan in New York, but not what. And he wasn't inclined to ask. He only hoped the latest news he'd got from the Germaine girl was going to cheer him up. He headed for the coffee.

'Have you seen the farm?' Morgan's voice suddenly cut coldly into the sluggish silence, and Claus almost dropped the spoonful of sugar he was heaping into a mug.

'*Ja*,' he said. 'They have workers all over the place. Carpenters, roofers, electricians.'

Morgan nodded. 'She doesn't waste much time, does she?' he asked, his voice gritting past clamped teeth.

'We gonna do her in?' Bruno asked hopefully.

'No,' Morgan said sharply. 'I want the money for the cause. Getting Germaine out of the picture is only the beginning. If we're going to get our message across we have to have the clout. Buy up a small but respected newspaper for a start. Fund some documentaries. Buy off some politicians. It all takes hard cash. Ventura cash.'

'That shouldn't be hard,' Greg piped up, from his pile of wires and detonators, stop-clocks and acids. 'Buying politicians, I mean.'

Claus, unhappy with the way things were going, decided to give his information and get out. 'The girl tells me that her brother is in love,' he said matter-of-factly, totally unprepared for Morgan's reaction.

'*What*?' he screamed, leaping off a chair and making even the solid Bruno jump.

Claus blinked nervously. 'The sister – Vanessa. As you said, I've been getting close to her. I . . .'

'Damn the sister!' Morgan raged. 'What was that about Kyn being in love? That man's never been in love in his life. Hit and run, that's his motto. Always has been.'

Claus shook his head. 'Not this time. Vanessa says he introduced this girl to her, something he's never done before apparently, so she thinks it must be serious.'

Morgan sank back down. His knees felt weak. 'No, he's never taken one of his flings home to Vanessa before,' he agreed.

Bruno and Claus exchanged looks, wondering just how well Morgan knew Germaine. Greg grinned smugly into his detonator. He knew, of course. He knew all Morgan's secrets. But he'd never tell. Never.

'What else does the girl say?' Morgan asked. 'Who is she?' he added quickly. 'Does she live locally?'

Claus took a sip of coffee. His throat was suddenly dry. There was violence in the air, and a coldness he'd never felt before. Claus loved the country – he loved mountains and clean air and skiing. He hated developers ruining the environment, and had always been a man not only of convictions but of action. Now, though, he was beginning to wonder if he was into the wrong action. 'Her name is Bryony Rose.'

Morgan stared at him. 'The same Bryony Rose who sold Coldstream Farm to that bitch, Marion Ventura?'

'I imagine so.'

Morgan frowned. 'I don't get it. Why would she sell to Ventura and not to Kyn?'

Claus shrugged. 'I don't know. I only know what Vanessa tells me. According to her, Bryony Rose is from Yorkshire in England, and her brother is crazy about her.'

Morgan grunted. 'Kyn. In love . . .' It was so hard to believe, but, if true, how could he best take advantage of it? He sensed that here was an opportunity to twist the knife, to add another psychological element of torture . . . He began staring into space again. Claus quickly drained his coffee and left. Perhaps it was time to get out of Deep Green. His mind made up, he zipped up his parka and strode into town.

Inside, Morgan was frowning. He'd heard the name of Bryony Rose before. Who'd been talking about her? Then he remembered. Mike Woods, the retired schoolteacher who knew nothing about the subversive goals of Deep Green, and who was the respectable face of the Society, had mentioned her. Aparently, she'd come to the office some time ago. Quickly he dialled Mike's number.

'Hi, Mike? It's me, Morgan.'

'Hi, Morgan. Did you hear about that waste dump over at . . .?' Morgan let him ramble on. Only slowly, and very carefully, did he bring up Coldstream Farm. 'Oh, without doubt that's one of our greatest triumphs,' Mike gushed.

'The company who brought it are brand new. I've seen the plans for the new centre there, and there's hardly any new building being done at all.'

'I know all about that,' Morgan lied. 'What I was interested in was how the last owner, Miss Rose, came to sell to Marion Ventura?'

'Well, it's funny you should say that,' Mike said slowly. 'Miss Rose was most anxious to sell to a good company, and asked us particularly about Germaine Leisure.'

Morgan tensed. 'She seemed keen to sell to them, then?'

'No. Quite the opposite, in fact. It seemed to me that she didn't quite believe me when I pointed out that Germaine Leisure has quite a good record. In fact . . . I may be wrong, of course, but it seemed to me that she was quite anti-Germaine Leisure, although of course she acted impartial. Anyway, I'm glad she sold to this new company. They've even kept old Elijah . . .'

'Well, thanks, Mike,' Morgan cut in quickly. 'It puts my mind at rest.' His eyes narrowed thoughtfully. Kyn was in love with Bryony Rose. But what was going on in Bryony Rose's mind? He had to find out. And quickly. Very quickly. 'Mike, perhaps you can invite Miss Rose to tea one afternoon. I'd like to meet her, and if she's going to buy and sell regularly, we need her in our camp.'

'Sure. I'll invite her right away. You'll enjoy meeting her, I promise you. She's really quite, quite beautiful.'

Morgan smiled. She *would* have to be something special to net Kyn. Slowly he hung up. He was looking forward to meeting the woman who had captured Kynaston Germaine at last. Almost as much as he was looking forward to getting his hands on Marion Ventura, and all that Ventura money.

Now that he'd had some time to think about it, it was

341

better grabbing Marion here. Fewer witnesses – the farm was way out in the woods. Even Leslie Ventura had played right into his hands by following his daughter out here. It meant he'd be right on hand to gather the money together and hand it over. Quickly his mind turned to practicalities. He'd have to bring Lance Prescott down. It wouldn't be a problem, since Lance had 'inherited' a lodge in Stowe as part of the divorce settlement. Morgan began to feel better. Greg, watching him, began to smile. He was only happy when Morgan was happy.

Bruno, who'd taken off his boots and socks, gently scraped the stiletto under his toenails.

Hadrian ran his hand up her bare leg, his fingers curling caressingly around her calf. 'Hummm,' Marion said.

They were in their rented cabin, a simple, modest but comfortable affair, on the outskirts of town. They were lying in front of the fireplace, totally naked. The flames cast intricate, infinitely fascinating shadows across Marion's bare white back. He lowered his lips and kissed the indent in her spine. 'Hummm,' Marion said again.

'Is that all you can say?' he asked, his fingers curling around to stroke the side of her small, pert breast.

'Hummmm.'

'We should be trying to find out what your dear old dad is up to. He's too quiet.'

'Hummm . . . *Hadrian*!' she squealed as, parting her legs, he quickly slipped his tongue deep into her, his hands around her waist lifting her just a little off the rug. Helplessly her legs thrashed weakly either side of his bent dark head, but he didn't stop until she gave a low, long moan of sheer ecstasy, her small, pale body shuddering in delight. Gasping for breath, she slowly turned over

342

and looked up at him, her face flushed from the firelight and her orgasm. Gently she reached up and ran her fingernail lightly around one thrusting male nipple. 'Not fair,' she said.

'So sue me.'

'I'll do more than that,' she threatened ominously, and, suddenly lowering her hand, she clasped his throbbing shaft in her palm and gently squeezed. Hadrian threw back his head with a moan. Quickly taking advantage, Marion pushed him backwards and moved over him, her other hand slipping down to cup his silky-soft balls. Hadrian's head thrashed from side to side on the black rug, his handsome face gently contorting with his growing passion. Marion loved to watch him lose control. His mouth fell open slackly, and his eyes turned so dark they looked like midnight. His cheekbones became pale, while the fleshy part of his cheek reddened, and when he came he moaned in such a way that it always turned her whole insides into liquid honey. Suddenly wanting more, much more, Marion let him go but quickly climbed over him and, her bent knees on either side of his thighs, lowered herself on to him, impaling herself with a small cry of pleasure. Hadrian arched upwards, thrusting himself more deeply into her, his hands grasping a handful of rug on either side of him, his knuckles going bone-white.

'Marion! *Marion!*' he screamed, bucking madly as she clenched her inner muscles around him, shuddering again as yet another orgasm rocketed through her. She felt his hot seed pump into her and slowly, like a wilting flower, she fell on to him, her cheek pressed against his shoulder, their gasping breaths heavy in their ears. 'Do you still want to go and see that the contractors are working to spec at the Farm?' she asked, grinning against his skin.

343

Hadrian groaned. 'Yes. But not now.'

'No. Not now,' Marion agreed. She already knew that the Farm was going to be all she and Hadrian wanted it to be and more. She'd had the finest architect draw up the designs for the conversions, and the new stables being built out of sight of the farm had rustic charm written all over them. With Elijah keeping a beady and fraternal eye on things, Marion wasn't worried about not being there to constantly oversee things. Besides, she had other things on her mind.

'Hadrian, I've been thinking about where we go from here. Once the Farm is sorted.'

'Hummm.'

'And we're going to Gstaad and Lech.' Burying her head further in his shoulder, she added quietly, 'Tomorrow.'

He gave a deep, long-suffering sigh. 'Mind telling me why?'

'I've been thinking,' she began earnestly. 'If there are people like Mr Ellsworthy over here, then there are probably people like him over in Lech and Gstaad, and St Moritz, and all the other "in" places too.'

Hadrian lazily ran a hand over her sweat-slicked back. But his voice was interested as he said, 'Go on.'

'Well. What do not-quite-rich people want most?'

Hadrian laughed. 'I give up. What do not-quite-rich people want most?'

'To live as if they were fabulously wealthy, of course. At least for two weeks every year. Now, these people can't afford to stay at the grand hotels. But . . . What if we can approach all those farmers with cabins up in the hills, most of whom have three or even four bedrooms doing nothing, and make a deal . . .?'

'Such as?'

Marion turned her head, resting her chin firmly on his sternum and staring at his strong, slightly rough, chin. Absently she ran her index finger over his bristles. 'Imagine you are an older couple, living up in the hills. Your children have gone and there you are, with plenty of room, a working farm but very little income. Now, suppose someone came along and offered to re-do the bedrooms to a luxury standard, gold-taps, individual showers, add on a balcony if the rooms haven't already got one, etc. Do the whole place over, upstairs and down, to resemble a really de-luxe *gasthof* – that's guesthouse to you . . . What would you say?'

'I'd say yes, please. But I'd wonder what they would get out of it.'

'We'd get seventy per cent of the profits from paying guests. They'd get the other thirty percent, plus a plush new home. And, once they retire, their children can take over the running of the *gasthof*, giving them an income. Our customers would get a luxury-hotel-type accommodation, in the "real thing", run by the "real" Austrians, Swiss, whatever, at all the top resorts. They'd get to boast about going to Gstaad for their winter break; we'd get the reputation of providing first-class luxury accommodation, plus a true "ethnic" experience for them. What do you think?'

Hadrian thought. 'We'd have to check out the lie of the land first.' He slipped a finger between the crack in her buttocks and shivered with pleasure when her firm flesh clenched instinctively around it. 'Your father would be proud of you.'

Marion snorted. 'I doubt it. He's probably still sulking. And plotting to take over Germaine Leisure.'

* * *

Bryony tore open the hand-delivered note, surprised to find it was from the Green Vermont Society, inviting her to tea. She'd learned from Marion that her father was hell-bent on taking over Germaine Leisure, but it didn't hurt to keep the Greens on her side either. She quickly penned an acceptance to the invitation. The phone rang. Even before she picked it up, she knew who it was.

'Hello, sweetheart. You haven't forgotten we're having dinner tonight at my place, have you?'

Bryony smiled grimly. 'No. Of course I remember.'

'Good. By the way, what are you doing for Christmas?' Kyn asked suddenly, taking her by surprise. 'It'll be our first Christmas together,' he added softly. 'So I was wondering if I could tempt you to Aspen for the Christmas week. I have to go to oversee the big Christmas celebrations we always give at our hotel there, it being our flagship hotel.'

'Aspen?' she echoed, stunned, desperately trying to pull herself together. 'But what about the hotel here?'

'Everything's all but done. We open on New Year's Day with a big party. But we'll be back from Aspen on the 28th. Say you'll come, Bryony.' His voice lowered huskily. 'I want you there with me,' he added, so softly he was almost whispering.

'All right,' she said, and took a deep, fluttery breath.

'Good. I'll see you tonight, then,' he added and quietly hung up. She could hear the happy satisfaction in his voice, and knew she should be rejoicing. But somehow she couldn't manage it. He was so sure they were now 'a couple'. He seemed so damned *happy*. She walked slowly to the window and looked out. She was getting used to the constant snow, and had fallen in love with Vermont. Beautiful Christmas lights added a fairy-tale magic to

346

the night. Christmas trees with coloured lights stood in almost every window. She remembered Christmas at Ravenheights. Holly bedecking every mantel. A huge tree in the front parlour. The huge turkey she used to cook. And Katy always came up from London for Christmas, sometimes only arriving on Christmas Eve and leaving on Boxing Day, but always she'd come. Now, this year, there would be no Katy, and no John Whittaker. Just herself and Kynaston Germaine. The man she loved and hated. The man she was going to destroy. And the man she was going to make love to.

For Bryony had already decided to make love with him. She wanted him so badly it hurt her. And if she didn't do it now, she'd never have the chance again, for soon he'd hate her. And there'd never be any other man for her, that she also knew. No, she had no other options. No other choices.

She'd make love to him once, then destroy him.

CHAPTER 30

Lech, Austria

Gstaad had been wonderful, and, for Hadrian at least, a real eye-opener. He'd been surprised by its smallness, and the air of community spirit kept up by the locals. Marion had been hellishly busy, badgering estate agents, looking at electoral rolls, persuading guides that they really did want to see the 'outer, real Gstaad.' They'd managed to locate ten possible sights for their planned 'Luxury *Gasthofs*'. They'd left Gstaad reluctantly, but they still had to check out Lech before the holidays. It was hard to believe Christmas was only four days away, Hadrian thought as he and Marion checked into their hotel, where Princess Diana had stayed previously.

Too excited to give their room more than a cursory examination, they quickly left to explore the town, and Hadrian took pictures of the beautiful murals painted on the ever-pastel-shaded walls. 'This isn't any poky little Alpine village, is it,' he mused, looping his arm around Marion's waist, looking out at the sprawling, ultra-clean and tidy streets. 'What's up in the mountains?'

'There's a satellite village of Oberlech,' Marion had done her homework well. 'You can get to it by cable car or road, so I suppose we'd better start there first.'

Lech had very well-maintained pistes. As the sun began

to set, they realised that, while most resorts stopped using Ratracs at night because of the cost, here in Lech the piste-bashing went on round the clock, providing the greatest skiing Marion had seen in a long time. Splitting up to cover more ground, Hadrian made notes as he went.

Several miles away, a plane landed at Zurich airport. Leslie Ventura disembarked with his usual ease, and soon his rented limousine was speeding up the main, well-gritted road towards Lech. He should have been a happy man. Hadrian had been right about one thing – he had not been wasting his time in Stowe. Apart from researching the possibilities of mounting a successful takeover of Germaine Leisure, Leslie had started a second project going. From the moment the very beautiful Bryony Rose had told him she was Boulton's cousin, Leslie had smelled a rat. What was the English beauty doing with Germaine? And why, exactly, had Hadrian Boulton chosen to work at Ventura? It reeked of a set-up, and he'd sent out an army of private investigators to dig up the dirt.

He knew work at Coldstream Farm was going on apace, and he admired Marion's ideas. She really was turning out to be a first-class businesswoman. As this trip to Europe indicated. Far from faltering now that she was no longer protected by the Ventura name and fortune, she'd gone from strength to strength. His spies even informed him of Boulton's own worthwhile input into the venture. The man was a genius with accountancy, costs and figures. But all thoughts of business had been wiped from his mind when his investigators had faxed over their findings from Yorkshire. They had been thorough, as he'd have expected. They'd even, ironically enough, stumbled across another team of investigators, this time Kynaston Germaine's, presumably, also doing a bit of checking. But according to Leslie's report, they were concentrating more on Bryony Rose Whittaker's dead sister.

Leslie shuddered suddenly in the heated, luxurious limousine. Like Keith, Katy Whittaker had committed suicide.

Well, Leslie was determined to spare Marion. And at all costs. And now that he'd found out all about Hadrian Boulton and his damned treachery, Leslie Ventura should have been a happy man. He was on his way to get his daughter back and send Boulton packing. He should be singing a happy song fit to raise the rafters. Why, then, did he feel so down?

Back at their hotel, Hadrian lay fully clothed on the bed, watching Marion make up her face. Hadrian loved watching her get ready. In the mirror, Marion saw him and smiled.

Suddenly there was a knock at the door. It made both of them jump, for it was a short, sharp, somehow angry-sounding noise. Hadrian got off the bed and answered it, his face registering his surprise at the figure who quickly pushed his way past him. Hadrian felt a sudden sinking in his stomach, as if he'd just entered a lift that had then descended six floors much too fast.

Leslie stopped dead centre. The room was a plain and simple room. No luxury bathroom, just a small toilet and washbasin, which he could see clearly through the door that had been left open. He wondered how Marion liked having her fully-fledged luxurious lifestyle curbed.

'Daddy!' Marion said happily, as surprised as Hadrian to find him suddenly in their room.

'Marion,' Leslie said, suddenly feeling awkward around his own daughter. One of the reasons he'd worked so hard had been to provide his children with all they could possibly want. 'This is hardly what you're used to, is it?' he asked, not even looking at Hadrian, who had quietly closed the door behind him and was waiting, not a little apprehensively, for him to come to the point. Leslie Ventura had the look of a man with a mission, and suddenly Hadrian's heart began to beat with a hard, quick, sickening thud.

Marion glanced around the room, obviously puzzled. 'What's wrong with it?'

Leslie stared at her, clearly taken aback. 'Nothing, I suppose,' he said finally, wondering why the hell they were talking about accommodation when he had far more worrying things on his mind. 'But I want you to pack up and come back to Stowe with me. I have things to tell you.'

Strangely enough, Leslie was not in the mood for a confrontation with Boulton. He glanced at him only once. He was as tall and good-looking as he remembered. And he still looked at him in that unafraid, unimpressed way that so irritated, and, perversely, made Leslie respect the Englishman more than any other of Marion's past suitors.

'Daddy,' Marion sighed, glancing at Hadrian, surprised and unnerved to see a worried frown creasing across his brow.

'I'm not going back to Stowe until we've finished our business here. Hadrian and I . . .'

'I know all about your venture,' Leslie interrupted quickly. 'But that's not what I want to talk to you about. And I want you away from him,' he jerked his head in Hadrian's direction, again without looking at him, 'when you hear it.'

Hadrian sat down in the nearest chair. He felt like a man about to be executed, for he suddenly knew exactly what Leslie Ventura was going to say.

'What are you talking about?' Marion said sharply, more alarmed at Hadrian's sudden pallor and unusual silence than her father's odd, ominous words.

'I'm talking about the real reason Boulton came over here,' Leslie said, wondering where all his anger had gone. Instead of feeling victorious, he felt miserable. And then he looked into his daughter's questioning, frightened eyes and knew why. Marion loved the man. And he was about to smash that love. For a brief moment he wondered whether or not to go through with it. But Marion had been tricked once, over Lance Prescott, and he wasn't going to let her walk into marriage a second time unless she did it with both her eyes wide open. 'He didn't apply for a job at Ventura just out sheer chance. Did you, Boulton?'

Hadrian didn't flinch. 'No,' he admitted heavily. He could, he knew, get his version in first, but he'd always known Marion would have to know the truth sooner or later.

Marion's fear began to escalate. She could feel her wonderfully warm and solid world beginning to crumble beneath her, like a sidewalk in an earthquake. 'What do you mean?' she asked, her voice suddenly small and afraid.

'He deliberately plotted to join the company,' Leslie said flatly, 'in order to help his cousin get her revenge on Kynaston Germaine. I have gotten it right, Boulton?' he added, at last looking the Englishman in the eye.

Hadrian stared back at him, his face totally blank. Only the darkening of his eyes and the tensing of his hands gave away the pain he was feeling, and Leslie's spirits sank even lower. It was then, in that moment when their eyes met, that Leslie finally realised that this man loved his daughter.

'You have it right,' Hadrian agreed, his voice hollow.

'Bryony?' Marion asked, bewildered. 'What has Bryony got to do with all this?'

'Do you want to tell her, or shall I?' Leslie asked, staring now at a space on the wall just above the Englishman's head.

Hadrian sighed. 'Do you remember I told you about Ravenheights?' he asked softly, looking at Marion, willing her with all his heart to understand. When she nodded, he took another deep breath. 'What I didn't tell you was that it was Kynaston's company that bought the farm, and that the shock of losing it contributed to the heart attack that killed her father. My uncle John.'

'Oh, God. How awful,' Marion said, her heart going out to her new friend.

'It's worse than that,' Hadrian said flatly. 'Bryony's sister, my other cousin Katy . . .' He faltered, then took a deep breath. 'She'd been living in London but things hadn't been going very well. She desperately wanted to come home but . . . Ravenheights was lost. To cut a long story short,' Hadrian finished bluntly,' she killed herself.'

Marion gasped, and Leslie winced.

'After that, Bryony seemed to go into a decline. But after I took her to my flat in York she began to rally, or so it seemed. She went on a crash diet and lost all her weight. She got contact lenses, and had her hair done. I thought she was all right at last, that the trauma was passing. What I didn't realise, until she suddenly went missing, was just how much she hated and blamed Kynaston.'

Marion shook her head. 'But I thought you said she was seeing Kynaston socially? We've seen them together, in Stowe. They always looked so happy together . . .'

'She's acting,' Hadrian said, his worried voice showing just how much he disliked the situation. 'She only wants to destroy him, as she feels he destroyed her whole family and stole her home from her.'

'And you wanted to help her, didn't you, Boulton?' Leslie said heavily. 'That's why you followed her to America. That's why you got a job at Ventura, and courted my daughter. You thought you could help swing our takeover bid of Germaine Leisure.' Marion, suddenly, went totally still. Her face drained of all colour. 'With you at Ventura, pushing for the takeover bid, and Bryony in Stowe, working on the personal front, you thought that between you you could crush Germaine. That's what it's all been about, hasn't it?' Leslie insisted, getting more and more angry as he spoke. 'Right from the beginning. From the very first day you met her, you've been using Marion. Isn't that . . . ?'

He never finished. Marion gave a harsh, grief-stricken sob and rushed for the door. Hadrian shot off the bed to run after her and found his arm taken in a firm grip, swinging him around in mid-step. He found his face barely an inch away from Leslie Ventura's, tight, angry visage. 'Leave her alone, Boulton,' he snarled. 'Haven't you done enough to her already?' Hadrian opened his mouth, then closed it again. Slowly he pulled his arm out of Leslie's grip. He walked heavily to the window and stared out into the darkness.

Marion, hurtling blindly down the staircase, rushed to the main door and stopped. Through her tear-impaired vision she saw the big black limousine waiting outside and realised, with the only part of her numbed, shocked brain that was still working, that it was her father's. She walked shakily towards it and the chauffeur opened the back door, his eyes carefully averted from the beautiful woman who had tears streaming down her lovely face.

354

From his window, Hadrian saw her get into the car. 'I'll leave her alone,' he said quietly, his heart cracking in his chest. 'At least, until she's calmed down.'

'You'll stay out of her life for good,' Leslie corrected grimly. He'd never seen Marion so totally devastated, and all of his previous good feelings about the Englishman had vanished. 'I'll look after her now. And she's coming back to Ventura. As my heir,' Leslie added. 'She's proved she has the right.'

Slowly Hadrian turned and looked at Leslie, his eyes sad. 'You don't know your daughter at all, do you?' he said softly. 'She was always capable of running Ventura. And as for looking after her . . .' Hadrian again shook his head. 'I seem to have more belief in her in my little finger than you do in your whole body.'

Leslie stiffened. 'What's that supposed to mean?'

'I mean, Mr Ventura, that when she's had time to calm down she'll begin to think. And when she begins to think, she'll realise that things just don't add up to that cold, nasty little scenario you just outlined. I think that when she's got over the unnecessary shock you just gave her, she'll remember how much she loves me. And how much I love her.'

Leslie stared at the Englishman, realising he meant every word he said. 'You're insane,' he said bluntly.

'No,' Hadrian said, his voice unaccountably weary. 'I just know Marion. And I know how strong our love is. She's only briefly forgotten it herself. When she remembers, she'll come back to me.'

'Are you prepared to bet on that?' Leslie asked, trying to summon up some savagery, but not finding any in him. The Englishman's faith was awe-inspiring and somehow humbling.

355

'I already have,' Hadrian said heavily, turning back to the window, looking down at the long black car, imagining Marion inside, sobbing with pain and disillusionment. Think, sweetheart, he urged her silently. *Think*. 'I've just bet my life on it,' he said quietly. Because life without Marion, Hadrian thought sadly, was really no life at all.

Stowe

Bryony followed Mike Wood's directions to his house easily, but, when the door was answered, the man standing in the doorway was definitely not Mike Wood. Instead he was tall, well-muscled, with longish dark hair and a handsome face in a vaguely sinister kind of way. 'Hello, I'm Morgan,' he added, holding out his hand. 'I hope Mike might have mentioned me?'

'Oh, yes, he did,' Bryony said, taking his hand and walking into a neat hallway.

'Please, go inside.' Morgan indicated the neat little living room. He sat behind a coffee-table and poured her a cup of tea. 'Biscuit? Mike just stepped out, I'm afraid.' He'd taken in every inch of her appearance and was impressed. 'Actually, I was the one who asked you to tea, not to discuss the Farm,' Morgan began silkily, 'but to ask you something totally different. Tell me, was Coldstream Farm a one-off thing or do you really care about the countryside?'

'Oh, I really care. I grew up on a farm until . . . we were forced off it.'

'Forgive me if I'm reading you wrong,' Morgan began silkily, 'but I think you can do the Society a great deal of good, Miss Rose. I'm going to be totally honest with you. Germaine Leisure has been causing us a great deal of concern for many years.'

'Oh, but I thought they had a good reputation?' Bryony asked, perversely angry to hear someone putting Kyn down.

'That's the official version, yes,' Morgan said, getting quickly in his stride. 'But quite simply, although we know of environmental atrocities perpetrated by Germaine Leisure, we haven't been able to prove any of it. So when we heard about a secret meeting of the Germaine board, we became quite excited.' Morgan watched her face closely. He was right! She *was* out to get Kyn. He could see it in the sudden gleam in her eyes.

'Oh? When is this meeting?' Bryony asked. It was the first she'd heard of it.

'Oh, Mr Germaine is very clever,' Morgan said cunningly. 'He's using the opening of his newest hotel as a cover. When everyone is at the New Year's Day party in the main dining room, we have it on good authority,' Morgan lied smoothly, 'that the board is going to meet in the main conference room to discuss diversification into strip mining in Argentina.'

'Strip mining?' Bryony said appalled. 'But why would Germaine Leisure go into mining?'

Morgan smiled. 'We believe Germaine Leisure are into many environmentally harmful things. The trouble is, we need solid, irrefutable, documented proof. And that's where you come in, Miss Rose. Or rather, I hope you do.'

Bryony blinked cautiously. 'What do you want me to do?'

'You are invited to the opening party, aren't you?' She nodded. 'Then we want you to place a hidden camera and tape recorder in the conference room. It won't be bulky,' he hastened to reassure her. 'Just a box about so big,' he indicated a size with his hands. 'All you'll have to do is slip

357

away from the party and put the box on one of the side-tables facing the conference table. Hide it behind something, but make sure the little black window is facing the table. That's where the lens is hidden,' he lied skilfully.

Bryony's throat was dry. Now that the proof of Kynaston's greed was there to be seen, she suddenly felt like crying. But she could not afford such weaknesses. Kyn was not weak; she couldn't be either. She nodded. 'All right,' she said, her voice small. 'I have a bag big enough to hide the parcel. I'll slip away while Kyn's still at the party; that way I know the conference room will be empty.'

'Good girl,' Morgan said softly. Kyn was going to be destroyed by his own lady-love. He'd place the warning call five minutes before the bomb would go off. Nobody would be hurt, but his new, expensive hotel would be gone, and his own beloved Bryony Rose would have planted the bomb that destroyed it. The bad publicity alone would ensure his guests would leave his hotels worldwide in droves. He'd be finished.

Bryony got up, her knees weak. 'Well, I have to go now. Where shall I meet you to collect the parcel?' Now that it was settled, she was anxious to get away from the mysterious Morgan. And the empty house.

'Right here,' Morgan said.

'Has she gone yet?' The voice sounded tinny and mechanical, and Bryony jumped, looking around nervously. She could see no one. 'Sorry, that's the intercom,' Morgan said, gritting his teeth angrily. 'It goes up into the attic. We have a workroom up there,' he added, quickly hurrying to a small box on one wall and pressing a switch. 'Not yet,' he said quickly into the box, his voice angry. It was true about the workroom. What he didn't tell her was that it now also housed Greg, and his nearly completed bomb. 'Let me walk you to the door,' Morgan smiled at her warmly, ushering her out. He'd kill Greg for nearly blowing it.

But Bryony was hardly giving the intercom or the unknown voice a thought. She had Kynaston at last. A sure-fire way of exposing him to the world for the liar and manipulator he was.

And tomorrow they were going to Aspen, and Kynaston would become her lover.

CHAPTER 31

Morgan looked up as Lance Prescott sighed deeply. They were in his lodge at Stowe, and he was not happy. 'I'm not sure I can do it again,' Lance said nervously. 'Last time I had a good excuse for calling her. Now . . .'

'Now your darling ex-wife is suffering from a broken heart. You shouldn't have any trouble convincing her to meet you out at the Farm. Just say what I told you to say. She'll come.'

Lance smiled smugly. He was glad Marion's romance had failed. Now, in a few hours, she'd be safely bound and gagged, and stored out of the way. They might suspect his part in it, but they wouldn't be able to prove a thing. He was only going to make a phone call, after all.

Morgan stared thoughtfully at the ceiling. Kyn was away in Aspen and for once he was glad. Kyn had a way of always messing up his plans . . .

Aspen, Colorado

Red-cheeked from the skiing, Briony and Kyn enjoyed a fine dinner at the Charlemagne and afterwards walked down Main Street, Kyn's arm curled protectively around her shoulders. All the trees were draped in white fairy-lights. She loved the way he watched her face, as if he could never see her enough. She loved the way he always dropped twenty dollars' worth of coins in the charity tins he passed and she loved listening to him laugh and chat to the shivering Santa Clauses. In fact, she simply loved him. And wanted him. 'Let's get back to the hotel,' she murmured, her heart beating so fast in her breast that it made her feel light-headed.

When they stopped outside her room, she kept her hold firmly on his hand. Quickly his eyes sought hers. What he saw there made his heart leap like a gazelle. 'Bryony?' he said, his voice cracking.

Wordlessly she pulled him into her room and closed the door behind him. Kynaston watched her, his eyes turning a darker, sea-blue. Now that the time had finally come, Bryony felt no fear, only a soul-deep excitement and heartfelt happiness. No matter what happened tomorrow, or, more accurately, on New Year's Day, this was her moment now, and nothing could change it or take it away from her. She had been working her way towards this moment every day of her life. All those lonely years in Yorkshire had hurtled her towards this hour. All the pain, anger and fear she'd felt had been the price she'd paid in advance for this one night. It would be all she'd ever have, and she was not going to be ashamed or regret one moment of it. Later, she could do both. Now, there was only Kynaston. Their eyes met and held like two elemental forces – hers orange fire, his the pale blue water of a tropical, warm sea. She shrugged the heavy coat off him, her hands shaking just a little as her hands brushed against his grey cashmere sweater, warm with the heat of his skin. He watched her, his throat going dry, a deep, shaking excitement invading every limb and muscle. 'Bryony?' he said again, as if unable to believe it was finally going to happen.

Wonderingly, like a blind woman learning Braille, she ran her hand against his chest, feeling the rippling muscle beneath the soft wool, sensing his heartbeat against her fingertips, pausing to explore the sudden hardening of his male nipple. Kynaston shuddered. When she lifted her fascinated eyes from her own fingers to his, she saw that his pupils were dilating with desire, and a slow, sexual flush of pleasure was staining his cheeks. In that second she felt power – raw, elemental, thrilling feminine power – rush across her like an army of tingling pulses. Her lips fell open as she leaned forward, but instead of reaching up to his own waiting lips, she dropped her aim at the last moment and pressed her mouth against the pulse beating in the side of his neck. He smelt wonderful, a tangy blend of pine-scented aftershave, musky sweat from the exercise they'd taken skiing, and a unique, totally male scent that she knew she would never forget as long as she lived. Wanting more, needing more, she pulled his V-neck sweater down, gaining access to his throat, which she explored with tiny, sucking kisses, enjoying the movement of his Adam's apple as he swallowed in desire. Turning her head, she moved back up the side of his neck and to his ear, nibbling a little on his lobe before darting out her tongue to explore the whorls and infinitely interesting indents of his ear.

Kynaston dragged in a deep, shaking breath, his heart thundering in his chest. His hands rested gently on her waist, lightly moving up her back, following the line of her spine, gently caressing. His touch was feather-light. He was frightened of scaring her by holding her too tightly. After all that had happened between them, all the coldness and hostility on both sides, her passion seemed almost too good to be true. He needn't have worried. Bryony was shaking with desire now that she'd let go of everything except her want and need of him.

Less leisurely now, she awkwardly pulled the loose-fitting grey sweater off one shoulder, marvelling at the tanned, firm skin and muscle. Her tongue swooped down, licking and tasting, loving the way he moved his head to one side to give her better access, delighting in the small, gasping moan he gave. Quickly she turned her attention to the other shoulder, then, frustrated by the sweater, quickly grabbed its hem and lifted it off him. The static electricity crackled as the garment came off, clinging to his hair, and her fingers went straight to his scalp, running frenziedly through his clean, cool hair. Then, distracted by the hardening nubs of his nipples pressing into her, she stepped back, staring at his naked chest. Slowly, and watching his eyes all the time, she placed her hands against his skin, her sensitive fingertips swirling in the light smattering of coppery-coloured chest hairs before finding his nipples. She laid her palms squarely over them, pressing hard, loving the way his muscles tensed in masculine strength, and knowing again that feminine, age-old power; although his strength was superior to hers, it was also hers to command. The truth of it was there, in his eyes, both glittering with passion and yet yearning. Only she could give him what he now craved, and when she moved her lips towards him, holding his gaze with her own for as long as possible, she felt herself soaring, free and fierce.

Kynaston closed his eyes as her mouth closed around him, her tongue flicking his nipple like an aggravated wasp. He shuddered and moaned with each near-painful nip, and his stomach and loins exploded into heat. He threw his head back, a wordless cry escaping his parched lips. His hands tightened on her back convulsively, and Bryony too moaned against his skin as her legs suddenly collapsed under her. Slowly she slid down on to her knees, her lips trailing down his stomach as she did so, kissing his abdomen and finally plunging deep into his navel. Kynaston cried out and quickly sank down to his own knees, taking her face in his hands and dragging her lips onto his. Ruthlessly he forced her lips open, then thrust his tongue into her honeyed mouth, the sound of his own heartbeat pounding in his head. Bryony clung to him, her hands on his shoulders, then moving across the wide, muscled planes of his smooth, tanned back. Her fingers found the ridge of his spine and moved down, stopping at the waistband of his trousers. She felt his own hand at her back, lifting the cape and polo-neck jersey beneath it, and obediently she raised her arms, their lips breaking contact briefly to allow the cape and jersey to be flung off her and thrown across the room. Then their mouths were fused together again, and his hands were once more on her back, unclipping her bra and tossing it aside. He groaned in satisfaction as her bare breasts rubbed against his chest, and his hands curled around, cupping them, each thumb gently rubbing her nipples. Bryony arched instinctively, her cry of pleasure and delight reverberating against his lips. Quickly he raised his mouth, and, pushing her back down against the carpet, reared briefly above her before swooping, his lips fastening on to one breasts, sucking one nipple deep inside his mouth.

Bryony's back arched off the carpet, her nails digging into his shoulders in unthinking abandon. She scored his skin, but neither of them noticed. Bryony's head whipped from side to, her hair splaying out around her head like fire. Feverishly, Kynaston's hands went to her trouser buttons, snapping them off in his haste to rid her of her last clothing. Quickly her hands too went to his trousers, her fingers no more nimble than his as she fumbled with his belt, managing to get it undone. Her fingers found the warm, hard bulge and stroked delicately, feeling the heat and power of his loins through the material, her natural female curiosity wanting to know what lay beneath. Kynaston groaned, and, awkwardly shifting their positions, he first tugged her own close-fitting trousers and panties down and yanked them off her feet, then, twisting quickly, he shed his own clothes. For a second they were totally still, each awestruck by the other's beauty. Kynaston stared lovingly at her pale, voluptuous body against the white carpet, the hair on her head and the lush triangle between her thighs, glowing like deep copper. Reverently he reached for her, cupping her quivering calf in his palm and then moving upwards, over her knees, and towards her thighs.

Bryony gasped, but wasn't totally distracted from her own perusal of him. She had never seen a naked man before, and Kynaston was superb. Muscles rippled under tanned skin, his nipples tight and dark, his thighs sturdy columns. Her eyes glanced shyly at first at his manhood, then more wantonly. How strong and proud it looked, she thought dazedly, then he was moving over her again, his hip brushing against hers, his chest covering hers, the hairs tickling her nipples. Putting his hands on either side of her head he stared down into her eyes. 'Bryony,' he said her name, and suddenly she knew she'd always wanted to hear him speak it like this. With want and desire, with a harsh edge due to their urgency, and yet a soul-deep longing within it. He really does love me, Bryony thought, her eyes widening, her heart breaking.

'Oh, Kynaston,' she said, and reached up to cup the nape of his neck, at the same time lifting her own head. The kiss was sweet. Unbearably sweet. Gently she felt his legs slip between her own, firmly prising them apart. Her body leapt with desire in the sudden knowledge of what was to come, and her thighs fell apart eagerly. Gently, with extreme patience and care, she felt him move against her, the head of his penis slowly entering her, filling her, making her whole body quiver with awareness. She felt an explosion of desire ripple out from her stomach, spreading down and up to heat every part of her. Kynaston, aware of her virginity, moved slowly and careful, ready to stop at the least sign of pain. It was torture. He wanted her so badly – needed to feel her hot tightness around him and yearned for the ultimate consummation – but he kept himself under strict control.

Bryony could only marvel at the feeling of completeness that assailed her. Far from him being an invader, her body accepted him like a long-last part of herself. There was a brief spasm of pain as he sank more deeply into her, and immediately she felt him tense. He began to draw away, and desperately she clutched his back. 'No,' she said quickly, her voice a panting plea for understanding. Quickly she looped her heels around the back of his calves, opening herself ever wider to him. Still afraid he might not understand, her hands pressed urgently against his quivering buttocks, but Kynaston already knew. With a small moan he buried himself inside her, the sensation of pleasure more than just physical. It was mental and emotional as well. For all the times he'd made love with a woman, he'd never felt this total joining of entity. He couldn't tell when he began and she ended.

Bryony cried out. It felt so good. So wonderful. No wonder men and women were prepared to die for this. Suddenly, as she clung to her lover, she understood all those great love stories in a way she never had before. She knew now why Juliet gave up her family for Romeo. Why Heathcliff was so cruel with Cathy. What drove Edward VIII to give up his throne for Wallis Simpson.

But if she thought this was all there was, Kynaston quickly began to show her differently. Gently at first, beginning as almost nothing more than a gentle rocking, he began to move. Slowly he started a rhythm that began to tighten and curl in her vagina, creating a tension that was at once frightening and addictive. When he began to withdraw she cried out in fear, but he quickly thrust back into her. His face was tight with tension, his eyes glittering electric-blue in his flushed face. His jaw was clenched with pleasure and concentration, and Bryony couldn't look away from the raw, elemental power and yet total vulnerability apparent on his face. Her heart contracted with love for him. She wanted to hold him inside her like this forever, but the desire was too demanding.

Faster now, his thrusts deeper, she felt herself begin to shake. From the tips of her toes to the last follicles on her head, she felt energized. Her eyes began to open in surprise and then in wonderment as she felt a tidal wave of ecstasy racing closer, like an out-of-control train. She clung to him, her sharp cries of desire sweet in his ears. He cried out her name in triumph. She bucked beneath him with a scream of ecstasy as her first orgasm washed over her, sobs of joy racking her already shaking body. He felt his own pleasure sweep him up and away, and together they rode the wave, their hoarse cries of pleasure echoing

367

CHAPTER 32

Hadrian arrived back at the Stowe cabin and turned on the lights. As he made the fire up, the glow of the flames flickered across his face, cruelly illuminating the dark smudges under his eyes and the bleak expression in their depths. He glanced at his watch. It was nine already. Did she know he was back? He walked to the telephone and dialled.

From his own place, Lance too dialled Marion's number. On the other side of town, Hadrian listened to an engaged tone. In the hotel, Marion answered the phone. 'Hello?' Her voice sounded tired.

Lance swallowed hard. 'Hello, Marion? It's me, Lance. I'm at the lodge. Isn't it a small world?' Morgan quickly crossed his line of vision, pointing at his watch. 'Look, I have to see you, Marion. Now. It's important.'

Marion sighed. 'I can't. I have an important phone call to make.' In her suite, Marion sat slowly down on the sofa. She wasn't lying. She'd been ringing Hadrian's cabin on and off all day. She'd done a lot of crying since returning from Lech, and even more thinking. That day in Lech, her father had done most of the talking. Hadrian had said very little. At first she'd been angry. Why hadn't he denied it, unless it was true? And then, as she began to pick over the

369

bones in a grisly, painful post-mortem, she began to see glaring holes in her father's analysis.

When Hadrian had first met her, and rescued her from those ridiculous dogs, he hadn't known who she was, of that she was now sure. And that very first encounter had been where it had all begun for her and, she was damned sure, for Hadrian as well. That left all the lies he must have told her. But when, last night, she'd gone over every single moment they'd spent together, she couldn't remember him telling her any. He'd told her all about Bryony, only omitting one detail – the detail about Kynaston Germaine. Apart from that, he'd been scrupulously honest. Which brought her to her father's main contention – that Hadrian had been using her to make sure Kynaston Germaine was brought down by Ventura. Except, Marion realised, he hadn't ever encouraged her to do so.

But Marion's growing and new-found happiness had been short-lived. Why hadn't she trusted him right away, when it really mattered? Looking back, remembering his taut, white face, his pleading eyes . . . why had she listened to her father instead of to her heart? Instead, she'd run out on him. The Ventura Princess running back to her throne. But how to apologize? How to beg forgiveness for such treachery? *He'd* never have believed anything bad of *her*, no matter who had said it. *He* trusted *her*. She had to see him. To explain . . .

'Look, Lance, I'm hanging up. I need to use the phone . . .'

In his lodge, Lance gave a nervous glance towards Morgan. 'Marion, I have something important to tell you. About Bryony Rose. She's in trouble, and I mean big trouble. She's gotten herself into something and . . . look, I can't talk about it over the phone. Can we meet somewhere quiet? What about that place of yours? The Farm? The roads are clear out to it, aren't they?'

'I think so. Lance, how did you – ?'

'I'll meet you there in half an hour.' Lance hung up quickly, knowing she'd been about to ask awkward questions. He looked at Morgan. 'It's all set.'

'I'll get Bruno rolling,' Morgan grunted reaching for the phone. By the time he'd hung up, Lance had already left for New York.

Marion tiptoed past the ajar door of her father's room. Inside she could hear him dictating into a mini-tape cassette recorder. Nevertheless, he heard the front door open and close, and sighed deeply. He was worried about his daughter. Suddenly he remembered that Boulton was due back today. Was it possible that she'd gone back to him? Angrily, Leslie grabbed his coat. Back in his cabin, Hadrian redialled. This time the phone rang and rang.

Marion hailed a cab. But, as the town lights slowly fell behind her, she began to feel uneasy. What exactly did Lance mean – that Bryony was in trouble? And how the hell did Lance know anything about it?

Bruno arrived at the farm at break-neck speed, parking his car off the side of the road under a bank of snow-laden pines. He knew the plan off by heart and quickly made his way to the farthest of the old 'stables' now being lovingly recreated into a rustic cabin. Bruno had no objection to doing the snatch here: the place was deserted. A few minutes later, Morgan joined him. 'Everything's set.' Morgan would go back to the cars and hide there, just in case something went wrong and the girl got away from Bruno. There'd be no quick escape by via car for her if it did. 'She'll be here any minute.' Nothing could go wrong.

Neither of them gave Elijah P. Ellsworthy a second thought.

In his cheerless cabin, Hadrian leapt to his feet as an angry pounding sounded outside his front door. 'Where is she?' Leslie Ventura stormed the moment he opened the door.

At the farm, Elijah's dog began to growl. Elijah, comfortably ensconced in front of his fire, glanced at the bloodhound in surprise, and clearly saw its hackles rise. Slowly he put his book down. Elijah trusted dogs, and when his hound was nervous, he became the same. He walked to the window, and carefully pulled back a little bit of the curtain. Blackness and snow. But . . . There. A light. It was coming from the stables.

Elijah pushed back the curtain, his mind working quickly. Thieves? Elijah glanced at the dog, now standing by his side, his unafraid eyes waiting for his master's word. Elijah glanced past the bloodhound to his ever-present shotgun. The world was going to hell in a bread-basket and no mistake. He retrieved his gun, checked it was loaded, and then paused. Elijah glanced at his faithful mutt. He didn't want to get his dog killed. And he didn't want nothing to do with cops. Suddenly he remembered the Englishman. He liked Hadrian Boulton. There was something capable about the big, good-humoured York-shireman. And his family came from farming stock. Yeah, the Englishman would know what to do. Besides, Elijah realised a bit belatedly, the farm did actually belong to him and his pretty little lady now.

Outside, Morgan had Bruno run through the plan one more time. 'Remember, she'll probably come by taxi. If she asks the driver to wait, I'll take care of him. You just make sure you get her. You have the stuff?' Bruno held out a bottle of colourless liquid and a clean white handkerchief. Morgan nodded. 'Don't pour it out until she's almost in here. If she gets a whiff of it it might spook her.'

Bruno nodded eagerly. He was shaking now with excitement. 'OK, Morgan,' he added quickly. This was going to be fun!

In his cabin, Hadrian stared at Leslie Ventura in amazement. 'What's going on?'

Leslie swung around. 'Marion. Where is she? I know she came here.'

Hadrian smiled wryly. 'I wish she had. If she . . .' he stopped as the phone rang, its piercing shrill ominously strident. Impatiently Hadrian picked it up. 'Yes?'

'Mr Boulton? This is Elijah. Over at the farm. Look, Mr Boulton, there's somebody out here. Out at the old stables.'

'Marion?' he asked sharply. What was she doing out there?

'I don't think so. Yon hound likes your little lady. But right now he's growling fit to scare the scarecrows. I don't like it, Mr Boulton,' Elijah said, his slow, worried drawl finally beginning to communicate itself to Hadrian. For some reason he felt a cold, hard wave climb up his spine and the hairs rose up on the back of his neck. In his peripheral vision he noticed Leslie Ventura coming back into the room, his search of the cabin over.

'Stay there,' Hadrian said abruptly. 'Don't go out and challenge them. I'm on my way.' He hung up quickly. His heart was beating fast and a sickening wave of fear spread over him. He glanced across at Leslie Ventura. If his hunch was right, and Marion was in some kind of trouble, he needed all the help he could get. 'Come with me,' he said shortly, making Leslie, who'd been about to demand again that he leave his daughter alone, blink in surprise.

'What? Now look . . .' he began, but Hadrian was already striding to the door.

'I think Marion's in trouble,' Hadrian said shortly over his shoulder. 'Have you got a car outside?' Leslie had. Quickly he ran after the Englishman, yanking open the passenger door and getting inside even as Hadrian was squealing away from the kerb. 'What's going on?' he demanded. 'What was that about Marion?' Briefly Hadrian told him about the call.

'That could be nothing. We don't even know if Marion's out there,' Leslie scoffed, but even to his own ears his voice sounded unconvinced. Hadrian looked briefly across at him and said quietly, 'I have a bad feeling about it, Leslie.'

Leslie opened his mouth, then closed it again. He nodded. In the glow of the streetlights his face looked suddenly hawklike. 'Drive,' he said grimly.

Marion stepped out of the cab and peeled off a ten-dollar bill. 'Please wait,' she said quietly and began to walk away.

There were no lights on, but surely Elijah was home? She was surprised his big dog hadn't bounded out to meet her. The affectionate bloodhound was quickly helping her overcome her aversion to dogs. But where was Lance?

Her booted feet in the snow made a steady 'crunch, crunch, crunch'. In the shadows of the old stable, Bruno felt his heart beat like thunder in his chest. He fingered the bottle of chloroform nervously. Marion's footsteps slowed. The whole place was eerily quiet. Perhaps she should go to the main farmhouse first and see Elijah.

Bruno took a quick peek. In the taxi's headlights, he

could see her look towards the house. She had just started towards it when a strange sound made her stop abruptly. Had she imagined it, or had she heard a slight grunt? She strained to look into the woods, but all she could see was the taxi and its driver, who was now leaning back in his seat. His head was lying back against the headrest at an odd angle. No doubt the poor man had dropped off. It couldn't be any fun, working on Christmas Eve.

Hadrian felt the car beneath him begin to skid and grimly turned the wheel into it. They were going stupidly fast, but by his side Leslie Ventura made no complaint. With every second the sick feeling in his stomach worsened. Marion, he thought silently. Marion, wherever the hell you are, don't do anything stupid.

Marion smiled at the sight of the sleeping driver and turned back towards the house. 'Pssst . . . Psst.' The sound was unmistakable and she swung towards the dark skeleton of a building to her right, recognizing the old barn.

'Lance?' she said, craning her head to get a better view. It was no good. Inside, the place was black with shadow.

Elijah Ellsworthy squinted from behind the curtains. Damn his failing eyes. Against the taxi's lights he could see a small figure. Carefully, he moved to the back door and opened it a crack. Instantly the dog's nose pushed it wider and the dog was through and running out into the night. 'Damn stupid dog,' Elijah muttered, his heart swelling with pride at the mutt's courage.

Marion moved towards the stables. 'Lance, this is ridiculous,' she hissed, feeling both foolish and suddenly afraid. 'What is this all about anyway?'

Inside, Bruno put on his torch, shining it briefly in her face, blinding her, then lowering the beam on to the floor.

He stretched his arm out of the open doorway and beckoned her inside with a waving motion, mindful of Morgan's warning not to say anything, in case she realised it wasn't her ex-husband's voice.

Marion sighed. It was just like Lance to be so theatrical. With an impatient sigh, she began to walk towards the dark, gaping doorway.

Hadrian spotted the turn-off to the farm and took it, almost on two wheels. Less than a mile to go now. Beside him, Leslie's lips firmed into a thin, grim line. Like the Englishman, he too was beginning to have a bad feeling about all this. If something happened to Marion . . .

The bloodhound stopped dead in his tracks. He'd smelt the woman at once, of course, a familiar human smell amongst all the others. He liked the woman. She gave him biscuits. But there was another smell, further away from the woman. Near the woods. The dog didn't like that smell. Slowly he took off towards it, ignoring the hot, oily smell from the car. Behind him he could hear the woman's voice, but in front of him he could hear something else. Something stealthy.

Morgan, having given the surprised cab driver a fairly expert karate chop to the side of the neck, was anxious to get a better view of what was happening. He moved forward and saw Marion heading towards the stables. Good. Very good. It was going to work. No woman stood a chance against Bruno, esp . . . Morgan's thoughts skidded to a halt. Was that a car he heard? He turned his head quickly, peering through the gloom. In intermittent flashes through the trees he saw the white-yellow lights of an approaching car. Damn! He glanced at the cab. Could he block it?

Inside his cabin, Elijah pulled on his boots. It was very

quiet out there. Why hadn't that cowardly mutt of his bit one of those thieves in the ass by now?

Marion stepped inside the empty doorway, peering into pitch darkness. 'Lance? What's this all about?' She smelt something sharp and acid and fear suddenly washed over her as she sensed something coming out at her from the darkness. Her first instinct was to turn and run, but she realised, almost in the same split-second as the instinct hit her, that it was too late. Instead she ducked, crouching down on her knees and tucking her head in.

Bruno lost sight of her. One moment she'd been standing in the doorway, the next she was gone. He gave a growl of anger, took a quick step forward, and bumped into something soft. Marion knew that Lance had not made that sound; it was too deep, too angry, too . . . primitive. She gave a small whimper of fear that turned into a gasp as something incredibly solid bludgeoned into her. She felt a hand reach out and grab the scruff of her neck. She screamed.

Hadrian slewed the car into the courtyard and switched off the engine. 'Did you hear something?' he asked sharply as Leslie, already opening the passenger door, suddenly froze.

'I thought so. Yes. A scream,' he added. For the briefest of second the two men stared at one another.

In the stable, Marion screamed again, this time because she felt herself being lifted off the ground as if she weighed nothing. Elijah crashed through the door and on to the ground, reacting instinctively to the high, purely feminine scream of distress. He rolled, coming to rest by the old cattle trough. Elijah had fought in the army during both world wars. In spite of age and arthritis, he hadn't forgotten how to move. Some things you just didn't forget . . .

377

Morgan stared in disbelief as two male figures sprinted across the courtyard towards the sound of the screaming woman. Quickly, he decided to cut his losses and ran at a low crouch to the taxi. He opened the door and heaved the unconscious driver out on to the snow-lined road.

Bruno laughed. In his excitement he hadn't noticed another car arriving. 'What's wrong, pretty little lady?' he sneered, holding Marion's face close to his own, leering at her, just able to make out her wide, frightened eyes. He loved the sound of her small, scared gasps of breath. 'Expecting someone else, were you?'

Morgan slipped into the driver's seat of the cab, fumbling for the car keys. Suddenly, in a flash of brown fur and white, snarlingly bared teeth, the dog was on him. He yelped with pain as fangs bit into his arm, but his padded coat protected him from the worst of the bite. Cursing angrily he kicked the dog's back legs with his foot. The dog grunted and loosened his grip. Morgan kicked out again. The bloodhound, enraged, promptly sank his teeth into the nearest object – Morgan's ankle. This time there was no protective padding and Morgan yelled out in pain.

Elijah, Leslie and Hadrian all heard it, but Leslie and Hadrian, knowing that Marion was somewhere in the darkened buildings, ignored it. Only Elijah, seeing Hadrian Boulton racing towards the stables along with another man, turned and began to scramble on to his feet, heading for the sound of wild cursing and deep growling. The mutt had got one after all.

Marion felt a cloth over her mouth and at once an astringent scent began to choke her. She gagged as she realised what was happening. It was every rich person's worst nightmare. She was being kidnapped. Suddenly

378

anger overcame fear and she kicked out, her sharp pointed boots connecting satisfactorily with a shin, and she was abruptly dropped. Falling on her backside, she quickly scrambled backwards out into the yard.

Leslie and Hadrian saw her at the same moment. Then a squat, brutal-looking figure lunged forward and Hadrian gave a yell of outrage as the brute grabbed Marion by the front of the coat and half-dragged her up. Bruno looked up, stunned, and dropped her again. Two men, two *big* men were bearing down on him from nowhere. Where the hell had they come from?

At the cab, Morgan gave a mighty kick and sent the howling dog bowling into the snow. He turned the engine on and gunned it, and roared off up the road. Outraged both by the sight of his yelping dog rolling across the road, and one of the bastards getting away, Elijah aimed his shotgun and fired. The blast recoiled him back into the snow beside his dog. Nevertheless, he heard the splintering of glass and metal, but the car didn't stop. The bloodhound licked his face. 'You're a good mutt,' he said, then quickly looked over his shoulder as he heard angry shouting. Struggling to his feet, he grabbed his shotgun and puffed back across the courtyard.

'Marion, get up!' Hadrian shouted, seeing that she was still lying stunned in the snow, the big hulking figure standing, equally stunned, only a step away from her. Marion felt a brief burst of joy on hearing Hadrian's voice. Then, registering his shouted, anguished words, she turned on to her knees and began to rise, pushing herself forward, feeling her feet slip beneath her. She was sobbing with the effort of trying to get a grip on the icy surface, everything in her screaming to move faster than was humanly possible.

Older and less fast, Leslie Ventura was a few steps behind Hadrian when he saw the squat figure drop the cloth he was holding and reach for something else. In the light from the open doorway where Elijah had crashed through, Leslie saw something glint. He knew immediately what it was. 'Knife!' he shouted, knowing there was no time, and that he had no breath, to say or do anything more.

Hadrian saw it at the same moment Leslie screamed the warning. Running up behind both of them, Elijah heard the shouted warning, and his anger boiled. Goddamned spivs. He hated gutter-rats who used knives. But they'd soon find out a knife was no damned match for a good shotgun!

Marion, still running forward, her gaze fixed firmly on Hadrian who was pelting towards her, heard nothing. Her heart was thudding in her chest, and she only knew she had to get to Hadrian. No matter what else happened, so long as she could get to him, she'd be all right.

Bruno, seeing the girl getting away, knowing he'd let Morgan down, knowing he'd probably go to prison, flipped the knife over in his hand and drew back his arm in a perfect knife-thrower's position. Leslie saw it, and knew Marion had only a second to live. His heart screamed out in denial. Never before had he felt so helpless, so desperate or so mortally afraid.

Hadrian, too, saw Bruno's hand whip back, but he was already reaching out for Marion. Although it was all happening in a matter of seconds, his mind was clear, his thoughts totally calm. If he didn't do something, *now*, she was going to get a knife in her back. 'No!' he screamed. His fingertips brushed hers. Lunging forward, he grabbed her hand and swung with all his might. Marion screamed in surprise as she found herself moving sideways, being swung like a pendulum. Then she was moving forward again. Hadrian began to turn, putting his own broad back between Marion and the man with the knife.

Leslie saw it all. Saw how the Englishman swung his arms around Marion, burying her head against his chest, holding her safe and protected. He saw the Englishman's shoulders tense, waiting for the knife that was surely going to hit him square in the back. In outrage Leslie looked at the knifeman who was pitching forward now, about to release the knife. '*No!*' he bellowed.

Bruno ignored the cry of outrage. Someone was going to die tonight. He was right. Elijah lifted the barrel of the gun and fired off the last round. It caught Bruno square in the chest, knocking him backwards, spraying an arch of blood against the pure white snow.

Marion screamed at the sound of the explosion and Elijah once more found himself on his backside in the snow. His dog once more gave his face a sympathetic lick.

Hadrian almost leapt out of his skin when he felt something touch his shoulder, but it was only Leslie. White-faced, he said, 'It's OK. The bastard's dead.'

Hadrian heaved a sigh. 'Thank God. I love you, Marion,' he said quietly. 'Oh, how I love you,' he choked, his hands smoothing the hair away from her wet cheeks, holding her so close. It was all wonderfully *right*. Desperately she tried to say something vitally important, to beg him to take her back, to say that without him she'd *want* to die, but shock had blocked her voice. 'It's all right,' Hadrian said gently, instantly understanding. 'I know you love me too.'

Gently he lifted her chin and kissed her.

CHAPTER 33

Bryony and Kynaston pulled into the parking lot of the new hotel, and when she glanced at the building her eyes widened in surprise. On a long black piece of ebony, etched in gold was the name. 'The Bryony Rose Hotel'. Inside, the party was about to start. It was the first day of a new year.

'You named it after me,' she whispered.

Reaching across, Kyn put a gentle hand under her chin and turned her wide-eyed face to his. 'Happy Christmas, darling,' he said softly. 'Didn't you wonder why I hadn't given you a present?'

Helplessly, she looked back at the hotel he'd named for her. And soon she was going to slip out and get the video camera from Morgan and secretly tape him in order to wreck his career and company. Quickly she opened the door and stumbled out, unaware that Kyn watched her, a puzzled frown creasing his forehead as he followed her up the snow-lined path.

It was one-forty, and the place was packed. She was wearing a dark green velvet dress that went so well with her hair, and Kyn was not the only one who watched her with admiring eyes. Huge evergreen arrangements and red and white poinsettias bedecked every room, along with groaning platters of food, every kind of alcoholic drink imaginable. In the ballroom, a band was playing everything from 'Santa Claus is Coming to Town' to 'Moon River' and 'Lady in Red'.

Leslie Ventura smiled and weaved his way towards Carole. He'd invited her down to Stowe, and was relieved to have her back. 'Dance with me?' she asked softly.

In the quietest corner he could find, Hadrian glanced around the room. He couldn't see Bryony anywhere. He sighed. It didn't seem right that he should be so walking-on-air happy when she was still in so much pain. He'd seen her only once since coming back from Aspen, and for most of that time she'd been listening wide-eyed and angry as he told her about the kidnap attempt. She'd been as angry and upset as Hadrian, but very evasive about her growing relationship with Kynaston Germaine. Still, he'd known something had happened at Aspen. Something had changed her.

'Hadrian, what's wrong?'

By his side, Marion looked ravishing in a red dress with her hair swept up in curl after curl in an intricate chignon. Her dancing eyes were proof that she was already back to her old self, and he could only marvel at her recuperative powers. On the night of the kidnap she'd been understandably shaken up. He and Leslie had taken her into Elijah's house and called a doctor and the police. Elijah, understandably a little worried after killing a man, quickly learned that Leslie Ventura was not a man without influence. Three hours at the police station giving a detailed statement was all that was required.

The next morning, it had been Leslie who'd told her about how Hadrian had been prepared to take a knife in the back for her, and she'd promptly burst into tears.

Leslie had left them locked in one another's arms, a happy man.

'You're worried about something,' Marion said now. 'Oh, Hadrian, I love you so much it hurts,' she said, her voice cracking. Looking into her brimming, big dark eyes, Hadrian swallowed a lump in his own throat. A lump of fear.

'Marion . . . I wanted to ask you something.'

'What?'

'Now that your father has come around . . .'

'Come around?' she interrupted, laughing at the understatement. 'I thought he was going to start a Hadrian Boulton fan-club,' she laughed. 'He's done nothing but praise you to everyone we meet.'

Hadrian grinned. Leslie's attitude certainly had changed since that night. 'So, I was wondering . . . now that there's nothing stopping us . . .' He trailed off and swallowed again. 'Oh, hell, I'm not doing this right.'

'Doing what right, you idiot?' Marion asked, grabbing his knee and squeezing. 'Take a deep breath and just blurt it out,' she encouraged.

'OK. If that's the way you want it,' Hadrian said. 'Will you marry me?'

Marion's mouth fell open. She stared at him. Slowly, a huge, wide, thousand-kilowatt grin almost split her face in half. 'That's some kind of romantic proposal, Boulton,' she said. 'Just blurted out, in the middle of a drunken party, in broad daylight. You couldn't even wait until there was a moon! What about going down on one knee?'

Hadrian had begun to laugh the moment she started speaking. 'Is that a yes or a no?'

'What do you think?' she said, her voice suddenly soft, and in a moment she was on his lap, her arms linked

384

around his neck, her lips nuzzling into his throat. 'Of course I'll marry you, you nut. Who else would have you?'

'No one,' Hadrian admitted forlornly, ignoring the laughing looks the guests were giving them. 'Now that's settled, do you think we should break the news to your father?' he asked, lovingly pushing a stray lock of dark hair off her face.

Marion grinned. 'OK. But I don't think it will be much of a shock.'

'So, we'll tell him that you're already pregnant,' Hadrian said off-handedly. 'That should make him turn that lovely puce colour he always goes when he's in a snit.'

Morgan was waiting when Bryony turned the corner and walked quickly up to the house. He rushed to the door. 'I was beginning to think you weren't coming,' he said, his mild voice cleverly disguising his very real fear.

'Sorry, it was hard to get away,' Bryony said truthfully, her voice distinctly lacklustre. 'Is that it?' she asked, nodding towards the brown-paper-wrapped package on the sideboard. Morgan nodded. Bryony walked towards it reluctantly. As she reached for it, Morgan limped towards her. 'Careful,' he said quickly, his heart jumping up into his throat. 'The video camera lens is set against that black-covered "eye",' he lied. 'If you jog the box too much, it might move it, and then all we'll get is a videotape of the inside of a cardboard box.'

Bryony nodded. The box felt strangely light to be holding a video recorder and tape cassette recorder. It felt . . . wrong, somehow. It seemed so . . . sneaky. So . . . dirty. 'Well, I'd better get going,' she said reluctantly. 'Nobody has made any move towards the conference room, but I shouldn't waste time. What happened to your leg?' she added, as Morgan limped to the door and held it open for her.

'Oh . . . you know, the usual skiing mishap.'

Bryony nodded. 'Well . . . I'll come back with this . . .' she held the box out in front of her, not noticing how Morgan paled and took a step back '. . . as soon as the meeting's over.'

'Right,' Morgan said, a strange, anticipatory smile crossing his face. He was looking forward to seeing Kyn take the fall. And what was wrong with that? she asked herself angrily. It was what she wanted too. Except it wasn't, and she could no longer fool herself that it was.

Morgan watched her go, then painfully climbed the stairs to the attic and tuned into the local radio. At five o'clock precisely, the bomb would blow. He'd place the warning call at four-fifty. Enough time to get the people out, but not enough time to find or disarm the bomb. Outside, Greg quickly re-entered the house and shut the door. Seeing Morgan nowhere in sight, he pressed the button on the intercom to the attic. 'You there?'

'Yeah,' Morgan's voice crackled back. 'Come up.'

Greg nodded, and walked to the hall, forgetting to turn the intercom switch off. He then all but skipped up the stairs to the attic. All they had to do now was wait.

The first person Bryony walked into back at the party was Marion. 'Oh, Bryony, I have to tell you. I know Hadrian would want to but . . . oh, hell, we're going to get married!' Marion laughed, throwing her arms around the stunned, taller girl and hugging her. The bag in Bryony's hand swung and bumped against a passing waiter.

'Oh, Marion, that's wonderful!' Briony said, recovering quickly from the surprise.

'You will be my chief bridesmaid, won't you?'

Briony laughed in delight. 'Try and stop me.' They chatted for a long time about the wedding, and it was only when Marion rushed off to tell Carole Ballinger the news that Briony remembered the camera. Sticking close to the walls, she managed to get through the crush without jiggling the bag too much and found the door to the main conference room. Opening it, she glanced inside cautiously, but the room was empty. Quickly taking the box from her bag, she set it down on a cabinet, making sure the black square pointed at the large centre table. Then, reaching for the large framed photographs of famous personalities staying at other Germaine Hotels, she placed them around it. Satisfied that only somebody looking for the box would see it, she walked to the door, took one last look around her, and left.

Outside, the party had become, if anything, even more manic.

'Let's get out of this menagerie,' a deep voice said right behind her, and her heart leapt. He took her arm and led her through the mêlée, and within moments they were in the quiet of the office. Kyn leaned against the door, giving an exaggerated sigh. 'Every year it gets worse,' he grinned, and, yanking off his tie he let it drape across the chair. His eyes became smoky. 'Come here,' he said softly, and on shaky legs she moved across the room. He took her hands in his. 'They're cold,' he said softly, his fingers rubbing briskly over hers. 'You know what they say, though,' he said gently, bending and rubbing the back of her hand against his cheek. 'Cold hands, warm heart.'

Bryony felt a lance of pain hit her straight in the heart. 'Kyn . . .' she said, then she was kissing him, her lips

387

frantic against his, her arms holding him so tight her fingers hurt.

'Now that's what I call a kiss,' Kynaston said, laughing gently as they finally pulled apart. 'In fact, after that, I don't feel quiet so nervous giving you this.' Slowly he reached into his jacket pocket and pulled out a small red box. Bryony's heart stopped then started again.

'Kynaston,' she said, his name a warning, a plea. Inside was a single but exquisite diamond, set in a plain gold ring. He glanced up, and the fire in his eyes put the stone to shame.

'Bryony Rose Whittaker, will you marry me?'

Bryony cried out. It was a wordless, indecipherable cry, but then she was in his arms, holding on to him as if something was threatening to suck her down. Kyn held her, a wonderful warmth and happiness in every atom of his being. He'd never thought love could be like this. 'Oh, Bryony,' he murmured against her glorious hair, his lips kissing her temple, moving across to her closed eyelids, then down to her lips. Bryony clung to him, her heart breaking. Slowly, gently, he held her away from him and; holding her shattered eyes with his own, slipped the ring on to her finger. It fit perfectly. Bryony stared at it and began to cry, and for once in his life Kynaston Germaine totally misread the situation. Laughing softly he took her in his arms. 'You silly puss,' he said gently. 'I've been telling you for weeks now that I love you. And after Aspen . . . what did you think?' he asked gently. 'That all I wanted was another affair?'

Suddenly the door opened, and the shock of it was like a blast of unexpected arctic storm on a tropical island. 'Oh Mr Germaine . . . Er . . . I'm sorry to interrupt, sir . . .' Both Bryony and Kyn looked up to see the red-faced head

388

waiter looking very unhappy. 'I really am sorry, sir, but Mr Colquist has passed out. I know he's had a lot to drink, sir, but I don't think that's all there is to it.'

'He's diabetic,' Kynaston said sharply. 'Call a doctor. At once.' He turned to Bryony, but she was gently pushing him away.

'It's all right. Go. You have to see to your friend. I'll be all right.' In truth, she was never more glad to have an excuse to have a few moments alone.

'I'll be right back,' he promised, and quickly followed the relieved waiter from the room. Bryony felt a sob well up in her breast and leaned forward, hugging herself miserably. It was no good. She couldn't go through with it. Kynaston loved her. More, he trusted her. He'd asked *her* to marry him. It was the ultimate gesture of love, commitment and loyalty a man could make. And she simply could not betray all of that.

'I'm sorry, Katy,' she whispered, drying her eyes with her fingers, her hand shaking. 'But I love him,' she whispered. Slowly, feeling stiff and battered, she made her way to the conference room. Immediately a half-naked woman and a red-faced man leapt off the table where they'd been lying. 'Oh! Excuse me!' Bryony muttered, going betroot, and drew back. Damn. She'd have to leave the camera there for the moment. But she'd take it out the minute she got the chance. She'd have to tell Morgan, she thought, the very next instant. It was not fair to ruin all his plans without at least apologizing in person. Besides, Kyn would find her at any moment and she was still in no shape to face him and tell him what must be said. Outside it was dark, and, surprised, she glanced at her watch. It was four-twenty already.

The drive to Mike Wood's house seemed much shorter

the second time. Nobody answered when she knocked, so she pushed the door slowly open. 'Hello?' It was dark inside, empty and deserted. Then a strange voice said directly behind her, 'Turn it up. I want to make sure we don't miss it.' She spun around, gasping in surprise. The hairs on the back of her neck stood up. There was no one there! 'Don't worry. The moment it blows, it'll be all over the radio. Besides, I haven't even phoned in the warning yet.' That voice she instantly recognized as belonging to Morgan, but what . . .? Then she saw the small red button on the wall and remembered the intercom. She walked towards it and as she opened her mouth to tell them she was downstairs, Morgan spoke again. 'You sure the timer was set for five?'

'Of course. Don't worry, I was trained by the navy. When I blow something, it blows when I say, and blows as much as I say. Don't worry, Morgan, there'll be nothing left of that hotel but rubble come five o'clock.'

Briony stared at the small red light. She felt suddenly numb, as if she'd been frozen in ice water. A bomb. They were talking about a bomb! Not a camera. Not a recording device. A bomb. At the hotel. *With all those people*! Bryony opened her mouth, but luckily no sound came out. The next second, she found herself running, slipping on the icy sidewalk before flinging herself into the car. She checked her watch as she switched on the ignition. Not quite four-thirty. She drove back like a maniac, and when she pulled up in front of the hotel she left the engine running and the doors open as she raced up the wide, elegant path. The words 'The Bryony Rose Hotel' were lit up in gold lights now, illuminating the porch, but she didn't notice.

The party hit her like a wall. Solid heat, noise, and laughing people. Kyn. She had to find Kyn. Oh, God, where was he? Pushing aside people she barged past a surprised Marion, who, noticing her wild eyes and pale, stricken face, quickly charged after her. 'What's wrong?' she yelled to be heard above the din, grabbing Bryony's arm. Quickly Bryony shook her off. There was no time to explain. Suddenly she saw a familiar fair head, moving about three yards ahead of her. Blindly she rushed off in pursuit. 'Kyn! Kyn!' her shout was lost in the noise. The band started to play 'The Party's Over', and Bryony found herself laughing hysterically at the aptness of it. She glanced at her watch. Four forty-two. She was wasting time. 'Kyn,' she shouted again and suddenly the fair head turned, and over the dancing mêlée of heads, his eyes met hers. Quickly he shouldered his way to her.

'Where've you been?' he shouted, but Bryony shook her head.

'A bomb! There's a bomb!'

He shook his head and pointed to his ears, indicating he couldn't hear her. Quickly she grabbed his arm, ploughing off in the direction of the conference room where she opened the door and all but fell inside. Luckily, the room was now empty. 'There's a bomb in that package,' Bryony gasped, out of breath with all the shouting, barging and fear.

'*What*?' Kyn yelled.

Quickly Bryony went to the cabinet, thrusting aside the photographs. She pointed at the brown paper package. 'There's a bomb in there,' she said, her breath coming out in short, panicked gasps. 'I though it was a video camera and that you were going to hold a secret meeting . . .' She stopped, suddenly realising she didn't have time to go into all this now. 'But it isn't. I heard Morgan talking.'

'*Morgan?*' Kyn gasped, grabbing her shoulders. 'He's here? Here in Stowe?'

'Kyn, listen to me,' she cried, grabbing his hand. 'It's going to go off at five o'clock!' she all but screamed. Just then the door flew open and Hadrian stood there. Marion had fetched him, insisting something was up. 'What's going on?' he asked suspiciously, his eyes flying from Bryony's distraught face to Kynaston Germaine's suddenly tight and ice-cold one. 'If you so much as . . .'

'Get everyone out of here,' Kynaston interrupted, his voice and tone cutting across the room like a scythe. 'There's a bomb in here. Get everybody out. Get the waiters to help. Shut the band up and open all the doors first; there's bound to be a panic, and the more exits there are, the better.'

Hadrian didn't hesitate. 'Right.' He swung around, grabbed Marion, and was gone. Kynaston turned back. His eyes were like electric ice again and she could see his thoughts racing.

'How do you know it's going off at five?'

'I heard Morgan say so. Over the intercom. They didn't know I was there. I went back because I couldn't go through with it after you gave me the ring . . .' She stopped and looked down at the diamond on her finger. She wasn't making much sense, but Kyn didn't doubt her.

'All right. We . . .' He paused as outside the noise suddenly stopped, then quickly started again. This time it was not the sound of revelry, but of panic. Kyn swore. He knew what a mass of panicky people in a small space could do to themselves, but his first thought was to get Bryony safely out of there. He walked quickly to the window and opened it. 'Come on, get out this way.' Bryony did as she was told, her mind still numb. Once out in the snow she turned, but he was already striding back into the room. 'Where are you going?'

'To help get the people out,' he called over his shoulder, never breaking stride, and promptly disappeared into the corridor and the chaos beyond. Bryony leaned against the window sill, shivering. The hotel would be destroyed, that other voice had said. It would be nothing but rubble.

Slowly, she lifted her head and looked into the room at the brown cardboard box. Somewhat belatedly, her brain began to function again. If she had carried it in, she could carry it out again. Quickly, before she could give herself time to talk herself out of it, she scrambled back into the room and ran towards the box, her legs feeling like water. Her hands shook as she reached out for it and lifted it up. The time! She'd forgotten to check the time. Too late to worry about that now. Carefully, she walked to the window and lowered it onto the wide sill. She clambered out, careful not to knock the box with her knees or hands as she did so.

Once outside she picked the box up again and looked around. It was pitch-dark. Think! She had to get the bomb as far away from the hotel as possible. Numbly she began to walk away, the snow getting thicker and thicker as she did so. It was soon up to her calves, then her knees. It became very hard to move, especially since she was holding the box out in front of her, terrified of dropping it.

Back at the hotel, Kyn picked up a frail older man, who'd fallen under a table. He saw Hadrian and quickly thrust the older man into his arms. 'Is everybody out?'

'They soon will be,' Hadrian shouted back. 'Where's Bryony?'

'I got her out,' Kyn yelled back. 'Make sure everyone's

393

outside, then shut all the doors. If the bomb goes off we're going to have trouble with flying glass so get everyone as far out into the street as you can. And call the cops!' he added over his shoulder, for he was already sprinting back towards the conference room. When he got there his eyes flew to the cabinet and the bomb . . . which had gone. He blinked, stunned. Then a gust of wind blew the curtains out and he stared at the window, his heart leaping into his chest. 'Bryony,' he whispered, his face going totally white. '*Bryony*!' he screamed, racing to the window and all but throwing himself outside. On the snowy ground, he peered out into total darkness. He screamed her name again.

In the distance, Bryony heard her name being called. It sounded far away. Good. That meant she must have put a good distance between herself and the hotel. Slowly she lowered the box to the ground and quickly dug a hole in the snow, placing the bomb inside. Then glanced at her watch. Her heart stopped. Four fifty-nine. Oh, God! She turned and began to run, stumbling and falling along the tracks she'd made going out. Kynaston, who'd found her tracks in the snow leading out into the night, began to run after her, staring out into the darkness. Suddenly there was a bright flash of orange and yellow, and the whole night was lit up. Then there was a great loud crack, like atoms splitting and hammering painfully at his eardrums, and he felt himself being knocked backwards by an invisible hot wall into the snow.

For a second he stared up at the sky seeing dancing patterns where the flash of light had temporarily blinded him. Then he scrambled up on to his knees. 'Bryony?' he said, his lips, his body, his heart totally numb. '*Bryony*!'

EPILOGUE

York

Lynnette opened the door the moment the doorbell rang. 'Bryony,' she said gently, holding out her hand. 'Come on inside, and let's get you a cup of tea,' she added, her worried professional eyes running over her friend. Minor concussion and a few cuts and bruises, Hadrian had said, filling her in on what had happened. But the ashen face, the wide, bruised eyes . . . these had nothing to do with physical pain. Bryony smiled wanly and let herself be coddled. 'Now, tell me everything,' Lynnette said a few minutes later, handing over the sweetened tea. Wearily, Bryony did so, leaving nothing out. Her love for Kyn, Morgan, the bomb . . .

'So it was the snow that saved you?' Lynnette asked when she'd finished, and Bryony nodded.

'Yes. People think of snow as soft stuff, but when it's packed metres thick . . . I fell over at the first blast, and most of the flying debris from the bomb went over my head – the bits that didn't cut my back, that is.'

Lynnette bit her lip. She had to be very careful now. 'Didn't Kynaston . . .?'

Bryony quickly interrupted. 'I haven't seen Kynaston since . . . the bomb.'

Lynnette looked quickly away from her friend's stricken

eyes. 'Let's put a drop of brandy in the next one, hmm?'

Bryony sensed that Lynnette was going to offer some advice, probably about going back to America and talking it out with Kynaston. That she simply could not face, so she very quickly changed the subject. 'Did Hadrian tell you he's going to get married? And that's he's going to be a father in eight months' time? Her name's Marion Ventura. Don't worry, she's really nice. I'd be the first one to come out of my corner, spitting and snarling, if someone horrible got their claws into Hadrian, believe me.'

Suddenly, Lynnette slapped her forehead. 'Talking of Hadrian . . .' She got up and began to search in the drawer of her writing desk. 'Now where the hell did I put . . . ah, here it is. You remember he went down to Katy's London flat to get the rest of her things, and that nice neighbour of Katy's helped him?' Bryony nodded, staring at the small package Lynnette was holding. 'I've been seeing to Hadrian's mail, and this came yesterday. I was just about to post it on to him when he phoned, so I'll give it to you instead. The neighbour found it under the table . . .' Aware that she was babbling, Lynnette sighed and said flatly, 'I think it's Katy's diary, Bryony.'

Bryony took the package from Lynnette's hand, and tears warmed her eyes. She stood up hastily, coughing to hide her suddenly choked throat. 'I think I'll go next door now. Hadrian said I could stay in the flat as long as I needed it.'

Once alone, Bryony collapsed onto the sofa, wincing at the cuts on her back. She'd woken in hospital, and Hadrian had been there to tell her everything that had happened. Apparently, after the explosion, he had found Kynaston holding her unconscious body in his arms, screaming for a doctor and ambulance, and rocking her back and forth. He was crying, Hadrian had told her bluntly, but she'd turned her face on the pillow, facing the wall, not wanting to think of it. Kynaston Germaine, crying? It was so . . . unlikely. So . . . horrible! What had she done to him? Bryony gave a dry sob. She wouldn't think of it. She wouldn't. At least he hadn't come to see her. She didn't think she could have taken that – to see the hate in his eyes and hear the disgust in his voice.

Slowly, painfully, she dragged her thoughts back to the present and looked at the parcel in her hands. Slowly she unwrapped the brown paper and stared at the smallish, leather-bound book. It *was* a diary. She suddenly felt so close to her sister, it felt as if she could reach out and touch her.

'Katy,' she whispered, and opened the diary. Half an hour later she put the book down, tears streaming down her face. Katy had been having an affair with a married man and he'd called it off. She'd been devastated, pouring out her misery on the pages of the diary. The phrases she'd used sounded so familiar now . . . Her heart stopped for a second, then began again with a sickening, heavy thud. Feeling numb, Bryony reached into her bag for the single, folded piece of paper that wasn't Katy's suicide note at all, but a scrap of paper from her diary. And understood. In a blinding flash, she saw it all. Katy had not been talking about Kynaston. The 'he' of the 'suicide note' was her married lover. And for 'home' read the London flat that she so bitterly resented losing.

Bryony gave a small, defeated moan. It had all been for nothing. She had hated Kynaston for nothing. Had betrayed him for nothing. For two hours Bryony lay on her bed and cried. Eventually, though, she got up and methodically collected her sister's private papers together, put them all in one big brown envelope and sealed it. She would never open it again. She could mourn her properly now. Katy had been very unhappy, but it was not her fault. She, Bryony, no longer felt responsible. She could say goodbye to her sister now. That left only one more 'goodbye' to be said and then she could get on with her life . . . such as it was. Without Kynaston . . . No, she wouldn't face the prospect of that empty void now. One thing at a time.

A minute later, Bryony knocked on Lynette's door. 'Can I borrow your car? I have to . . . go somewhere.'

'Of course you can but . . . are you up to driving?'

Bryony nodded, and Lynnette, sensing it was something important, quickly handed over her keys. 'Drive careful-ly,' she said softly. Bryony did. It was wonderful to get back deep into the Yorkshire countryside again. Although it was January, there had been no recent snowfall and the hills looked green and lush. The windswept dales, the miles of dry-stone walling, the white dots of sheep were all as familiar as her own voice, and yet it was not home any more. She found herself remembering Vermont – the trees, the mountains, the clear lakes, the sheer beauty of it.

She drove steadily north, down roads that led back to the past. Then she was taking the turn to Ravenheights . . . Suddenly she slowed and stopped. What was that? A flash of colour where there should be none. Moving fast. But she knew that sight – the way the colours moved, zig-zagging . . . they were people skiing! But skiiing on what? Bare grass . . . no, the colour was not *quite* the same. But so close, she'd never even noticed the difference. So these were the hated dry-ski runs. So well concealed they were almost invisible. Shaking her head at yet more evidence of her blind prejudice towards the man she loved, Bryony drove on. She braced herself as she crested the hill, expecting to see a barren waste where the house had once stood. She was ready for it.

She crested the hill and stamped on the brake. There was Ravenheights. As solid, as real, as beautiful as ever. And there was smoke coming from the chimney. But if people could carry on living there, why had he taken it away from her?

She sighed and drove slowly the rest of the way, parking just before she got into the courtyard. She walked into the familiar quad and stopped dead. In the centre of the courtyard was an old well. The original had been filled in long before she was born, but now, once more, there it was, looking exactly as some old photographs had depicted it. Slowly, hardly believing her eyes, Bryony walked towards it. She hadn't gone a yard when she stopped again, her heart leaping in shock. Gambolling towards her, as fast as her old legs could carry her, came a familiar black and white figure. 'Violet?' Bryony breathed, and the dog's plumy tail lashed back and forth in confirmation, her tongue lolling happily from her open mouth. Bryony bent down, tears falling down her face as the old female sheepdog began deliriously licking her face. 'Violet . . . what are you doing here, old girl, hmm?' she murmured, stroking her hands lovingly across the dog's back. 'I thought you'd gone to stay with old M – '

'Violet? Look what you've done to that lady's nice clean coat, you bad dog,' a voice said, but not unkindly, and both Bryony and the dog looked up. The man approaching was in his mid-fifties, with a beaming red face, a thick crop of dark blond hair and kind brown eyes that twinkled at them. 'Sorry about the dog, miss. She's very friendly, though. She used to live here, you see, and kept turning up. When the museum opened permanently, and I came to live in . . . well, I kind of adopted her.'

'Museum?' Bryony whispered.

'Aye, it's open to everyone. Free, too. We get most of our customers from the ski-slopes, of course. Feel free to look around. That's what we're here for. Show people how life used to be . . . come on, Violet, there's a good girl. I've got them lamb bones left over from the stew in the kitchen.'

Bryony gave the faithful dog a gentle push towards her new master and the sheepdog happily trotted off. Bryony straightened and glanced around. She went first to the old barn, which was now a showplace for old farm machinery that had been lovingly restored. Leather straps and horse-brasses hung from the walls, polished and well-tended, just waiting for the big shire horses that had used to pull the machines. Shaking her head, Bryony walked across the courtyard to the house itself.

Inside, the kitchen was transformed. The Aga was gone, and in its place the old fire hearth had been reinstated, a huge cauldron hanging over a burning fire. A neat placard in front of the hearth described how all the cooking was done in the old days. In a daze, Bryony moved on to the front living-room. There, in one corner, was an old-fashioned spinning wheel and loom. She had always wondered what the small, scratched indents on the floor had been made by, and now she knew. Again, an infor-mative placard explained how fleece was combed and spun and made into wool that in turn was made into clothes. Out in the hall, Bryony stopped, listening. The house was happy. She could feel it. Lovingly restored and changed back into its original shape and purpose, the house was almost purring.

When Bryony stepped back into the courtyard she was smiling gently. She nodded goodbye to the man who was watching her from a converted barn, now made into a pretty little cottage for one. Bryony turned and looked at the house one last time. Goodbye, Ravenheights, she thought sadly. I'll miss you, but my time with you has come and gone.

She walked back towards her car, her head bent against the cold wind. When she looked up there was another car parked next to hers, and getting out of it was a tall man with fair hair and ice-blue eyes. Bryony stopped dead, her throat going dry, her heart racing wildly. 'Kynaston?' she whispered.

Slowly he walked towards her, his eyes never leaving hers. 'I thought I might find you here,' he said softly. 'Why did you leave me?' he asked softly, not stopping until he was only a hand's touch away from her.

Bryony shook her head. 'I don't . . . know what you mean.'

'The police kept questioning me for days. Why did you think I wasn't at the hospital with you?'

Bryony's stared at him, her eyes wide. 'I didn't think of that,' she said, her voice small. 'I just thought . . . well, that you didn't want to see me,' she added dejectedly.

'You can be very stupid sometimes, Bryony Rose Whittaker,' he said gently.

'I know. Morgan fooled me . . . What happened to Morgan? Did you catch him?' she asked urgently, suddenly realising she had no idea what had happened since she'd left.

Kynaston's eyes flickered. 'Yes. Once I gave the police his name and description they found him within an hour. He was behind Marion's kidnapping too, by the way. He

401

confessed it all and implicated Lance Prescott. They arrested him last night in New York.'

Bryony gasped. 'But why? Why Marion?'

Again Kynaston eyes flickered, an odd look darkening his iris's. 'Because he thought she was going to take over my company, and he couldn't let her do that. Morgan couldn't let anyone destroy me except himself.'

Bryony's back went icy cold. 'Kynaston . . .' she said softly. 'That sounds . . . so . . . personal.'

Kynaston nodded his head. 'It is personal,' he said quietly, then took a deep breath. 'Morgan is my brother.'

'*What*?'

'It's a long story,' he said softly, and he didn't want to go into it now. He wanted to take her into his arms and kiss her until they both gasped for air. When he'd discovered she'd left the country, he'd been frantic. Instinct had told him to come here, and he'd been right.

'Why would your brother hate you so much?' Bryony asked, longing only to go to him, to close the tiny but chasm-wide gap between them, but not daring to.

Kynaston nodded. There had been so many misunderstandings between them, there could be no more. He owed it to her to explain. 'Morgan was always . . . unstable,' he began. 'When we had to leave our farm and move to New York he . . . got worse. At first he took it out on me, beating me up when Mom and Dad's backs were turned. Hell, I hated the slum too, but not in the same frantic way Morgan did. He became obsessed with getting out, with moving back to Vermont. I think that's where his twisted mania about the environment began to form. Anyway, one day I came home from school and heard Vanessa screaming. She was only two, but there was something terrified about her crying. I searched the house, but couldn't find

402

her. Then, from the window, I saw Morgan out in the alley.' Kynaston ran a hand through his hair, his face bleak with remembrance. 'I ran outside and saw him scooping up water from the gutter and forcing it into Vanessa's mouth. Bryony, you have to understand the place we were living in. The alley was filthy and rat-infested. Old cars leaking oil and gas rusted on the pavements . . .'

'My God, she could have died!'

'She nearly did. That was what he was counting on,' Kynaston said wearily. 'He had this crazy idea that if Vanessa got sick, the city would move us somewhere better, maybe even back to Vermont. It was all madness. Nobody would have cared. Nobody would have done anything . . . That slum was a hell-hole of apathy and depravation. Anyway, I pushed Morgan away, grabbed Vanessa and ran straight to the nearest police station. They got her to a hospital and a stomach pump, but I had to tell them about Morgan. Mom and Dad refused to believe there was anything wrong with him, though they must have known. He was so obviously disturbed . . .' He shook his head sadly. 'Anyway, the authorities put him away in a mental home. I can still remember driving there with Dad. I was . . . fourteen, I guess. The place was a red-brick building. I waited in the car while Dad went in with him . . . When he came out he never said a word to me. We never really talked much after that. A few years later he and Mom died in a train wreck and . . . well, that left me and Vanessa.'

'But why did they let him go if he was still dangerous?'

'They didn't. He escaped with another inmate, a guy who'd been trained by the navy in explosives. I had no idea he was in Stowe, hiding under the banner of a "green" society. He's back in a mental hospital now –

one of the best. I can afford it. Who knows . . . one day . . .'

Bryony nodded. She, too, could only hope his brother could be cured. 'I'm so sorry I believed him and not you,' she said, her voice breaking.

Kynaston slowly looked up into her eyes. Tense and heart-sore, she braced herself, but there was no anger in the sky-blue depths, only pain and puzzlement. 'I was wondering about that,' he said softly. 'Why did you do it?'

Slowly, carefully, Bryony explained about Katy, finishing with her discovery of her diary. 'You poor kid,' Kynaston said gently, pulling her into his arms. 'It's been a rough few days for you, hasn't it?'

Bryony, her cheek cushioned against his chest, laughed grimly. 'You could say that. Oh, Kyn, I'm so sorry. I . . .' A sudden twinkle of light caught her eye and she looked down at her ring. She had not been able to bring herself to take it off. Slowly she took a step back. 'I suppose you want this back?' she said quietly, her voice harsh with pain.

Kynaston followed her gaze down to the ring, then looked back into her lovely eyes. He nodded. 'Yes. So long as you're attached to it.'

Bryony gasped. 'You can't . . . still want me,' she said. 'Not after what I did.'

Kynsaton smiled. 'What did you do?'

Bryony blinked. '*What did I do*? I put a bomb in your hotel and . . .'

'Carried it out again, risking your own life. And I still want to strangle you for that,' he said harshly, reaching out and taking her shoulders in his hands, his fingers strong and nearly brutal. 'You nearly gave me a heart attack,' he said, his voice like granite. 'When I found you in the snow, unconscious . . .' His voice softened suddenly, and she felt his whole, big, beautiful body shudder. 'I thought at first you were dead, and I wanted to die too. You're going to have a lot of years to make that up to me, Bryony Rose,' he added warningly, his voice gruff.

'But I . . . lied to you,' she said uncertainly as her heart began to sing with renewed hope. Was it really possible that he still loved her?

'And I always knew,' he said simply. 'And in the beginning, I was prepared to break you in half. So I was hardly blameless in all of this, was I?' he smiled ruefully.

'I said I loved you . . .' she began, her voice barely a whisper.

'But that wasn't a lie,' he said softly. 'Was it?'

Mutely Bryony shook her head.

'So . . . you're going to come back home with me. Aren't you?'

Bryony nodded.

'And marry me?'

Bryony nodded.

'And make love to me every night?'

Bryony nodded.

'Good. Now come here and kiss me.'

Bryony did, and as she did so she felt the old Bryn Whittaker come flooding back, her heart warm and free now, and filled only with love and happiness.

As their lips met, and she felt his strong arms holding her close, she knew, at last, that she was *truly* home.